House of Shadows

THE FRENCH LIST

House of Shadows

DIANE MEUR

Translated by Teresa Lavender Fagan

LONDON NEW YORK CALCUTTA

Seagull Books, 2015

First published as *Les vivants et les ombres* by Diane Meur
© Sabine Wespieser éditeur, 2007

First published in English translation by Seagull Books, 2015
English translation © Teresa Lavender Fagan, 2015

ISBN 978 0 8574 2 028 2

British Library Cataloguing-in-Publication Data
A catalogue record for this book is available from the British Library

Typeset by Seagull Books, Calcutta, India
Printed and bound by Maple Press, York, Pennsylvania, USA

Behind me are the grounds, the fields. In the summer a hot haze covers the hills, and above the wheat fields the air, filled with wasps and butterflies, trembles. There are farm cottages too, whose roofs descend so low that when the grass is tall, when I can no longer see the windows or the doors, they appear to be billowing skirts out of which frail bodies of smoke emerge.

Sometimes the farmers' children come here to steal a pear, a handful of cherries. In Gavryl's time, they would have been pummelled with stones and insults in their language, perhaps even with the threat of a complaint to the bailiff. They would have run off towards the skirts, dogs yelping; and Gavryl, stopping at the gate, would have thrown out a final curse; and I would have seen his boots slowly turn around and come back towards me.

It's been some time since old Gavryl joined his Ruthenian brothers in the cemetery of the Uniate church, whose humble wood steeple rises up among the farms; and only the stela of his grave, dominated by a sullen-faced saint, still frightens the children after Sunday services. Many years after him there was Mr Jäger, an Austrian from the Low Countries whose nasal accent, metal pince-nez and urbane retired-engineer manners seemed to the Zemkas to be more worthy of their status. Mr Jäger didn't shout, didn't wear boots; he knocked politely on the cottage doors, but when they saw him the women shrank back along the walls on which hung a lithograph of Franz-Joseph, as if to call upon His Imperial Majesty's protection against the trouble that was to come.

Mr Jäger finally went away too, one night in 1869. He went away with the salaries of the three hundred workers at the sugar factory and a large stack of railroad stock; he left behind only his useless pince-nez which, being a fraud in all things, he apparently wore only to make himself look respectable. The investigation revealed doctored accounts, doubtful morality and a woman he kept in town.

The history of the estate could be told through its successive overseers—they would not be a footnote, rather the heart of the subject. Who better than an overseer sums up the changing interaction between power, money and ownership in a given period? Who knows better the decaying foundations of a fortune, its secrets, the patient addition of blocks of wood, sacks of wheat, pears and cherries, of which that fortune is only the sum?

But I feel utterly incapable of such a strictly chronological account—for me, time is a very abstract notion. Rather than memories, I have a wealth of sensations that are all equally present, and it is through an effort of will that I am able to date them to a certain period or a certain day. People and things come and go; I am always here.

In the front is the colonnaded portico, the main entrance, the gate that is opened wide on days when the family is receiving guests. To my left are the sixty chestnut trees that line the road to the train station which is hidden from me by a bend in the road. They say it is magnificent—too much so, perhaps, for such a secondary route. From here it takes more than twenty-four hours and who knows how many connections to get to Vienna. During the day I hear only three or four trains go by, and they scarcely need to stop, so slowly do they move. It's a common line for business travellers, a road to the scaffold for students returning to boarding school after the holidays, a one-way trip for so many girls who go to the city to look for a position, a husband, the feathers and bad cognac of an outlying brothel. A one-way trip too, for the soldiers who, in the near future, will leave wearing their *hechtgrau* uniforms and won't return, or, if they return, won't recognize the world they left behind—changing borders, new governments, emigration and civil wars—like the boy who thought he had been only seven days in Fairyland but could no longer find his house when he returned, having spent seven times seven years away.

I don't know if it's because of those departures without returns, but the sight of those chestnut trees always saddens me a bit. I prefer looking straight out in front. In the winter and on rainy days, it's an empty space, a cottony white space that allows me to understand, I believe, what humans mean by 'the future.' But the rest of the time you can see tall roofs and bell towers, a bit of a wall, the grey and red mass of the little town of Grynow.

The houses in Grynow are lovely, with their gables and their caryatides. The entire canton envies our market square. There are twenty shops; barrels, fabrics, pottery, all strut for customers under balconies of wrought iron on the floors above. I know, because in my green salon a series of small paintings reproduce it from every angle. *Market day in Grünau*, a kaleidoscope of colours, cows and pigs, is there above all to remind us of the time when the dual monarchy had not yet returned to the towns of our province, along with a certain autonomy, their Slavic names. But I rather like *Flour Balance at Dawn*, *The Drapers' House* and especially *The Jewish Quarter Seen from the Church of St George*, in which two children dressed in black are playing jacks, seated on the ground. Everyone considers it the very best, for the sense of life that pours out of it—one of the little fellows, concentrating, is preparing his next shot while the other, from over his shoulder, is staring at the viewer, his eyes shining with mischief. 'Rubbish!' Jozef Zemka had nevertheless shouted in front of his daughter's masterpiece (Wioletta, the third, who never married). Facing that pair of little eyes, breaking out of the canvas to taunt him, a feeling of injustice and impotence had seized him, blood had risen to his head, as it so often did, but that time it did not go down again. The infamous painting had remained in the salon, and it is still there; the old man was confined to his bed where he died a few days later, his eyes troubled, his brow furrowed. 'Rubbish' had been his last intelligible word.

Oh yes, the masters pass through as do the overseers. But in this beautiful balancing act, in this apparent order—with the overseers in the background in the fields, and the masters in the foreground in the green salon with its realistic gouaches—a note of disorder already slips in, because history, in my experience, does not progress in a straight line. Here, there have been those who became overseers because they could not remain masters, others who became masters after having carried out the duties of the overseer. The world is indeed ever changing, that is the lesson I have learnt, even if on a human scale it does not appear so.

On my own scale, this is quite striking. I was 'born' at the beginning of the eighteenth century, in Poland, out of the sumptuous whim of a

Count Ponarski (relative of the Ponarskis of Volhynia, but belonging to a younger branch that had settled here for generations). Costume balls, chamber orchestras in the English garden, neoclassical splendour on the roiling ocean of the Galician plain—all of that seemed destined to last until the end of time. Sixty years later, Poland, carved up by its three neighbours, had disappeared from the map of Europe; Count Fryderyk had fallen under the blows of his serfs' scythes; and his heirs, to pay off his debts, had to sell his *dwor*, his land, and his thirty-eight horses.

And so people come and go, and I remain; indissolubly connected to their fate without, however, resembling them. I belong to them, of course, insofar as they wanted me and made me. But there is something else in me, something they do not suspect and which owes them nothing.

I can't quite explain what that 'something else' is; at most, I am able to feel it physically. In those moments, for example, that precede storms, when, oppressed by the heat, both animals and humans fall silent, I sometimes feel the air of the fields enter me through an open window, go down a hallway, cause a door to open onto an empty room; its breath moves the pendants of a lamp, silently blows at a bit of unglued wallpaper. Then what I have once only heard of, becomes a feeling again, and I *am* once again that 'field of the dead tree' that spread out here before I emerged from the land.

It wasn't a field, and there wasn't a tree, either dead or alive—our peasants cultivate the art of preserving for centuries toponyms that, in human memory, no longer correspond to anything. Even the oldest among them have always known it as a damp prairie, scattered with reeds and smelling like peat. Regardless of what one thinks of Count Fryderyk, he did a great service to the entire area by draining this fever-prone marshland.

And under my white cornices, my bevelled glass, my façade that resembles a Greek temple, that is what I was and could be once again—a desert land, where mosquitoes and frogs love to sing in the sunshine.

I
IN THE SPRING

I met Jozef Zemka in 1820, at a gathering hosted by the Baron and Baroness von Kotz, my owners at the time. There were many guests and I wouldn't have paid any more attention to that one than to the others if the women working in the field across from me hadn't put down their hoes and, with their hands on their hips, started shouting flattering remarks: 'Dear me, isn't he handsome!'

'Blond and pink, a true baby Jesus . . .'

'And his hands, my goodness, aren't they white!'

Yes, the man who was approaching the gate on foot was indeed a good-looking fellow. His wavy hair, without powder or wig, was as shiny as glass. A layer of soft hair covered his cheeks, ending in the folds of the scarf around his neck. His trousers were moulded to his shapely legs, his stomach was flat and muscular; and the hand holding his walking cane was indeed exquisitely white; this should have made me realize there was blue blood coursing through his veins.

The beautiful Ulianna, the one closest to the road, even went so far as to boldly shout: 'Hey, my little sugar pie, aren't you just the most adorable thing!'

The cheeky woman could well have been his mother. But her solid forty years, her rosy cheeks, her heaving breast inspired other than maternal thoughts in men, and she knew it well. Yet the young man turned his head away; and if he blushed, it was out of irritation.

It was that odd reaction that immediately inspired me to slip inside his head; and I saw that the word 'sugar' (the only word he understood of what the Ruthenian woman said), far from flattering him, had cut him to the quick.

Little sugar pie! Wasn't that an allusion to what he still was in the eyes of the world—the son of a candy-maker? The 'Pastilles de la Vierge—the Secret Formula of Tadeusz Zemka'—that sweet speciality, sold in pretty tin boxes at the apothecary shops in Grünau, Freistadt, even Lemberg, at that moment summed up his social hopes, his claims to nobility. And just when he was invited to the *dwor*, these harpies had to remind him of the fact in their nasty patois!

Evidently, this isn't the only thing that is bothering him. It is the second time he has pulled out and looked at his watch, and he moves faster as he climbs the front steps. While a servant is taking his cane and his hat, he catches a glimpse of himself in a wall-mirror and blushes again—the overall look is good but his boots have become muddy on the way, the cut of his vest looks like it came from a country tailor, and his suit, although very clean, has obviously seen better days.

'Mr Jozef Zemka,' announces the lackey at the door of the grand salon.

The room falls silent—women are not the only ones aware of someone's beauty and attraction. But the boots, vest and suit quickly ruin that first impression and a moment later, all eyes, or almost all, look away from the newcomer. It is to an expressionless face that, after kissing the hand, he pays his compliments. But Caroline von Kotz suddenly has a thousand other conversations to attend to, a thousand other smiles to deliver; he receives only a quick 'Charmed, I'm sure . . . so kind . . .' then, like a door that shuts, she turns her back on him. A glass of Madeira in his hand, he walks from the fireplace to a window, from the window to the piano and ends up joining another odd man out—the young Jewish doctor of Grünau.

He listens distractedly to what the doctor is saying, discreetly looking around at the other guests. There is no trace of his uncle, the one who had advised him to be there on time. Richly coloured uniforms, a few dark suits; the baron, among various other bureaucrats of lesser status, is proffering some political aphorisms—some words on Metternich, other words on the difficulties of the Ottoman Empire. For the time being Jozef is the only Pole there—after forty-eight years of occupation, the Galician magnates are still keeping their distance.

He looks around the reception room carefully, at its large, dusty, pink and white stucco panels, its wooden parquet floor with interwoven, inlaid flowers. He had never seen all this before; but I begin to have the impression that he recognizes them, or at least that he is studying them with greater concentration than he should have been.

'A beautiful interior, isn't it?'

'Admirable,' agrees Salomon Weinberg. 'The baron had it renovated and furnished with a great deal of taste, I find. The loveseat and the chairs are really quite beautiful.'

The loveseat! These Jews know about such things, Jozef grumbles to himself, not happy to realize that the doctor speaks much better German. Of course, the doctor has been to university, and many of his courses must have been taught in that language. But that explanation only manages to irritate Jozef further—behind that word 'university' is a lot of abstruse and perhaps useless knowledge which immediately arouses his aggressive instincts.

'The baroness is one of your patients, I believe,' he slips in, to remind his interlocutor of the ancillary nature of his status that has earned him an invitation to the festivities.

'The baroness, thank God, has no need of my services,' smiles the other, with an involuntary glance at the woman who, indestructible, continues to spin around among her guests. 'But I've had the honour on occasion of being asked to attend to Miss Clara, her daughter. In fact, there she is, getting up to play the piano.'

Quite the ugly duckling, thinks Jozef—square shoulders, a flat chest, bowed head, as if she feels the critical eyes of her parents, watching her movements from a distance, weighing down upon her. Yet she resembles them but in an unfortunate way—from her lively mother she has only the thin mouth; from her father, the protruding eyes and a physique that is too robust for a girl. She begins to play, but the music is scarcely audible; she seems to be begging pardon from the entire earth for her cumbersome body and her lack of beauty.

A great slap on the back brings Jozef out of his observations, and he turns around: 'Ah, Uncle, here you are!'

For me, it is a thunderclap; and I finally understand the vague feeling of déjà vu I experienced upon seeing the seductive young blond man for the first time. The man he has just called uncle is none other than Krzysztof Ponarski, a grandson of Count Fryderyk, who, since he came of age, has been the overseer of his family's former estate. I don't know why—perhaps Christian charity or the prestige of great names—the successive owners allowed him to hold that position. They all sold after a few years, often at a loss, and I am persuaded that the deleterious influence of this incapable man had something to do with it.

Seeing his nephew brings tears to his eyes; he hugs him, kisses him, pinches his cheeks, 'Jozef, my dear boy, you are here, that's wonderful!

Right on time too. *La politesse des rois* . . . Oh, I'm the one who is late
. . . I'm very sorry, but you see I had so much to do out there . . . My
accounts . . .'

He thoughtfully puts his watch back in his pocket and takes a glass
of wine as the server passes by.

'And what do you think of the von Kotzes? I admit they've given a
little cachet back to this old salon, even if I find their Empire furnishings
somewhat questionable. A sphinx as an armrest, what an idea! . . . I hope
you've already paid your compliments to the baroness?'

His comments are drawing attention, and Jozef murmurs: 'Of
course, Uncle. By the way, I trust you know Doctor Salomon Weinberg,
from the University of Kraków?'

'Oh, oh, how well you said that—Doctor Salomon Weinberg! There
is no doubt, my boy, that you know your world. My little Elzbieta has
raised you as a worthy Ponarski. My poor little sister, my poor sacrificial
lamb . . . But, of course, nephew, I know the doctor, we eat together at
the same table more often than you might think. Weinberg, so this is
my nephew, Jozef Zemka, who will be following me in my duties . . .'

He nods his head and empties his glass in one gulp.

'Really! Let me congratulate you,' says the doctor in the silence that
follows.

'Oh yes, oh yes,' Krzysztof continues, his voice lilting, his eyes filling
with tears. 'Oh, congratulate him, Weinberg, for it is a prestigious duty
to administer a property such as this one. I'll have many regrets when I
leave, but I'm getting too old, because, you see, I've had a hard life . . .'

To have had a hard life for Krzysztof meant having been born the
son of ruined aristocrats; to have grown up amidst tales of past parties,
hunts, but under a shingled roof (his father had only three serfs, whose
work was scarcely enough to feed everyone); to have had the status to
claim the title of Galician count per the ordinance of 1775 but not the
means to pay the taxes that the title implied; and to have attempted to
forget the cruelty of his fate, and the misfortunes of his homeland, in a
flood of drink—Madeira, tokay, kontuszowka and substandard beer, for
he never drank alone although his company was more than mixed.

In thirteen months Baron Franz von Kotz had developed a good
sense of the man. The week before the party, he had asked him to find

a successor as soon as possible. He, himself, was the administrator of the State Salt Reserves, he knew all about administration, but because he was often absent he needed a reliable lieutenant. Krzysztof, stunned, but lucid enough to be grateful to the baron for merely pointing out his advancing age (he had just turned sixty), quickly proposed his nephew so that the position would at least stay in the family.

'Jozef Zemka, Excellency. A stupid name, I grant you, but of noble blood. My poor sister . . .'

'You can introduce him to me on Tuesday at my wife's reception,' the baron interrupted before lowering the lids over his bulging eyes, a sign that the meeting was over.

And here we are. Arriving late, the last of the Ponarskis (I'm speaking of the younger branch of the family and not of the Ponarskis from Volhynia who are still doing very well) has exhausted every possible means to stall this humiliating duty. The lackeys are beginning to avoid him when they walk around, trays in their hands, among the guests. Krzysztof tries to beckon them over with a glance, then calls out their names, but they ignore him. With nothing left to drink, with nothing left to say, with the young girl of the house having just finished playing and the audience clapping half-heartedly—it is time.

'Nephew, I think it is time I introduce you to the baron,' he blurts with another loud clap on Jozef's back. 'Oh, I'm sorry, you hadn't finished your drink. Don't worry, Madeira doesn't really stain, you'll just have to soak your tie for a while . . . Weinberg, please excuse us . . .'

It is quite a feat to make their way over to the head of the house. An officer with a ruddy face and the bishop of the district are forming a barrier around him and move away only while scrutinizing from head to toe the intruder who they know is beneath them; Krzysztof, who has already swallowed many bitter pills in his life, doesn't react.

'Excellency, here is the young nephew I spoke to you about.'

There follows a litany of Jozef's abilities, talents, and accomplishments, which Jozef is wise enough not to interrupt and tempers only with the raising of his eyebrows. He has already established the art, when he is among men, of hiding his looks behind an austere mask—his seduction is at work but unbeknownst to those concerned.

And the baron is in fact thinking: has character, seems serious. This nephew from Grünau is a nice surprise, I expected worse . . . A bit young, perhaps; but you can see right away that he knows how to count and has a head on his shoulders. He's the man I need.

'Very well,' he concludes loudly. 'Mr Zemka, come back next week to start work under your uncle's supervision. He will bring you up to speed. And in two months I expect you will be able to stand on your own feet . . . I thank you.'

Without transition he resumes his conversation with his important guests. Jozef and his uncle bow, slowly retreat to the bay window that looks out over the grounds. Side by side they look at the view, their thoughts following the same course, and Jozef is hardly surprised when he hears his uncle murmur: 'My God, and to think we are at home . . .'

This is in a low voice that I have never heard before. Without effusion, without tears of nostalgia, it comes out of a stratum of pride buried deep inside him and preserved from the dissolution, from the alcohol. Jozef, like me, is impressed. And by 'at home' it is clear that the uncle is not just referring to this impressive salon, the windows, the cedars, and maple trees that are already over a hundred years old but also to the entire vast land that spills out as far as the horizon; the rivers, the prairies, the ponds, the towns which, under Austrian, Prussian, or Russian rule (no one seriously believes in that new 'Congressional Poland' of which the tsar was king), separated my walls from the distant Baltic.

Jozef nods. He also has that pride but it is buried less deep. His mouth curves, he bids farewell to his uncle and presses his hand in a silent promise.

Walking to the door he again passes in front of Salomon Weinberg who is speaking almost familiarly with Clara von Kotz. The homely girl seems quite happy to be talking to someone who is nice and whom she knows a bit. The doctor gestures in Jozef's direction but Jozef escapes with a slight bow. Enough niceties for one day—all he needs now is to be beholden to this surgical rabbi for doing him the honour of introducing him to the daughter of his future boss.

He keeps going. Behind him, two shining brown eyes silently grow larger but their shine is not that which causes a man to turn around.

Once again the piano can be heard—the officer's wife is going to sing some lieder, accompanied by Lieutenant von Berg (her lover, as everyone is well aware). The scraping of chairs being moved and gossipy whispers escape from the great room while Jozef collects his cane and hat in the foyer.

'Meine Ruh' ist hin, Mein Herz ist schwer . . .' sings a rich and sonorous voice, as he is walking under the windows.

His gait is firm, his head full of new impressions, bitterness, appetites. Only when he is farther away, almost at the grove of weeping willows at the bend in the road, does he turn around. His profile is tiny, but I distinctly see him raise his arm to focus his view, like a marshal studying the terrain before launching the attack.

2

I have mentioned the large Empire salon, its chairs, its parquet floor, the von Kotzes and their guests, with their various titles, statuses and positions. The people, in sum, and the rooms they inhabit. But sometimes I like to mention other things I also know—those places, for example, that no one has ever seen, except the carpenters and masons to whom I owe the light of day.

Up there, between the ceiling of the attics and my roof, is a space left empty for insulation. Two round holes provide fresh air for every little bit of the building. I could tell the story of the hundreds of birds that find shelter in this space, the bluish eggs in their nests of twigs, the little open beaks, the fatal falls that cut short their little lives, the raids of cats that destroy so many families, the successorial quarrels around the nests from the preceding year.

It would be a wonderful story, full of protagonists, infinitely long, a bit monotonous too, perhaps; ultimately, it's a question of point of view. Being what I am, I don't have a point of view. I'm content to borrow those of others, and you can't imagine the disturbing pleasure there is in changing it so often.

And so from time to time I like to gather myself completely in this burrow beneath the roof where the winter snow and frost find shelter, and where, in the summer, myriads of dust particles swirl in a luminous ray of light, silent, eternal, indifferent to the heat that I can easily describe as inhuman. Seeing them frolic, sometimes only rising, other times falling and forming piles on the ground (dust bunnies), as if they possessed free will and an embryo of social life, I begin to imagine the vast burning desert governed by a dust that has become intelligent, which the Earth perhaps will be in a few billion years. (Now, that is a radical change in point of view, the extreme limit of my imagination in that domain.)

But this diversity of perspectives does not imply any indifference on my part. I can move around everywhere, into everything, but once I am there I am completely involved in what I am observing. It is not that I consider humans *like* dust or little birds—they all interest me equally.

I'm sure that such a confession wouldn't please people, as every man and woman takes pride in the Copernican revolution while remaining the centre of his or her own universe. They would never be curious enough to look at that world from the point of view, say, of their clocks, lamps, draperies or other everyday objects in which those naive creatures see only a prolongation of their beings. Yet, that is what I do, sometimes. And what strange colours the world takes on then! How little it seems, how little it changes, and how the movements of the animate beings appear mysterious and empty of meaning! Yes, that point of view is no doubt a bit sad; but I try to understand it as I understand all others.

For when I add up everything I have learnt by assuming the multiple sensibilities of animals, men, chairs and cups, when I listen simultaneously to everything that has ever been made, said and thought within my confines, it is like an enormous symphony; I feel so full I could burst, I feel I understand everything and understand it with unparalleled depth, a wealth of vision. Everything then forms only one single great story, in which the role of the mice in the cellar is no less important than that of the Counts Ponarski or the Miss Zemkas. Everything resonates together, beings and scenes of the future blend with those of the past that explain and prefigure them. I anticipate, at the time when my existence will finally come to an end (because we objects die too, even if our deaths occur much more discreetly and gradually than those of organic beings), the mouldings and wooden objects I had known when they were new, will be worn, chipped, ravaged with age; I can see, underneath the rosy cheeks of the young man, the death mask of the old, I can see the tragedy beneath the comedy or the comedy beneath the tragedy (that happens too); I see those who come later bear the weight of the errors, prejudices and crimes of their fathers; I see others accomplish what their fathers strived for in vain; I see the unfortunate women pass down from mother to daughter or from aunt to niece the blindness that will make them slaves . . .

And words, bits of song, liberated from mouths that emit them, float in me like old sensations, find a nest in a hole in the wall for a few decades; then one day they emerge and go off to whisper in the ears of a living being who doesn't hear them but who will be affected by them nonetheless. 'Your Grace, open up, don't be so cruel . . .' *Poland isn't lost yet* . . . 'You'll never make anything of this boy.'

While I am describing a reception at the von Kotz's five years after the Congress of Vienna, you must understand that I have in my mind an infinite number of other scenes linked to the first through analogy, contrast, conflict or continuity or even without any connection at all. I have trouble staying in one place, that's also true—if I follow my desires, I would continuously jump from one period to another. Of course, to fully explain causalities and relationships, the march of time is necessary. But I can't tame myself entirely, and while seeing the young Jozef set down his empty glass on a windowsill before leaving, I simultaneously see that same salon, one rainy day in the 1880s.

The shutters are closed, the furniture is under dust covers; the musty, damp odour is that of rooms that have not been warmed by fires for a very long time. Oh, yes, the good old days have been gone for some time, days when no fewer than three maids were assigned simply to clean the house. The one who remains (a slattern, the great-granddaughter of the beautiful Ulianna), already has difficulty keeping only the classroom, the green salon, the bedrooms and the dining room clean. And the library? It is cleaned only when she feels like it.

A little girl has just opened the door. She is nine years old, with shiny hair that escapes from the ribbons attempting to hold it back. Her everyday apron is stained with ink, strawberries, dirt from the yard. She walks silently in her little wooden clogs—her nurse makes her a new pair every year—lifts up a dust cover, looks in the drawer of a chest. Yellowed letters, dried flowers, a little ball-and-cup game that was all the rage, one winter, at meals with her grandmother and her four great-aunts Zemka. She looks around, hums, blows on the dust. It's not very interesting, and yet it absorbs her to the point that she forgets to swallow . . . And a little spit bubble forms between her lips while her eyes fix upon a point in eternity . . . in these moments it almost seems as if she *sees* me.

'What are you doing in here?'

A jump, a tinkling sound—the von Kotz's last Madeira glass falls to the ground, but what was it doing there among those old papers?

'Good job. Now you're breaking things. Don't you have anything better to do than poke around in drawers?'

She straightens up, her hands behind her back. Above her, a red-headed adolescent is glaring at her sternly.

'Of course, you're not answering. The cat's got your tongue. The lady hangs around the kitchen gossiping all week long, but has nothing to say when she is asked a simple question. And . . . oh my heavens, you're still wearing those nasty clogs?'

'Kazimierz!'

Her voice is a bit shaky, but through the tone of objection there pierces an enticing note of submission and complicity.

'I don't want to see those on your feet any more. A slovenly Ruthenian maid, that's what you look like. I won't let my own sister— my sister!—lower herself in such a get-up.'

She tries an appeasing smile, teasingly moves the stool. After all, he isn't going to prevent her from wearing her clogs!

'Stop grimacing, you're making me ill! And I forbid you to pick up those pieces of glass. First, you'll cut yourself, and it's Nikolaïa's place to do it. Go on, leave them alone.'

She follows him into the hallway, her eyes fixed on the cut of his student tunic. She admires him hugely. He is tall, much taller than she. She would like to be tall too. She would like for her voice to have the same effect on others, to make them tremble or, more rarely, to swell with happiness. And she would also like a tunic like that, cinched at the waist.

But to be locked up for ten months a year in a school in Lvov, to be punished, to wash in cold water, to no longer run in the fields! No, never mind the tunic, she prefers to remain what she is—a slovenly maid who plays the piano badly and doesn't understand his Latin quotes. To be inferior, in the end, is not without its advantages. So little is expected of you!

And yet her stomach clenches a little when Kazimierz, as haughty as an emperor, disappears into his room and shuts the door in her face.

What to do? It's raining again. Walk on the tile floor, avoiding the black tiles and jumping from white to white?

But that game from when she was younger isn't fun any more, and suddenly the awareness of her boredom comes crashing down on her. She goes down to the kitchen, explains that she has broken a glass— someone grumbles—then goes upstairs with a broom and dustpan. She hesitates, should she take advantage of the servant's absence and steal a piece of bread and quince jam? But her eyes fall on her boots that Nikolaïa has just polished and which are waiting against the wall.

She sits down on the bench, looks at her feet in their black cotton socks, slips both into the boots with great concentration, her neck bent, her lips already curving into a slow feminine smile.

She bends down a bit more and buttons the tops. There are twelve buttons on each boot.

3

Clara von Kotz was already twenty-six the first time she saw Jozef Zemka. The age at which a young lady, if she isn't yet engaged, begins to cause serious concern, as the youthful glow that is perhaps the only beauty she will have is already beginning to fade.

She was pious, and at fourteen had even experienced a mystic episode in the Viennese convent where she was completing her education, and had thought, to the great dismay of her mother and father, that she would become a nun. That was out of the question, she was told; in any case, the crisis passed, Clara lost her taste for incense and baroque trappings. However, she read a great deal, and ultimately developed a true passion for music which until then she had considered a mere accomplishment demanding fastidious scale practice every day. She timidly asked for high-waisted dresses; though they flattered her small bust, they also emphasized her thick and masculine body. From a distance, in the straight folds of the white muslin, she resembled a Doric column.

How do I know all this? I know more than might be imagined. There is the portrait that was made of her by a painter who was fashionable at the time, in which she is seen standing against a background at dusk, her glance dreamily focusing on some Roman ruins. There are the books that she put on the shelves in her room when she arrived here—an *Imitation of Jesus Christ* and the *Confessions* of St Augustine, whose cover had suffered but which I hardly ever see her open any more, *Werther*, Schiller, and even Ossian, who followed one another assiduously on her bedside table. And then there were the letters of a novice who had been her teacher and who implored her to be courageous, while regretting that her vocation had been thwarted. Reading her prose, which I do sometimes by slipping into the envelope, I don't really like that Sister Angelika. Beneath her calls for Christian humility and obedience, I sense a good dose of pride, a haughty scorn for secular joys, a bit of perverse pleasure in controlling the conscience of a girl who had been born well above her and whose father remained faithful to Josephian ideals.

That nun, however, was no doubt the first to understand Clara's soul, the advantage that could be taken of such passion allied with a loving and tender heart. But the correspondence stopped after several letters—it was perhaps her family who put a stop to it.

It was perhaps something else as well. At eighteen, Clara debuted in the world, a world reeling from the events that were shaking up Europe. That was in December 1812; everywhere, people were talking only of the retreat of Napoleon's army; such talk floated over the silk and pearls of balls, over the languid and slightly scandalous twirling of waltzes, like the disturbing smell of smoke and the grumbling of distant canons, all of which caused many hearts to race. Nothing is more conducive to love than troubled times.

I know nothing about the first man Clara fell in love with, except that his name was Adalbert. But from the blank and hesitant way she pronounced that name in the shelter of her bedroom, I guessed that she had never had the opportunity to say it in the real world. It must have been a love she kept hidden from the fellow himself, either because it wasn't shared, or was impossible, or was undesirable for some reason. A glove, an ivory dance card, a dried flower perhaps picked from under the trees of the Prater in memory of a moment of happiness—these were the relics that she kept in a hidden drawer of her desk. A mere touch of the hand would have been enough to enamour this imaginative girl so starved for affection; and she harboured enough emotion in herself to keep a fire alive for many years without external stoking.

When the von Kotzes moved in here, she was so used to that love that she identified it with her being and would have given it up only upon her death. Heated discussions with her father told me that her hand had been asked for several times (the daughter of a high functionary, of old Carinthian nobility, she was, all things considered, an excellent catch) and that in refusing she had deployed the sweet but inflexible obstinacy of a Christian martyr.

'I order you, do you hear? I order you to accept Councillor of State Menzel. He is a dignified man who appreciates your qualities, he will be like a second father for you. Do I have to remind you how old you are? Do you know that you are putting your reputation on the line by inexplicably refusing the suitors whom so many envy you for having?'

'Father, Councillor Menzel honours me greatly but I won't marry him.'

The wars had ended, it seemed to her that the world had regained its order and would no longer change, fixing for ever in her heart a passion born of the troubles; she resigned herself to it.

I see her again, in the evening, contemplating the treasures in her little drawer. She takes them out, looks at them, sadly realizes that their power is dwindling with time, that they bring to her mind only fewer and fewer memories now growing dimmer and dimmer. She regrets this, but also realizes that she is suffering less; one day perhaps she will be able to cherish them as serenely as her prayers every night. She would like the day to come when she will be at peace, when she will finally be old, or at least definitively considered an old maid; in any case, it already seems to her that she has lived a very long time.

After lunch she takes her exercise on the grounds, on the recommendation of the doctor from Grünau. She complains to him of neuralgia, oppression. The delicate kindness of the young man keeps him from telling her what he is really thinking—that she should quickly put an end to her celibacy. Everyone around her is already tormenting her enough on that subject. She walks under the trees with the gait of a soldier, something she has never been able to avoid or to render more feminine. She stops under a cedar, breathes in the air, feels a few drops of rain, smells the mushrooms; her little floppy hat is ruffled by the autumn wind; a few strands of hair escape but she doesn't bother to put them back in place. Sometimes she walks along the fence on the inside, her eyes fixed on that part of the horizon where one day, long after her death, there will be a line of chestnut trees on the road to the station. The children of the serfs, thinking she is watching them, take off their woollen hats, wave and quickly return to what they are doing; in truth, she doesn't even see them.

People think she is proud; she isn't very well liked. Her alms do not elicit gratitude; the furtive way in which she distributes them suggests she is expiating her sins rather than being truly generous. Her greatest pleasure is to sit at the piano when no one is there to hear her, and I am the only one to know how she is transformed when she plays impassioned sonatas for herself alone.

I love listening to her, watching her back when she thinks she is alone. Poor Clara! I would like her to have a bit more happiness in her life, but she is ill disposed for that. Too much passion, too much imagination—happy people are indifferent and placid, and nothing could have described her less.

'. . . Your Grace, I find you quite pale. The reception has tired you. Please, ask your father to allow you to be excused.'

'Do you think so, doctor? I don't know if . . .'

'You have made your presence known. Believe me, it is enough.'

She can't help biting her lip when Jozef's head disappears through the door. Like everyone else she saw him arrive and like everyone else she had turned away—but not out of scorn. From that moment she has been shivering, she knows that she has never played so badly in public, has never walked with such little grace or said niceties with such little conviction. A feeling of disaster is rising slowly in her. You will have only one God, you will not adore idols, she repeats to herself, horrified, it seems to her that everything she has been has been reduced to nothing.

The new love is already taking hold, speaking to her, subtly making her see that for years she has been adoring only a ghost, a chimera, a childhood fantasy; that for years the space in her heart has already been free to love a flesh-and-blood person, that she, too, is a flesh-and-blood person who can no longer be fed on memories and ideas. She is paralysed by these thoughts, only her lips continue to respond mechanically to what Weinberg, whose presence suddenly seems endowed with immense power, is saying to her. He greeted him, knew him, he already knew his name—how rich and powerful he is, that shy young doctor who calls me 'Your Grace' and who himself doesn't dare to claim his own honours! He knows what I'm burning to know, he knows what is waiting for me, a single word from him will make me the happiest or the most desolate of creatures . . .

'Who was that young man you waved to, doctor? Isn't he the new district commissioner?'

'I'm sorry, but you're quite mistaken, Your Grace, Mr Zemka is your father's next overseer.'

'The next overseer . . . Oh! I see.'

'But you're trembling, Your Grace! Go on, leave the duties of hospitality to your parents and go to your room and rest. As your doctor, I order you!'

She gives him an awful smile, because she is shivering in spite of the cashmere shawl around her shoulders. She agrees with a simple bow of her head (anything more would be impossible) and docilely walks away. It should also be pointed out that she has great reserves of docility with certain people. That powerful Saint Blandina, withstanding for months the matrimonial demands of her father, becomes meek before the advice of Salomon Weinberg, does not utter a word. Under the circumstances, she does the right thing—a good practitioner and psychologist and compassionate about the illnesses of everyone, the doctor is indeed a good advisor and would never lead her astray. If only she could always show so much discernment!

She goes up to her room and closes the door behind her without a sound. There isn't a fire in the fireplace, but she decides not to ring and ask someone to come light one. All the servants are busy downstairs and, in any case, her bell is the one they respond to last and with an ill humour that her embarrassed apologies do little to dissipate.

So without a fire, in the cold of the dusk that filters through the windows, she collapses in front of her desk, takes out her old treasures and strokes them sadly. Then she blows out the candle, lies down fully dressed, on her pink bed cover. Seen from the ceiling, in the dark, with her arms spread out on either side of her, she looks like a big doll.

One last time she whispers 'Adalbert,' but in a tone of definitive farewell.

Fate, chance, design; the shape of a human's body also plays a large role in their lives. Longer lashes, a more oval face, a more svelte body, would no doubt have endowed Clara with a completely different existence. I who am shapeless, or in a certain sense proteiform, I am always surprised and a bit shocked by this.

But let's allow our minds to wander. At the moment we are leaving her on the path of life, let's imagine Clara, not pretty (a physical variable that means little to me and which I'm not interested in changing) but exposed to other circumstances, to a better-suited love. Let's assume, for example, that instead of Jozef she had encountered Jozef's brother, the less handsome but more sensitive Adam. A fervent patriot who, working a bit in the family candy business and starving for heroism, hurried off to Lemberg in 1809 when the Polish troops allied to Napoleon occupied the city. The results of that campaign did not live up to his hopes. The grand duchy of Warsaw thenceforth extended to the banks of the Vistula; but Lemberg, Przemysl and his native Grynow remained under Austrian rule. Adam Zemka no longer wished to live on his occupied land. He settled in the grand duchy, took a wife (a love match, according to what I heard) and stayed there even when Warsaw passed under Russian control again. He pursued a brilliant military career there and maintained contact with the Ponarskis of the elder branch.

That man—whom I saw only once, but who is indirectly a part of the history of the estate—is no doubt the one who, of this entire familial constellation, would have suited Clara best. Both were burning with passion, they would have loved each other, a beloved Clara would have increased in charm and would have perhaps inspired passion, in turn. In Paris (where Adam later emigrated), her modest salon would have attracted crowds, the entire romantic world would have come to admire that Romeo and Juliet from Galicia, that tall radiant Austrian woman who, reading the ardent looks of her Polish husband, would have sat down at the piano and, with a loving smile, played a piece by Chopin or Liszt for him.

This was completely unlikely, but the reality was scarcely less so.

4

When in the summer of 1821 the marriage of the overseer Zemka with the daughter of the administrator of the State Salt Reserves was announced, there was but one cry heard in the surrounding countryside: 'Sugar is marrying salt!' The tithe, labour, taxes and fees—under those pressures the Ruthenian or Polish serf bends his back and to his masters appears lowered to the rank of a beast; but, far from their presence, he thinks, he laughs and sings, all the same.

Neither the von Kotzes nor their overseer would have been pleased to hear the malicious epithalamium that circulated during the four weeks preceding the event. Four weeks—such haste said as much as did the scandalous inequality of the two parties. For anyone who could count, it was just enough time to throw together the trousseau (all the peasant women who were not spry enough to harvest were assigned to the task) and to have the wedding so that the little token of love could still pass for having been born preterm.

Not once, however, did the Slavic song reach the ears of their Graces, who, in any case, wouldn't have understood it. The baron, crushed with shame, spent all his time during the rapid engagement at the mines of Wieliczka, where the collapse of a gallery had opportunely caused some damage; the baroness locked herself in her room to avoid running into the unworthy Clara. And within these walls, no one would be permitted such impertinence. It was as if a glass wall had been erected two hundred feet around the house, in front of which mustachioed men and their robust wives stopped, heads lowered; and they never would have taken one more step without having been expressly invited to do so.

But in the evenings of these long August days, when Clara walked around the exterior fence, she heard in the distance the choir of the peasant women in their embroidered smocks, their large red skirts blowing around them, returning from their work in the fields. How lovely it is, she thought, almost overwhelmed by happiness—because she was happy, in spite of everything. Didn't she have what she wanted? The warm polyphony opened up an abyss of tenderness in her, a desire to cry, she thought of the child she was going to bring into the world, trying to hum the melody whose words seemed so happy:

> My little bird, oh, my turtledove,
> Fly to the field of my love,
> Tell him to come to the wedding on Sunday
> And that I'm waiting for him to go dancing,
>> Because sugar is marrying salt!

> And tell him too, that if he wants my mouth
> It's not enough that he be clean.
> A true gentleman brings an offering,
> I need at least a little necklace.
>> Because sugar is marrying salt!

> And if he really loves me, he should bring candy,
> And caramels and dragées.
> For all those sweets he will have my mouth
> With something else that is more salty.
>> Because sugar is marrying salt!

> You, my dove, remain pure,
> Don't let yourself be tempted by sin.
> God blesses salt, God blesses sugar,
> But it is the Devil who mixes them
>> When sugar marries salt!

Out of what bitter transactions did the marriage contract result? I alone can say (apart from the father, his future son-in-law and the old lawyer, of course). But try as the baron did to lower his heavy eyelids in reprobation, to attempt to address the schemer only through the mediation of the old lawyer, to call on his honour and integrity, Jozef was in a position of strength—the sugar and the salt had already been mixed.

Clara brought eighty thousand guldens and a usufruct for the estate which, on the death of her parents, would be handed down to her as well as to her husband. Jozef brought only his handsome face, the tangible proof of his reproductive capabilities, and, in an uncertain future, the patent for Pastilles de la Vierge. A rather one-sided contract. Into the marriage coffer, however, he did put not the vulgar coral necklace of which the peasant women dreamt but two diamond earrings

which had belonged to his dead mother's mother—through them the
Ponarskis returned to their home. And on the evening of the wedding
(a modest event to which even Jozef's father was not invited), Jozef
finally allowed himself a discreet smile of triumph.

It remains to be explained how the very Catholic Clara, the aspiring
nun, the pupil of Sister Angelika, had consented one evening to allow
her father's overseer into her bed and steal her maidenhead. Are we
surprised? I'm not. Under the same roof was a girl whose most fervent
desire was to give herself (she gives herself to her God, to her music and
soon, to several children) and whose emotions all came together in her
senses—and a young man less inclined to passion but burning to
succeed, still inspired by a strong social and national resentment. Under
such conditions, the outcome was established in advance; only the
opportunity remained to be found.

It nevertheless took several months before it arose. In the beginning
Jozef followed his uncle around, visited the estate, began learning
the accounts and thus to appreciate the prosperity of the von Kotz
family, scarcely affected by the damage from Krzysztof's drunken
administration. He listened, observed, recorded and was very quickly
able to suggest efficient measures for improvement.

As often happened in Galicia, the estate was badly laid out, scattered
into multiple parcels of land and invaded each day by starving people
who gathered wood in the forests or brought their goats to graze on the
fallow lands. Such activities obviously could not be legally taxed; but
Jozef instituted a sly system that granted the right for those animals to
graze on the masters' land only after a veterinary examination, and
forced the wood collectors to undo their bundles under the eye of an
official responsible for verifying, by breaking each branch, that there
weren't any green ones.

Jozef was also able to convince several small landowners to sell their
contiguous lands at a low price; he had the hedges removed and new
paths put in. Gradually, the estate grew rounder, it became possible to
employ the manpower more rationally over the large, almost continuous
wheat fields. Over the roads of the estate there was a coming and going

of families who were displaced for the needs of the season, men at the front pulling large carts filled with furniture and chickens, women behind with their bundles of clothes, their icons and their children.

Thoughtful, energetic, Jozef met all the expectations of the baron who congratulated himself for having found such a pearl; as for Krzysztof Ponarski—he had been thanked and, with the help of a small pension, settled in lodgings in the outskirts of Grünau, which also contained a public house.

Jozef went everywhere—to the mill, to the stables, to the county tribunal too, when the affair being judged involved theft, a material problem, or any other attack on the property of his employer. The imperial and royal state ordered landowners to organize conscription. Far from seeing this as a burden, Jozef cleverly knew how to choose the shirkers, the difficult father or the cumbersome fiancé of a pretty girl and send them off to war. In his idle moments, he visited other properties to study how they functioned, had treatises on agronomy sent to him from Prussia which he deciphered in the evening in his room, located—out of a consideration that he could appreciate—not on the floor with the servants but on the second floor where there was also the library, the useless nursery, the bedroom of Miss von Kotz and another room often occupied by visiting guests.

He went up to rest after his day of work, smiled to himself distractedly in the mirror over his basin, was satisfied with his appearance but without being vain; and then, with a bilingual dictionary at his side, he dove into recipes for fertilizer and descriptions of steam-run machines, sometimes into a comedy by Platen or a tragedy by Grillparzer to improve his conversational German. He went to bed very late, got up early. He had not been taught how to relax when he was a child—his artisan father had inculcated the cult of work in him, something that had always horrified his mother who was born a Ponarski.

'You will kill my sons, making them work like that, Tadeusz. It's Sunday, and those poor boys have been outside only to go to church. More studying? But Jozef is pale, Adam is yawning out of weakness. Let them have some fun, give them a few kreutzers to go spend in town! Boys their age should also have their little pleasures.'

'Don't worry about them, my dear,' grumbled her husband, who loved her too much and who had too little wit to remind her what such principles had produced in her brother Krzysztof; he was content to place a clumsy kiss on her lazy white hand.

'Oh Tadeusz, don't do that, you're getting my hand all sticky,' Elzbieta complained even more lazily—arguments weren't her forte, they tired her, actually; nothing, not even her sons' cause, could distract her for long from her favourite activity—lying on her Turkish cushions next to a dish of candy, with a novel she wouldn't read, her eyes half closed in happy tranquility. Her three men respected her indolence but didn't imitate it. In short, from his mother's example, Jozef had derived the idea that rest was something for women and the dying.

He was seen all over the estate. The strict regime he imposed on his body gave him great, though cheerless, joy. He hated his master whom he essentially saw as a usurper but paid him all due respect; he had very little to do with the baroness. As for their daughter, he had quickly formed his judgement of her—a proud girl, who averted her eyes when someone looked at her, who left the room when someone entered, who closed the door of the library quickly when she found her father there in the company of the overseer.

'That proud "lady" is above all this, of course,' he said to himself with the bitterness of his rank and the pride of his usefulness. 'She has her piano, her novenas, her healthful walks—the rest of the world doesn't exist for her.'

The attention she paid Dr Weinberg, at whom she smiled, spoke at length, lent books, argued against his theory but didn't refute it.

'Flatterer, insinuating the true behaviour of a court Jew. That's who receives the lady's attention—it's the crowning of her scorn for us.'

There came a day, however, when Clara didn't shut the door to the library; but Jozef didn't see her. His back was to her, busy as he was speaking to the baron who was listening to him attentively while examining his nails.

'Allow me to tell you with all due respect, Excellency—such excesses should be banished. Last Saturday, your bailiff sentenced a certain Tarass to fifty lashes. They were applied so badly that the boy, although young and vigorous, remained unable to work for the entire planting. And a few months ago, a pregnant woman subjected to the same treatment lost her child, thus depriving the estate of an additional soul. The serfs are an asset, Excellency, and one must take care of one's assets . . .'

Clara trembled behind the open door, her eyes filled with tears. 'He is good, I knew it, she said to herself fervently, oh, my God, he is as good as he is handsome.'

'I hear you, Zemka,' responded the baron. 'I don't approve any more than you do of those corporal punishments which we are allowed by rights and which unfortunately bring us closer to our great Russian neighbour. But what would the peasants think of such an abolishment? They are used to the whippings, they consider them, after all, a form of legitimate authority. I even heard them say that they prefer them to a fine in good money.'

'*Don't ask of your purse what your back can endure.* Yes, Excellency, I know their proverb, I know the power of custom and I know the dangers to which power is exposed when one tries to alter that balance. But there are other things to take into consideration here.'

'Such as?'

'In this matter, Excellency, it is the overseer who is speaking to you. The estate is thriving.'

'Indeed, and you've had a lot to do with that.'

'You flatter me, baron. But I listen to things, and I have spoken a great deal with my counterparts during my last stay in Lemberg for the signing of the contracts on the coming harvest. It is not just that the merchants are stealing from us, Excellency. Our Galician wheat tends to sell less well—this is a universal fact.'

'Yes, but what does this have to do with . . .'

'What does it have to do with it? In order to maintain your revenue, it will soon become indispensable to force our peasants to work another day during the week. I've studied the issue, I've thought a great deal about it, reformed all that I could in other areas. There's no option—an extra day a week is imperative. And what better way to have that measure accepted than by accompanying it with a solemn renunciation of corporal punishment throughout your lands?'

The baron continued to ponder; and Clara, who saw only Jozef's blond hair, was nervously wringing her hands.

'. . . Consider too, Excellency, the economic advantages of that benevolence. Your serfs, treated as men, will serve us more willingly and their good physical condition will benefit us.'

The baron listened with his eyelids lowered. These ideas were in fact his own, and those of the missed Maria Theresa whose influence had marked him in his youth. 'One can get anything out of them, on the condition that they are treated well and with friendship,' the sovereign of Austria once said of her peoples. Why shouldn't he enlarge that maxim socially? This Zemka was astute, he thought, reasonable; and he had the good taste not to resort to philanthropic jargon that was becoming the fashion in certain circles.

And the baron saw even further. What a lesson for the Polish aristocrats of the region! One didn't beat serfs on an Austrian's land, it would be said in the countryside. The Austrian treats his peasants better than the Polish masters treat their countrymen; the idea would take hold. All those magnates looked down on him, scorned the Habsburgs. Too bad for them if, here and there, their serfs broke some of their windows or set fire to their land; it would serve them right.

'We can think about it,' he said with a gesture of dismissal; something that, from a man who was inclined to say no without hesitation, was almost an agreement.

Having reached the door, Jozef was surprised to fall into the arms, so to speak, of the young lady of the house.

'Thank you, Mr Zemka,' she stammered, while a bright red invaded her cheeks. 'You have convinced him—it was . . . a good action, worthy of a truly Christian soul. Thank you, oh thank you!'

A strange girl, he thought while curiously looking at that face which he was seeing so close for the first time. How deeply she is breathing! I was wrong about her; she is, in fact, a fanatic.

That night in his room he didn't read a line. He was thinking.

5

After that encounter in front of the library door, things moved very quickly. Jozef soon understood, and he, too, saw into the future. Ever since he was nineteen he had caused many a head to turn but he had never tried to seduce a woman he wasn't attracted to. The challenge was stimulating.

As for the prey, she had less of a challenge—the love was already there; she had only to conquer modesty and appearances. A bit of aggressiveness, perhaps a little force sealed the deal. The first kiss, applied with passion, as if it were beyond his control, onto a mouth that was mute with stupefaction, was slyly followed by a two-week silence during which Jozef carefully avoided any visual contact. Clara was in despair. The burning memory that had no follow-up was poisoning her body with depression and her soul with uncertainty.

He must surely regret it, she first said to herself, noticing that Mr Zemka was avoiding her. He thinks he has offended me, he is ashamed, perhaps he is suffering? And she sought out his eyes during meals, she wanted to tell him or make him understand that she wasn't angry; but he remained elusive.

He loves me, she concluded desperately, after a few days. That's why he's avoiding me. Aren't we forbidden from each other? He loves me, and our love is impossible, he knows that and knows that I know.

She couldn't sleep, her eyes had dark shadows beneath them, her skin grew leaden. A massive despair pressed on her heart, a despair that neither prayer nor macerations could dispel. In any case, what would she have prayed for? What she wanted was impossible—dead ends surrounded her, her life had no horizon.

When Jozef, who was monitoring the progress of her deteriorating condition, saw that she was shattered, destroyed, almost seeking death, he had only to gather her up one night like a perfectly ripe fruit. She wasn't sleeping and was easily convinced to open her door to him, persuaded that he had resolved, through despair, to leave the estate and had come to bid her his final adieu. His kisses and caresses shattered any weak resistance; she felt reborn; they had finally found a luminous issue for their unhappiness. No, their lives weren't over, no, the horizon wasn't closed for them . . . I won't say that she derived extraordinary pleasure from the act but she was overjoyed—they had sealed their fate.

In the end, Jozef wasn't such a bad husband. There could have been much worse—a Lovelace who would have fled, leaving her an unmarried mother; or a simple dowry-thief who would have left as soon as the wedding Mass was said. Jozef was neither of those things. He cheated on her, bullied her, sometimes mistreated her; but she would always remain his wife. He chose his mistresses from among the serfs, later from among the workers at the sugar factory, but never from among his equals, and so Clara shut her eyes. (She shut them often. Her existence from the time of her wedding essentially consisted of shutting her eyes, of shutting herself.)

Yes, she had got what she wanted—Jozef. It goes without saying that she soon lost any illusions about the nobility of her husband's soul and his attachment to her—he was neither good as she had thought, nor loyal, nor a man of integrity. As the months passed, the virtues she had seen in him fell away like so many scales, she then saw him only as he was—handsome, mean, determined. And her love was tainted with bitterness and shame, even though it never died.

She too caused Jozef some disappointment. In spite of her excellent education, her music, the French she spoke almost fluently, she was always a dull mistress of the house, embarrassed and ill at ease when it came to entertaining. After the baron and baroness left (they preferred to resume their life in Vienna after the scandal), the estate stopped being one of the poles of social life in the district. The Zemkas' dinners were not enticing; people avoided that ill-suited couple whose union had been consummated in a very ambiguous manner. Someone other than Clara would have conquered such reticence over time, but she seemed on the contrary to be delighted that their salon welcomed only relatives, vague friends and a few employees. In that closed circle she was relaxed, became more social. In the end, she would never be anything other than a good wife and mother.

But even in the maternal realm she was a disappointment to Jozef.

Their first child—'the child of sin,' as was whispered in the countryside—was born seven and a half months after the wedding. A daughter; and Jozef experienced an annoyance that, to his own surprise, quickly turned into pride and tenderness.

'Maria, my little Maria,' he says to the little creature wrapped in blankets whom the nurse brings to him every night. And he is eager for the child to be able to walk so he can take her into the garden, for the atmosphere of the nursery is oppressive.

But when two years later Urszula is born, he is seized by a stronger regret. Maria is now walking and babbling, he takes her outside for rough games from which the little girl returns flushed and delighted— they play horsie, later climb trees, throw stones at the birds and indulge in other marvels that neither Mama nor Pelagia ever know. Healthy, energetic, robust like their mother, the little girls grow up and create a lot of hubbub. Jozef doesn't object, after an hour or two, when he returns them to their governess—a Madame Denisot, from Nantes, chosen for her French, her piety and her impeccable discipline.

Moreover, he is absorbed by his new functions as property owner— planter, entrepreneur, tax collector for the coffers of His Imperial and Royal Majesty, even, in a certain way, the gatekeeper to heaven—before celebrating Mass every week, the Uniate priest must ask him for the key to the church and pay him a little fee for his trouble.

Jozef has hired a man called Gavryl as his overseer, a former soldier from the region. That dour man, whose words fall out of him like the blows of a sickle, is useful for conveying orders, in his dialect, to the flunkeys and dayworkers. The son of a peasant himself, he knows how to push a plow, forecast the weather and isn't easily fooled. But Jozef has no intention of relinquishing control because he has conceived new projects for the estate for which he has a usufruct. In an attempt to grow his father's candy business, he comes up with the idea of producing sugar on his land so as not to have to depend any longer on the vagaries of colonial trade (the blockades are still a bad memory). He increases his investigative trips, brings in an agronomist from Silesia and sugar beet plants. Everyone says it will be a disaster but the Galician soil welcomes the foreign plants—they thrive, grow round, even though the peasants grumble about the kohlrabi that are no good for eating.

In between two series of inspections of the building intended for the sugar factory, Jozef finds time to pat his daughters' blonde heads and to perform his husbandly duties; but this time it takes some time for the pregnancy to occur.

'That's what happens when you marry a woman in decline,' he thinks every month in a bad mood. Now thirty, Clara does her best, is in despair, prays; but her stomach remains flat. Then, after three years, she again begins to have some hope. Jozef starts to become assiduous, becomes solicitous, watches what she eats.

'Have some more asparagus, Madame. Gavryl found them for you at a very high price—you can't find them anywhere at this time of year. Take some more, please, and don't tell me you don't like asparagus! Who doesn't like asparagus?!'

And Clara, ever obedient, has some more asparagus, caviar, wine from Somlo and everything else that is reputed to favour the conception of a male child. Which is why the birth of Wioletta would occur as a great blow, a betrayal. I can still hear Jozef shouting loud enough to shake the windowpanes, in front of the doctor who is covered in blood (the poor woman has wide hips but her births are horrible butcheries, she always wants to do well, too well, too quickly, she is clumsy even in childbirth):

'This is too much, Madame! You have trapped me in this marriage and you are good for nothing. Zounds! I am able to make sons, I had one, six months ago, with the Doroshenko girl. You're the one who is bad luck—you're doing this on purpose!'

The newborn was crying, the mother's pulse was weak, Weinberg thought it best to intervene.

'Please, Your Grace, let your wife rest or I can't speak for her recovery.'

'Fine, fine, mister medical artist,' growled Jozef, somewhat ashamed of his behaviour. He certainly didn't want to become a widower; she was his wife, after all. But he didn't look at his third daughter for a week.

He was making a mistake, because even in the first days the child proved to be quite lovely, more so than her older sisters. And, something that would console Jozef and ultimately soften him, she resembled strikingly his great-uncle Krzysztof—a Krzysztof with clear eyes, silky eyelashes, the skin of a peach, just as he must have been before Poland was split up the first time.

Poor Krzysztof had been buried three or four months earlier. And Jozef, although he didn't cry (I can say that I saw Jozef cry only once), did express his devotion to the old good-for-nothing by paying for an extravagant funeral. All the people on the estate had to pass in front of the coffin, their hats in their hands, and bow low in front of the mortal remains—the master demanded it. Then a long requiem was played in the chapel before the procession accompanied the dead man to the Ponarski family tomb.

Thus Jozef consoled himself for the absence of the truly guilty ones by increasing his victims. Because it was indeed the von Kotzes he was aiming at by putting on that funereal show. Oh, how he would have loved to see Caroline von Kotz kneeling on the ground, bringing the fat hand of the drunkard to her pursed lips, when, while he was alive, she had never deigned to address a single word to him! And the baron—his hat off, the baron, on his knees too!

Clara did kneel and kiss the hand but for her there was no humour—she truly did have a good heart, she even spilt a few sincere tears on that practically unknown man who had been so dear to her husband.

And so the months, the years go by without really bringing those two beings closer together. There is always a tension in Jozef, an aggressiveness, due, perhaps, to his remaining in the role of morganatic husband. In fact, he resents his wife for the promotion he owes to her.

6

But Jozef is not a monster. His conjugal bullying most often remains immaterial, I would even say that it is growing more refined with time. He willingly spends money or uses complicated strategies to torment his wife. In the end, apart from rutting with the peasant girls this is the only enjoyment that tireless worker has.

One morning, for example, while he is going out the door through the columns at the front of the house, pulling on his gloves, he sees a little group of people on the road. He isn't happy to see them: he doesn't like his workers gathering and fomenting disorder. He approaches them and with even more displeasure realizes that it is a group of women. For a moment, he has the horrible vision of a delegation of mothers who have come to beg for their brats—'each one smaller than the next, God have mercy on us!'—whom they can no longer manage to feed. You can divert men by passing around some free liquor, after which they begin to argue amongst themselves and leave you alone; but mothers are the bane of anyone who hopes to maintain order.

Once through the gate, though, Jozef discovers the quite-innocent reason for this gathering—a peddler with his wares. He doesn't have much to sell, considering the worn ribbon and the filthy almanac he is holding out as if they are the best of his offerings. But he is very young, handsome and funny, and the women are laughing and forgetting to barter and the younger ones are blushing when he gives them a trinket for the price of a kiss.

'. . . I win again!' he adds gallantly, one hand pressed against his caftan where his heart would be.

He speaks to the Ruthenian women in their dialect, and to the Polish women (because there are also some on the property) a fairly good Polish; he even throws out for everyone's amusement a few words in Armenian and Hungarian. This vagabond seems to have travelled everywhere between Transylvania and the banks of the Vistula.

Jozef is standing behind the buyers who, upon seeing him, begin to scatter without asking for their change. From the look on his face, the young man seems to want to do the same. He has taken off his cap, lowered his eyes and is trying to back away with small, imperceptible steps.

'Hey, Jew, not so fast! I have something to say.'

For all his fellow Jews who live in small towns, this type of encounter with a landowner can sometimes end with a fatal beating. The young peddler seems well aware of this but also just as aware that it is too late to run away.

'Very good. Tell me, Moschko, I don't recognize you. I might be wrong, but I don't think you're from around here.'

For now Jozef doesn't really know what he plans to do—he has an opportunity to have some fun and intends to take advantage of it. But the young man, resigned, is looking at him; then raises his arm and—no doubt counting on the laughter that, more surely than pity, can soften hearts—points up at the sky: 'You're quite right, master, I've come straight from there. A stork dropped me from the sky and I ended up here, like an idiot. So I cried out to the stork: Now what do I do? And see how good she was—she turned around and dropped—boom!—a complete range of merchandise!'

'Hmm. I don't like people who make fun of me. What's your name, and be quick!'

'But, master, you already know it—Moschko. As you and your peasants know, all of us Jews are called Moses.'

Something, a flicker of amusement, perhaps, keeps Jozef from slapping the insolent youth as he deserves.

'Stop your joking. I'm asking your name, you idiot, the one your father gave you.'

'Efraim.'

'That's better. And who is he, that father? And don't tell me he's a male stork, or you'll feel my hand!'

The young man reveals a set of white teeth: 'You're getting warmer there! My father is a horse trader, near Wadowice.'

'That's far from here.'

'Far? I don't really know any more. We were hungry at home, and I prefer the roads.'

An idea is forming in Jozef's head. He studies the boy in front of him, from his gaping boots up to his shock of black hair that has certainly not seen a comb in a long time.

'The son of a horse trader, eh? So you know something about horses.'

'Not just something. I was born in a stable, so to speak.'

'Excellent. What would you say about coming to work for me?'

'Work for you, me? In your chateau?'

He involuntarily glances towards me, looks at my three storeys of cornices and white statues; I sense that restive wanderer is hesitant to stay for a long time under the same roof.

'Don't worry, I won't ask much of you. I need a coachman, and that should be something you can do. You will drive me, you will take care of the horses. The rest of the time, well, you will only have a few errands to run. So you will be my Jewish *faktor*, like in the great houses of Lemberg.'

The young man scratches the back of his head to give himself time to think.

'Your *faktor*. But . . .'

'Fed, lodged, laundered. And I won't ask you where you spend your nights. You can go wherever you wish.'

That phrase seems to make up Efraim's mind. He happily spits on the ground, puts his peddler's cap back on his head and swings his merchandise up onto his back: 'All right, I'm your man.'

He is, and over the next few days it seems he has lived in the house for ever. He already knows the outbuildings like the back of his hand, has won over the cook Leokadia (and all the cooks who come after her), has an assigned place at the servants' table where he eats like a horse and drinks like a fish. He never learns how to suppress his plebeian manners, continues to spit on the ground, to sing out loud, regardless of the hour or the place, expressing his joy—he is irrepressible. And when Jozef is confident in him, there he is, one fine noon, accompanying Jozef into the dining room and sitting in the place of honour at his left while a shudder travels through those elegant ones seated around the table.

Elvire Denisot stares at the newcomer and turns away in horror. What an example for the little girls! That boy seems to know nothing about how to use napkins, he even cuts his bread with a pocketknife he takes out of his caftan. What could Madame be thinking?

Madame watches the newcomer with surprise, as a disapproving lackey places a bowl of consommé before him. Ephraim sticks his spoon into the clear liquid, sadly contemplates the von Kotz monogram at the bottom of the bowl and then looks at his neighbours as if to ask them: 'Where are the meatballs?'

She turns towards her husband who, over the table, smiles at her slyly. 'You see?' he seems to say, 'I have a Jew too.' Everyone at the table sees it, their eyes then turn towards the doctor who, every Thursday, joins them for the noonday meal.

It is indeed Jozef's style to employ this devious method to wound his wife. It isn't easy to humiliate Clara since she has a humble soul; deep down, that is her strength. She can only be struck obliquely. At that moment she is suffering for Salomon Weinberg to whom Jozef has just provided a vivid reminder of his own origins. 'Look at what you are, look at what all of you are to me,' the master mutely proclaims by defying their guest with his look. 'I'm not taken in by your polished shoes, your suit jacket or your short-sighted spectacles. You are a doctor, you speak German to your children, you proclaim your friendship with my wife and eat at our table. But you won't be the only one to eat here. I've brought your younger brother, Salek. What do you think of my gift?'

And Salek, understanding the full meaning of all that, suffers for Clara whom he senses is the target through him. A strange husband, who goes to so much trouble to harm his other half, he thinks, before looking back at the object of the scandal. The new guest, who has already finished his bowl of soup, is waiting for the next course, moving his legs around nosily under the table. Weinberg smiles imperceptibly— he gives this child of the *shtetl* three days before extracting himself from these interminable meals of the masters, even if he is beaten to a pulp.

Once again, the doctor is right. Two days later Efraim has disappeared; he sleeps for a few nights in the ditches in the area and then agrees to resume his duties only if he is allowed to eat in the kitchen.

Jozef agrees. After all, the shortest jokes are the best. And as a coachman and groom Efraim certainly earns his wages—he gets the horses to behave with a simple click of his tongue, rubs them down lovingly, knows all the recipes for treating their minor wounds. He has the same success with women, the same talent for persuasion, and Jozef is happy to make him his agent for his many trysts. Efraim has no peer in telling the girls, even their mothers, what an honour such a liaison would be for them. Sending him on an errand in Grünau is a bit riskier—sometimes he does fulfil the errand but most often he lands in a gambling parlour, plays the little money he has been given, loses everything and returns without his shirt. He is beaten; but his skin is thick and his mood joyful.

It is a true pleasure for me to watch him at rest. Leaning against the door of the stable, his cap over his ear, looking at the bluish line of the Precarpathians, slowly munching on an onion . . . his simple way of just being, bringing the onion to his mouth after dusting it with a bit of salt, is an insult to any idea of order and domestication. He exudes anarchy.

There are indeed shadowy zones in Jozef's soul. Because really, that autocrat truly appreciates the outbursts of his new recruit; I would even say that Efraim is the only one who can make him laugh and, sometimes, change his mind. Where does that attraction for everything he disapproves of—obstinacy, freedom of gestures, total absence of reliability—come from? And, furthermore, the doctor had an inkling of another interesting possibility—ultimately, what does it mean when one *harms one's other half*? Doesn't it show a hatred for a part of oneself?

(This is what makes Weinberg such a good doctor—his interest in the depths of the human psyche. Any old barber is capable of reducing a fracture, of stitching up a wound; Weinberg, however, also knows how to guess the cause for alopecia in a forced marriage, for a broken voice in an inadmissible secret. What makes men the enemies of part of themselves, what makes them become ill when they think they want to live, falter when they think they are moving forward? A complex alchemy between the body and the soul, he is convinced of this. But he keeps his hypotheses, which the faculty disapproved of, and which his patients would laugh at, to himself.)

A taste for that which resists, a need to harm that which belongs to him—these are the traits that are constants in Zemka's life. I see him well, the nights when he goes into his wife's room, becomes aroused by that body which, still asleep, is hiding and closed to him. When Clara, realizing that she has her master, her husband, *the one she had wanted*, lying next to her, becomes an inert mass of good will and resignation in his arms, Jozef senses his pleasure as hunter turn into bitterness. And he isn't sorry, then, to hurt her a bit.

Because in every situation this man wants to possess, to bend others to his will. But in bending to his will, the others become part of him and cease to interest him; his satisfied desires then leave him only with a feeling of emptiness—he is doomed to dissatisfaction. Is this what leads him, like Efraim, to put bits of sand into his cogs, to always rub up against alterity?

He isn't really sure what he wants. He likes to establish order but order bores him; he likes to conquer but possession tires him. So he cannot really be called a 'parvenu'—a man like him will never climb anywhere, will never look back with the feeling of having arrived. When he does look back, it will be during the latter part of his life, when his star will already be in decline. Jozef, through his longevity, is one of those people who will go directly from ambition to nostalgia.

But I'm exaggerating and making generalizations. He is also able to experience those stages that mark an existence and, at least temporarily, leave room for pure joy. We are now approaching such a stage.

7

For shortly after the birth of Wioletta, the baroness died from a stroke right in the middle of a ball; two years later, stricken by a sorrow that up to then no one thought he was capable of, the baron in turn expired. And the Zemkas inherited the entire estate.

One day in 1829, then, here is Jozef in mourning attire, very energetic, tackling the redecorating of the large salon and foyer. Three servants are busy under his orders, climbing ladders, grunting under the weight of the paintings they place on the walls. All this activity represents the marking of a passage of power, and isn't power incarnated best through family portraits?

Respect still prevented Jozef from removing the portraits of his late in-laws. But the clique of Carinthian ancestors is invited to leave the premises as soon as possible, along with Maria Theresa of Austria and the reigning emperor. In their place are hung a small profile of Elzbieta Zemka, an oil painting showing her son Adam and his Warsaw wife, as well as a few portraits of the Ponarski counts painted at the height of their glory. The lighter spaces where the previous paintings had hung remain on the walls, so Jozef puts up a copy of *Tadeusz Kosciuszko in the Uniform of Major General of the Polish Army* and another of *Bonaparte at the pont d'Arcole* which until then had been languishing in a room upstairs.

Then he falls into an armchair and contemplates his work.

But he remains seated only for a moment, because he is eager to survey the estate which, ever since his visit to the lawyer the day before, is officially his. He puts on a warm jacket, goes through the columned entrance, whistling, jumps into the briska next to Efraim, takes the reins from him and sets off on the road to the bailiwick, exuding a satisfaction that can be seen even from behind. He is a landowner, and the world, for him, is transformed.

The world transformed! I've always found it a bit laughable, the importance most humans attribute to such things. Depending on whether the land belongs to them or to others, they have a completely different way of looking at it, even of moving on it. And yet, in truth, to whom does it really belong? If I were asked, I would say—to the wind, which covers many more acres than the Radziwills or Zamoyskis will ever possess, bends the wheat in long waves over the fields, knocks over trees, taking away its tithe of shingles. The wind that turns every man into a peasant forced to fend for himself as he goes along, and every woman a serf whose legs it uncovers and hair it tangles on a whim.

But humans see this issue of ownership through prisms that I find quite abstract: To whom did the land belong fifty or one hundred years ago? What State did it fall under? Who holds that piece of paper? I am talking about charters, diplomatic treaties, titles of ownership and other scraps of paper to which they attribute so much value.

Of course, I, too, am subject to that regime. Somewhere, and Jozef is thinking about this intensely at the moment, there is a scrap of paper stating that I am (temporarily) his property and that of his wife. But I admit I am not very concerned with those pieces of writing. Their property! They make me laugh. They think they own me—it is I who own them.

Because I have seen them all pass through. Each one of them takes over with the idea that something infinite, immovable is beginning on that day; but, on average, their reigns do not exceed thirty years. Most have been happy, Jozef is extremely happy; others less so. Urszula's son, for example, will feel only a lukewarm joy. At thirty-five, he will have seen his father, Agenor Karlowicz, waste almost his entire life waiting for that inheritance. From this he retained the idea that the existence of a non-owner was a long punishment to endure and, in killing time, he had slowly killed himself, through alcohol, women and who knows what else (I wasn't there). His enthronement is already almost a wake—he is pushed from room to room in his wheelchair, placed in front of the bay window so he can enjoy the view before going back to his nursing home. He should have been happy but he is only exhausted.

And, not long afterwards, there would be the two offspring of that insignificant creature. Frail in their mourning clothes, sticking together like the orphans they had become over the past few days, they look at their new home with new and unhappy eyes. Tessa is shivering and, for the first time, all these large, empty rooms reveal, rightfully, the spectre of a poisoned destiny. Kazimierz, older and more experienced, is thinking about everything their tutor has just been saying to him, is feeling overwhelmed by the weight of this property that is as impossible to exploit as it is to sell. They go into the yard. On the other side of the gate, the inhabitants of the hamlet are putting hay up on carts, the pitchforks are moving, there is laughter, the people are talking to one another in Ukranian; and that evening, perhaps, there will be dancing in front of the church.

It is a peaceful tableau, and yet it threatens the sister and brother in mourning who feel, behind the gate, terribly alone, terribly oppressed. Without my walls, my panelling and my lamps, what would they be? Nothing—two Mohicans besieged on their last bit of land, heading towards extinction. To an objective observer it is obvious that they should immediately run away as fast as they can, preferably in separate directions, and never come back. Except now they are landowners; and their vague wish to flee is paralysed. The scrap of paper that holds them is there and, in their turn, they are chained to the glebe. How strong is people's belief in those scraps of paper!

It is out of such a belief that Jozef, today, is exulting in the briska next to his *faktor*. He has got his land back—for him, it is a victory for all Poles over their occupiers. In his private happiness, he sees the destiny of his entire nation through rose-coloured glasses.

'What do you think of the Austrians, Efraim?'

Efraim shrugs his shoulders.

'So you don't think anything?'

The young man is watching a heron which, as they go by, takes off over the marsh: 'I think they're leaving us alone. But I don't like their government officials.'

'Really? Why?'

'Because of the rotten patronym they have forced us to take. My grandfather had long ears, so now we are called Lan—'

'I couldn't care less about your last name, I'm talking politics. You see, I sense the wind is changing. The Austrians are trying to get on our good side now that they are in a delicate position with the tsar. Giving us Prince Lobkowitz as governor was a sign and . . . But I'm not going to get carried away—a free Poland will probably not happen overnight. All the same . . . Do you know that they're talking about offering the Polish crown to the Duke of Reichstadt? These are only rumours, I'm sure. But Napoleon's son, king of Poland! How great that would be, Efraim, how wonderful!'

'Don't pull so hard on the bit, master. She knows very well where she's going—leave her alone, you're going to hurt her.'

'What? You've confused me, I can't remember what I was saying . . . Well, all of this makes me regret that I wasn't able to have a seat on the Lemberg Diet. I am the great-grandson of a count, after all. For the time being, of course, such a position doesn't mean much, it is only honorific. But that could change, that could change . . . Doesn't it seem to you too, that the times are changing, Efraim?'

'There, there, Jolie, there there! Let me have the reins back, master. You'll be able to talk more easily.'

'Quiet, idiot! I want my peasants to see me holding the reins—today I am the master and I want them to remember that.'

'How could they forget it? With all due respect, you make them sweat enough.'

Jozef doesn't even get angry. At most, he pushes the irreverent man out of the carriage into the ditch. Efraim gets up and in three leaps catches the rig; but he has time to shoot an inspecting glance at the mare's shoes.

'She has lost a shoe. We need to stop at the next crossroads, master, at the forge, to fix that.'

'If you say so . . . So I make them sweat, eh? You're talking like that young idiot Prince Dubinski who is always going on about the people, preaching that we're pressuring them too much, that their sweat, it would seem, is sacred. It is precisely to outdo that odd person that I would like to have a seat in Lemberg. I make my serfs sweat? That's nothing. Who sends them his own doctor when they are sick? Who pays for the wet nurse when their wives die in childbirth, who lends them seeds for their plots when they've eaten everything, who bothers to settle their obscure disputes without receiving any fee?'

'You're forgetting the most important benefit you provide them, master—the grain alcohol that they have to buy from you by the head, women and children included, whether they want it or not.'

'Are you insinuating that I'm forcing them to drink? Is that what you're saying? They would buy it somewhere else, and no doubt it would be more expensive. From the innkeeper at the Three Oaks, from old Nathan at the travel stop, in the taverns of Grünau. As if you Jews didn't sell alcohol! I don't know any tavern-owner in the area who is Christian. What do you have against liquor? This is new.'

'Oh, I don't have anything against it. Liquor is good, it warms the heart. Except, you see, if it is to make them happy, you should do better—you should give it to them free.'

'What are you saying! What would I live on, then?'

Now they are too far away, and I can't hear what they are saying. And a moment later, the briska disappears round a bend in the road. I remain alone to think of Jozef's question, which I find relevant, even if he asked it in the form of a retort. Oh, yes, what would he live on? It's the happy mortal who for the time being doesn't have to ask himself that question.

8

The times were going to change, yes. But I, who watch things from this isolated corner of the earth, don't allow myself to be overcome by the agitation my guests feel when they receive those letters and dispatches, because it is rare that the winds of History blow directly on me. The fall of Charles X in France must have been a shock for the world; for me, July 1830 was marked, above all, by the storm that struck down the elder statesman of my cedars.

True, the following months brought many repercussions, even here. There was a constant coming and going of horses and carriages. A day didn't go by that a neighbour, a relative or a friend, top hat in hand, didn't erupt into the entryway shouting: 'Have you heard the news?'

Thus we learnt of the uprising in Brussels, the response of the Dutch army, the tsar's military preparations to support his ally Nassau. For his part, Adam Zemka, from Warsaw, wrote impassioned letters to his brother, commenting with horror on his mobilization among Russian troops: 'Are we going to crush the young Belgian revolution? Jozef, tell me: Can Poles battle freedom?' At the same time, one sensed he was in the grips of an enthusiasm which, out of caution, he did not explain. But all was understood when, triumphantly, he announced the success of the conspiracy, the flight of the Grand Duke Constantine and the liberation of Warsaw. National renaissance seemed on the horizon.

Jozef was beside himself, was neglecting his estate and his family, was living entirely in expectation of those letters that came from the kingdom of Poland. They came one after the other, at a frenzied pace, for almost a year. Each courier who arrived at our door had the mail ripped from his hands by a feverish Jozef and then sent away with a large tip, while the wax seal was already being broken and the lines, written in a hand that was almost illegible through haste, jumped off the page.

At first Jozef devoured them without understanding a word; then he went up to the library and read them again more calmly. But I did see that often that second reading left him even more agitated—he paced, opened and folded the letter, stood in front of the window as if to seek out all that was happening in the north.

'What has got into that Chlopicki, with his bowing and scraping to the tsar?' I heard him mumble. 'And there he is sending back home all our brave volunteers who ran to lend their support . . . He shouldn't do that, not at all! The Patriot's Club is right to censure him, although, all the same, Gurowski is too much . . .'

Or: 'Place Lelewel on the bench! But he is a madman, a democrat! Those people are capable of ruining everything, to lead us back to anarchy . . . No, absolutely not!'

Then Adam's letters grew more disturbing, the news more tragic— Warsaw was attacked, Warsaw surrounded, the infighting, he wrote, preventing any military intervention . . . Once I even saw Jozef—this was in June—throw down his brother's letter in despair, run to his cupboard to put on a travelling suit, kiss his wife, then pregnant for the fourth time, go down to the stables and have one of his swiftest horses saddled and bridled. Two pistols stuck out of his belt—he jumped on the horse, spurred it on and sped off at a gallop in a great cloud of dust.

But when he was at the top of the hill that blocks my view to the north, he slowed down and stopped. From that side he looked out at the mosaic of woods and fields where the shoots of wheat, the little leaves of the beetroots, the white trunks of the birches basked in the sun. Women were cutting, men in billowing trousers were felling trees with great blows of their axes, big draw horses were straining against their yokes; and Jozef sat there. I don't know what battle was raging in his heart, but after a long time, his shoulders lowered, he slowly returned home. And this aborted departure was never mentioned again.

Soon, moreover, news of the fall of Warsaw reached the house and Jozef made the entire household go into mourning—it was the hope of a people, he declared, that had just been buried.

I then have the memory of a long period of calm, or at least of an absence of events. Because, can you call the birth of Jadwiga an event? Jozef received this fourth daughter from the hands of the midwife with only a mumbled 'I expected as much.'

There was the baptism, the planting, the farm work; there was still no news of what became of Adam. It was only in December 1831 that a letter finally arrived, this time from Paris.

'Our big sister, France, has opened her arms to us,' wrote the eldest Zemka son, who was dismayed by that exile but who never lost his verve. His wife and young son were safe and had joined him there, at the same time as thousands of other compatriots; but the Ponarskis of Volhynia, their distant relatives, had been cruelly tested. Three brothers, three young men who had conspired and taken up arms, were hanged, Count Eugen sent to Siberia with all his children, two of whom died from the harshness of the journey. Poor cousins, through retaliation, had their titles of nobility revoked and had definitively sunk to the status of peasants without land, subject to taxation and conscription.

Luckily, Adam had fared better. During a battle in Wola he had received a wound that had threatened his life but about which, each month, he gave more reassuring news. Jozef stopped shuddering when he received his letters—in time, they became just parts of the landscape. His brother seemed to have a wonderful life in Paris, at least in his connections—his bravery had almost made him a friend of Prince Czartoryski and he had entrees at the Hôtel Lambert where he hobnobbed with other notable exiles. From a financial point of view, however, his situation appeared more delicate, if one made the effort to read between the lines:

> Ah, Jozef, you can't imagine how much the French like us. We are spoiled here, courted, a week doesn't go by that we aren't invited to a dinner or a ball. But you know my poor Lubina, so proud, she pretends she doesn't have anything to wear . . . How goes father's business? We received your letter of credit last month, but you mentioned exceptional profits . . .

His brother scrupulously shared the profits from the candy business with him and henceforth sent him thirty boxes of Pastilles de la Vierge every New Year, which Adam said were very popular among the Poles of Paris. Jozef had mixed feelings about this correspondence. Thanks to it part of his heart was beating on the other side of Europe where the embers of their destroyed homeland still glowed; but that salon gossip, those quarrels among emigrants, the attacks against the 'Versailles clique' and the 'agitators' of the Polish Democratic Society, they seemed very distant to him, even a bit irrelevant. More concrete and more serious were his own concerns, his daily life as landowner—here it wasn't a matter of castles in Spain but of real land, of real harvests and real returns. He thought back uneasily about his heroic impulses during the terrible year. What was the result of them? The substitution, on the mantle of the blue salon, of the antique barometer with a monumental bust of Adam Mickiewicz. In secret he envied his brother's ardour, felt small next to that officer who, for his ideas, was forced to lead a difficult life and whose wife was forced to turn her dresses inside out to make them last longer.

He was also jealous that, though without a fortune, Adam had a son, a legitimate male heir—Jan, who Adam said had become 'a true little Frenchman'.

> Everyone here calls him Jean, just yesterday the prince pinched his cheek and suggested he would help when it comes time to send him to military school. Oh, not right away, he is still very young, but you know that these things, in our situation, must be planned for . . .

Later, there were reports of Jan's success, his teachers' praise of his strength and intelligence:

> He has grown some more, you know. His lungs seem to be completely healed (unlike those of Lubina who, alas, has declined a great deal), he is now a handsome young man, and believe it or not, he has begun to grow a moustache! We have had a miniature of him painted, which I'll send to you, for your von Kotz wife and all my little nieces whom I don't know.

As proof of this, in the library there was now the portrait of a handsome fourteen-year-old adolescent with ruddy cheeks, on whose lip only the eye of a father could discern the shadow of a moustache. Often, while he was working, Jozef felt the weight of the gaze of this nephew whom he had never seen and for whom he felt a tenderness mixed with a bit of shame. That gaze was shining, confident and full of expectations: 'Uncle,' it said, 'I am here! What are you doing for us?'

And it was very softly that Jozef, in his head, responded: 'What am I doing? I am paying, young Jan. You are fighting, and I am paying. You see, you need everything in a cause—brave soldiers, but also experienced managers. But don't think that we have forgot you . . .'

No, he didn't forget them; but for his peace of mind he sometimes would have liked to.

9

And Clara?

Clara no longer believes in happiness, Clara no longer believes in love. She continues to believe in God but even that belief requires a certain effort. Most often, in her daily life, she doesn't believe in very much—she doesn't have the time.

She had five children, actually seven, counting those she miscarried. She was overjoyed with the first birth, and almost as much with the second, in spite of her husband's disappointment. The third brought her a joy tempered with regret—she too had been hoping for a son! When Jadwiga was born (it was already four years after the last birth), in all honesty, she felt only weariness. Her body is marked by the many pregnancies, each has cost her dearly; her hair, which had never been beautiful, has grown thinner, her brown eyes no longer shine.

And Zosia, the last, came into the world in silence. What could have been said that wouldn't have exasperated Jozef? He contemplated what would probably be his last legitimate offspring, thinking that his name would die off on the estate and that he would eventually have to provide dowries for all those girls.

And so Clara no longer believes in what life might bring her. In the past she once waited feverishly for new things (children, changes, world events) which would perhaps bring her a transfiguration, a second coming. But her life, she has now understood, will be only a long dusk.

That doesn't prevent her from being loving and attentive—her five daughters give her few true joys and much concern; there is always something to worry about involving their health, even matters of life and death for one or the other. She stopped sleeping for eleven nights when her eldest two contracted smallpox—they recovered, but Urszula still has scars on her face that will later make her difficult to marry off. (Clara is already thinking of that—she sees the future only from the angle of difficulty, problems that she would have to solve). Wioletta had the croup, Zosia scarlet fever. Each winter Dr Weinberg, married and a father, spends more time at their house than he does at his home in Grünau. I see him arrive, holding the reins of his phaeton himself—

calm, reassuring, he jumps to the ground with his big leather satchel; the sight of him always brings relief to Madame Zemka in serious cases, and pleasure when he comes for routine visits. Because those people who knew her when she was young are rare now; Weinberg is now her only childhood friend.

He is also called upon, more discretely, to take care of his master's conquests and occasionally his bastards. Clara knows this, she even knows that one of those children was a favourite of Jozef; he offered the mother (that Doroshenko girl of whom he tired as soon as she prematurely took on the physique of a matron in her pregnancy), a haberdashery in Grünau, in the town square. Clara is curious about that little boy that she was unable to have. One day, she went so far as to have herself driven to town to see him with her own eyes. She found him cute, that Vasyl, with thick hair and Bohemian traits. But he stuck his tongue out at her before hiding behind his mother who was standing in the doorway with an insolent smile. (Clara's maid, who accompanied her, later told the story in the kitchen, chuckling at the details of the scene.) Clara isn't upset at them. What did it matter? She also smiled inside at that stuck-out tongue, pink like that of a little kitten.

She ultimately cherishes the memory of that little incident, a ray of strangeness and audacity in her predictable, everyday life. And when (rarely) she loses herself in a reverie in front of a window, it is towards Grünau that she lets her eyes wander, Grünau where her dear Weinberg and the naughty little boy live.

That horizon where, in the distance, she once saw a swarm of lives, lands, unknown people, and towards which she would have so much liked to fly like a wild goose—why does it now appear so naked and flat to her? It hasn't changed, however. The same farms, the same hills, and the same trees are still there, although those have grown considerably. But it appears to be fixed; beyond the windowpanes it has become like a painting which one has seen a hundred times and which one hardly notices any more. And doesn't she have better things to do than stand there dreaming in front of the window, which needs a good cleaning, by the way? So many things weighed on her. She must check on the condition of the reception rooms, greet her guests, chat and smile. She has to pay visits to the neighbouring chateaus, sometimes go into town to pick out fabrics, coffee, tea and oriental condiments (this should have been done by the overseer, but Gavryl knows only about cutting and farming and would have bought ochre instead of saffron). She must constantly approve menus, hand out alms, undergo endless fittings for new outfits. She also has to dress the little girls, and then console one, listen to another practice her catechism, listen to scales and the complaints of the French governess.

That woman irritates her. Her way of crossing her hands over her stomach, never looking directly at a man, giving every little trifle the importance of an affair of state, secretly weigh on her. But to silence Elvire Denisot, to fire her, to replace her? Come now . . . Clara might be the mistress here, and in theory, all-powerful, but she is quite incapable of putting an end to what displeases her and even more incapable of obtaining what she wants. Anyway, she doesn't want anything, or, if she does, such a wish is so obscure that it does not reach her consciousness. And so the landscape is not the only thing that appears fixed to her—it is everything, everything that surrounds her, her entire life has taken on a cadaver like rigidity, an immovable weight. Nor can her half-hearted attempts change anything.

'The mistress is sad today. She hasn't touched her eggs.'

'Sad! Why would she be sad? In her place I would sing—the master slept with her last night, I saw him in his nightshirt, taking up water.'

'Oh, yes! He continues to plow his field. He's a stubborn one, our master. He still wants to grow wheat on a barley field.'

'He's as stubborn as a true Pole.'

'*Poland isn't lost yet . . .*'

Stifled laughter goes around the kitchen table, hands reaching for the piles of beans to be shelled.

'Oh, I think this time Poland is really lost. The mistress is entering the change. Yesterday, at dinner, she grew all red and strange. I went through that too.'

'The change? Ha! It's because the Jew was looking at her.'

'The mistress has a thing for him. On Thursdays she always wears her pretty frilly dress. And I have to curl her hair. I'm paid to know this.'

'It's a pity to be so well groomed when you're so unattractive. Give me a frilly dress like that, and you'll see whether Marko makes me dance or not!'

'Careful, my dear. We know how Marko makes girls dance—on their backs in the barn!'

'Don't worry, old woman. He won't do you any harm any more.'

'And you'll never have a frilly dress, you viper!'

'Bah, you're right. And I'm not the one who will get married, like the mistress, if I get pregnant. It's always the same ones who get everything.'

'That's right: *The devil always shits on the biggest pile.*'

'Speaking of piles, hand me some more beans, I don't have any more.'

'Take mine. I hear the governess ringing, I have to see what she wants.'

And even further below—I'm not speaking of floors, since we're still in the kitchen, but of frequencies. What follows is inaudible to human ears:

'What are they doing at the table?'

'They're putting little white things in a bowl.'

'Those will be for you. You have a copper bottom—it's best for the stew.'

'I don't like being heated up.'

'Idiot! That's what we're made for!'

'I would really like to get out of the room, like them. And then come back in, because I would be a bit scared, all alone without you.'

'Leave, come back! Little sister, you're talking nonsense. Do you think you're a serving platter?'

'Well, *I* did leave one day. I had a hole—they took me to a boilermaker.'

'Don't listen to her, she's babbling. Did you ever hear about one of us having a hole?'

'You're too young to know all that. But I'll tell you—it does happen; sometimes, we too, have holes.'

'And what is there outside, since you've been there?

'Not much. Jars, strainers, rabble, you know.'

'Then it not really worth it! I think I'm better off here.'

'My ass is all black. When arc they going to rub us with some whitener?'

'You priss, wait for Sunday! That's when we're cleaned.'

10

While going up the stairs the chambermaid runs into the handsome Jozef and, as she moves aside to let him pass, she gives him a coquettish bow. But he hardly notices her, he is preoccupied. He goes into the library and shuts the door, lights a cigar and looks out of the window, deep in thought.

Planning, building, planting—that is all he has been doing since he arrived here, and the results have surpassed all his hopes. He is the only master on the land, the beets are producing, the sugar factory is functioning full-force—ten new serfs have come to work there. And not only does the sugar factory supply the candy factory (a few rare connoisseurs find the Pastilles de la Vierge different since cane sugar is no longer used, but those are old timers, those who love the old world, the types of people Jozef doesn't want to deal with—the horrible old Princess Dubinska, and the music teacher of the young Wytockies, one of those Swabians implanted in the region for a century and who would be happy if nothing had changed since. He even considers Mozart a dangerous agitator, a Robespierre of harmony, he pretends to plug up his ears, shouting 'Dissonance! Dissonance!' when he hears Mozart being played), not only does his sugar supply the candy factory and the estate but his less expensive sugarloaves are selling wonderfully in the surrounding towns.

A booming business, a well-managed estate, healthy male and fecund female serfs; aside from the ideas that are germinating among the people, and which are held by a few irresponsible types among the elite, nothing can disturb Zemka's optimism regarding the future of his fortune.

But—there is a 'but'—what is this all for? What has he planned, built, planted for?

He picks up his brother's latest letter, which relates the little celebration held at their home for Jan's eighteenth birthday.

The prince was there, Jozef, our great Czartoryski! Well, he was there in the person of one of his secretaries, who proved to be divinely friendly and full of charming attentions for my poor Lubina. And do you know what he promised us? As soon as the prince reigns again, he will see to it that I go by the name of 'Zemka-Ponarski'. Zemka-Ponarski, Jozef! My heart is bursting with joy, I couldn't wait one day for the pleasure of telling you this huge news . . .

Oh, yes, he has a son.

Jozef gets up, walks around the room, touches the bindings of the beautiful books he loves to own but has never read—Plutarch, Titus Livy, Herodotus, authors whom neither the counts Ponarski nor the candy-makers Zemka needed to be what they are and to live in dignity. He too is what he is and lives, he believes, in dignity. Why, as the head of his lineage, should he have to defend himself against his lack of education and curiosity?

It is the times, he thinks vaguely. We are all ill, we have lost the peaceful moral health of our ancestors. Everyone feels obligated to justify what he is, what he does, as if no one in the world had an assigned place any more. We plunge into past eras to understand what we are, what we should be . . . Nothing is assumed any more, everything must be questioned—we are *moderns*, and that forces us endlessly to prove ourselves better than our predecessors, to never be content with ourselves.

And yet everything could be so simple. I have the advantage over my ancestors of being determined, ambitious, full of ideas. (My poor father had only one idea—to name a candy 'pastille,' and to have the Virgin painted on the tin boxes. That was enough for the final thirty years of his life. Even on his death bed, his final words were: 'Never change the formula!' May he rest in peace, I didn't listen to him.) I see much further than they did, my world is infinitely vaster—I have interests as far as the Pacific Ocean through the stocks I hold, I am interested in the number of hours workers in Manchester work, in the yield of the wheat fields in Ohio. My world is vast, and it is not just that which surrounds me—it is the projection of my will, of my wishes, of my hopes. It is me, in the end. I should be its master, its ruler, its demigod. And yet I have failed in getting what I want most—a son.

Maybe I should pray to God? Pray to God to have a son, that's what our fathers would once have done. I am no longer capable of that. (A little voice is saying: 'It's your liver.' Such thoughts always come after I've eaten too much. I'll summon Weinberg tomorrow, after I go to the sugar factory). Pray to God, but how? I don't like getting on my knees, I don't like asking.

He looks out the window and sees his wife below who is going out, accompanied by the governess and their three eldest daughters. She knows how to pray. As if it did her any good!

He held her in his arms the night before; now he's watching her adjusting her large shawl over her shoulders, smiling at Maria. He can't hear what they're saying, he only sees their lips moving, their steps moving them towards a destination he doesn't know. That night Clara was his thing; today she is coming and going, making plans—those minuscule plans that are in her domain. But plans nonetheless, from which he feels excluded. A small irritation grows in him, he quickly opens the window: 'Where are you going?'

'To Grünau, to the seamstress. Do you want to come with us? Efraim hasn't finished harnessing the horses yet.'

'That's fine. Go ahead.'

He was in Grünau yesterday. He has a son there, that's true. But what does that matter?

He sees his former mistress who, when he entered the shop, closed the doors, took him into the back room where he sat down, kneeled down to take off his boots and replace them with a pair of embroidered slippers. Vasyl was there, and at a gesture from his mother he stopped playing and got up. He looked at her when Jozef questioned him, playing with his hands behind his back; his schoolwork was horrible. His mother, to quell the storm, went to get a carafe of liquor and served Jozef while letting the front of her blouse fall open. He was irritated at the sight of those already-soft breasts, that chubby arm that he so loved to bite and whose armpit he loved to smell, already twelve years ago. She would no doubt have liked to have him back, become pregnant again . . . He got up with a sigh and left a few coins on the table so she could buy the boy a new coat.

(The images of the scene scatter in the library where I gather them with curiosity, like children who cut out pictures from an old book that the adults don't want any more.)

Should he raise that Vasyl, recognize him, give him his name? Jozef keeps thinking while he sits down at his desk. What's the use! They are only slaves. At best, I will have a freed one.

But he abruptly puts down the pen he is about to dip into the ink jar, because his eyes have passed over the already old portrait of young Jan Zemka on the desk.

What if—suddenly the affection he feels for this unknown boy becomes terribly concrete and overwhelming—what if he makes Jan his heir, the future master of the estate? How? It now seems extraordinary to him that he has never thought of this. Quite simply by requesting a dispensation for him to marry the eldest of his first cousins. (Another little voice pipes up: And why not Wioletta? The beautiful Wioletta, who looks more like the Ponarskis . . . Be quiet, bad advisor, we don't always do what we want, and Maria will inherit the estate. Be quiet.)

New images, encouraging and colourful, blossom before his eyes. An autumn evening—it would be in the autumn, during a beautiful, late season dusk—Jozef would be there, in the middle of his fields, an arm around the student who, for the occasion, has jumped out of his portrait frame and opened his young lips in a delighted smile. Jozef would raise his cane to show him, here the parcels of grain, there the parcels of sugar beets, the roofs of the farms and the dark line of the woods. And his outstretched arm would make his biceps stand out, because Jozef is a forty-one-year-old man, a man in his prime. Just because his daughter is going to be married doesn't mean he has one foot in the grave.

He would have to teach Jan everything, because he wouldn't know anything. He would listen, mouth open, to what his uncle taught him, would be full of attention and gratitude. He would no longer look like the son of a hero but relaxed, like a future landowner. Jozef would make him look like him.

He would also share Maria's bed but for the time being Jozef has trouble associating that with the portrait of the beardless youth he has before his eyes. He sees the situation as a child's game in which they sweetly play husband and wife or give each other little kisses through the bars of a chair. Hum! There would always be time to think of that . . .

He stands up, rubs his eyes, puts a piece of paper in front of him to write to his brother. He dips his pen, thinks only for a moment about what he will say. The ink is black, his hand steady; the lines come one after the other, *t*'s crossed with light bars and all the letters formed with firm downstrokes.

This time, again, he'll do without Weinberg.

11

Maria is her mother's favourite, and she knows it. Indeed, Madame Zemka has never been entirely able to hide her preference for her first born, her child of sin. In Maria there survives a remnant of that time of passion that has now passed. When Clara studies that face, which is really quite average, with the large mouth and bushy eyebrows, it is herself she sees offering her bed, on so many nights, to that bold conqueror.

Maria wouldn't need to know that to make her way—she was born with the assurance of the eldest child and solid good sense, and she is content. Not a lot of humour, not a lot of talent for analysis, but she learns and understand easily. She is growing like a beautiful plant and is successful in everything she does.

Wioletta is her father's favourite but she doesn't know it. Jozef is one of those men of action who is ill at ease with emotional attachment, seeing it as a sign of weakness. So he treats her harshly, is cutting and easily sharp with her. At twelve, this has made her fearful and timid; it will take her several more years to be convinced that she is pretty, prettier than her four sisters. And yet she will never exploit that discovery. Whenever she finds herself exercising her charms, she feels weighing upon her a critical and almost malevolent eye: You see? She wants to seduce, she's on a mission!

She is ashamed of herself, retreats into an inner life inhabited by obscure demons, phantasmagoria. She reads a great deal and has many unusual, independent thoughts on many subjects but which others attribute to worthless fantasy and suggest she keep them to herself; she has thus grown used to speaking little and to acting in secret.

She can spend hours painting. Concentrating on the movement of her brush, she feels at peace, no one asks anything of her. An alert observer would see in her flower arrangements and landscapes the embryo of true artistic talent, and something more, a bit frightening and haunted. But there is no such observer in her family—everyone shows sincere but superficial admiration for her little paintings.

Everyone is so aware that Urszula's place is not easy, in between the eldest and that pretty girl, that in fact she enjoys every privilege. It's not enough for her, because her view of life is clouded by a sense that she has been disadvantaged. It would take a lot of determination to cure her of her passionate envy, but nothing is ever done to do so. She is openly favoured—she always has the best place in the salon, in the carriage; she is always allowed to win at dominos and blind man's bluff (when she is caught, the catcher pretends for a long time not to recognize her pockmarked cheeks and her stringy hair). And she doesn't like the ball-and-cup game that their father brought back from a trip to Bohemia, which her sisters adore. A game of pure skill, it is impossible for others to coddle her by 'losing' so she can win, as with other games. And when it is brought out of the cupboard, she crosses her arms and pinches her lips in ill humour and feels that she has been personally slighted.

As for Jadwiga and Zosia, they quickly understand that they can count only on themselves in this life. These two latecomers, greeted as burdens, would ultimately be the ones who most quickly find their way. I can already report, because the thing happened all at once and without any incident, that at nineteen Jadwiga would become a postulant in the convent of Staniatki (a decision that would have undoubtedly touched her mother, if she had still been among us). Not through a penchant for mysticism but out of a taste for the life of a gynaeceum, which she had always had and which she had no desire to change. Once she had taken her vows, she would show talent for administrative tasks, great endurance for deprivations, an always even temper and a perfect indifference to the places and protagonists of her former life. For me, then, her life ended in 1850. For her, it would be only twenty-six years later, when at a relatively young age she succumbed to pneumonia. Her calm and peaceful death earned her a posthumous reputation as a saint. Wrongly? I couldn't say. I try to stay away from questions of sainthood.

For Zosia, the youngest, I don't want to look ahead. I am content to watch this little girl in a lacy dress walking around with her wax doll, 'Cordelia'. (I don't know where she got that name: she can't read yet.) She takes up so little space that she goes around unnoticed, observing everything with those big eyes that understand little and admire everything. Standing in her mother's room, she blends into the wall and watches Clara cry softly when she thinks she is alone. Even when they are sad, grown-ups are beautiful, she thinks, everything they do seems so full, all their words seem true. Her older sisters seem like princesses to her, the poems they recite a coded language, the mazurkas they play a celestial harmony. She lives in perpetual wonder, and that faculty would stay with her for ever. A happy nature! Happy Zosia!

In the early 1840s, my interior is a constant chirping of young ladies. Oh, none of them are really loud, but the combination of all these fluted voices produces a din that, at least for my inhabitants, covers another, more serious choir—still sotto voce, a choir of the millions of men who will soon rise up in the four corners of Europe. Only Jozef from time to time hears a few notes from this choir; it seems to him that there is a lot of grumbling outside, that people are demanding things, being aggressive. But these stirrings don't frighten him, he likes hitting the table, showing his authority. If he could get these six females to be quiet as easily as he silences the leader of the peasant community when he arrives, fiddling with the crucifix he wears on his belt, to ask Jozef for some favour for his people; or the young Prince Dubinski when that half-wit, at his mother's receptions, brandishes a Bible and admonishes his peers to 'give back the land to those who work it'!

But it's impossible—in his house they can't even hear him.

I'm returning to the henhouse, he thinks with some weariness when, in the evening, he leaves the taciturn Gavryl, his sugarloaves and his fields. As they grow older, the sight of his daughters gives him less and less pleasure.

Why is that? Sometimes he wonders. He did adore them, even though they were girls, when they were little. He bounced them on his knees, played hide-and-seek with them under the trees on the grounds, put them up on the back of Jolie, the white mare who with age had become a placid sheep. He took them for rides in the briska driven by Efraim, who encouraged the horse to trot quickly with a joyous clicking of his tongue (he felt it dishonourable to use his whip) which made the little bells on the harness ring loudly for the girls.

He used to love their noises, their little animal-whims, he brought them back trinkets and picture books from his trips; he had truly loved his girls—his girls when they were two, four, seven years old. How did it happen that, as the years have passed, he now looks at them only with boredom, even distaste?

Of course, there is *that*—which Clara, that old bore of a woman, would announce to him discreetly each time, with emotion and a stifled pride. Another nubile girl: What is there to be proud of, really? Each time he cursed that very female indiscretion; those stories of blood disgust him, make him sick, how could his wife, after fifteen or twenty years of marriage, not know that? He avoids his mistresses when there is the slightest suspicion they have *that*. It is better to do without than to risk falling upon that soiled linen and those pins, the sight of which appall him. A miscarriage makes him abandon a woman; anyway, there is no lack of peasant women and he likes a change.

And now his daughters, his own daughters! They could easily spare him these sorts of details. It remains to be seen how the thing would affect their bodies, perhaps even their characters. Maria is growing puffy and stuffing herself with poppyseed cake; Urszula's appearance is worsened by the development of a large posterior. They are all asserting themselves, they all have ideas on life, are all beginning to take themselves much too seriously. When he sees the faces they make, he sometimes wants to give a good slap to those creatures who charmed him when they were children but whose physical presence as women he detests. Find husbands for all these females, let their husbands take over: I've seen enough lowered eyes, sad smiles and hot-water bottles accompanied by knowing looks.

One thing calms him down—that at least their eldest is spoken for. Adam immediately and enthusiastically agreed to the plan for the cousins to marry. They only had to wait for the couple to get a bit older, for Jan's beard and sideburns to thicken and for Maria to have finished growing. New portraits were exchanged, letters too. Maria finds her French cousin very much to her liking and is delighted to marry soon; Jan appears to combine his intended and his Poland into a single and same ardent yearning. He has never seen either—or if Poland, at least not the Galicia of his ancestors. He says he is dreaming of its fields, its towns, its mountainous forests where bear and ermine are hunted; all of this seems very far away and very exciting to him.

When he would arrive here in 1844 to meet his future wife, he would prove to be less juvenile than his letters made him seem. Jozef was expecting a nice young student, putty in his hands, but the reality proves quite different. First, he appears one evening, unannounced, in a sleigh with three horses that seem to belong to him whereas (this was all too well known) his Parisian family has absolutely no means to buy him such an expensive vehicle. Next, apparently he has been in the area for six long weeks, has stopped in the small republic of Kraków, then in the districts of Bochnia, Tarnow and Sanok. Everyone is surprised, but he avoids their questions with much ease, kisses hands and explains that on his way here he wanted to pay his respects to the families of the émigrés he knows in Paris and to get acquainted with his homeland.

'What would you have thought of me, cousin, if I had turned up as I am, a poor Parisian who grew up on rue Jacob? You would have shrunk back from my pale cheeks and my awkwardness in the hunt, you wouldn't have wanted me . . .'

'Oh, but yes,' cries out the naive Maria, who excels in many things but not in flirting.

'Allow me to differ. You would not have wanted me any more, I'm sure of it. In order to please you I had to become Polanized first. And it has been done.'

And he kisses her hand again.

That gallant tone is new in the house, they will have to get used to it. Jozef wasn't expecting so much style, so much urbanity. The little Parisian from rue Jacob goes from a refined Polish to the purest of French, his manners are exquisite. Even Princess Dubinska wouldn't find anything to criticize. In any event Jan knows her through intermediaries, and says he has already decided to pay her a visit during his stay as well as to other magnates in Galicia. Jozef finds himself a bit humiliated. He thought he was going to offer this boy a great gift, do him a huge favour, and here he is, connected to the crème of the aristocracy, with a life and activities around which there hovers a certain mystery; moreover, Jozef is convinced that he isn't telling them everything.

In the end, there is good reason to congratulate himself, he thinks, while his nephew is charming the other women in the family, making his little cousins laugh, getting a smile out of Clara, even conversing with her about Paris and its fashions. He is good, he is very good, he repeats; and yet this evening he feels something blowing through his still-thick hair, through his still-straight back, something like a cool wind, a foretaste of old age.

12

I feel more connected to those whose emotions pour out when they come in contact with my objects and furnishings. For example, I will never *feel* Kazimierz Karlowicz whom I have nevertheless intermittently seen grow up. There will indeed be a time when, sporting a fine moustache, he will have a habit of placing an elbow on the mantle when there are guests in the salon—a gesture learnt, practised, perhaps, in his rooms when he was a student at Lvov. But I do not learn anything from that contact with his elbow. I am thinking of those backs that press against a door frame from the shock of a fright, those burning cheeks that press against cool stone hoping to find temporary relief—such emotion does not come from Kazimierz. Only once will I feel his trembling hand pressing on the wall in one of my hallways while his mouth stammers in the darkness: 'My God, my God, what have I done?' But that night, it will already be too late for me to feel anything for him.

The young Jan Zemka in the 1840s is something else. It is also much earlier. Perhaps chronology plays a role here? It seems to me that, with the generations, the people here developed an increasing tendency to hold in and control their emotions. Jan still belongs to the generation of those who pace the floor in large strides when they are conversing, or simply thinking, raise their arms when they speak words such as 'fatherland' or 'hope', stamp their feet when they are not understood. It is perhaps by virtue of a process of civilization that his great-nephew Kazimierz will be as discreet as a snake, stingy with gestures, detesting raised voices.

When Jan is in the salon, everyone takes notice. His boots pace the floor, impatient and polished; his smiles radiate everywhere, fall like rain on his cousins and his aunt (whom in the beginning he approached with caution but whom he did not find the stiff Viennese woman he expected her to be). He is unbeatable at cup-and-ball, eats like four men, although elegantly. His eyes shine even more brightly than his boots; and when he sings, it is in a vibrant, sensual baritone. What a handsome specimen of a man! Maria is a lucky girl.

From the time he was here for the engagement announcement, a year later at the most, I especially remember a long conversation he had with his uncle Jozef in the library. This time, by contrast, Jan speaks almost in a whisper; but his tone is all the more burning and his eyes are shining with a glow that is even more impassioned than usual. The cold Jozef is almost warmed while listening to him, his eyebrows are furrowed, his beard is moving. What are they discussing? And why did they think it necessary to lock the door?

It is certainly not to discuss the terms of the marriage contract, as one of them had done in this same place twenty-four years earlier. This time the contract is a family affair—there is nothing but common agreement and shared benefits in which everyone wins. This family marriage is a true game of Edenic baccarat.

No, what concerns them is much more important than the hand of Maria—may she forgive me, if she gets wind of it, for this objective opinion.

'. . . an emissary, you are an emissary! But for whom, since when?'

'Shh, shhh, Uncle, please don't speak so loudly, my cousins are delightful but they are too young to keep a secret, and what I am telling you must absolutely remain between us—our lives depend upon it.'

'Explain.'

Jan clears his throat: 'You are no doubt aware, Uncle, of the work that is going on to resuscitate a national movement among our compatriots. My father has always kept you up to date on these things.'

'Ah! I understand now. You are the emissary for our future king, perhaps you have a diplomatic mission here, a secret dispatch?'

Jan stifles a look of annoyance, moving in his chair.

'Let me explain, Uncle. I know, of course, everything that my family owes to Prince Czartoryski. Nor am I unaware of his role, the importance of the contacts he has been able to make with foreign courts, what he has done to advance our cause over all of enlightened Europe.'

'But? . . .'

Jan pulls up his chair, pushing back a lock of hair from his forehead.

'But the diplomatic route has its limits, Uncle. You must agree— the times no longer allow for the destinies of peoples to be decided by palace intrigues.'

'Palace intrigues! Is that your view of our national struggles, the Confederation of Bar, the struggles of our great Kosciuszko?'

'Uncle, all of those things, whose importance I do not under-estimate, have failed because they were the affairs of a tiny minority. The nobility . . .'

'God help us, the nobility among us are not a tiny minority. We are a people of nobles, the most aristocratic of all the nations in Europe.'

'Now, Uncle, those are very fine thoughts, but is it the nobles who, here, bring in the harvests and work the land? "The republic of nobles" was a myth, and a dangerous myth; it hastened the end of Poland. And our fatherland will not rise again without its people, the true people.'

How frankly he is speaking, the son of his brother, to him, who is however his uncle and future benefactor! For the first time in his life, perhaps, Jozef must take into account the arguments of an equal, and he loses his bearings. How, what? Everything he has learnt to venerate would be a myth? A dangerous myth?

He takes out his handkerchief and wipes his forehead: 'What does your father think of all this?'

'My father, whom I adore, is a man of the past. He has shown the greatest courage, and I hope I can prove to be a worthy son in that regard. He is also capable of generosity, and the cause of freedom ignites him, even when it is not his own. With what selflessness did men like him fight in the Napoleonic legions to deliver the peoples who were nothing to them, I am the first to recognize. But—and this is what dissuaded me from telling him what I am telling you now—his view is deformed by the principles of another age. He confers the march of History to a few knights errant, to a handful of death-defying heroes. Whereas I am convinced that freedom is everyone's concern.'

What troubles Jozef so much in what Jan is saying is that he recognizes ideas that have once passed through his own consciousness. Yes, it has happened that in reading his brother's letters he has felt a critical annoyance; and isn't that which kept him from going to Warsaw in 1831? Jozef is also aware of the fact that Jan is confiding in him what he thought best to hide from his father. Because that is something Jozef absolutely doesn't want—to be considered a man of the past.

'Everyone's concern, everyone's concern . . . No doubt, but how do you see all that? Are you aware, you and your companions-in-arms, of the strength of the enemies you will have to fight? The Austrian army, the Prussian army, the Tsar's army . . . Who will support the poor Poles against them, who will support David against Goliath?'

'Who? All of Europe, the true, the Europe of peoples who hope to emerge into the world. Uncle, open your eyes. From Denmark to Greece, people are waking up. The fools, the reckless ones, are those who don't want to see, who hang on to the old world and who will be swept away when the time comes. What examples we have been given by the peoples in America, Mexico, Bolivia, who are waiting for our people to break free of their chains!'

'That isn't incorrect . . . But really, a nation such as ours, broken up, isolated . . .'

'Isolated? But Uncle,' Jan whispers, leaning forward, 'Don't you understand that everything is going to be set ablaze? Wait—a month ago, I held a secret meeting in an inn near Krosno . . .'

'You're holding meetings in inns!'

'Of course. The people are waking up but there's nothing like the cock's crow to get them to arise. And it is precisely here that aristocracy and intelligence have a role to play. We are the apostles of the national faith, we are preaching freedom, we propagate hope . . . So, I was giving a speech in a room in an inn, you know the kind, black with soot and lit by a few naphtha lamps. While I was speaking I knocked over a lamp, the naphtha spread and in a few seconds the flames shot up. We laughed, threw sand on the flames, and my heart rejoiced at this omen. Uncle—Europe today is a flask of naphtha that is waiting for its spark!'

'So you are counting on the serfs of Krosno . . .'

'Serfs? *Poles*, Uncle. What does the inequality of rank matter when the fatherland is at stake? They cherish freedom as much as we do, and freedom is for all—in the near future, here there will no longer be serfs or masters, but one people free, strong, and unified.'

The young man has got up and is pacing back and forth, while Jozef, sunk in his armchair, follows him with his eyes. What a gulf, what an abyss has opened under his feet! Why this terror? Might he, like Adam, be attached to principles from another age?

In a toneless voice he answers: 'So you ultimately recommend an end to serfdom?'

'Of course. Such bonds between men are unworthy of the new world that we want to build. Emancipated beings, equal before the law, working side by side to earn their living, that is what you base a modern society upon. You, yourself, are aware of the odious archaism of such an institution. Haven't I heard that you once ordered corporal punishment to be stopped on these lands?'

He isn't wrong, thinks Jozef, I've felt for a long time that this ship was taking on water, and I am the captain. But what? Such an upheaval . . . Ah, my God! No, my thoughts are reeling, I must think . . . And then his argument has weaknesses that I owe myself to reveal.

'Dear Jan, if only I had your youth! Listening to you, I feel like an old man, a sceptic, a cynic.'

'You, Uncle? An old man? You're joking.'

'I wish what you are saying were true, dear Jan, but you see, like an old man I see only obstacles and impossibilities.'

'Such as?'

'Your peasants in Krosno were no doubt Poles for the most part. But here, for example, and in all the districts to the east, what will you tell the serfs? Tell them of a free Poland? They couldn't care less. They are Ruthenians, you won't understand anything of their dialect, nothing of their world. Even their religion isn't ours. Their priests get married, they still follow the Julian calendar. Although they recognize the Pope, those Uniates will never be anything but a type of orthodox sect.'

'Excuse me, Uncle—Greek Catholics. And Slavs, like us. Aren't we cousins? Don't cousins share their plows and their oxen, at least for the time of planting?'

'Their plow and oxen! . . . Good God! My boy, you have become more Galician than we are! I'm not surprised that you fill the inn rooms in our countryside.'

'You mock me, Uncle, but deep down I think you know that I'm right. I won't be dissuaded by your objections, objections you don't believe yourself. Because, ultimately, in the near future, the Ruthenians will also rise. And why won't they fight for their father Poland, since they have practically never had their own state? They who don't even have an owner class, industry, in short, their own elite? Why will they not be open to loftier views than the defence of their dialect and their customs—to national views, in fact, if only we educate them?'

Why, why, why? It was interesting, but at that precise moment I had had enough listening to them. Because I too, sometimes have enough. I left them in the library where they had just lit their cigars, and I went up to the roof, and I looked out upon the great celestial vault. The air was dry and glacial, and far off into the distance there shone, mockingly, stars without fatherlands.

13

Europe may well have been a flask of naphtha, but those years when Jozef's five daughters were entering the prime of their young lives were truly the great era of the estate, the one that was always nostalgically known as 'the good old days'.

Five daughters to marry, a curse in a certain sense; but their youth times five, their high spirits, their awareness of being fresh and ready to be picked, radiated over the region and infused it with a shudder of desire, a general appetite for life. The old people forgot to die, as if they were waiting for the ladies of the *dwor* to get married. The poor were less poor, or at least they could think they were—there were endless, joyful sounds of parties and dancing, an abundance which everyone could share, beautiful toilettes that were still practically new, which the girls gave to their maids so they could be passed on to their sisters, daughters, nieces and cousins. So much velvet and satin had never been seen on the peasant women at the Grünau marketplace, so many flowers in their hair. In the local population, 'the good old days' were also marked by a spike in marriages and births.

And right here it was a ballet of carriages, pomaded lieutenants, widowed notaries who, dreaming of a second life, girdled their stomachs in the corsets of supplicants, noble mothers who came to assess the family and to scout out suitable wives for their sons. Raffles, ball-and-cup games, handing out Pastilles de la Vierge in a silver bowl. The times were very good.

'Wioletta, Wioletta, give me your hand . . . If I were fifteen years younger, Miss Zemka, I would kiss the hem of your dress. By granting me this dance, you've made me the happiest of men . . . Zosia, my little dove, where is your sister? If you tell me, I'll repair your toy . . . Seweryn! Where is Seweryn? We need him to dance a quadrille!'

Clara no longer knew which end was up. She was already dreaming of the moment when they would all be settled, as once she had dreamt, out of a desire for rest and calm, of being an old maid. While she waited she had to soldier on, accept that the house would be full of strangers— those suitors who practically moved in; the seamstresses arriving with their arms full and leaving even fuller; the new tutor, recently hired to teach the older girls, to provide an education and enrich their aesthetic senses, a realm upon which Madame Denisot had quickly given up.

Clara had reluctantly agreed to hire Zygmunt Borowski. Young, much too young; if she had been asked, she would have pointed out that a man of twenty-seven, whatever his talents and merits (because he came from a Polish family of the Russian empire, it too decimated by the repressions of 1831, and whom Jozef, for that reason, had wanted to help), a man of twenty-seven without means had no place in a house full of marriageable girls.

She didn't think this without being ashamed—she was very well placed to know what nature can do under these circumstances, however excellent until then the principles of moral education had been. In the beginning, she had watched the tutor carefully, had slipped into the nursery now rearranged into a classroom to espy any signs of guilty attraction on her daughters' faces. It was for naught; she had even smiled upon hearing her daughters protest against the dictation of a phrase that was too long and filled with metaphors. It was very clear then that the young man was entirely focussed on his work, and the minor shaking of his voice came neither from a desire to please, much less from the assurance that he had pleased, but from the contentment of having been able to beautifully formulate the truth: '. . . And so the Sarmates' tranquility and indolence soothed the noble Poles in the erroneous certitude that their world would last for ever: more horrible would appear to them, in 1648, the series of political and military catastrophes that would befall their land . . .' The voice dictated, and dictated, and Clara continued to listen, out of simple linguistic pleasure mixed with curiosity—she hadn't been taught history like this at the convent; she remembered only lists of pontificates and royal marriages whose protagonists were as meaningless as the royal figures in a game of cards. When the tutor spoke, Clara thought she really saw the ages go by, the men live, the causes and motives stand out with force from the magma of facts. Some things, however, troubled her a bit, seemed quite bold to her. Is this how one spoke of the decisions of a king, of the responsibilities of a caste? This Zygmunt dealt with his national history, and even all others, with the implacability of a young, ardent judge.

'Bah, you don't understand a thing,' Jozef had grumbled when she told him of her reservations. 'Anyway, it's not as if those girls understand anything he's saying . . .'

And the humble Clara of course had to agree, since she herself, an adult, did not understand everything. Moreover, the young man must have had the sense that he was preaching into the desert. When Urszula took notes with grudging sighs, Wioletta in dark silence and little Jadwiga asked for help with each complicated word; when Maria, with her pen in the air, dreamt of her betrothed with a sweet, absent smile, Clara detected a hint of bitterness on the tutor's face, something . . . a little mean, that was it. When he saw them reacting so badly to his history lessons, it almost seemed that he didn't like them.

Only Wioletta had caused her mother some concern, because she grew animated and loquacious when young Borowski studied her drawings and watercolours with her, helped her fix a perspective or taught her the rudiments of composition. Their heads, in those moments, came a bit too close above the sheet of paper, and more than once Clara had thought it a good idea to stand behind them. But their whispering, when she heard them better, was quite innocent. It was very technical, and in his comments the young master proved to be as impartial as one could have hoped. And Clara was astonished to hear him frankly criticize the little painting that, the day before in the salon, had raised a chorus of male praise.

'That group of trees is fixed, rendered too carefully, like on a botanical plate. It doesn't capture the light, that light of the dusk that you have suggested rather well on the side of the hill.'

'But I wanted . . . no, I'm silly.'

'Not at all, go on.'

'I in fact wanted it to be completely grey, dark, in the golden light. I sometimes see it in the summer, at sunset—the fields are aflame, become yellow and pink, and it is so beautiful . . . but the little woods already belong to the night, it is as if they have already been extinguished, already dead, you see?'

'I understand the intent, but I don't find it in your painting. You must work on it, try to achieve that. It is an interesting idea.'

In the absorbed nodding of Wioletta's head it was truly impossible to see anything other than artistic preoccupation. And so much the better, Clara said to herself, if Mr Borowski manages to pull a few words from her, a few thoughts. That child is not happy, that's obvious, her beauty embarrasses her and I am unable to give her confidence. Maybe he will be good for her?

And when he then raised his head and encountered Clara's gaze, holding it with the impassibility of a pure conscience, she smiled at him, without really knowing why.

Not very dangerous, then, all things considered. And the day when Princess Dubinska, paying them a visit, had looked at him carefully, then whispered: 'Hum! So that is the Borowski who is teaching your daughters?' Clara immediately answered: 'Oh, Princess, rest assured, he is harmless.'

'If you say so,' the dowager had sniffed. 'At least he isn't handsome, you must admit. In my time, a man with such a mediocre face would hardly have made his way in the world. But today, that's all that you see, isn't it?! Horrid little trolls who become bishops, ministers, and who knows what else . . .'

'Dear Princess, Mr Borowski is only our tutor.'

'Of course, of course,' muttered the other woman before dipping her fingers into her tobacco tin and noisily sniffing—a habit she had kept from her time, and still engaged in with a haughty indifference to new customs. 'You have always been trusting, that is very touching. But in your place, I would keep my eyes open. I have already heard bad things about your protégé.'

'Bad things?'

'Oh, yes. He was seen in Kraków in very questionable company. Be careful, my dear, not to harbour a snake in your household.'

'You're nothing but an old gossip, keep your nose out of things that don't concern you.'

That is, at least, what Clara would have replied if the laws of hospitality and good manners had not become second nature to her. I, fluttering around the trimmed neckline of her dress (whose adept cut succeeded in making her large shoulders appear to be sloped, following the style of the moment), I felt under her skin the murmuring of those words; but she halted their progress before they arrived at her lips, and instead replied: 'Princess, I am grateful for that information. But you are perhaps attributing too much importance to it. What man that age doesn't have some youthful follies behind him? In the lessons he gives our daughters, Mr Borowski is entirely satisfactory.'

And with that she stood up with an agreeable goodbye to give some instructions to the servants and to allow herself a moment of solitude in the hallway. Never did she feel the weight of her social obligations so greatly as in the presence of the Princess.

14

I would, however, like to describe a ball, one of the great moments of that great era. It will give me the opportunity to recall something from the winter. For, as might have been noticed, I remember what happens more easily in the warm season—which is rather short, especially, in our land. Ah, those torrid days in August when my rooms imperceptibly exude the wood, the varnish, the badigeon, when my particles join with human effluvia, their thoughts, their desires . . .

But I digress . . . For now, it is a glacial afternoon in November which a feeble sun has too quickly deserted. The hills are resting under a thin layer of snow, out of which here and there a tuft of grass emerges, a fence on which a crow is perched. The wind has fallen with the dusk; the smoke from the cottages climbs straight up into the sky. It escapes from a simple hole in the roof, because the peasants around here still do without the refinement of a chimney. Why lose the good heat of that smoke which fills the top of the room and gives blankets, hair and clothing an agreeable odour of smoked pork fat?

I can't see them in the one-room cottages but I can easily envision the scene. At this time of the day, the grandmother and grandfather are already asleep next to the stove; the others are huddled on benches that line the walls; one person is asleep, another is sewing, a third is repairing a tool. Outside, it is almost dark; wood and candles are rare; soon everyone will be asleep, the head of the family holding his wife in his arms in the only bed. It's unnecessary, this evening, to beat on a pan to frighten the wolves. In a little while, the brouhaha of the carriages arriving at my gates will take care of that.

Efraim is giddy as it is also a big day for him—there are some thirty new animals for him to admire, rub down, warm up with a few handfuls of oats sprinkled with alcohol! He is seen coming and going out of the stables, wearing a cloak made of bits of fur sewn together, going to greet the new arrivals with great slaps on their necks.

In the grey hood that covers his head, and which at a distance gives him the appearance of a dishevelled old man, I recognize the remains of an old fur-lined coat from the late Baron von Kotz—a chambermaid must have made this Nordic harlequin outfit for him, or perhaps he made it himself, looking at the large bits of thread that hold it all together. His still youthful face, though roughened by life outdoors, shines—a communicative joy, winning over, unbeknownst to them, chaperons and dowagers who make their entrance into the grand salon with as much excitement as the girls looking for husbands.

There are a lot of high-society people and noble families here. Princess Dubinska, who had to be begged for a long time to come, and finally did agree to come, said, only to please her son ('He so loves to dance! . . .'), is nevertheless among the first to arrive—nothing in the world would make her miss those uncertain minutes when there are still few guests, when servants hasten to serve you, when the lack of taste, the insufficiencies of wardrobe stand out, not yet hidden by the animation of the event. In these moments she, herself, triumphing under the tiara and the lace wimple that her mother wore at the coronation of Stanislas-August, felt she was truly what she considered herself to be— the first among equals.

As usual, she has settled down in the best armchair in the best location, inspecting from top to bottom each girl of the house, demanding that she be introduced to all those who have the nerve not to be known by her; but she really speaks only to Clara, whose titles of nobility are irreproachable and weigh more, in her eyes, than her lapses in conduct in the past. The princess maintains a sense of what is essential, and what is essential is blood—the rigour of the younger generation appears quite silly and bourgeois to her.

'So you say that Urszula will soon be engaged? That is what might be called good news,' she croaks, while her little grey eyes pitilessly compare the girl in question to her sister Wioletta, very pale in her white dress (because this is her first ball). 'And who is the lucky gentleman?'

'Here he is now—quickly, quickly, Agenor Karlowicz, come here so I can introduce you to the Princess . . .'

'Thank you, he looks charming,' the princess interrupts while turning her head away. They can't really expect her to honour every man in attendance with her conversation! It is already quite enough to have to endure that Zemka, playing at the master here with as much ease as if his father had not been a candymaker. (There is a reciprocal antipathy between her and Jozef, and she never misses the chance to give him an insolent smile when she takes a 'Pastille de la Vierge' out of the bowl).

Maria has come over to pay her respects, and is now moving gracefully among the groups of guests. This season is good to her—the cold, which she does not mind, reddens her cheeks and makes the make-up her mother would have forbidden in any event, unnecessary. And the absence of her fiancé, on such a festive occasion, adds a bit of melancholy to her features; it gives her an *interesting* look. Several young men surround her but their gallantry remains purely pro forma. This beautiful girl is already taken, they know, and they all ask her to save a dance for them out of pleasure but expect nothing more.

Wait, wait, the violins are tuning up. Wioletta's heart clutches, she would like to loosen her flowered sash, unlace her corset, go hide in a corner where no one will see her. Who knows? Maybe after the first dance she will feel better. And she still needs a partner; but as soon as an admiring glance settles on her, she lowers her eyes, bites her bottom lip and turns away; this discourages the candidates and keeps her dance card empty. (Let it stay empty! She almost wishes, while also fearing it.)

The voices grow a bit louder, a general movement is made towards the dance floor, black suits on one side facing a wall of softer colours, and suddenly there is silence. A couple emerges—the young Prince Dubinski will open the ball with Miss Zemka.

Music. Clara is beaming with ease because her eldest daughter proves perfect in her role. She dances well, she is at her best, a single person is missing but she knows he is close, at least in thought. ('My sweet Galician flower', began the last letter from Jan which she had just reread while Lubienka put the final touches on her hair). Maria is enjoying this moment which will no doubt be, along with her wedding, the apogee of her life as a woman.

As for the prince, he is completely enjoying the dance. His mother didn't lie; he enjoys dancing almost as much as he does hunting. He has found a partner equal to his abilities, and a large smile never leaves his face. He remembers a bit belatedly that he should exchange a few words with his partner, and thinks for a moment: 'It's been very cold lately, hasn't it?'

'Oh yes, quite!'

'True seasonal weather.'

He wants to say something more but lacks inspiration. This tall strapping fellow is not at ease with women, and if his mother expects him to marry honourably, she will have to keep an eye on him because his timidity, his awkwardness and his democratic ideas make him the dream of any slightly scheming woman. Jozef was perhaps correct—Prince Dubinski is kind but he's not the sharpest of tacks.

Jozef is however now looking at him with kindness, that Galician magnate who did not refuse to open the ball with his eldest daughter. For him it is a triumph, a consecration: Who could have predicted this a quarter of a century earlier? Aristocrats or peasants, old people will die one day and no one will remember any longer that Jozef was once one of those blue-blood servants so often seen in old Poland.

He thinks of this with satisfaction, his shoulders are straight, his calves firm; the girls in the kitchen, who are moving around behind a service door, devour him with their eyes and have to admit that he is still the most handsome man in the group.

'Do you think he'll dance?'

'Aniela, move, you've already seen the first four waltzes . . .'

'Shhh! Be quiet, he's moving. He's going forward. He's asking someone.'

'Who? Who? I can't see a thing.'

'Bah, it's only the mistress.'

Indeed, Jozef is dancing with his wife. He hadn't planned to do so but he had the misfortune of seeing the youngest Wytocki girl, who, like Wioletta, is debuting this winter. Hips that are still straight, moistened eyelids and mouth—instantly, the forty-year-old undressed her in his thoughts and pushed her naked body onto a bed before pulling himself together, his cheeks on fire. Careful now, my neighbour's daughter! She was still playing with dolls two or three years ago! Clara is unwittingly benefitting from that stifled lust. Still stifled, moreover, because they dance a quadrille whose steps don't lend themselves to the frank embrace Jozef needs. It doesn't matter—he jumps, he gallops, he catches hands. There is nothing like movement to cool one's head.

'Excuse me, may I get by?'

The tutor also wants to see the spectacle. The servants move aside, because he can stand in the frame of the door to watch. Given the hour he is not called to any duty, so why not watch the dance a bit?

Clara is smiling vaguely, she didn't expect to dance this evening, either, and it seems that her breast is undulating in the dress she has chosen, in a way that is not entirely suitable. When she can, she places a hand on that rebellious bosom, but what can she do when she has to give both arms?

Oh, Mr Borowski is watching them. Poor boy, perhaps he would like to dance, she thinks. It must not always be pleasant to serve. But she chases away those thoughts—it is not the time to dwell on the injustice of fate, she must seem happy and be attentive to her daughters.

'Do you see Wioletta? Does she have a partner?' she whispers to her husband who for the moment is facing her.

Jozef grunts. That little fool Wioletta is already making a spectacle of herself. An under lieutenant had succeeded in cajoling her, she came forward on his arm and, with her eyes riveted to the ground, had begun to dance. A few minutes later, she abandoned her partner and disappeared into the crowd of spectators. What had got into her? The man blushed under the affront and dryly took his leave; among the mothers lined up along the wall, the tongues began to wag.

Now Wioletta is glued to the wall, a wall into which, I sense, she would like to disappear. How she would like to be flat like a leaf, invisible, completely shapeless! She curses them, these contours, her plastic dimension. Never having waltzed with a man (because the stiff old German dance-instructor didn't approve of that dance), she couldn't imagine that an arm around her waist could be so eloquent, nor that she would be held so close. The under-lieutenant's eyes glistened as he looked at her; and when he wasn't looking at her it was worse because he then had a smile that was even more disgusting. And his breath, which she felt in her hair! That warm breath on her was torture, an abomination. She pushed him away, and her partner, thrown off balance, had held on to her while squeezing her waist—it was too much, she fled in a great commotion.

And now she is mortified with shame because of that contact, and because people are whispering about her. My God, let this ball be over! She feels her eyes filling with tears.

She backs away even more, her shoulder brushes against a black suit, oh no, please, not again! But it is only Agenor Karlowicz, her sister's almost-fiancé, she knows she doesn't have anything to fear from him. He isn't tall or handsome or blond. His brown eyes look at you with indifference, instead of leering at you, like that awful under lieutenant. His thick brown hair looks dishevelled no matter what he does. And when he speaks, it is with a flat, nasal voice that, in a tone of friendship, is perfect for putting you at ease. Wioletta takes a deep breath, fans herself, smiles at him. He whispers in her ear: 'I'm dying of thirst, and you?'

'Oh, yes!'

'I think supper is going to be served soon. They're bringing the lamps into the little blue salon. Aren't you going to dance any more?'

'No, I don't think so . . .'

'I certainly understand. I'm also bored to death, and, on top of everything, my boots are hurting.'

Wioletta laughs behind her fan—what a funny boy! But there's Urszula who sees them and is not pleased they are conversing. That sneaky Wioletta can't really imagine that my love is here to dance with her! She weaves her way over to them, looks at them sternly, the blue silk of her dress giving her complexion the tint of a lemon and her furrowed brow not making things better.

'So, dear Agenor?'

'I couldn't find you, my dear. Will you do me the honour of dancing with me?'

'Of course!'

He kisses her hand, leads her to the middle of the room. In fact, he is limping, and when he looks at Wioletta, he gives her a little grimace of pain, making her laugh.

She's feeling a bit better now, the blood isn't beating at her temples any more. Behind her people are talking, two mothers are looking at the couple that has just moved away: 'Engaged?'

'No, not yet, he hasn't asked her yet. But it will no doubt happen soon. Look at them!'

'That little Urszula knows what she wants, at least.'

'Oh yes. She is only too happy. With her pocked face, there were no guarantees.'

Wounded for her sister, Wioletta moves away. Those mean women! May she never become like them. (Her wandering mind moves off.) What she would really like is to never become anything, to remain always what she is. To read, to dream; to enter into one of her paintings, to be one of those groves precociously seized by the dusk, yes. Or one of those birds that she allows to float, hardly visible, above the fields. Before her eyes the dancers blend into a kaleidoscope of taffeta, satins and silks. It would be nice to paint this whirlwind. In her reverie her face relaxes, her lips part—at that moment she is amazingly beautiful.

Supper will soon be served. The most avid dancers continue, they want to take advantage of their final moments. Fathers and mothers enter the fray, and those who aren't dancing are standing watching them, this is the height, the acme, the strongest moment of the party; the gates are shaking at the other end of the grounds.

In her room on the second floor, unaware of the din and the excitement, Jadwiga is sleeping the sleep of the righteous, her hands peacefully crossed on top of her quilt.

In the next room, Elvire Denisot is nodding off, her hands in a less modest position. This prude, a widow for so long, has secret pastimes (that I am the only one to know) and therefore unutterable reasons to fear the looks of men who may detect them in her eyes.

Little Zosia has slipped out of her bed and gone down one flight of stairs in her nightgown and slippers. Crouched low, she pushes her little face through two bars of the staircase and tries to see a bit of the ballroom, some couples gliding by. The music intoxicates her, she is very sleepy, but she struggles with all her might to keep her eyes open.

Outside, it is snowing again.

15

If, as is generally believed, a ball is held to promote legitimate unions, this one was only a half-success. People in the district talked for a long time about its elegance and animation, and the Zemkas climbed another rung on the ladder of Galician high society; but pretty Wioletta remained without a primary suitor, and Urszula's admirer, contrary to what the matrons predicted, did not seem in a hurry to declare his intentions.

This was very much in his character. Agenor Karlowicz was a calm man, a sceptic, little inclined to reveal himself. Jozef imagined he wouldn't ask a girl for her hand without first being assured of the desires of the young lady, of her interest in him and of his own ability to meet the needs of a family. And on that last point, things remained a bit unsure. One of his uncles who had no children had a large shawl factory near Jaslo, but he was a man in the prime of life who might still want to start a family of his own.

From time to time Agenor mentioned the possibility of going into the Austrian administration, but no one here encouraged him. What Pole did that? People without a conscience, without patriotic feeling, or those who were starving and couldn't do anything else. Jozef was grateful that he discussed that extreme measure with them, it was a compliment to his daughter, a proof of motivation and good will; but he was almost just as grateful that he didn't execute it. Furthermore, there was no hurry. Urszula wasn't going to get married before her older sister, and the winter months were not very favourable for engagement parties. Clara herself agreed—it would be nicer in a season when the grounds and the lawns would be in full splendour.

While waiting, Agenor was now part of the furnishings. He was living in Grünau for business that must have not been very demanding, because three or four times a week he arrived here after noon, joining the family circle, and left only late in the evening. And yet he was in no way a frivolous swain, didn't wax on worldly or artistic issues, even called himself, and they believed him, blasé on pleasures, receptions and the theatrical seasons of Lemberg where he had lived up to then. Jozef found him calming—an attentive listener, an equal player, a delightful companion to his daughters, including the youngest whose wildness and teasing didn't bother him because he had grown up with three little sisters.

The young ladies watched for him every afternoon—his arrival marked the end of their lessons. When they saw him from the window of their classroom, the wise Jadwiga wiped her pen, blew on the page and crossed her arms, waiting for the signal to stand up. Not all of the girls had as much discipline. Maria was already happily leaving, walking languidly to the door; Urszula, concentrating, smoothed out her curls, Wioletta was fidgeting on her chair and nervously chewing on her pencil. And so the tutor closed his book with a discreet sigh and said, 'You're dismissed.'

They didn't have to be told twice. A moment later the classroom was empty and the hallway filled with the rustling of their four skirts.

One day, Clara found him silently watching his pupils going out. Leaning on the door frame, a finger still stuck in a book, he seemed serious. She muttered 'hello,' walked by him, then turned around, 'Are you . . . satisfied with them, Mr Borowski?'

'Madame, (he coughed), I am as satisfied as possible.'

It was an awkward question, Clara regretted having asked him. She hesitated, then went on, 'No doubt your abilities deserve better than the situation we can offer you.'

He looked at the floor, 'Madame, I cannot complain of a situation without which I would have nothing to live on. Besides, it leaves me with free time. I can ask for nothing more.'

He turned over and over the book in his slender, adolescent hands. His entire body, from his narrow chest to his clean-shaven, rather hollow cheeks, evoked the remnants of an adolescence that was surprising in someone who was almost thirty. His eyes, however, were more mature. They had a reserve, an aloofness, a resolution that belied the rest. A bit taller than he, aware of being his employer and his supervisor, Clara nonetheless felt small in front of him; small and, in an obscure way, judged. Judged negatively, she was ready to admit. She also felt that, at that moment, he would have preferred that she go away. It wasn't out of nervousness that he was fiddling with that book—he was waiting to be alone to return to his work.

'Free time? Yes, I know that you read a lot.'

'My profession demands it, Madame.'

'Good heavens, please don't defend yourself, I have the greatest respect for what you . . .' While she was searching for the right words he silently bowed and concluded for her, 'I have no doubt, Madame.'

It was a discreet end to the conversation; Clara should have recognized it. He was refusing, declining her attentions, perhaps he found her as much a fool as her daughters. And why not? She was indeed a fool, she knew that. She wasn't surprised to be seen as such, that had always been her lot. It didn't matter, because *she* knew how to be generous; she didn't need to be appreciated, admired, to admire herself, she would show them (here, her movement of pride had already enlarged into an indistinct cohort the 'they' in which in the end only the tutor and her husband were included) her moral superiority—she would treat this young man as a son to whom one gives without receiving, she would watch over him whether he wanted it or not, protect him, with her discreet care, the blossoming of his talent, the achievement of a book, perhaps . . . But where should she begin? He was already taking his leave, getting ready to shut the door.

'Mr Borowski! Mr Borowski. There's something else. Are you sure you have everything you need?'

'Everything I need?'

'I mean, in your room. Do they bring you enough wood, enough hot water?' It wasn't at all the level of conversation she had anticipated, she felt herself blush in front of the young man's stupefaction.

'But . . . of course, dear Madame.'

He was almost smiling now. This first attempt wasn't very good, she would have to be more adept in the future. With burning cheeks, she drew herself as tall as her training had made possible, raised her chin and said dryly, 'Very well, I am delighted. Good day, Mr Borowski.'

It was several days before she returned to the classroom—the awkward conversation weighed on her. She carried out her activities as muse and patron behind the scenes. She had her own maid inspect the condition of Mr Borowski's shirts and handkerchiefs in the laundry, and mend them, if necessary. Then she became bolder, dared to leave the domestic realm that was hers alone, and, this time openly, attended an entire history lesson, at the end of which she stood up and declared to the instructor: 'If you might need to acquire any book for your lessons, I invite you to ask me. We will do what we can.'

'Madame, I thank you. But the library already contains almost all the classics that your daughters need to know, and . . .'

'I understand. But, you see, I would like them to leave your care a bit less ignorant than I am. *What girls need to know* is not very much, as I am all too aware.'

'Madame!' the young man protested, agitated.

'Come now, you know this better than I. And, however ignorant I may be, I am aware that a schoolmaster, to do his work well, must know considerably more than his pupils to be truly expert. And so do not be held back in your research, pursue it, don't hesitate to provide yourself with the means—I even ask you to consider it part of your duties as far as we are concerned.'

He remained uncertain; Clara's final words seemed to make him decide.

'Well, in that case, there are, in fact, a few books that would be very useful to me and which I would find some way or another if I were still living in the Kraków republic . . .'

Clara had winced at that name which reminded her of the princess' insinuations and made her see her employee's earlier life; a life of debauchery, no doubt, of the escapades of a student, of 'questionable company' . . . But she pushed aside those thoughts. Generosity is unconditional; and the man seemed to have settled down nicely since his student days.

'Which books, sir? Wait for me to sit down and get a pen—you can tell me the titles.'

He opened his mouth, thought again. He observed, at the table, the lady of the house seated in Jadwiga's place, her pen in the air, and, like her daughter, waiting for his magisterial word to fall; the similarity was a bit comical. And yet, seated in that way, Madame Zemka indeed looked something like a schoolgirl. The imposing fall of her skirts had disappeared under the wooden table, a little spot of ink already soiled her ringed hand, her ribbons docilely framed her face which was lowered. At that moment she looked up, 'Yes?'

'Madame, I have some hesitation. My personal research leads me to subjects that I am not supposed to be teaching your daughters. What would your husband think of these expenses paid in a goal so beyond my official functions?'

'Oh, you needn't be concerned. Money isn't an issue.'

The look he gave her was full of meaning. That phrase, which she had just nonchalantly uttered, had contracted the face of the young man like lemon juice on an oyster. And she noticed it, regretted her indiscretion while noting the degree to which the young man's black jacket, seen close up, was worn, ratty, almost reddish in places.

'It will not be a problem for me,' she corrected in a shaky voice. 'My daughters' education remains my responsibility, and I will take it upon myself personally to carry out this request. Between us, my husband couldn't care less what my daughters read, within the limits of decency, of course. Beyond that, he leaves everything to me. So have no fear, he won't pay very much attention.'

He was still thinking.

'All right, Madame. Faced with your insistence, please note the following titles . . .'

'Wait. All right, I'm ready.'

'Stanislas Worcell, *On Ownership*.'

Worcell; it seemed to Clara that her husband had sometimes spoken this name, along with disapproving commentaries. She regretted launching without reflection into such a daring enterprise. Perhaps it wasn't a good idea?

'Alexander Ivanovich . . . Herzen.'

Totally unknown. Clara breathed easier. Her pen was flying now, quick and careful, adding the little bar over the *t* and a dot over the *i*.

'Herzen . . . yes?'

'*On Dilettantism . . . in . . . the Sciences*.'

She nodded her head, impressed. All of that seemed very serious. And she smiled to herself thinking of the carousing and debauchery of

Mr Borowski's former existence that she had imagined a few moments earlier which he had given up to come work for them.

'Is that all?'

'My goodness, if it's not asking too much, then add *Histoire de dix ans* by Jan Joseph Louis Blanc.'

'Jan . . . Joseph . . . Louis . . . Blanc. Oh! You read French too?'

'Yes, Madame. You see, we are somewhat from the same world.'

She raised her head, her eyelids were fluttering. Should she acknowledge that bit of humour, show that she was amused? Deep down, she found it to be rather hostile. But fifty-one years of reserve and diplomacy had not gone by in vain for Clara von Kotz, now Zemka. She ran her tongue over her lips and smile, 'I'm a bit surprised, you see, because you have never made this knowledge known to us.' And then she was quiet and blushed violently while thinking of the commentaries of Princess Dubinska, of which he must have heard every word.

'I didn't, that's true. Madame Denisot is responsible for teaching French to your daughters, and that seemed enough to me. And I really just read the language, but speak it badly—it is only a bookish knowledge.'

On that cold explanation, the conversation was over. Clara left with the satisfaction of having acted, and the vague sadness of having been paid badly for her efforts. The hostile phrase remained in her mind, and it was not before several hours that she realized that there was also, in that half-offence, a note of intimacy.

16

The order was indeed placed with a bookseller in Kraków whose address the tutor had given her, but then Clara completely forgot all about it. There was so much to do in this season! Christmas was just round the corner, Christmas was almost here—a festive wind was already blowing within my walls, a warm wind scented with cinnamon, poppy, cloves, rivalling the cold storm that raged almost continuously outside. In 'the good old days' everyone here kept so much hope in their hearts that the great day would be endowed with even more exquisite magic. Zosia and Jadwiga were not the only ones to feverishly await it—even their elders felt excited and jumpy at the prospect, at that of the coming new year too, and what it might bring!

Laughter, clapping, excited murmurings; on the afternoon of 24 December, the crèche that had been made by some Polish peasants on the estate in honour of their masters was installed; the artisans had outdone themselves. There were no pearls, no glass, no sequins or tissue paper—everything in it was made of unfinished wood but the result was only that much more powerful. It was created mainly from a large block of beechwood, carved out in the front into a sort of grotto where tiny figures moved, like an army of dwarfs leaving a mineshaft.

Everything was there: the donkey and the ox, the shepherds, the magi, Joseph and Mary surrounding the infant . . . Maria started dreaming while she looked at the marvel; soon, oh! soon she would be in her glory as bride and perhaps as young mother—what beauty, what a wonder is Christmas, she said to herself, and she felt igniting inside her a fire of piety whose fuel, without her knowing it, was rather profane.

They got closer, cried out as the details grew even more enchanting. The sculptor (an old infirm serf who had spent an entire month working on it was now blushing, mute, from the praise) had been able to make use of every knot in the wood, every spot on the bark to suggest the slightest movement, a facial expression. For a moment everyone felt they were truly in the midst of the biblical scene and part of the crowd of amazed shepherds; there were even a few seconds of complete silence. Then the young people began singing a Christmas carol, the flames of

the candles trembled, the servants told Clara that Madame was served—
reality took over, the shepherds became serfs, servants and masters again,
and the latter hoped to break their half-fast by attacking the twelve
courses of a sumptuous supper. A great noise already came from the
kitchen, silver platters rattled against one another, the kitchen help ran
in the service stairway—the feast was beginning.

The supper was marked by an even more joyous event. As the fourth
course was being finished, conversations died down, and in this interval
of calm a ringing of bells was heard. Zosia couldn't sit still, ran to open
the curtains under the disapproving eye of Madame Denisot, and came
back shouting, 'Papa! Mama! Maria! I think it's my cousin!'

It was Jan, in fact, who was getting out of the sleigh, covered in furs.
Everyone ran downstairs to greet him—pink from the cold, his eyes
shining, his boots clacking on the tiles of the entryway, he was even
more alluring than they remembered, and Maria, stunned with
happiness, remained in the background, not daring to be the first to
greet him.

He conveyed the good wishes of his father, the prince, etc., shook
hands, dispensed embraces, explained his unannounced arrival. He was
going to have business in the region at the beginning of the new year
1846 and, when he had learnt that, could not resist advancing his
departure to come join them for Christmas. The letter that announced
his visit, mailed before his new decision, would no doubt arrive after
him.

'The postmen don't have my reasons for travelling so quickly,' he
observed with a meaningful look at his intended, who was even more
moved; and, walking right up to her, he took her hand: 'Merry
Christmas, cousin. May it be the last that I call you such.' And he placed
his lips on her open palm while everyone sighed tenderly.

Jozef was happy. This time they were keeping Jan, he wouldn't leave
from here without becoming his son-in-law—this engagement had
lasted long enough. And then, he could take care of Urszula, and
Wioletta perhaps. Almost three out of five! Life was indeed good!

Then he decided to introduce Agenor Karlowicz to his nephew. A
strange meeting between the effervescent Pole from Paris and the placid
Pole from Lemberg. At first glance, the comparison played against the

latter who seemed quite serious next to Jan Zemka. At second glance, however, Agenor improved his image. First, because he had visibly sparked the interest of his interlocutor who prolonged the exchange beyond what politeness required, listened to his answers while nodding his head, adjusted his tone of voice to his. He seemed to shrink imperceptibly, regain his human proportions, descend from that Olympus where the admiration of the entire family had placed him. At the end of this little conversation, everyone had to note deep down that they had two equals before them. Because what Agenor lacked in physical presence he made up for in ease, calm, and above all in a quality that Jan completely lacked—irony.

'Come on, let's go back to the table,' Jozef commanded to close these formalities. They went back upstairs, Jan sat down at the place that on Christmas Eve was always left empty for an unexpected visitor; and in front of the now complete table everyone felt the soothing emotion that is inspired by a miracle when it arrives right on time.

It happened that this year Jozef had prepared an extraordinary event. For the first time he had arranged with a troupe of artists to play right here, on Holy Innocents' Day, a mystery of the Nativity.

'I am very sorry not to have known you were coming,' he said to his nephew, 'or I would have chosen Saint John in your honour. You are our son, you know.'

And Jan protested, thanked him, acknowledged the allusion and responded beyond all hopes—in two days a date was finally chosen for the marriage which would take place at the end of spring.

So there was a rising tide, a true flood of new joys. In his enthusiasm, Jozef even had a message sent to the young Prince Dubinski, asking him to join them for the performance. A bit of supplementary status wouldn't be too much. One could say that the year was ending on a very high note.

On the appointed day, the artists arrived very early to clean out the barn, the only place big enough to contain their puppet theatre and the audience. Because, in addition to the household, the master had generously invited the inhabitants of the hamlet, including the Uniates and the Ruthenians, considering that religious schisms and linguistic chasms should be forgot, at least from time to time.

At first glance, the troupe was not very impressive. Amidst its stage, its curtain and its worn marionettes, the leader extended greetings in bad Polish with a strong Moravian accent; he was, moreover, as he said, originally from the outskirts of Brno. The others spoke better but they all still looked like poor wretches who slept in ditches and rarely had enough to eat. Their smiles lacked sincerity, and Jozef thought they looked a little suspect, in short, he had the disagreeable impression of having gathered onto his land a tribe of gypsies, even without women and children. But it was too late to cancel, everyone would be too disappointed; but he almost sent another message to Prince Dubinski to dissuade him from coming.

When he returned with his family for the performance, his fears disappeared. The barn was unrecognizable—a dozen good armchairs, in the middle, awaited the masters, paper decorations covered the walls and the beams and the theatre structure was hidden by a great deal of fabric that formed the wings. Seen from a distance, the stains and spots on the faded Turkey-red curtain disappeared; and when it opened onto a little, still empty stage, it revealed a row of pendants above that knocked together and shone in the light.

An admiring 'oh' escaped from Jozef, his wife, the young ladies and the prince (a good audience member, who was, moreover, an avid fan of popular customs). Jan and Agenor were content with an indulgent smile; but behind and around them the standing crowd was silent with delight.

And the spectacle began.

Everyone knew the story, everyone knew the protagonists, they knew by heart almost every line; the pleasure here was entirely in the recognition. They liked that Mary was wearing white and blue, Joseph a long coat of Oriental cut; they wouldn't have wanted it to be otherwise. All these figures recited or sang, Mary above all did so with so much grace that everyone in the audience felt their eyes fill with tears. They quickly became accustomed to not seeing the puppets' features move or their lips open up; very quickly that group of ventriloquists and paraplegics had established themselves as the very quintessence of reality. And when through the glass dais a member of the audience caught sight of the hand of a puppeteer, he jumped with fright, so large did the hand appear next to the little characters of cloth and cardboard. One might have thought it was the hand of God Himself, floating up in the sky to pick out the good and crush the evil.

At the end of each act the curtain fell, one heard the clicks and crackling of the planks but the illusion was not broken. Mouths opened wide, eyes even wider, no one dared say anything—holy, each time more holy was the scene that came next, the infant Jesus on his straw cradle, the three kings, their silk and jewels, the terrible Herod whose evil intent could already be anticipated.

There was at that moment a somewhat funny interlude that dissipated the fervour a bit. Two Franciscans arrived arm in arm, then a man and woman from Kraków, a couple of Hutsul mountain people in embroidered costumes, a Jew with a cap and a Jewess with a pearl headpiece; and they all began to dance, in a din of metallic sticks that could not cover the accompanying choir.

But the laughter stopped, because armed soldiers carrying spears had made their entrance, accompanied by Death brandishing its scythe. In no time at all, the dancers disappeared, Herod cried 'Kill!' and the spears plunged into the wings from which one heard the cries of the Innocents and the shrieking of mothers.

'Papa, stop them!' cried Zosia, before putting her hands over her mouth. It took Agenor, her great friend, to pull on her dress to get her to sit back down and whisper a few reassuring words in her ear.

Soon, indeed, a devil arrived and stabbed the evil king, dragging him off to Hell—in the audience, there were shouts of joy. And when they saw the Virgin on a little wooden donkey carrying her Son across the stage, the audience gave free rein to their delight. Zosia laughed with pleasure. The old women, standing in the back of the barn, clasped their hands and thanked God in a sonorous Ruthenian chant. As for the big Marko, he moved away from the wall and said to Efraim above all the other heads:

'That's good, they've escaped. But wait for Easter! . . .'

It was becoming a bit too boisterous for Jozef's taste, and he gave the signal for the applause to begin. The curtain fell while hands clapped endlessly as the masters stood up, and some women, eager to go light the fires under the soup, started to move towards the exit.

But everyone stopped in their tracks, and the applause stopped, because the curtain was rising again. Was there an epilogue? The masters sat down again, calm returned; and then Death reappeared on the stage.

It slowly raised its scythe; there was complete silence. And suddenly, behind the stage, a voice rang out, 'To the people of the countryside!'

That voice no longer sang out but cried feverishly, as if knowing that it would not be allowed to express itself to the end. And what was that voice crying out? It was shocking, it was unbelievable—everyone wondered if they were hearing correctly.

'Peasant men and women, Christians of Galicia! You cherish Jesus and Jesus cherishes you. Yes, you know this, it is for you that he died, so that there would no longer be slaves on earth who plant and masters who reap the rewards. For God did not want men to be slaves, God refuses it, God repulses it!'

The handle of the scythe struck the floor loudly and, in the audience, everyone jumped.

'. . . God created the earth so that it would be for everyone, He created you equal and gave you free will. And so, Galicians, listen to His message—you alone can make yourselves free once again as God made you. So take back your land and chase off your masters, and God will bless you, for it is His will!'

17

Then the master was seen leaping from his seat, racing towards the ramp and seizing the puppet that first resisted, then fell into his hands. Jozef should have climbed onto the stage and pulled down the set to unmask the guilty party; but too stunned, or fearing he would seem ridiculous, he simply raised the little Death up to his face.

At the end of his arm, it really no longer frightened anyone, it was only a package of fluff and papier mâché. But a murmuring now arose in the barn and Jozef, furious, turned around, 'Silence! To your places! No one will leave here until this horrible joke has been explained.'

And following a gesture by Jozef, Gavryl went to stand against the closed doors, joined by the bailiff who was wiping his forehead.

People were obeying but the calm was tense. Wioletta began to laugh nervously, Zosia was weeping, the Ruthenian peasants in the audience were having people translate phrases they couldn't understand, no one could stand still. They of course began by questioning the artist, but to no avail. The Moravian swore to all gods that he had nothing to do with this horrible thing, he almost began to cry, called his associates to his aid who declared they knew nothing about it, really nothing! At the time it happened, they were all grouped together at the left, waiting to take their bows. All? Yes, all, at least they thought so—but it was pretty dark in the wings, and then the children of the hamlet had gone behind to see how the puppets worked, and the other side of the scenery, it was a real mess back there, with all due respect.

Yes, yes, Jozef admitted; and none of their voices seemed to be the right one. It was a clear, young voice, which had reminded him of that of the Virgin Mary. But when he questioned the adolescent who had that role, his hypothesis crumbled—the lad fixed his interrogators with a stupid smile, had not understood a word of the *Appeal to the People of the Countryside*, was scarcely capable of articulating a sentence in Polish if it wasn't part of his repertory, in short, it could not have been him.

Then who was it?

They tried to remember the scene. People clearly saw Marko standing up against the wall on the right after having shouted about

Easter, and Efraim on the other side of the barn, stuck in an attitude of fear, anger and scorn. Those two at least seemed beyond suspicion.

Furthermore, it wasn't the voice of a Ruthenian serf or that of a Jewish footman. It spoke to the serfs here, it spoke for them and with words they understood; but one could guess that it was the voice of a man who knew other words, a man much more educated than he wanted to appear.

These deductions, in the end, were not reassuring. Gradually the master and the bailiff felt an unease rising in them, their sentences were pocked with silence; soon they were quiet, merely looking at one another.

It can't be Prince Dubinski! thought Jozef. Come on, he was seated . . . three seats away from me, but at that moment everyone was standing and moving towards the exit. But that's absurd! The prince, slide into the wings and make a puppet give an incendiary speech? . . . And yet, how many times have I heard him in his mother's salon call for the abolition of forced labour while citing the Gospels! But no, no, no, no! The prince is a well-intentioned twit, incapable of such devious plots. This type of appeal to insurrection isn't like him at all.

But in that case . . .

Suspicions one after the other took form in his mind. The good Agenor Karlowicz? The idea was laughable. Young Borowski? Jozef frowned at the memory of strange things his wife had told him. But a moment later he shrugged his shoulders. No, that voice full of pride and assurance was not that of an employee, even educated; never would an employee have so hastily risked his position, nor called upon the hoi polloi to overthrow the one he depended on.

What a pity, all the same, not to be able to put the affair onto Efraim! A word from Jozef would no doubt suffice to have him thrashed by everyone around. But no one would be fooled, and his seigniorial authority would in no way be restored.

Jan, Jozef finally thought, his heart clinching.

Then his blood flowed again.

Jan, his nephew, Jan the candid, the clear—Jan, indulge in that dark masquerade? He is not as candid as you think, his little internal voice whispered to him. He doesn't tell you about all his activities, he plots, he conspires, you know. He lies to his father, why wouldn't he lie to you? Who has told you that in Paris he doesn't frequent the worst Communist riff-raff that can be found, alas, in the ranks of our compatriots? He holds meetings in inns, don't you remember? He knows how to speak to the peasants, he works the plow and the hoe with his words, so why wouldn't he also wield the scythe?

But really, the scythe! Whoever Jan might really be, never would he have chosen such a symbol. He himself is aware that his great-great-grandfather died, here, under the blows of the serfs' scythes, massacred, torn apart . . . No, no, it's impossible. Since when did the descendant of Count Fryderyk, my future heir, turn into a leader of peasant revolts?

We have recently seen stranger metamorphoses, continued his voice. You said so, yourself—times are changing, and they don't change without men also changing, at least some of them . . .

It was insane; at that moment, Jozef noticed that the bailiff was saying something to him, what was he babbling about? He was wondering, the imbecile, if it might not be best to defer this matter, which seemed very serious to him, to the Austrian police.

'What are you saying! Have you lost your mind? Am I not master of my land, responsible for rendering justice and maintaining order?'

'Of course,' stammered the unfortunate man who, not daring to explain, looked at him meaningfully.

'You are an ass, a coward and a bad patriot,' shouted Jozef who, having finally someone to yell at, let loose upon him. 'The Austrians don't need to stick their noses into our affairs! As for the rest, I am not worried in the least. The guilty party is among this handful of artists—that is obvious. They are protecting one another, of course, but they are lying—that is as clear as the nose in the middle of your face. Riff-raff! The wings are to blame! Bring them here, beat them and get rid of this crowd. And in the future, these Moravian brothers better not show themselves around the estate or it will be the rope.'

And so the master's orders were followed. The crowd was dispersed, the puppeteers were beaten, the hamlet was thus as diverted by their punishment as they were charmed by their art; it was a sort of addition to the spectacle, the cherry on top. But contrary to Jozef's expectations, the page was not, however, turned. The matter had been hastily buried, everyone was aware of that. The atmosphere inside these walls became heavy with it; and beyond, on Zemka's land, the calm that apparently reigned could not hide a dark stirring.

When Jozef made his rounds in the sleigh driven by Efraim, the little bells no longer rang gaily in the midst of the winter silence. They rang lugubriously, like the voice of a child lost in the dark who is singing to make the invisible monsters believe he isn't afraid. And yet, the region greatly resembled what it had always been in this season, and nothing brought to mind the tumult of the year 1786, a very dark memory. There was no one on the roads, aside from a solitary peasant who greeted them from afar by removing his leather cap and, close up, showed a moustache covered in ice. In the hamlet there was a muted silence, snowy cottages inside which people quietly carried on their winter tasks.

On New Year's Day, as usual, Jozef had been received by the leader of the peasant community, an almost hundred-year-old man who had this position since the time of the von Kotzes. As always, the visit was carried out following a complex ceremony. The master entered behind Gavryl, the inhabitants of the cottage pretended to be extraordinarily surprised and not at all prepared for his visit, the women kneeled to kiss his elbows; then Jozef gestured for them to stand up and exchanged courteous formulas with the leader that never varied by a word.

'Praise be to Jesus Christ!'

'For eternity, Amen.'

'You honour us with your presence, master. My women are stricken with shame because my house is not worthy of a guest such as yourself.'

'I came, Roman, to present you with my wishes for the New Year. Health and prosperity to you and to all of yours!'

'Bless you, master. And to you and yours, may God give joy and wealth for the coming year.'

'Amen,' muttered the women. And with that they had the master sit at the table, where, as if by magic, there appeared an abundance of food in front of which he pretended to be delighted: a borscht with sour cream, golden cheese, onion rolls and various sweets. But the ritual dictated that he not touch anything before the eldest of the daughters-in-law (an old woman herself, acting as mistress of the house ever since the leader had become a widower) had ostentatiously poured into the soup a handful of salt to indicate that they were truly sparing no expense. Then, on a final compliment, the master picked up his spoon and attacked the soup amidst the smiles of those around him, and everything was thus perfect.

. . . Everything thus had been perfect in man's memory; but this time the reception lacked warmth and sincerity. The soup was good, even if a bit too salty; the nuts and raisins were served abundantly, the rolls were crusty. And yet Jozef felt imperceptibly watched; at one moment, even, he held up his spoon and looked into its back but saw only the reflection of the stiff Gavryl who, as usual, had refused the stool that had been offered him.

And contributing to the tension of the situation, the leader, after so many years of vigour, was visibly beginning to decline. To Jozef's questions he responded distractedly, or did not respond at all; or in a wavering voice he launched into digressions in which he mixed up dates, people and places.

'It is a dirty bird who soils his nest,' he repeated from time to time, and Jozef was angrily impressed by the return of this proverb cited out of context. He asked for more soup, emptied his bowl, noisily accepted more glasses of vodka to mask his unease; and the old man watched him eat and drink with a pensive, distant, and, it seemed to him, pitying look.

'Have some more, master, do honour to these humble dishes, they are your due, God forgive us our sins . . .'

'Come now, old Roman, your sins must fit into a handkerchief, and God has surely pardoned you for them already. Peace be with you, and have a glass with me!'

'I told them: *You will not take God's name in vain* . . . have some more, have some more! Yes, *it is a dirty bird who* . . .'

'But what is he talking about!' interrupted Jozef, pounding on the table. No one made a sound, the women continued to stare at him with a humble and empty look, the clock tick-tocked. It was time to leave.

'Be well, Roman, and may God keep you in His grace.'

'Bless you, bless you,' muttered the leader with a vain effort to get up from his bench. 'God keep you, God keep the Ponarskis . . .'

And Jozef, who had been startled by that lapse, thought he had seen between those wrinkled eyelids two tiny tears.

Yes, OK, I am allowing myself to indulge in a bit of fantasy because it is quite obvious that I didn't see all that. I have never seen the little cottage of the leader, much too far away for me even to have an idea of its exterior. I only saw Jozef leave one grey morning next to Gavryl, and return sombre and reflective, hardly touching his lunch; when his family expressed concern, he responded, 'It's nothing, the Ruthenians stuffed me again;' and to his wife, who asked for news of the leader with whom she sometimes dealt for her charities, 'My goodness, he is declining a lot, poor old Roman.'

Yes, I admit I have copiously embroidered that thin story. But I don't think I am very wrong. Perhaps the rolls were not as crusty as all that, there were perhaps not nuts and raisins but cheesecake. So what? Isn't it almost as convincing as if I had really been there? Thanks to what I know of everyone concerned—the local customs, Gavryl's roughness, Jozef's condescending familiarity with his inferiors, not to mention what is said in the kitchens . . . aren't I capable of extrapolating and having an idea that is almost exact, I'm convinced, of what happens beyond my little horizon?

And so my guests are worried, even if they don't admit it. Nothing can erase that incident at Christmas which they so want to forget. It is like the spot on the little key in Bluebeard (in that terrible story that Madame Denisot reads and rereads to her pupils to teach them, while working on their French, that curiosity is a horrible sin). Nothing removes it, because they are continuously reminded of it when they expect it the least. One day Wioletta is looking in a drawer for some drawing paper, and falls upon a piece of paper printed in Latin characters but written in the Ruthenian language. The young girl is able to decipher a few sentences and jumps when she recognizes the text of *Appeal*. Her hands start trembling, she doesn't dare tell anyone, and throws the paper into the fire. A line remains legible for a long moment: '. . . God refuses it, God repulses it.' Wioletta Zemka doesn't know yet, but that line would always remain engraved in her memory.

Another day some twenty pieces of paper fly off, like a flock of birds, from under the peristyle of the Uniate church. The wind carries them off, then they fall back down into the snow. Luckily, they have not flown too far—in ten minutes, Gavryl has picked them all up (except for one that would be found at the foot of a tree, all washed out but still recognizable, after the thaw). He hurries to bring them to his master, who almost chokes with rage, 'In front of the church now! Ah, but this is going too far! Who is the joker who put them there?'

Under Jozef's harsh interrogation, the Uniate priest protests, defends himself—they weren't there the day before, that's all he can say about it. Who put them there? Well, someone who had time to waste, no doubt, because none of his parishioners knows how to read. He has never seen them . . . or at least . . .

'What? Speak!'

Well, he had, in fact, had in his hands a copy that a peasant had found under his door and wanted to have read to him. So he had read it.

'Ah! You read it to him. And what were your comments?'

'I told him,' the priest responds while imperceptibly raising his head, 'that these writings were very impious, and that someone was taking advantage of their faith in order to trick them. We are all in the hands of God, that's what I told him. And God's representative on earth is the emperor, isn't he? That they should look to him, that they should have confidence in our Ferdinand to ease their misery, and if they should take up weapons it is only to support him. Their true enemies were those bad Polish shepherds who want to take them over the brink . . .'

'Who told you,' Jozef replies heatedly, 'that those shepherds, as you say, were Polish?'

'My word, it is not difficult to guess. Otherwise, why are these sheets printed in Latin characters?'

Jozef doesn't much like what he has just heard, nor the impertinent tone of this lousy pope. He stares at him in silence, whips the tip of his shoe and asks, 'This sheet of paper, what did you do with it?'

'What did I do with it? My goodness, I think our maid lit the fire with it. Or no, it seems that the peasant took it back with him when he left, or . . . I really don't know.'

'I thank you for your help, Father,' Jozef says, enraged by his new off-hand manner.

What will please him even less is to receive, a few days later, a visit from the commissioner of the district—a visit that, going by the important way in which the man is rolling his moustache, is not a social call. Furthermore, going into the small blue salon, he immediately clicks his heels and bows before the lady of the house, excusing himself, in German, for having to bother her for an official matter. Clara understands and gets up, followed by her daughters and their governess; only the male members of the household, Jozef, his nephew and Mr Borowski, remain.

A few niceties, and the commissioner comes to the point. He slides a hand into his uniform, extracts a piece of paper, gives it to Jozef Zemka, with a bow, 'Have you already seen this paper?'

'Good God!' Jozef moaned, 'that cursed tract again!'

'Dear sir, I then take it to mean that you have already seen it?'

'Oh, yes! I can't move my foot without stepping on one . . .'

The Austrian interrupts him—of course with a smile that dissipates the brutality but interrupts him nevertheless. In that moment, no one can ignore it—he is there as a policeman, not as a social acquaintance.

'Allow me, dear sir, to be surprised by this. Because if you had this printed paper in your hands, it was obviously incumbent upon you to notify the authorities. Is it possible that you haven't noted the subversive nature of this so-called pious discourse?'

Jozef opens his mouth but, an exceptional thing, finds he doesn't know what to say.

'Luckily,' the other man continues, 'there are in these lands good subjects of the emperor who seem better advised.'

'Sir!'

'Excuse this reproach, but it is deserved. The man who gave us this paper is one of your own serfs. I won't tell you which one out of regard for him. Well! Serf or not, that man proved a discernment and a civic sense that are frankly and unfortunately lacking in the elite of our province.'

This is an official reprimand. Jan Zemka can be heard coughing, perhaps upset at witnessing the scene, or getting ready to intervene. The commissioner turns towards him and slowly passes a finger over his moustache.

'I can guess your hesitation. *Birds of a feather flock together*, don't they? And a Pole does not denounce one of his compatriots. But not everyone thinks as you do. Imagine that this tract, whose presence on your land interests us greatly, has circulated in Polish in the western districts of Galicia: a dozen copies were brought to our colleagues by serfs of your nationality. This should show you that, even among your own, there is loyalty.'

On the faces of my three inhabitants one can read only their effort to remain impassive. With variable degrees of success—a new cough shakes Jan's shoulders, Zygmunt Borowski is taking a few nervous steps to the window, his hands crossed behind his back.

'That is all I have to say to you,' concludes the commissioner. 'I will not trouble you any further with this matter—I had nothing to reproach you for, dear sir, except your slight negligence. All the same, on a more personal note . . .' (his glance passes distractedly over each of those present before resting, impenetrable, on the bust of Adam Mickiewicz), 'on a more personal note, I could not recommend *prudence* too strongly. The times are agitated, sirs, many things are unstable. No doubt they have always been so in this region of the world, as Poles you cannot forget, can you? But this time, I think it is necessary to remind you with a bit more urgency. I repeat: Be careful.'

The 'thank you's that Jozef addresses to him ring terribly false; in his heart he is seething. What, this little commissioner has the gall to remind them of the worst hours of their history, the massacres of 1768, the even more bloody trials of Chmielnicki, as if . . . (As if what, then? If Jozef were forced to say what he is thinking deep down inside he would admit—as if he didn't think about it all the time, himself).

Was it a threat, or a simple warning? What game is being played here, what dark ghost is haunting Galicia?

18

Until now I've always felt like one of those doll's houses without a front, where the eye can enter innocently right into each room. Now it seems that everything has been shut up. Before, the many doors were opened and closed with no one paying attention; but now everyone has had occasion to question their thickness, to shut them carefully before holding some meeting, or even—oh, yes, one would be wrong to believe this pastime is reserved for servants—to stick an ear against a door to find out what is being said by two others who think they are safe. This explains why even I, who normally knows everything, sometimes followed the wrong path or omitted to see what was happening right in front of me.

And I too, in my fibres, felt this atmosphere of threat, of mystery and also of hope. Yes, of hope—I am persuaded that every human, however attached he or she may be to the present state of things, harbours a hidden taste for a shaking up that will change the world and alter lives. This still unshaped shaking, I assert that everyone here wanted it without necessarily admitting as much, just as the body ends up desiring the blow that it knows is inevitable, or the virgin ultimately desires the pain that will make her a wife or a fallen woman. Something different.

Because everyone, including the youngest, will be decisively marked by those two years. Jadwiga, because they will appear to her as enough of an experience of turmoil. As soon as she is able to take her young life in hand, she will peacefully withdraw from the game, far from the cruelty of the world and the heartaches of womanhood. Thus, the same causes can have opposite effects—the irruption of history into individual existences, that climate of effervescence that throws one into passion and adultery, alarms another and turns her into the most zealous of Benedictines.

And Zosia, who is almost twelve, will retain from the events the yet different idea that things are not always the rule and the law, as she has been taught; that the order of the world is only one order, and that it can be changed for another. Her faculty for wonder is not diminished by this; rather it is enriched. Henceforth, she will reach for the possible, for the unknown, no longer only for what she has before her eyes and for that which has been the life of her family for generations. It is these two years that will later make her the loving wife of Emil Elfenbein, a converted Jew, but the grandson of a Kosher butcher from Bucovina; then a well-respected Viennese woman known for her taste in the arts and new ideas; and still later, the mother of two great pioneers in their domains—a jurist, enemy of the Historic School; and a playwright who will destroy, with a pen used as a sword, the remnants of dying romanticism.

My little Zosia. In her final portraits, which one day will hang on the walls of the greatest museums in the world—not because of her particular beauty but because of the talent and fame of those who painted her and were her close friends—I assume that she still keeps, in her old woman's eye, the spark of that love of the world, of that universal curiosity that she acquired in this family, between these walls, in the midst of this undulating plain, and that she perhaps owes a bit to me.

But for now it is Jozef and his nephew whom I follow with my gaze, believing, in my naivety, that for a time they will be the only protagonists in the story. Who would have doubted this when, after the departure of the commissioner, Jozef is seen leading Jan under the trees on the grounds, in a state of agitation that I had rarely seen in him?

It is bitterly cold these early days of February, and their breaths form little clouds in front of their mouths. Jozef vigorously rubs his hands to warm them, hesitates, seeks an entrance into the subject. And Jan, grave, ends up speaking first, 'My uncle, I see you are worried . . . Is it the visit from the police? I admit that I, too, was disturbed by it. But must we give in so quickly to the intimidations of our enemies?'

Jozef raises his head quickly, looking at his nephew's face.

'What is it, Uncle?'

'Ah, I can't help myself, this doubt has been nagging me for weeks . . . Jan, I beg you, swear to me—swear that you had nothing to do with the propagation of that *Appeal to the People of the Countryside*?'

He doesn't dare ask his question more directly, and he is right. For now his nephew is truly angry.

'What . . . What? Are you joking, Uncle?'

'Oh, my poor Jan, you can't know how that extravagant suspicion has caused me sleepless nights, how I trembled when that accursed commissioner looked at you . . . It seemed . . .'

'It seems to me that this matter has troubled your mind,' Jan interrupts, still frowning. 'What do you think there is in common between our hopes and that vulgar Communist propaganda, beyond the fact that it might be the work of Poles such as us?'

'*Might be*? What do you mean?'

'I mean that things must be taken with circumspection. We have recently seen such attacks circulating in other places, in Prussia, in Hesse, and their authors appeared to be authentic radicals. But you know as well as I do the truth of these circles—for three sincere sans-culottes there are two agents provocateurs who risk very little throwing such crazy and enraged rhetoric around.'

'So that is your hypothesis? A provocation by the police? But see here, who here . . .'

'I don't know, I don't know . . . and yet . . . that Agenor Karlowicz, for example. He immediately struck me with his intelligence, an intelligence that he camouflages behind, let's say, a down-to-earth exterior. Not that I find him unpleasant—far from it. But what is he doing at your house, do you really know?'

'My goodness, he's courting Urszula, or at least . . .'

'He isn't in much of a hurry.'

'He is hesitating, and I understand. He is a sensible young man, and our poor Urszula is not a woman to cause a man to lose his head. And really, Jan, why would the Austrian police come and bother me on the subject of a tract that they, themselves, put into circulation here?'

'Oh, you underestimate their taste for intrigue. Why? To intimidate us, to sow discord and fear among us. So it is said in the region that you are suspect and that the authorities are watching you, or in I don't know what even more obscure goal, because their Machiavellianism goes beyond my imagination.'

'So you think it was Agenor? I will keep an eye on him, if you say so. But I'm ready to bet you're wrong.'

'You might be right, Uncle,' Jan sighed. 'The habit of conspiring has made me suspicious.'

A pile of snow falls from the tree under which they are standing, they move away, take a few steps, each one feeling his heart secretly clinched.

'I should also tell you, Uncle . . .'

'Yes?'

'You must have understood this—this unrest foretells of events I have touched upon. Our enemies are preparing, we have just seen proof of this. But we will be ready before them, because it is faith that carries us, and not the vile reasons of State. Soon . . .'

'Yes?'

Jan lowers his voice, glances towards my walls and sees only, as he should, a mute façade under the winter frost; then he turns back, and his movement makes the folds of his coat move.

'Soon national deliverance will come, Uncle. Rejoice for us, for you, for me! Oh, what joy, what intoxication, that moment when we finally feel that we can act on the destiny of our people, throw the weight of our courage, our ardour, the entire weight of our lives into the movement for the highest of goals!'

Oh, my God, thinks Jozef. Obviously he expected this, he knew well that an uprising doesn't take thirty years to prepare. But already, so soon! He almost regrets these weeks of Advent when nothing yet darkened the horizon, when the future seemed a succession of weddings, engagements, in short, games and laughter.

'And so it is . . . imminent?'

'Imminent, yes. In one, two weeks, all of Poland will rise up. And without your active help, upon which I allow myself not to count— because I understand the responsibilities and the duties of a father and husband—I would like to ask you (his voice thickens) for your blessing.'

'You have it, my boy, you have it, how could you doubt it?' Jozef's eyes begin to fill, his chest is trembling—the hour is decidedly historic. The two men embrace and Jan continues, largo, con anima, 'I am infinitely touched, Uncle, by the tenderness you have shown me since you have welcomed me into your family. This blessing, you see, I couldn't ask it of my father, who still doesn't know anything . . .'

'Your father, come now! Am I not almost your father?'

Jan looks away, and clenches his jaw.

'It is cold, let's go back,' says Jozef in a gruff voice. It seems he must give the example of the male hardiness with which his brother, the Napoleonic soldier, would no doubt have said adieu to his son if he had been in his place. Because too much emotion cannot be good here, and Jan will have to go off to battle with a hardened heart.

From then on, Jozef will forbid himself that type of effusion, will be efficient, will provide his nephew with some money, an excellent horse and the best weapon. He constantly feels something like a drum beat in his chest; but he doesn't allow anything to show. And when Jan sets off a few days later, under the pretext of a business trip to Kraków, Jozef, alone let in on the secret, will be the only member of the family to hide his sadness and his anxiety. He will even go so far as to slap the neck of Jan's horse and say in a hearty tone: 'Go on, you rascal, and sow your oats while you can!'

19

Clara went through those troubling times in a very different way. Like the others, she perceived the climate of urgency and instability, and the *Appeal to the People of the Countryside* had upset her as much as anyone else. But her timid spirit did not go so far as to be launched onto a concrete terrain, to wonder who, why, in what goal and for what consequences this was happening. It stayed inside and simply suffered to see that the people here were showing ill will towards them, as masters, an ill will that, moreover, was rather justified. The religious tenor of the *Appeal* had struck her, struck her with fright, at first, and then her with its truth. Yes, it was no doubt true, God had intended no man to be a slave, and despite Clara's good works, her care, and her constant concern, weren't their serfs slaves all the same?

She summoned her spiritual advisor who protested, made her understand that a good Catholic shouldn't have such thoughts that verged on heresy—a good Catholic made her husband happy, took care of her home, watched over her children, their physical and moral health, not forgetting, obviously, to support the poor; but beyond that, she was overstepping.

Seeing his penitent grow pale and stifle her tears, the Jesuit recalled too late what a sensitive soul he was dealing with and changed his tone, 'Now, now, my daughter, where did you get such fantastical notions? You have once again taken even more upon yourself, I can guess, and overloaded your soul with tension and worries. Take care of yourself, my child. Don't be so hard on yourself—God wants us to love others as we do ourselves, but for that we must first love ourselves. And so leave to others these questions that disturb you and are beyond you. Calm yourself, and your strengths (because you have more than enough, my daughter, you are a courageous Christian, full of energy for the good), concentrate your strengths on the happy events to come, which at present demand certain preparations of you.'

It is true, he is right, Maria is getting married, thought the poor mother who, in her inner torment, had almost forgot that. Henceforth she spent a large part of her days checking on the completion of the trousseau, reflecting on how the wedding would unfold. She often went to Grünau to compare fabrics, to look at porcelains and silver. She found, moreover, that the workers nearby were getting lazy, that they were sewing hems less carefully, forgetting the stays in the dresses, embroidering less richly; but she didn't dare say anything because of that vague feeling of guilt of which she was unable to rid her soul.

She was also aware that Maria's wedding was not the apex of her duties as a mother but only the first step. The times were perhaps not propitious for matrimonial plans, for pleasure parties in which so many unions were concluded; since Advent they almost never entertained, unlike in other winters, and invitations were rare in the neighbourhood. But it was her duty to supervise her other daughters, the ones who were not yet engaged, so that this missed season would not embitter them. In the current circumstances, it was better that they devote themselves to their studies, finish their training, occupy their minds in a worthy and fruitful way. She was well aware that, afterward, it would be too late. Already Maria was growing uncontrollable, refusing to work at any discipline that she would not be using directly in her future life as a wife. If she practised the piano, drew a little, showed some interest in domestic planning and accounting, she would hear nothing of Latin, geography, classical or modern history.

'Ah, non, maman, ne me demandez pas ça!' she had protested in exquisite French and with a pout that was no less so, to defend her cause; and her mother, indulgent, gave in to her. But her example should not contaminate the others.

And so Clara continued to spend an hour every morning in the classroom before leaving to attend to her prenuptial tasks. She deplored Urszula's intellectual laziness, belatedly assessed that they had badly served this girl by placing her disadvantages and her ugliness at the centre of everything. She encouraged her softly from the back of the room, whispering: 'Come on, my daughter,' and sighed with irritation when the girl was unable to remember a date or a name. And by listening every day she ended up knowing a few things, herself, so that Mr Borowski sometimes raised his eyes up at her with a bit of surprise, 'That's correct, Madame, but please, don't answer for my students—you are preventing them from making progress.'

I am preventing them! Clara was astounded, since she had never in her life encountered a reproach of the kind. Then she observed the tutor who, with a frown, was now questioning Wioletta, and she said to herself: I may very well be annoying him.

One day when the young man had several times looked with a sombre glance at Maria's vacant seat, Clara drew up her courage and said, at the end of the lesson, 'You have lost a student, Mr Borowski, I give you her excuses. You must understand, her mind is elsewhere, and she has passed the age, hasn't she, to be constrained in these things?'

'Rest assured, Madame, I put my pride elsewhere than in the attraction of my teaching,' he replied rather dryly, and he was no doubt lying. 'Moreover,' he continued in an effort to be amiable, 'I've lost a student, that's true, but it seems that I will have soon gained another.'

'Oh,' said Clara beginning to squirm and suddenly no longer sure of what to do with her fingers, 'I understand. You are scolding me . . . I shouldn't have . . .'

He was watching her and she fell quiet, crimson.

'I don't really understand, Madame, what reproach you are accusing me of. I am thinking of your daughter Zosia— it seems to me that in a few months she will be able to join her sisters. Or at least,' he corrected with a meaningful smile, 'those who, at that time, will not be engaged. I have heard her answer her governess' questions. She is bright, and I think she could already follow without too much difficulty.'

Clara made an effort to pull herself together. She was filled with relief, and with something else too, a feeling of emptiness, of a dissipated dream. The misunderstanding was indeed laughable, and she hoped with all her heart that the young man had not understood her.

'I will confer with her governess, sir,' she said in a clear voice that seemed hollow to her; and never again sat at the back of the room.

But this was not to take chance into account, nor the context, nor the consequences of what was already there. Shortly afterward, Clara had to break the vow of silence she had imposed on herself and stopped the tutor between the first and second floors. That morning, for a change, seemed quite normal—the sound of piano scales climbed up the stairway, and behind the door to the library one could hear Jozef and Gavryl as they studied some accounting or farming report together.

'*It's incomprehensible, my dear Gavryl. The Doroshenkos claim to have taken from the little field only two-thirds of the production of last year . . .*'

'*They are hiding it, master. Bad people, bad thoughts. And then, you are too easy on them because of your strumpet.*'

'*Yes, but they are not the only ones, the Pavlyks too . . .*'

'*Oh, they're hiding, I tell you. Bad times, bad minds! You need to look under their floorboards and you will see what you will see.*'

Clara had put her hand on the railing: 'Mr Borowski, may I speak to you for a moment?

'I am at your disposal, Madame.'

'I have here (Clara rummaged in her pocket) a letter from the bookseller in Kraków. He says he has received two of your books from abroad but hesitates to send such materials to me right now . . . Movements of troops, near their territory . . .'

The tutor had come closer to her and, at her invitation, went over the letter attentively.

'*Knock down the poplars, and then, if we divert the little river . . .*'

'*Listen to you! And where will we find the manpower at this time of year?*'

He read it a second time, absorbed; and Clara, who was standing two stairs below him, watched his teeth nervously gnaw at his lower lip.

'What do you think?'

'Of the delay? Oh, it doesn't matter,' he finally said, folding up the letter and giving it back to her. 'There are very few books that I would truly be able to do without, especially for a matter of a few weeks.'

And so she was bothering him for nothing. And the favour she had done for him was really not that consequential. Clara felt anger welling up in her, but that sentiment was so unfamiliar to her that she didn't know what to say. She remained there, one hand on the railing; and the young man, whom she was preventing from coming down the stairs, ended up looking into her eyes.

'*Three and a half quintals, and it's optimistic . . .*'

She discovered that she was trembling. Their silence continued. A more worldly man would have found some nicety to fill the silence, conclude the conversation on a polite and insignificant note. But Zygmunt Borowski (she would soon learn) was an orphan who from his childhood had known only institutions and student garrets. He had never known superficial kindness, the social habits learnt within a family. He had not even received that elementary assurance that a man acquires by being cherished by his mother. He was quiet.

'You seem to be . . . quite hostile,' she muttered, her breath cut off by the awareness that because of her the conversation was getting out of control, going onto an unknown and unsettled territory. 'May I ask you the reason?'

He blinked his eyes.

'Well,' he muttered, with the absent air of a man seeking the exact expression for his thoughts. 'How can I tell you? I think that, in a certain way, you are . . . I'll just say it: You are everything I detest.'

'All right, all right let's do it! Tomorrow I will go and see the builder.'

Clara grasped the young man's arm, led him into the hallway of the second floor and firmly pushed open the door to the classroom, stupefied by her own boldness.

'How can you say such a thing to me!' she cried out as soon as they were alone and the door had shut. 'To me, who have always only sought to help you! What do you detest in me?'

All of *this*, answered the tutor's eyes with implacable sincerity; they looked at the molding of the ceiling, the bound books, the velvet chairs, the large trees in the grounds, and Clara herself, tall, big and regal in her satin dress.

At that moment, he must have noted that his interlocutrice was stricken with movements very different from her dignified stature of possessor—wringing her hands, bringing them to her mouth, unable to express herself. In her thoughts the arguments swirled furiously, but she didn't know the words to speak of such things. She could only blurt out, 'I am not *all that* . . . I cannot be, myself alone, *all that you detest*, it's not possible . . .'

She wanted to say: You hate my class, I've finally understood. You hate my class, its power, its culture, its objects . . . But I am not *it*! No being is by herself all of the aristocrats and landowners, I am one, I am me, I am a human being!

If he understood, she didn't have the opportunity to realize it; because after that attempt to explain, which seemed so pitiful to herself, she turned around, tears in her eyes, and left the room without saying another word.

20

He remained fixed where he was for a few moments; then, mechanically, he sat down at the big table and opened the book he found on it, read a few pages, took two or three notes in preparation for his class the next day.

He worked for about an hour, engrossed in what he was doing; it was only when he heard voices outside that he raised his head.

He went to the window. In front of the gate, the groom Efraim was leading a horse that was saddled and bridled, a servant was bringing packages and putting them into the saddlebags. Then two other figures appeared in his line of vision the master of the house and his nephew, whom he held by the shoulder and to whom he slid, discretely, an object wrapped in cloth (a pistol, thought Zygmunt). The rest of the family followed, girls, governess. But yes, of course Jan Zemka was leaving today for a brief stay in Kraków.

He shivered when he finally saw Madame Zemka appear. She now seemed very much the mistress of herself, was the first to go up and kiss her nephew. Behind her, Maria was dabbing at her eyes, Zosia, the enemy of separations, raised her sad little face to her future brother-in-law . . . Should Zygmunt go down and mix with the family, convey his good wishes at the departure?

What would be the point, he suddenly said to himself with some emotion. I've just lost my position.

He undid the collar of his shirt, ran his hand through his hair. What had got into him, how could he have said to his employer 'You are everything I detest'?

Handkerchiefs were waving, Jan Zemka started his horse, and his uncle said a final inaudible word to him. Now they were returning to the columned entryway, the wife on her husband's arm. She was no doubt going to take advantage of the moment to mention the incident to him.

The young man sat down again. He waited for the knock on the door that would come at any moment, announcing a scene, insults, and, at the end, his dismissal. But the knock never came.

They've just bid their nephew goodbye, she is sad, she will wait for this evening, he thought. But dinner went by, then the evening, then the morning of the next day, and nothing happened. Had he dreamt that conversation?

He knew he hadn't, because Madame Zemka wasn't the same. She didn't look at him, didn't speak to him except in front of someone else. He continued to try to catch her eye to attempt to resolve the tension; he could never catch it. He no longer feared losing his position; but he was still worried without really knowing why.

And yet he didn't regret what he had said to her. It was true, it was at the heart of his beliefs, at some point someone in this house had to know about his deepest thoughts, a man cannot continue to live while hiding himself. It seemed to him, moreover, that what he had said to her, she could understand, she was even the only one here who could. The only one? Why? Why under her stylish jacket, under the Ruthenian kazabaika lined with fur that her husband had given to her and wanted her to wear on holidays, under the flowered shawl that she draped regally over her large shoulders—why would she have a heart capable of understanding him?

Why, I don't know, but she does. Such was the observation that went through his mind while he was still sleeping, on the morning of the third day.

He would have liked to continue that conversation, make her see that it wasn't to hurt her that he had spoken that way but because he believed it in all sincerity. It was an objective statement, without animosity and even, in a certain sense, fairly friendly. He tried to say the sentence again—'You are all that I detest'—by giving it other intonations. He would have liked to find the tone in which such a phrase could be said and seem amicable. It wasn't easy.

On the fourth day, while the entire household was gathered in the salon, a messenger, out of breath, came to inform them that, forty-eight hours earlier, the Austrian troops had entered the republic of Kraków. Zygmunt did not see that at this announcement the master of the house grew very pale and suppressed a gesture of concern. He didn't see, because at that moment his eyes, seeking those of Clara Zemka, had just found them. A flame seemed to spread within his chest—he had found her eyes! The brown irises, with their soft shine, and, yes, so familiar, were finally looking at him. And the two gazes said to each other: 'Kraków occupied! We almost knew it, didn't we?'

Almost immediately she turned her head away, but his joy remained. A joy strangely mixed with alarm. Or rather, it was a strange renting of his soul—pure joy on the one hand and fear on the other, fear for the fate of a city to which he had so many connections.

He moved closer to the master who was questioning the messenger, attempting to glean any additional details. Madame Zemka was just getting up, no doubt to avoid catching his eye a second time. As she passed behind him, the train of her skirts brushed against him and seemed to unleash an electrical current in his body.

He couldn't stay there.

Two such similar souls could not be satisfied with brushing together, glances. He needed words, he thirsted to hear the sound of her voice again, uttering words to no one else.

He followed her out of the salon. She had already gone up a few steps, a hand holding the heavy fabric of her skirt, the other hanging, full of rings, at her side. *All that I detest*, he muttered a final time; but those words no longer had any meaning. Because, unbeknownst to him, he was already on a terrain before the boundary of which stopped the firmest convictions; a terrain where nothing has the same meaning it has, sometimes simultaneously, in other parts of a single mind. When, without transition and without contradiction, a man in love with power can love to be enslaved, the enemy of inequality can see in his opposite an attraction—even become smitten with it.

What nobility in those shoulders, in the folds of her skirt, in her neck made heavy by her low chignon . . . She is a queen, he thought. And another voice, on this side of the boundary, tried in vain to warn him: 'What are you doing with a queen? You don't like queens!' But he didn't hear it any more, or it was so weak that it seemed no longer to concern him. Yes, a queen, he thought, this time with tenderness. Because queens love, suffer, are sacrificed too—Berenice. A loving queen, a sad queen, and sad because of me . . .

'Madame, excuse me . . .'

She turned around. He received the full power of those brown eyes.

'Madame, I fear, the other day, I said an unfortunate thing . . .'

No, no, no. She pulled herself up, her look relaxed him, she didn't want excuses, formalities; nor did he. That was to go backwards, to that very distant time when there was a tutor and the mother of his pupils. So distant? It was four days ago! Yes, four days—an eternity.

Their chests rose, their breathing came together while their eyes, finally, feasted on what they had come to understand. She smiled slightly, a transfiguration; and he touched her hand, the strong hand, a bit large, which hung at her side, took it, squeezed it in his own . . . But footsteps soon broke them apart.

'Oh, there you are,' said Jozef to his wife, while the tutor, once again invisible, went up to the second floor. 'I must speak to you. I'm going to leave for a short trip, as well . . . impossible to put off.'

'A trip?' Clara said in a mechanical voice. 'Where are you going?'

'It doesn't matter. Business.'

'Oh, and when are you leaving?'

'As soon as possible. May I ask you to gather up some things for me—toilet articles, a few pieces of clothing? Efraim will get me some provisions from the kitchen for three or four days.'

'As you wish—but why such mystery? Wouldn't it be better for me to ring for your valet . . .'

'Don't try to understand—just do what I ask you. I'd like to be gone in an hour—is that clear? Thank you.'

He left her there and she obeyed, her thoughts in chaos. It was without knowing what she was doing that she went into her husband's bedroom, opened the drawer of the chest and chose three shirts, went into the washroom and took some soap, a brush, a tortoiseshell-handled razor. 'He took my hand. He squeezed my hand,' she kept repeating to herself. It was inconceivable, it was miraculous, she felt beaten down while also supernaturally light.

When she went back downstairs her husband was waiting for her, an eye on his watch, close to the service door behind which stood Efraim.

'You aren't changing? Don't you want to put on your travelling suit?'

'No, there's no need. Clara, I bid you adieu. And if you are questioned, say only that I am taking a tour of the estate—you don't know where.'

Five minutes later, she heard the sound of the horse's hooves on the road. She remained drained, dumbfounded, shaking. Was it possible?

He had touched her hand.

21

Jozef didn't go far on the county road—at the first bend, he was stopped by an obstacle.

On the side of the road a group of men were warming themselves around a fire made from twigs. As he drew closer, two men stepped out—the tall Marko and a young fellow from a Polish farm—and stood in the middle of the road.

What terrified Jozef more than the scythe and the flail they had slung casually over their shoulders was that upon seeing him they did not take off their hats. He even had to stoop so low as to greet them first, 'Praise be to Christ.'

'For eternity, amen!' responded the group in an overly loud chorus.

'It's chilly this morning,' said Jozef, but his remark met with no response.

The horse was jumpy, Marko caught it by its bridle and put a palm on its nose, 'Calm down, Sultan, calm down . . . you're really loaded down! Hey, master, where are you going with all that?'

'Oh, my friends, I'm out for a ride.'

'He's out for a ride,' repeated Marko, turning back to the group, who burst out laughing. Then his acolyte stuck his hand in one of the saddlebags, took out a shirt, examined an entire ham with interest, then unfolded the razor and tried the blade on his thumbnail.

'You think of everything, master, when you go out for a ride. Maybe you're right. Because the roads aren't safe, these days, for you Poles.'

'Come now!' said Jozef with a forced laugh. 'As if you weren't a Pole yourself, Karol!'

Karol spat on the ground, 'Polish? Me? You make me laugh, master. The Poles are the gentlemen, the lords, those who can read and write. We are only peasants.'

Jozef squirmed on his saddle. In spite of the cold he was sweating. As he opened his mouth to reply, Marko said: 'You know what, master? You should turn around. The weather isn't good for a ride, there's going to be a storm. Look—over there, everything is grey.'

There was more laughter and Jozef, cautiously, turned his head in the direction Marko was pointing at. To the west, where the hills stood out, two columns of smoke darkened the sky, spreading into black clouds. He pulled at the reins in his hands.

'It's true,' added Karol. 'You should go home, take care of your family. They're maybe going to need you.'

'And take care of your children, especially. Children can break your heart.'

'And nephews too.'

'We haven't seen much of your nephew recently. He's probably out on a ride too, eh?'

Jozef sat still. Finally, he raised his chin and said, with the same tone of knowing irony, 'Hm, you're right, the weather is indeed threatening. Well, thank you for your advice, I think I will follow it. Good day.'

'Good day to you, master!' chuckled Marko, letting go of the bridle.

And so Jozef Zemka returned home after thirty minutes. But in thirty minutes, much had changed in his home.

In the blue salon, the young girls were chattering as they put the finishing touches on a play they wanted to present to their friend Agenor. Clothing was draped over the furniture, the large rug was strewn with feathers, bits of yarn and pieces of paper. Urszula was radiant in her Cleopatra costume, made out of all the shiny and golden things they could find in their wardrobes. Maria, using a burnt cork, was trying to give her sister the skin tone of an Egyptian woman. Wioletta, focusing intently on a paint brush, was painting an old belt to make it look like a snake, and the two smallest girls, in the background, squinted their eyes to look at it all when, suddenly, the one who was being adorned stopped moving and looked out of the windows. 'Oh! Did you see that smoke?'

Dumbfounded, the five girls ran to the window, opened it, then quickly closed it again, because the air outside stunk of things burning.

'There's a fire,' murmured Jadwiga.

'Two,' corrected one of her sisters.

Two fires, in this season? It was not the sort of weather to cause barns to go up in flames. They remained standing, sensing they were looking at something they should not have seen and that an adult would have hidden it from them. But, luckily, everything would soon be brought back to order, wouldn't it? The fire would be put out, or at least explained, repressed, pushed outside their world, like everything that was frightening and smelt bad . . .

But nothing happened. No adult came into the room; they all looked at Maria hoping that she, as the eldest, almost married, would know what to do. But even Maria seemed at a loss. They stood there, silently, and Urszula, automatically, pulled off her long veil and began to rub the soot off her cheeks.

'Hey,' grumbled the cook, 'my ham has disappeared. And an entire loaf of bread! This is unbelievable, my dear girls. People are doing whatever they want now!'

'And why not?'

The fat woman turned towards the three helpers who worked under her. 'Who said that?'

They lowered their heads, looking at one another. Finally Lubienka stepped forward and, her hands behind her back, muttered, 'I did. But I'm not the one who took the ham, I swear by the Holy Virgin, as my witness!'

'All right. Who, then?'

They shook their heads—they really didn't know. And then the youngest spoke up sanctimoniously, 'I saw Efraim come into the kitchen. Maybe it was him?'

'Of course it was him,' said Lubienka, emboldened. 'I saw him leaving by the back door with something big under his cloak. He was going to sell it in Grünau, that's obvious!'

'Or eat it himself,' suggested a third. 'That rascal, I wouldn't put it past him.'

The cook blinked. She didn't like the turn things were taking. Everyone knew that Efraim was somewhat her protégé. And she wasn't ashamed of it—she liked good-looking fellows, especially if they made her laugh. Under other circumstances she would have put an end to the mutiny with one of her shouts that made even the jars of jam in the larder cupboards tremble. But a certain something in the air kept her from doing so today, something new. She had to be on her guard.

'He'll see who he has to deal with, that one,' she growled. 'Oh! He can't make a fool out of me. He hasn't heard the last of this.'

It was good but it still wasn't enough. The helpers, instead of going back to their chopping and grating, stayed there, their heads lowered, looking suspicious.

'Have you all taken root? Go cut those carrots and chop the onions. I have a lunch to prepare. We're here to feed those ladies and gentlemen. And their daughters, their suitors, their Jews and everyone else . . .'

An approving murmur greeted her words; and while the women were getting back to work, she concluded, triumphant with the momentum, 'I'm not joking. Have you ever realized, girls, that without us all these people would starve?'

My husband is gone, Clara thought suddenly when the sound of hooves had faded away. An unknown land was opening before her, a void, a white space—her husband was on a trip, and she . . . He touched my hand. My husband is gone, I packed his bag, I offered him his travelling suit and he refused, I don't know why, I don't want to know. He is gone. Another life is opening up for me, it doesn't matter if it lasts two days or fifteen—it is here. It has already begun. And in this life I know I must go up into the classroom, that I am expected, that I am desired.

This new life was extremely simple. She didn't need to weigh the pros and cons. She didn't have any pros or cons inside her, no uncertainties, no considerations. It was a weightless life, where everything happened through instinct.

Clara climbed the two flights of stairs.

The hallway was silent. The five girls must be downstairs; yes, she now remembered she had heard them, from the vestibule, laughing and talking, they were in the blue salon preparing a surprise for Agenor

Karlowicz who was expected that afternoon. My girls, she thought, how I love them, how good they are! Yes, in that moment she felt like hugging them all to her breast, to show them that demonstrative tenderness that had never been her strength and which they no doubt should have enjoyed. I will do it—but later, she thought. And, with a horrible clenching of her heart that surprised her in the midst of her joy, she opened the door.

Zygmunt was there, his back to her. She had time to take in the sight of that back, to say to herself: How thin he is, how the fabric of his jacket shines on his shoulders, from wear, no doubt . . . and he turned around. And his eyes grew larger. And he walked towards her, and she walked towards him. And he moved closer. He wasn't taller than she, and so his face was exactly in front of hers.

'You came,' he whispered.

They continued to look at each other in silence, the time to probe their new certainty. Then he continued, in a voice hoarse with emotion: 'May I touch your hair?'

She nodded, because her voice no longer obeyed her. And so he raised his hands and touched her hair. A few silver strands were shining through, he moved his fingers to the wide, imposing forehead; then they came back down, caressed her eyebrows, which seemed unbelievably soft to him, her eyelids, darker brown, the corners of her eyes softened by a few fine radiating lines, her cheek, where a beauty mark struck him as troubling coquettishness on this so very chaste face.

Never had it occurred to her that she could be beautiful. Not to her or to anyone else. And yet she was. She was invisibly so, she was so only within the last hour, only in his eyes. He, Zygmunt Borowski, possessed a treasure, a hidden treasure—he suddenly trembled with joy and tenderness and finally dared to draw her to his chest. And she responded, her arm resting, soft and full of languor, on his shoulders, feeling the masculine warmth through the fabric, the somewhat rigid frame . . . She felt she had been reborn, that she was coming out of an endless dream filled with boredom and sadness, that she had finally been found.

When, much later, she turned her head to the window—to see what the world, her everyday horizon looked like when she was loved—and saw her husband on the road coming home at a trot, she wasn't even startled.

Who is that man? He means nothing to me, muttered an awareness deep inside her.

It was only when Jozef drew closer that she saw the expression of terror on his face, and later picked up an odour of smoke; and without yet knowing why, the terror took hold of her as well.

22

There then begin some very strange days for my inhabitants. They arise out of fear and ignorance; I say ignorance, because after Jozef's return, and for close to two weeks, no one here knows anything any more.

The roads are blocked—to town, to the bailiwick, towards the Wytocki estate, carts are stationed, guarded by men who are well known, or whom one thought one knew but who now have new faces, postures, ways of speaking. Here and there Austrian soldiers appear, but they seem to have received orders to observe and not to intervene.

Agenor Karlowicz doesn't come from Grünau any more—he won't see the play, won't help Zosia repair Cordelia's broken eye. In any case, it isn't the time for parlour games or playing with dolls. The girls wander from their rooms to the classroom where the voice of the tutor falls in a deadly silence; and when they attempt to go outside, they keep close to one another like detainees in a prison courtyard. Maria is becoming taciturn. She doesn't know anything any more, either, but the absence of her fiancé, in this situation that she guesses is almost insurrectional, has finally undermined her optimistic nature. She catches her father watching her with a worried look that does not bode well; and in her bed, at night, she often cries.

No more Agenor, no more dressmaker nor deliveryman nor Jesuit. Clara easily does without her spiritual advisor; she has even decided not to call upon his services any more—her conscience is doing very well, thank you, and doesn't need to be guided. They are also, for the time being, doing without the dressmaker, but the table, no longer being supplied by the town grocers, fish mongers and wine merchants, is beginning to look a little empty. And the cook derives a sly pleasure from feeding them from *what she has on hand*, as she explains in a somewhat aggressive tone at the same time as she increases the beet soups, boiled poultry and bean and mutton stews.

On one occasion Jozef becomes angry, calls her into the dining room and asks her what she is thinking, serving them only fried bread for dessert. But he backs down when Leokadia, her fists on her hips, insolently responds that if he wants a fancy dessert he can go have it prepared by his friends in the popular government in Kraków. From the hallway to the kitchen, one can hear the stifled laughter, the inscrutable lackeys passing around the dish, Jozef sits down like a man struck by lightning. And everyone, their forks in hand, dig docilely into the toasted bread fried in butter from their farms and powdered with local sugar—everyone except Zygmunt Borowski who, his face twisted with inexplicable emotion, has just excused himself and left the room.

So it is complete isolation. Only one person from town will come to visit them, one evening at nightfall, but only to give them a message without saying a word—standing outside the gate, he will look for a moment at the bay window lit by the chandelier in the great salon; then, after picking up a stone, will throw it through a pane of glass. When Clara, trembling, will approach the window, she won't recognize the young man who greets her with an ironic tip of his hat—her husband's bastard son.

And so they know nothing, and yet rumours, mysteriously, travel over the fields, fly over the barriers, filter through the kitchens and outbuildings and reach the master's quarters. My walls whisper, my fireplaces have ears, I feel a flow of obscure, contradictory news, perhaps entirely made up, trembling inside me. But when you know nothing, isn't false news better than no news at all?

They say that the huge plume of smoke from the day before yesterday came from the Wytocki estate, a wing of which was set on fire and destroyed. They speak of a true battle, in Bochnia, between the Polish insurgents and General Benedek's troops. They speak of mountain dwellers who, in the south, have risen up; but against whom in fact? A mystery. Some stories battle one another and fight hand to hand, which can you believe? Has Prince Dubinski abolished forced labour on his mother's land, parcelled out the fields? Or has he been assaulted by his peasants and saved *in extremis* by a detachment of Austrians who then, immediately afterwards, who knows why, threw him in prison? Jakub Szela, that Polish farmer who incites his peers to fight the insurrection of the nobles, is he a hero, a good subject of the Emperor or, as they say in the kitchen and as Jozef tends to think, a mercenary of the reaction? And is he really Polish? Perhaps he is actually Ruthenian?

In any case, he is attributed with cartloads of cadavers that, it seems, are scattered over the countryside west of our district. A vague odour of death seeps into my walls, without our knowing whether it is from all those distant victims or from an animal carcass left in a ditch—because chaos reigns, in these days when male serfs are busier forming militia than working the fields. (What Gavryl thinks of all this he keeps to himself. He walks along the fence, sadly observing the abandoned tools rusting in the rain, the wood that has been cut and is beginning to rot; but he doesn't lift a finger. Perhaps he fears for his life too, if he tries to talk to them.)

Over this continuous drone of fear, rumours and hypotheses, a sustained melody stands out—from two instruments which should never have come together but which now combine their music, creating chords of unreal harmony. Rare are the hours they can truly enjoy each other: they live in expectation, in the memory of those hours, which form a screen between them and the world, a prism through which events appear both stressed to the point of phantasmagoria, and abstract, because they are incapable of separating them.

When they are holding each other close and listening to each other's hearts, each other's breaths, one accelerated by that of the other, the sound of a gunshot sometimes reaches them from the edge of the woods.

'It's a hunter,' whispers Zygmunt, to reassure his lover.

'Yes, I hear it,' she murmurs as if she believes him. Neither of them believes it, and they hug each other even harder, for they are in love and read each other as open books.

It happened so simply, so quickly that Clara still can't believe it. And yet this haste was her doing. Zygmunt wanted her and she gave herself to him. If she hadn't offered herself, he would have wanted her all the same; but he would not have taken her—he worships her too much for that.

Yes, she offered herself to Zygmunt. Why wait? Their lives won't be so long, especially hers, she sometimes thinks in a wave of sadness that she is quick to drown in the more immediate and overall worries. At this hour, in these terrible days, what life in the Polish households didn't promise to be short? Who doesn't feel his or her life to be fragile, precarious, held together only by a thread?

She offered herself, and it came easily to her. First, there were words, those words of love that she had never uttered—My love, my dear, oh! how I've missed you since yesterday—an entirely unknown language that, magically, she immediately knew how to speak. And then the gestures—but here too, she realized that she already knew that unknown language, that she even spoke it very well. She needed only to go where she was expected, where she had a place—close to him, around him, her skin against his skin. It was so simple, so unbelievably easy! She was surprised but not ashamed. Something so beautiful, so good, could not be a sin.

One day, however, when they had seen the Wytocki's chateau burn, Clara's fear pierced through that screen of love that protected the two of them. Pressing convulsively against her lover as soon as they could be alone in her room, she couldn't help but break their tacit agreement not to speak about *that*, 'Oh, Zygmunt, I'm afraid! What is going to happen!'

'Sh! My love, calm yourself, what do you mean?'

'What do I mean? Do you need reasons—aren't you afraid too?'

He brought Clara's large hand up to his mouth, and caressed it with his lips, 'Of course. I'm afraid too, everyone here is afraid. But, you see, I think that all this fear is covering quite different thoughts and that it would be interesting to confront them. Why stop at your fear? Fear in itself doesn't mean anything, doesn't do anything. Explain it to me, let's look at the facts.'

'The facts? But Zygmunt, all of that!' she pointed at the sky filled with smoke, the red sun, 'That tumult, that hatred that I've felt hovering for so many weeks . . . Oh! Remember that *Appeal to the People of the Countryside*! It was so awful, so right too, but so awful . . .'

'So right?'

'You're right, I am silly to talk about things I don't understand. And yet I can't help it, that's what I feel—it was right, my stupid heart told me . . .'

'Don't speak badly of your heart, my love. First, because I love it, and especially because it is certainly not stupid, as you say, but strong, lucid and generous.'

'Oh, Zygmunt,' she whimpered, burying her face against her lover's shoulder, 'you are humouring me, you're appeasing me, when at this very moment they are perhaps coming to cut our throats . . . That *Appeal*, the one who shouted it out wanted us dead—I'm convinced of it.'

'Not at all. He only wanted that justice, the justice to which you yourself are so sensitive, to shake off the weight of customs and institutions, to rise up out of the grave where it has been buried for centuries . . .'

'What do you know about it . . .'

'It was I.'

Clara raised herself on her elbow. 'You!'

The man who today is her lover had thus slipped into the wings of the puppet theatre, chosen Death and spoke those incendiary words— was it possible? Of course it was. She is shocked now that she didn't recognize that voice that has become so familiar to her. So familiar, and yet . . . What an abyss she discovers now, what an abyss between him and her . . .

'You're not saying anything. You appear frightened, my love.'

'How could I not be? You've done something like that! And you've hidden it from me all this time!'

'All this time,' he repeats with a tender smile. 'Sweet Clara, have you forgot that we have been lovers for only ten days and that I have much more urgent things to tell you when we're together?'

'So you love me, in spite of everything?'

'Take back that "in spite of everything" or I'll bite your mouth, mean one,' he says, and then does so. 'Really, my love, is it possible that you never thought it could have been me? Weren't you the one who already knew me the best, knew most about me?'

So he loves her in spite of everything—oh, what does the rest matter? Tears of relief flow down Clara's cheeks, and she continues, shaking her head, 'But my dear, what madness! Don't you regret those words, now that, now that death has risen up around us, as if at your own call?'

'Regret? Why should I regret the words if they are true, as you yourself just said?'

'And yet . . .'

'I will tell you what I really regret—not having the time also to read the *Appeal* in the Ruthenian language when I had the text right in my hand, when I myself demanded that my friends print it in both languages. What is propaganda that stops at linguistic borders? If those things are true for Polish serfs, why shouldn't they be said to the Ruthenian serfs?'

'Shouldn't be said? But Zygmunt . . .'

'Dry your eyes, Clara. You who are so strong—why cry, why tremble? What I also regret, I'll admit it, is that our message was so badly understood. Because we were appealing to a sense of injustice, but we have only incited hatred which is something else entirely. I don't know what is happening further south, further west, but from what I see here, I find above all serfs whom hatred renders blind to the feeling of injustice, to whom it appears more important to kill or to deliver up insurgents if they belong to their masters' class than to become free men themselves. Rather than refusing hard labour, taking care of their own plots and reclaiming the land that, in the end, belongs to them, they are joyously lending a hand to the power of the State.'

Clara listens to him, still upset but attentive. Never has anyone brought up such subjects in front of her, used such language—her young lover seems to have forgot that he is speaking to a woman. She would almost smile at the thought if the circumstances were less serious; at the same time, she realizes that she understands everything. She even understands enough to detect the imperceptible nuances in Zygmunt's speech. Jozef would not have said 'the power of the State,' she thinks. He would have said, 'The Austrians.' And in saying that, he would have looked at me askance while showing the nice teeth of a handsome man . . . My lover is not handsome, no more than I am beautiful. He works his magic over me with his words, his character, what he is, what he wants . . . But what am I thinking! He is speaking, and I'm not listening any more?

'. . . Yes, I'm afraid too,' he is saying in a lower voice. 'I'm afraid for you, for us, for all my friends in Kraków, the Kingdom and Prussia, of whom more than one must have been slaughtered or are awaiting execution in the bowels of a fortress. I'm afraid, but my fear isn't important. It isn't strong enough to make me regret what we have done, or at least attempted to do. Sooner or later, justice will raise its head, will demand that verdict. Because the history of the world is a tribunal, that's true, but the cases it hears are never closed . . .'

Clara feels those words, now no more than a murmur, flowing into her ear. They rock her, imbue her with a peace that surprises even her. It is thus, it is our destiny, she thinks with emotion; history, a tribunal with limitless mercy, limitless . . . He hopes, he has faith, I want to open myself to his audacity, share his confidence. Fear is a bad companion between us, it distances us, separates us, I will chase it from my heart . . .

And sweetly, trembling, there rises up in her soul, in her transported senses, the image of a field without borders or walls, green from the rain, heavy with fruit, huge, as endless as their love.

23

The following Thursday there was a surprise—Dr Weinberg arrived at lunchtime in his little phaeton, as if nothing were wrong.

There had been a great deal of commotion. The day before, Efraim, sent into town to attempt to buy a few things, had returned covered in blood because people had thrown stones at him. From then on it was decided that they would not try to obtain such innocent things as cigars and new ribbons.

'Did you have any . . . problems on the way?' asked Clara who had come down to greet him.

'Oh, it was nothing,' he smiled, kissing her hand. 'But please forgive me for arriving just as you're sitting down.'

I had seen that *nothing* from the top of the roof. Down below on the road, a group had gathered around the carriage, had furiously shaken the rigging. They had laughed loudly, a man had shouted, 'Kill him, that damned Jew, he works for the Poles!' And, indeed, things were going badly, the doctor was already being dragged onto the embankment when a little old woman slowly came out of the second cottage. A grey scarf around her neck, a rounded back, her thick legs wrapped in rags—it was the one who, twenty-five years earlier, everyone had called 'the beautiful Ulianna'.

She didn't speak loudly, beautiful Ulianna, but she wanted something, that was clear. After a lengthy discussion interrupted by curses, the men finally released the doctor and hoisted the old woman up onto the seat next to him. The carriage took off again, this time in the direction of the cottages.

Was a grandson, a great-grandson ill? After twenty minutes Weinberg came out again, exclaiming over his shoulder: 'Don't put too many blankets on him, and watch the fever. If he is still having convulsions, come get me at the chateau—I'm having lunch there.'

Behind him, Ulianna was shuffling with two eggs in one hand and a hard bristled brush in the other. Weinberg accepted the eggs politely, took off his hat and allowed the old woman to brush off the back of his suit. So that upon entering the dining room of the *dwor*, he appeared as well groomed as ever.

'So, what news of Grünau do you have for us?' Jozef asked him after the soup was served.

'All kinds,' the doctor replied with a sigh, and began to describe events. The facts were not clear, but his calm, measured voice explained things, clarified rumours, put order to dates and places.

Everything had begun, it seems, with arrests in Prussia, then in Lemberg; but these had not, however, managed to nip in the bud a conspiracy whose members spread out over the three zones—Russian, German and Austrian—of Poland. A few days later, in an inn near Tarnow, a clandestine meeting had turned into a confrontation between the patriotic insurgents and the peasants they thought they had rallied. Then the riot had spread—in many places, serfs had risen up against their Polish masters, whether they were insurgents or not. Everyone knew what happened next, which was almost as bad as the horror of the peasant revolts of 1768.

Kraków? A popular government had in fact been formed there, before being joined and radicalized by a certain Dembowski. After a few days, the city had fallen under the assault of Austrian forces; in Podgorze, the last insurgents, counting on the mutiny of soldiers and the peasant militia supporting them, had attempted a sortie, with priests and crucifixes at the head; and all of them, including the priests, had been massacred, Dembowski was dead, most of the conspirators also dead or taken prisoner. Not much hope was held out for the survival of the little Kraków republic, now occupied by its great Habsburg neighbour.

Zygmunt was listening, without joining the chorus of those asking questions; his face revealed nothing. Only, upon learning of the death of Dembowski, his gaze grew a bit fixed, vague; and even so, only Clara noticed.

'And Jakub Szela, who is he?' Jozef continued, still frowning.

The 'king of the peasants', as he had been nicknamed, had been able to raise a true army of Polish loyalists in the countryside and launch a bloody hunt for the insurgents.

'They speak of two thousand dead,' the doctor said, and it seemed to Jozef that his eye sought his, but he pretended not to notice this discreet address. 'It has even been said that the Austrians were paying rewards for each head. But in truth, I don't believe it. After looking into it, I've come to understand that the imperial and royal army had confined themselves to reimbursing the peasants for the cost of their carriages and carts . . .'

'As if that weren't the same thing!' grumbled Jozef, incensed by these nuances and this little tone of impartiality. 'To reimburse the rabble for stifling the rise of freedom, that has always been the tactic of tyrants—I easily believe that. Oh, really, all of this is simply great! The empire is ultimately not going to look very good after this episode, that is the only thing that consoles me . . . But tell us, how about Prince Dubinski?'

Regarding him, all the rumours were true, as strange as that might appear. Yes, he had gone to preach before his serfs, promising them a distribution of land parcels. (Jozef could imagine him very well—dressed in the embroidered shirt and the long vest made by a tailor in the village, he must have muttered some Christian parable to them, some 'My brothers,' looking ridiculous.) The speech wasn't successful—they thought it was a trick, and also, around here people don't like men who speak of God without being priests. The next day the prince was ambushed on the road to Lemberg, wounded by several blows of a billhook. He was saved in time by some Austrian soldiers but was then accused of seditious actions. Waiting, he stayed in prison.

A scourge, that type of man, Zygmunt smiled to himself. Angelic amateurs, hugely naive . . . Lord, preserve us from our allies! Then he thought of Dembowski again, and his throat swelled . . .

Everyone was getting up from the table. Clara and her daughters headed to the salon, Zygmunt was getting ready to sit down again with the men to drink cognac and light one of the cigars that Weinberg had brought them. But he saw that the latter was taking Jozef aside, speaking to him softly, and he joined the ladies.

As if the presence of the doctor within these walls had subtly marked a return to normal, the salon exuded a domestic peace that it had lost since the beginning of the troubles.

On the large, green and white striped satin sofa, Elvire Denisot was seated between her two youngest pupils and looking at a collection of stories with them. From time to time, one of them laughed discreetly, her mouth hidden behind her hand. Maria, leaning on the mantle, seemed lost in contemplation of the bust of Adam Mickiewicz and in so doing showed her prettiest profile. The two younger sisters stood out in the light of the window, Urszula in pink and three-quarters visible, Wioletta in blue from the back.

Clara had sat down near her needlework table and was looking for the right colour silk to use. When she picked up the skein to look at it in the light, the curve of her hairpiece shone against her cheek, her arm was rounded, strong and supple, under the puff of her sleeve. None of them had seen Zygmunt enter.

They are all of one piece, he thought, taking in the harmony of the scene, the individual grace of their postures. He was an indelicate intruder into this interior tableau. This majestic woman in the midst of her children, he profaned her every night, saw her naked, plunged his hands into her long, brown hair . . . What awful game was he playing in this house—was this where he belonged?

But this was one of those thoughts that scarcely graze one's consciousness and that could remain hidden for many days, many months, content for the time being to pour the poison of a vague sadness into him. He sought a cause, and easily found it—Dembowski was dead, and the popular government with him. A profound sigh came out of his chest. Then Clara heard him, turned her head, put down her needlework and, with a meaningful look, slowly went and sat at the piano.

A week earlier, hugging his mistress' body against him through her batiste nightgown (the nightgown she found too elegant, too fancy, but which he begged her to wear), he had asked her why she never touched the instrument.

'You can play, I'm sure. I see it in the way you correct your daughters when they make a mistake, in the advice you give them. Why have I never heard you play?'

Clara had shaken her head, embarrassed. Yes, she had learnt, of course, but didn't have time . . . a practice she had long neglected . . .

'Why don't you take it up again?'

She ended up admitting that she didn't like playing in front of others; without pointing out that what weighed upon her was above all the memory of her years as an unmarried girl, when the baron and baroness, worried about her mediocre attraction, pushed her towards the piano so she could highlight what she did best, her musical talent, her artistic sensibility—as if she had been a disappointing slave but one whose impeccable teeth could be showed to advantage.

'But for me? Won't you play for me? *Meine Liebe*, I beg you. I would really love to hear you play.'

Clara, who had successively allowed the young man to hold her hand, caress her hair, kiss her face, then her shoulders, to take possession of her, in fact, without feeling any discomfort, had to overcome a violent modesty to satisfy that new desire. She was blushing, and assured herself that none of her family could hear her, as she approached the Bösendorfer and started playing unsteady scales. Then she grew bolder, and started playing the pieces she had studied in the past. And the walls, the curtains, the cornices that listened to her came together to form a protective screen, made her forget everything except the ardent young man for whom she wanted to play. The chateau, its inhabitants, its menacing surroundings, no longer existed . . . Clara's breathing accelerated, she abandoned herself, without stopping at any mistakes or clumsiness.

I am dreaming, perhaps, but I sometimes think that if the estate was spared in this month of February 1846, it was thanks to these notes full of love and hesitant grace that, during certain hours, escaped out of the windows of the salon, fell on the fields and put the birds into a questioning silence.

And so Clara sat down, raised the cover of the instrument, she was going to play for her lover for the first time because she had seen he was sad. She played a few chords, as a prelude; and as if to support her efforts to put him at ease, the intimidating tableau of familial harmony was instantly disturbed.

Urszula had recognized the Schubert impromptu she had been working on for six weeks. Upset at being subjected to such an insult by her own mother, she stomped off to the door and shut it behind her with a bang. Oh, if that's the way it was, she would show them! . . .

Between the two little girls, amazed at seeing their mother at the piano, Madame Denisot had put the book on the footstool and tried to set an example of the attitude they should assume under such circumstances. Sitting up very straight, she pivoted towards the musician, crossed her hands, stretched up her neck and assumed a look of profound boredom.

Wioletta, still standing, had jumped at the first notes. Then, her shoulders relaxed, her neck bent, she let herself slide onto a chair in the nook of a window and listened, her eyes fixed on the other side of the window. At the next piece she pressed her temple to the back of her chair and folded her knees between her crossed arms, closed her eyes— my goodness! If Madame Denisot, in turning, had seen her in that position!

Zygmunt had eyes, ears, only for Clara. This was a new voluptuousness, this sonorous caress that she was offering him despite those around them and in the presence of all. Kraków has fallen, Dembowski is dead, the people are killing the democrats but she is playing for me. I adore her, he thought while his eyes filled with tears. I adore her as she is there, her body leaning in to accompany a chord, a strand of hair escaping, falling onto the neck of her dress, her mouth opening when a phrase sings under her fingers, touching the right chord in my heart—because she can feel it, I'm sure.

He was a bit angry when Maria went up to the piano and did what he had been dreaming of doing from the beginning—put one arm softly around the shoulders of the player and, with the other, turn the pages of her music. But he consoled himself, because that was beautiful too, seeing them together; seeing Clara smile tenderly up at her daughter, blushing slightly—that imbroglio of thoughts and intentions, that tenderness she was receiving from her daughter while thinking of her lover. (Clara's conscience could rest easy—at that moment Maria was thinking of her fiancé.)

But suddenly the door opened wide and slammed against the wall— a pale Jozef, unrecognizable, his eyes shining with pain and anger, had just entered the room.

'I must ask you to stop that music, Madame. Gather your daughters, call in the servants, so we can let everyone know—we are in formal mourning.' His voice grew a bit louder, was almost hoarse: 'In formal mourning, do you understand?'

And then he left, leaving the door wide open.

Madame Denisot raised her hands to her mouth, the cover of the piano slammed shut, and Maria fell in a faint at the foot of her mother's stool.

24

Salomon Weinberg wasn't worried that evening when he set out for home. All those he met along the way were hiding out of fear of the bearer of bad news—the master had lost his heir. The news had already spread.

The same maids who, a few hours earlier, had been dressing the women, eyeing their finery and dreaming that it wouldn't take much for these trinkets to be theirs, were wiping their eyes and whispering behind Maria's back: 'That poor girl! And to think, they made such a nice couple!'

The next day Jozef could be seen riding along the edges of the property—he no longer feared physical threats, or, rather, he no longer cared. He needed air, he needed to move, he needed to escape, by moving, from the torment of this *idée fixe*. Fallen in Gdow, Jan, his nephew, his hope! Shot right in his chest, as Dr Weinberg had learnt from an eye witness; killed in battle, killed nobly, as was befitting a son of Adam Zemka, but dead, dead, he kept repeating while spurring his horse who was picking his hooves up high as he went through patches of melted snow. All this land, this black earth that reappeared in spots, these trees still naked in winter, these mournful and, for the time being, sterile furrows, would not be Jan's. Whose would they be? He didn't know; but he felt that another age had begun, a page had been violently turned in the great book of his family.

He saw, without joy, order returning to the estate, the serfs resuming their work, spirits calming down. The great spectre of the uprising seemed suddenly to disappear. What remained was detachments of imperial soldiers who were henceforth more visible, recalcitrant serfs returning to work, mutely proclaiming that the party was over. There were still rumours, money too; a lot was said about the sums that a certain peasant had earned by providing mysterious services, people nudged one another when they saw someone wearing a new vest, with a new cart, a few more animals than before. But they also thought, obscurely, that this couldn't be all, that *things* were going to happen. Things couldn't stay as they were, could they?

When Gavryl had taken his troops back in hand, there was some murmuring. The men who had done the most to stop the insurgents and instill terror in the aristocratic Polish homes, now lowered their heads and slipped away, stunned by this brief power they had enjoyed but of which nothing remained. But the women didn't want to return to their former positions—they were more stubborn and slower to come to heel. 'You'll see,' some of them shouted at Gavryl when he gathered them for the first time since the days of February. 'The Emperor loves us, the Emperor knows well what we have done for him. He will stop serfdom, the labour, and you will labour alone in the fields of the masters if that's what you want . . .'

'That's enough!' Gavryl had shouted, standing straight in the boots that in those days his calves still filled. He looked around with his bluish eyes at the rebels, spat on the ground, mumbled some vague threats of reprisal, of calling on the army; and everyone had set off to work, not without silently thinking that he who laughs last, laughs best.

But the weeks went by, and the great hope placed in the Emperor, that mountain from which one expected to see spouting forth an eruption of new freedoms, gave birth to a mouse—in the month of April, a decree announced that it would henceforth be forbidden to use serfs to work distant fields, as that would separate couples and disrupt families. From then on, the most stubborn were silenced because, this time, it was clear—they wouldn't receive anything more.

As if to confirm this, another curious piece of news came the following month—Jakub Szela who, with his peasant army, refused to resume hard labour and continued to cause disturbances in western Galicia, had managed to obtain a few acres of land in Bucovina.

'Land for that outlaw! The reward for his evil acts, oh, yes,' Jozef commented, outraged.

But when that night Clara broached the subject with her lover, he interpreted the affair quite differently. It was a banishment, no more no less—the man had served well, but he was dangerous, and consequently Metternich sent him packing elsewhere. The manoeuvre was clever and not surprising.

'But what do you think of him?' she pressed timidly—she so wanted to know his views, share these things for which he lived and which weren't hers.

'Of the "king of the peasants"? Well, I think that his motives are just, and that in getting the serfs to rise up against their masters he put his finger on the only real problem of this province, of the Empire, and even of a good part of the world. Not attacking this problem, the imperial and royal State resolved nothing. It showed its strength, brought back order, but it has only hastily patched a wall that sooner or later will crumble.'

Clara blinked her eyes. Was it possible that they were talking like this, without emotion or taking sides, about conflicts that were so important, that involved them intimately?

'And yet,' she continued—this new Clara who, with him, had lost the habit of being silent, dared to give voice to her thoughts without fear of being laughed at, or without fearing that laugh; 'and yet that Szela fought you ferociously. He allied himself with that State that is oppressing you and is opposed to your independence. It's because of people like him that our poor Jan is dead, that Dembowski, whose praises you sing, is dead. And think of all those unfortunate young people whom he helped to arrest and who are now rotting in imperial prisons . . .'

'The ally of the reaction,' he murmured pressing his cheek against that of his mistress. 'Yes, Clara, you are not the first to voice these ideas, you are even in good company, as many of my friends share them. But I think they are slapdash and, to be frank, wrong. Why are you smiling?'

'My poor love, I'm smiling out of sadness, because you don't even share the views of your friends . . . Must you always be alone in what you are?'

He looked at her silently for a moment, then held her closer. 'You are so fine . . . fine and tender, I don't know another soul like yours. Do you know, my clever one, that your uncertain air hides a formidable wisdom? Yes, my love, you see me clearly. *Always alone in what I am*— that is without a doubt what one can say most truthfully about me. And it is also why you are so dear to me—don't you see how our two solitudes are wedded and complete each other?'

She could indeed see it, and she laughed voluptuously as his gestures mirrored his words. She gave in, her long hair spread out on the pillow; but in the midst of her pleasure was a sense of concern, of maternal worry. Was it good for him to be so alone in the world? (And deeper inside her: How much longer would she be able to populate that desert?)

In the end, the sadness never left her. It was her nature—she needed a concern in her heart, she wouldn't know what to do with pure joy. Would she be as tender, moreover, if she didn't have that ability for sadness? Her tenderness came from her ability to see pain in others, to prevent it and console it; she recognized herself in it as in a mirror.

And the mourning that had just stricken them, dashing the hopes of her dearest daughter, appeared almost as a righteous outcome. This thought stifles her affection and prevents her from caring for Maria without guilt. She devotes herself to her, spends several nights at her bedside when her daughter, out of grief, falls ill, with a high fever that requires Weinberg to come several times. Clara could rub her hand, mix her tears with hers, get her to drink some tea or bouillon from a spoon; but not speak the words of Christian resignation that the circumstances demanded.

It is not that she thinks divine justice is responsible for Jan's death, as in the past she had seen in her adolescent lapses the original sin that she was paying for with her miserable marriage. All of that had become quite secularized in her mind, and the idea seemed almost as outrageous as that of a bearded God above who had stricken a young patriot in Gdow because his aunt was pursuing an affair and was shirking her spousal duties. What she feels is that there is in her, in her conscience, an invisible accountant weighing her joys and sorrows like debits and credits, comparing them, balancing them out. That accountant is none other than herself, and that is the problem. Because if you can fell an idol, what can you do against yourself, how can you be delivered of yourself?

(An idol? she is astonished at the thought. That God who since my childhood has accompanied me, to whom I had briefly planned to devote my existence—an idol, an idea? Have I already come to that? Have I changed to such a degree?)

So she tells lies coldly to her confessor—he would tell her not to see Zygmunt any more and to love her husband, which is impossible for her to do. Moreover, what duties is she shirking? She gave her husband five children; five daughters. She didn't give him a son, but it is too late. Is she keeping her body from him? It has been six or seven years since Jozef has set foot in her room, asked anything of her. Her soul? He has no rights over it, he who doesn't love and has never loved her. So what sin is she expiating with her sadness, why does she accept it as her just due? Her inner accountant whispers to her—what she is paying for is for wanting to be happy, for having been happy, for still being happy.

This is what Clara is thinking while her fingers are striking the keys of the Bösendorfer, while the chords make the crystals of the large chandelier tremble. Zygmunt, seated in his room, senses only the loving verve, the song that she is sending to him through two floors. He is listening, he is happy, he sets his book down for a moment. An enthusiastic future is unfolding before his eyes, made of this perpetual union, and also of new dawns, new harvests. A day will come when . . . he doesn't really know what, but he has confidence in history, in its unknown advances. And when in intervals the music stops, he hears the cries of the thrashers outside, the sound of two mallets striking a post, the squealing of a cart, the joyous symphony of the approaching summer.

25

And here is a portrait of a beautiful August night.

I love the night, its noises and its silences. I love its odours more than those of the day, which only follow people like loyal dogs—kitchen smells yap at the heels of the lackeys who climb the stairs, Jozef's eau de cologne wags its tail and knocks over everything as he passes, and, when a maid opens a sideboard, lavender, dust and mustiness jump onto her lap, like a pack of puppies demanding their food.

Night odours are more independent. You don't know where they come from, and they go where they want to, like a proud nomadic people who laugh at attachment and camp wherever they wish. They slip under doors and through open windows, visit cellars, inspect formal rooms while nudging one another—these pretty fixed things appear quite vapid to them.

Thus the great salon where, that night, a few windows are left open, all the perfumes of the grass and the flowers from the fields are invited to a secret ball, to spin around under the bow of a violin-playing cricket. Outside, under the moon, the haystacks await them, like large chickens roosting on their three wooden sticks. And they murmur, indulgent, 'Come on . . . come back . . .' but know well that, before dawn, they won't be heard any more.

Morose, depressed, the curtains of the little blue salon listen at a distance to the noise of the party. Their old percale flutters, they sigh; that joyful din only makes their concerns more cruel.

Poor curtains! Like most decorative objects, they primp and simper throughout the day. But at night, since no one is there to express the admiration they so desperately need, they reveal a soul tormented by the certainty that one day they will no longer please and will be *replaced*. Doesn't the man of the house speak of replacing them with *toile de Jouy*, of whose stylishness Adam, in his last letter from Paris, sang the praises. That letter, dated from the end of January, was still full of patriotic hopes, of plans and proposals. Adam didn't doubt at that time that he would be able to come to his son's wedding and thereby console himself for the loss of his dear Lubina, who had died eighteen months earlier. And the curtains were not the only things to fear that he had set out before having received the news of the second death, and that he would arrive here with a smile on his face, carrying the *toile de Jouy* for his future daughter-in-law.

In his room, Jozef is thinking about this too. Lying down, his eyes open, he ruminates on the mystery of that failed insurrection and of that premature death. The song of the crickets is weighing down on him—all he needs is such singing! And he gets up to close the window; but doesn't immediately go back to bed. Outside, the moon lights up the stones of the path and the trunks of the birch trees, and the haystacks are standing like miniature cottages on the expanse of the fields. It is beautiful, he thinks; but the sight grips his heart, just as everything grips his heart since he lost Jan. These deserted fields crush him, he thinks about the fragility of destinies, fortunes . . .

And then he suddenly sees clearly—the feudal system is dead.

He shivers. No, come on, how, why? His mind rebels. But louder than this voice, the grey cameo of that lunar rural landscape repeats its sentence—the feudal system is dead. One cannot eternally suppress the hopes of so many people, as has so brutally been expressed; and the rulers know it too, they aren't stupid. Jozef's world is living on borrowed time, why be blind to it any more? Didn't Jan, himself, tell him so during one of their last political discussions?

'Everyone's future is in ownership—for our peasants, in the land that they farm, and for us, in the factories and plants that are still so cruelly lacking in our province.' These words resonate in Jozef's ears, but without causing him the shock they once did. They are said today with the calm patience of a dead soul encountered in the underworld who sees further than you, who knows the distant future that awaits you.

Factories, plants? Yes, Jan was right. One must move forward, do away with nostalgia; triple sugar production, raise high the flags of modernity. Enlarge the building for that . . . or even construct another one, more spacious, more functional. Over there, Jozef suddenly decides.

And to his right, on the obscure edges that border the silver sky, he sets in his mind the brick foundation of a building with two or three smoke stacks bearing on its façade the inscription 'Zemka Brothers' in red and white ceramic.

'That's it . . . that's it . . .' he murmurs, while a weak smile, the first since Jan's death, appears on his lips, and he slowly goes back to bed. Under his heavy eyelids a few figures are still dancing the dance of a nebulous estimate, and he falls asleep—finally. The next day he will arise early to set all of this in motion.

My friends, the pots and pans, aren't sleeping, however. I've just confirmed this when I go down to the kitchen. Hanging from the wall like pipistrelles, they listen mutely to the drops of water falling from a cloth hanging to dry. The dark isn't easy on them, idleness, either; these metallic workers, as soon as they are at rest, think of their coming retirement, brooding, glance unhappily at the door panel. What will become of them, once they have crossed that threshold? What life is there beyond this?

And the cook, in her garret room, asks herself the same question. What did I do to that soufflé for it to fall like that? Was the oven heated badly? The egg whites not firm enough? Nothing like that has ever happened to me. My late mother had ruined an eel aspic like that before beginning her decline. Is it my turn? I don't like that smell of hay, I've never liked it, it's stuffed me up and made my nose run ever since I was young. Young, oh my! My poor legs, even at night they don't leave me alone any more. If only I could go live with my niece in Przemysl . . . But her husband drinks and beats her, he would let me die of hunger. If only I could go back to sleep, like Lubienka who is snoring and not thinking of her son who has joined the army . . . Lord give us peace, poor sinners that we are.

But from a blocked gutter there descends to the second floor another odour, the odour of earth and dead leaves carried by the wind. It is odd, damp, a bit carefree—wait, there's a bedroom, a young girls' bedroom! But one of them isn't sleeping.

Urszula, in fact, is listening with irritation to the sighs that her sister, after crying, is making in her sleep. She envies her that sleep, even envies her so noble, so poetic a mourning. For Urszula has only inglorious and humiliating anguish. Her own admirer didn't have the nerve to die, or even to be wounded; as the troubles were waning, he prudently decided to take the waters at Karlsbad, and they haven't heard from him since. And only little Zosia—the privilege of childhood—has the right to say out loud how much she misses him.

And it smells like dirty water, Urszula laments. She would like to cry too, but her body has never contained many tears and she must be content with a painful bubble that obstructs her throat. Even in that domain she has less than the others.

Returning to the little salon where the Bösendorfer is impatiently waiting, hiding under its cover, and is remembering the tunes it played today. How dark it is! Where is Madame?—it is secretly in love with Clara, and the nights seem long for it.

Madame is in her bed, my dear piano, and she is not alone. But your ebony soul knows no jealousy, and nothing would shock you in this display if you could see it—those two entwined bodies speak only of love, abandonment, mutual confidences. Zygmunt is almost handsome with his shirt open over his adolescent chest, in which there beats (we know) the ardent and wilful heart of a man. His breath is still quick, he has just fallen asleep; one of his arms is thrown over Clara's waist; she is not asleep and is watching him. She turns her head towards the window where a bit of moon is beginning to appear, sighs, blinks her eyes. Shouldn't I dye my hair? Some mixtures brighten the brown, she thinks, before falling asleep.

I come and I go without a great effort to be discreet. At night, no one is surprised at the creaking that goes through my floors and the wood of my beams. I slip through hallways where the shadow is almost palpable, where a bored *Hunting Scene* and *View over Kraków* are hanging on a wall, where a bouquet of wilted flowers is drying on a credenza. I go upstairs, I go downstairs; the clocks go tick-tock, mouths breathe, the tireless worms chew on the bottom of an armoire . . . They never stop, full of zeal and unawareness. Their final victory—the crumbling of the piece of furniture they inhabit—will be the death of them all as the ruined piece is taken out and burnt; but these little creatures are much too simple to worry about eschatology. They chew, and that's all.

But now the morning is arriving, the air of the great salon is cool. In their frames Kosciuszko and Bonaparte are relieved to see the dancers tire, the gypsies smooth their skirts and their long hair with their hands. What, dawn already? Yes, the violin has stopped. The perfume of a red clover thanks its partner with a pat on the neck before signalling to everyone to depart. They all try to be the first to slip through the upper windows, quickly, quickly! They climb, they push . . . 'I've lost a shoe!' 'Oh, we'll be back tomorrow night . . .'

On the kitchen stove the cat that was asleep opens an eye, stretches—the last embers have gone out and there's no reason to stay. He jumps to the ground, sniffs something he doesn't like, scratches the floor and goes out through the cat door. The night is his—he rushes into it, intoxicated, over the grassy expanse, chases a fallen leaf, climbs a maple tree. How wonderful it is up there! But it would be even better on the roof—in one jump he reaches it. He walks with small steps, questions the moon that is already low, goes down to the gutter and, with his tail unmoving, eagerly laps up that stale water.

And now the wind is picking up. From the hills, maybe even the mountains, it brings the odour of pine. The percale curtains of the blue salon swell, are happier—in a couple of hours, someone will come to open them, and tomorrow is another day, isn't it? The shutters groan, a current of air raises the pages of a book, makes the piano strings vibrate hopefully. And hands pull up covers, sleepers burrow more deeply to enjoy the last of their sleep—it is the moment when many of them begin to dream. Elvire Denisot has returned to Nantes, under the Directory, she is wearing the little organdy cap she used to wear as a girl. She is travelling over squares, walking in streets whose names she has forgot. Is it the wind or a flicking by Mr Jozef that has just carried off her cap and made it roll on the pavement across the street? She runs after it, it rolls even farther, and many passers-by stop to look at her. My God! My God! They can see the top of my head! she thinks as she runs, prey to a feeling of shame and guilt. But if she raises her hands to hide the top of her head, won't people see underneath her arms?

The wind blows, moving the leaves of the great maple, the moon has disappeared and on the fields there is a pearly dew.

In an empty stall in the stable Efraim is still asleep, his hands in his armpits, because it isn't warm. A big ram has been walking around him for some time—where did it come from? He pushes it with his arm, whistles to chase it away. The ram shakes its head, goes back against a wall; but it is only to get a better start, and here he comes from behind, goes in between his legs and then carries him off on his back. It gallops, it charges, Efraim hangs on to the wool on its shoulders, its spiral horns: 'Hey now, old fellow, stop, I want to get off!' But the ram in one leap jumps into the sky. And the ground fades beneath them, the entire district appears as on an official map, with its villages, its streams, its white stone churches and grey wooden churches, that dot the field like the tips of a curry brush. And over there, isn't that the San, that large ribbon that snakes between groves of willows?

'But you're crazy, that's enough! Take me back to earth!'

The ram looks at him maliciously over its shoulder, descends to the rooftops, then climbs again, even higher. It pierces the air, its nostrils flare, its mocking muzzle heads for the clouds:

'M-a-a-d . . . m-a-a-d . . . m-a-a-a-a-d . . . Are you going mad!!'

Then Efraim wakes up, snorts, and turns over on his other side, falling back asleep.

Above Grünau the sky is becoming lighter, the wind falls, the fields avidly drink in the colour that is returning.

And soon, among the farms, the first cock will begin to crow.

II

BUT NOTHING EVER ENDS

1

Four years after that night, oh how things have changed! Maria gone, Urszula gone, Clara will never come back, nor will Zygmunt. Jadwiga is packing her bags, and Gavryl is definitely beginning to show his age. He will still live for a long time, but I can already see the succession of more civilized overseers who will never stay for more than a few years and who will leave as soon as they have found something better elsewhere; like Rudolf Jäger, the embezzler with the pince-nez and dubious accounting.

Like a symphony for which the Galician troubles were the prelude, that is how the year 1848 passed here. It brought to the throne the little Franz-Joseph, a boy of eighteen who surrounded himself with ironhanded advisors who underhandedly took back a good portion of what his uncle had had to give up. But let's be clear the times were not the same. Forced labour, for example, was abolished. Forced labour abolished! That should silence the *realists* who always assert that nothing can change and that the struggle is in vain—don't listen to them, but try to find out the secret interests that tie them to the current state of the world. Listen, rather, to those, more isolated and with weaker voices (Borowski is one), who convey a completely different message—that the struggle is not in vain but has constantly to be resumed, precisely because things never really change.

Forced labour abolished? That should make the peasants on the estate rejoice, get the great Marko out of prison, he who in 1846 proved to be too ardent an emulator of Jakob Szela, reconcile poor Prince Dubinski with life, as he was quite affected by his misadventures and his few weeks of incarceration. And so now, according to the prince's wishes and those of Jan Zemka, the peasants are owners of their plots of land, connected to their former masters only by ties of money. They are also, truth be told, indebted for a long time—it will take them more than twenty years to reimburse Jozef and his peers for the cost of that labour from which those former masters had the goodness to free them. But the State is creating funds, will play the intermediary and, finally, things will go smoothly.

And yet, no, Prince Dubinski is not reconciled with life. Oh, he is dancing again, hunting in his forests, taking even greater pleasure in the delights of the table which has a tendency, as he has passed his fortieth year, to add a few kilos to his solid frame. ('I won't marry that fat fool,' Zosia would say, moreover, a few years later, when he decides to ask for her hand.) But under this external Epicureanism is a soul wounded by the evils of the world and tired of working to make it better.

Because, indeed, he was among the first to try to give his serfs the land they worked. His patient goodness saw in the riots of 1846 only the bad influence of a few agitators. Freed by the Austrians, and in spite of the excessive shoulder-shrugging of his mother, he set out to convert his peers and won more than one over to his cause during that intermediate year 1847. Then the uprising in Vienna, the fall of Metternich, the agitation of the other cities appeared to him like a gift from heaven—his ideals were reborn from the ashes, the impassioned crowds; indeed, those ideals opened onto an age of heroism and reason; the odious tyranny had been defeated.

He was told too late that in Lemberg a group assembled by Franciszek Smolka was preparing a speech to the emperor to request the autonomy of their province, the equality of their faiths, the abolition of forced labour. Thus he was not able to contribute to the preparations; but—a consoling thought—he was allowed to accompany the delegation that went to submit this proposal to the court. He retains an emotional memory of those few months in Vienna, filled with fraternization, common declarations, common hopes. They all supported Poland; the brave German insurgents increased their offers of solidarity; all the peoples crushed by the Empire were singing in unison. He was still there when the deputies of the first Austrian Parliament arrived in the capital; lauded, along with the students of Vienna, the peasant deputies of Galicia who had come to govern in boots and smocks; and shrugged his shoulders at the scurrilous anecdotes spread by the conservative nobles about those often illiterate unfortunates, lost in the debates held in German, and who had stupefied a Viennese innkeeper by wanting to sleep twelve in the same room, as they did at home, as long as they were given enough straw.

But bitterness overwhelmed him when, upon his return, he discovered the manoeuvre to which he and the other delegates had fallen prey.

While poor, weak Emperor Ferdinand was benevolently receiving their proposal on reforms, the governor of Galicia was carefully putting those reforms under the axe, forbidding owners to abolish anything themselves; and, after letting the situation deteriorate over several weeks, allowing the countryside to agitate, the insurgents to be divided between Polish and Ruthenians, Count Stadion (that modern Machiavelli) solemnly proclaimed the abolition of forced labour, like a special pardon by the sovereign of his deserving people.

Regarding their address to the emperor, their liberal proposal, there was no mention of it—the few large landowners who, like the prince, were striving for social justice saw vindictively removed that which they had wanted to give freely, and themselves mocked by the people who everywhere raised crosses gratefully commemorating the proclamation of 15 May. Instead of the messianic times that Dubinski thought he would see opening before him, the abolition had led only to petty quarrels in the Reichstag among those who demanded that the masters be paid back for their losses; and the 'deputies in shirtsleeves' estimating that the former serfs, beaten and starving for centuries, had already paid enough with their bodies and owed nothing more.

In short, Dubinski and the others had the rug pulled out from under them. But, far from seeing this as a reaction by the threatened state, a brilliant anti-revolutionary manoeuvre, the prince concluded that humanity was bad and henceforth decided to become a misanthrope. Oh, he isn't an offensive misanthrope—he continues at his own expense to take care of the sick day-workers, whereas nothing obliges him to do so any more, and he plans to build a school. But he has no more illusions and no longer expects anyone to like him in return. Never again, he assures my guests, while trotting out on each of his visits the great moments and problems of the year 1848, will he get involved in politics—he won't be taken in again.

'Pardon them, my friend,' he sighs when Jozef tells him about some new mischief by a peasant rabble-rouser, or some hateful declaration by a Ruthenian nationalist (a species that blossomed during the springtime of the peoples, granted themselves a 'Ruthenian Council' in Drohobycz, demanding that Galicia be cut in two and that the Ruthenian dialect become the official language here). 'Pardon them, for they know not what they do.' And, with a solemn attentiveness, he accepts a second piece of mocha cake and, sighing, sits down on the wing chair whose legs groan under his weight.

This occurs in the little blue salon. But if the lace cloths, the silver cake-server, the bust of Mickiewicz haven't aged a bit, they are the only things that haven't changed. The hand holding out the pastry dish to the prince is wearing only a single stone, its wrist is covered only by the sleeve of a sad dress pinned with a cameo. You're not dreaming—it is indeed Madame Denisot who now acts as mistress of the house, and, like Jozef, like Wioletta and her two little sisters, is in half mourning. Whom are they mourning here, and where have the others gone?

In Wioletta, it is her face, and even her morphology, that have changed. She has lost that bony look of adolescence, her eyes no longer have that fierce spark of a doe that a pack of dogs has just sniffed out— they are eyes that know life and, indeed, don't think very highly of it. Further, her hair still falls down her back in a braid, instead of a chignon that would point out a married woman. And then, my goodness! Why doesn't she do the honours at the table, in the absence of her mother and two older sisters?

Jozef isn't the same, either. His voice is a bit more serious, his blond hair is streaked here and there with grey. In the wrinkles of his forehead is a disturbing and questioning nuance. Our Jozef, that proud package of certainty, desires and ambitions, seems secretly undermined by a pain or a mystery.

Those four years have not, however, brought him only pain, far from it. In the middle of the summer of 1846, scarcely a few days after the night I have described, he even experienced the most violent joy of his existence, one of those joys that shock, upset and affect a heart worn out by fifty years of good and loyal service, perhaps as much as the announcement of a catastrophe.

It was one morning, rather early, as he was coming back from a farm alongside Efraim. On the side of the road, suddenly, a figure rises up, leaning on a stick. Jozef once again curses those beggars who wander about while there is abundant work in this summer season. 'You'll see the alms I have for you,' Jozef mutters, taking the whip from Efraim's hand; but his movement is halted and the wind goes out of his sails. Who is that there, what ghost is looking at him from under the hat whose wide brim is grey with the dust of the roads?

'Efraim, tell me I'm dreaming!'

But Efraim doesn't tell him anything at all—he has leapt from the carriage and is running in the opposite field, his legs flying, his features contorted by terror.

When he is out of my sight, I discover an inexplicable scene. Jozef has got off the carriage and thrown himself into the arms of the beggar. Then the two get back up on the seat, Jozef takes the reins and drives the carriage at a trot up to my gate. And it is then that I recognize, sitting next to him, the dead Jan Zemka.

2

Jan alive, Jan unharmed, Jan more handsome than ever, in spite of the beard devouring his face and making him unrecognizable (convenient for his security)! Jozef, who has closed the door to his rooms behind them, falls onto the bed and in a low voice peppers his nephew with questions. Wasn't he wounded, hadn't he fallen, in Gdow, under the bullet of an Austrian soldier, shot in his chest, as that scoundrel Weinberg, who claimed to have it from a sure source, had told them?

'That's all true, Uncle. I was indeed wounded, exactly as you say,' Jan whispers, raising his shirt to show him, on the right side, a still recent scar. 'My comrades thought I was dead, and I would have been if my wound and my fall had not caused me to lose consciousness for a long time. Because the Austrians were finishing off the wounded who were still moving.'

'But . . .'

'It was later, when they had piled up the bodies into carts that I woke up. I was lucky to be noticed by one of the women who had come to get the dead, the wife of one of those rare free peasants who supported us. She had me brought to her home, she took care of me as if I had been her son—the poor woman had just lost her own. The bullet, luckily, had only grazed my lung. After three months, I was once again on my feet, but they were still looking for us so I stayed in her house . . .'

'Aren't they looking for you now?'

'Most likely, but I couldn't endure it—I had to see you again, to see Maria . . .'

Jozef devours him with his eyes, asks for more details, both to regain his composure and to avoid the great question that has been nagging him for months: Why such a debacle, why these ruined hopes, why the failure of an undertaking that seemed to satisfy so many common interests? That is a subject he does not want to bring up with his nephew, but he sees with relief that Jan doesn't want to, either. The two men begin talking about military tactics, Jan grows heated as he explains to his uncle the errors of the insurgents and the deadly abilities of Benedek; he moves his hands across the bedcover to illustrate what he is saying, his vertical palm indicating the inevitable progress of a band of cavalry, his fingers galloping sideways in the image of the defeated patriots. Jozef almost thinks he is there.

Then there is silence.

'What will you do now?'

'Leave Galicia as soon as possible, I fear. Uncle—can you help me?'

They continue talking. The servants and, more important, the serfs, must know nothing, Jan's life depends on it. Jozef will himself go to Grünau for money and a rented carriage. The members of the family are informed of the secret one by one and there follows in Jozef's room a furtive parade of dresses through the door that then rustle against the body of the resuscitated one, get drenched with tears of silent joy. Maria, who is told the news gently, is the last to arrive. Jan hugs her, the two fiancés, mute with happiness, embrace in tears. All of this emotion has given Maria the spark of passion she was lacking and now she is perfect, vibrant, in love, like the woman she is becoming. They are allowed to be alone for half an hour—blast appearances! We're in the midst of an epic!

Jan must leave before dawn in order not to be seen by the harvesters going off to the fields. In the meantime, Jozef lets him stay in his room and does something he hasn't done in several years—he spends the night next to his wife. She derives no benefit from this. Engrossed in his happiness, he doesn't say a word to her, doesn't look at her, rolls under the covers and she can hear his eyelashes blinking on the pillowcase. She herself is moved, but her joy assumes a more serene and contained form. What happiness for Maria! How life, in the end, knows how to surprise us with its gifts! The burden that weighed her down, the remorse at having sinned and being punished through her favourite daughter have vanished. Her hands crossed on her chest, she falls asleep with a satisfied smile on her face.

It is almost the middle of the night when Jozef finally falls asleep. And so he doesn't hear the noise of wheels that, a bit later, wakes up his wife but which she doesn't immediately understand.

Shock the next day. The carriage has disappeared—Jan has left a few hours earlier, without waiting for the blessing of his uncle and aunt, and, as is soon discovered, has taken his fiancée with him.

'Mon cher Papa, ma chère Maman,' begins in French the letter that Maria has at least taken the trouble to leave behind on her bedside table. But immediately afterwards, giving in to the enthusiasm and no doubt the urgency of the situation, she reverts to Polish to excuse the indecency of what she has done and to promise to marry as soon as they have arrived safe and sound in the first town in Hungary.

Jozef is furious. Ultimately, his will has been done, it was he who had promoted the union of these first cousins. But he doesn't like them to be emancipated to this degree, to carry out the plans that were his idea in the first place.

'What was that hussy thinking of, how could she dispense with my consent? To set off on the road in these troubled times, without even going to a priest first! My compliments, madame—a nice morality you have inculcated in your daughters! And if that radical Jan is finally really killed and she is pregnant—what will she do? Have you thought of that?'

Clara reddens under this reproach which she secretly knows is just, pleads for her daughter, invokes extenuating circumstances but it does no good, Jozef's anger doesn't abate until three weeks later, when he receives a letter from Jan from Ungvar informing him of their marriage. And when he reads the detailed account of their journey over the Beskids on goat paths, and all the perils they had to overcome, he finally pardons Jan his indelicacy.

In the meantime, Jozef has been able to measure the justification of Jan's fears and the usefulness of the precautions he has taken. A few days after his eldest daughter was carried away, he had the disagreeable surprise of receiving another visit from the district commissioner, who, this time, left his moustache alone and kept his hands discreetly crossed in front of his uniform trousers. Jozef is surprised at the black crepe the officer is wearing on his sleeve. 'Have you lost someone, my friend?'

'Not at all, sir. It is on the contrary I who have come to convey my condolences to you, while excusing myself very humbly for having been so long in doing so. The measures of pacification, you know, and police operations didn't give me a minute, unfortunately, to carry out this condolence call. Your nephew, Jan Zemka . . . Poor young man . . . the folly of youth, bad influences . . .'

'Hum! It is indeed a very sad loss for us,' Jozef mutters, forcing himself to assume a troubled look but unable to hide his unease.

'You have no doubt already held a Mass in the memory of this unfortunate man?'

'Well, I mean, not yet. The troubles, you understand . . . all this tension, including among confessions . . .'

'Don't put it off. You see, I'm aware that Mr Jan Zemka was indeed what we must call our adversary. But my solicitude for you and your family,' he adds with a little bow in Clara's direction, 'would make me detest the idea that *your nephew's soul would not rest in peace.*'

There is a long, awkward silence, Jozef coughs.

'That is a thought, commissioner, that touches me deeply. I will take it under advisement, you may be sure.'

'I would be pleased. Would you be so good, sir, to invite me to the ceremony?'

'But of course, it would be an honour!' says the master of the house.

Because of this insinuating pest, he is now forced to undertake a farce that verges on profanation—to have a Mass said in the chapel for the eternal rest of a nephew who he knows, at that moment, is going through the mountains and despoiling his daughter. And all of this under the piercing eye of the commissioner who is ironically watching the master of the house, his wife, his four daughters, and who observes that the fifth must be unwell, too unwell to miss this ceremony in memory of her dead fiancé.

Thus when Jozef receives his first letter from the young couple from Hungary, he quickly writes back, after a somewhat grudging blessing: '. . . and above all, above all do not return right now!'

In time, however, his good mood returns, since all's well that ends well. Of course, the horizon remains dark: floods and bad harvests continue; in November 1846, Kraków is reunited with the Habsburg Empire. The last little Polish entity has lived, and Jozef is far from foreseeing the national uprising that, eighteen months later, would cause much of Europe to rise. But he is distracted by these public ills and devotes himself as never before to his projects of expansion. Behind me, I now see a few bits of walls, carts and masons—the new sugar factory is taking shape. Jozef has again converted some grain fields on his land into sugar beet fields, and the little river has been rerouted. It seems that this has inspired gossip in the area, that other landowners now see Jozef as a maniac or a bizarre innovator.

'Oh! He'll ruin himself,' asserts Princess Dubinska confidently to Jozef's wife. And that prediction causes her to smile broadly, because that would only be justice served—bankruptcy is the final destiny of all parvenus. Wanting to climb too high, they fall farther to the ground; it is indeed a sign of the times, this propensity for people to want to leave their ranks, deny their condition. What good can come of it, I ask you! And, sunk into the large winged armchair, she triumphantly sniffs a pinch of tobacco. (As her very old woman's body shrivels up, her meanness grows more concentrated; in a few years, when that body reaches the end of its long existence, that meanness in her will be, so to speak, in a chemically pure state.)

But Jozef Zemka could not care less about such sniping. He perseveres, and the future will prove him right.

What is also contributing to restoring his good mood is the increase in matrimonial prospects. At the end of the autumn, Agenor Karlowicz has returned from his water cure and once again proves to be determined, although in his slow and indecisive way. He is seen all winter serving as shepherd to the herd of young ladies, a bit lost by the departure of their head sheep, Maria. He brings from Karlsbad precious information on the latest styles—open sleeves with bits of ribbon remain very fashionable, he assures Urszula, who is wearing them for the first time. But the *sine qua non*, at the moment, is to wear in the evening a skirt of moiré gauze over one or two layers of tulle illusion.

For Jozef, in the library which is sometimes used as a smoking room, he reserves less virginal stories. A relative of the Troubetskois has taken up with an obscure but seductive officer; an English lord rented an entire floor of the hotel Pupp to lodge his two mistresses, his major-domo and his family of Malaysian servants.

That winter they organize several soirees, as if to make up for the preceding season. Nothing grandiose, nothing extraordinary. One feels that the riots have left their mark, and that the fortunate in the world no longer dare display their fortune as openly as in the past. Never more than eight couples, and without seated dining; the music is discreet and laughter muted. In this Lenten ambience, desires are born nonetheless, fates are established. An old and rich magnate begins to be interested in Wioletta and, in spite of her obvious disgust, Jozef intends to bring her around. After all, he is her father! As for young Karlowicz, his uncle from Jaslo is declining—he is discreetly congratulated on this hopeful news, and Jozef, believing that the good old days have returned, watches Agenor tenderly as he walks in the garden, Urszula holding on to his left arm and one of her younger sisters on to the other.

3

Urszula was engaged at Easter and married in August. Jozef wasn't unhappy at his plan. Having first been assured, through discreet research, that the bequeathing uncle would not be recovering soon, he hurried to conclude the affair. If they waited any longer, the death of the valetudinarian risked delaying the marriage for another full year in order for them to observe the required mourning; and in a year, who knew what could happen! Even engaged, Agenor remained visibly hesitant. His courtship of Urszula had been most discreet, had never gone beyond a tone of friendship. And if Jozef didn't complain about that, having seen, in his eldest daughter, the disadvantages of too great an attachment, he feared up to the last moment that the fish would slip through their fingers and contract a more lucrative union elsewhere.

Clara wasn't involved in this sordid strategy. She was delighted at the results, however, but cried during the wedding, which didn't surprise anyone in a mother attending the first wedding of one of her daughters. In seeing her poor Urszula walk up the aisle in her white satin dress, Madame Zemka had experienced both a great relief and a tightening of the heart of a fifty-three-year-old woman whose daughter, in turn, was going to become a wife.

During the Mass she met Zygmunt's gaze, and he smiled at her.

How long will he smile at me? was her terrified thought. What will I do when my daughters no longer need a tutor? When nothing will justify his presence in our house?

She worked it out, calculated. Zosia, smart and not at all unattractive, could be married at seventeen, even if the modesty of her dowry had a delaying effect. In five, six years at most Zygmunt would leave. And an even more bitter voice murmured: Six years? You're dreaming. Do you think he'll still love you in six years? You're getting thicker, your hair is turning grey—it won't take him even two years to notice. And in the end, isn't that what you should wish for him, if you really love him? Is it good for him to stay until his late thirties as a tutor for your little chicks, he who no doubt has a different future waiting for him? Are you out of selfishness going to turn him into a withered piece of fruit, a failure? His life is calling him elsewhere, as you know well. He still loves you, but you are an obstacle on his path. One day he will blame you for having held him back.

It is at that moment that she begins to cry.

Zygmunt adored her as ever, every night confided to her his political thoughts. She listened to him passionately, responded with the modest weapons of her good sense and sensitivity. When her objections revealed to her lover a contradiction in his thinking, a point that remained obscure, he hugged her tightly and said, '*Meine Liebe*, what would I be without you? You are the ideal interlocutrice. I'd like to take you away with me, make you our muse. Grounded by your presence, no group would be torn apart. Your sweet and righteous spirit would keep us from any doctrinal wandering. Why are there so few women in our ranks?'

Take me away, she thought. The young fool! He is still seeking to reconcile his love for me with the much more powerful interest the world has for him. Take me away? As if that were possible, or even desirable! He would regret it himself at the first town we stopped. Luckily for him, I am wise enough for both of us . . .

And while he explained to her, to Clara von Kotz, a divergence between the German Marx and the Russian Bakunin, passionately made her measure the stakes and the consequences, the caresses she gave to his neck while listening to him were already, in her mind, gestures of adieu.

And yet, what sweetness, what bliss . . . In the name of what should she put an end to all this, where would she find the strength to do it? The German words he liked to whisper to her, so devoid of any prejudice was he, and because he guessed (the *young fool*) that, for a human being, to hear one's mother tongue can be the most tender of caresses—those German words melted Clara's heart, made her weak, made her want to hold on to her happiness for as long as possible.

And she began to believe that everything was going to work out, that a new miracle would come to dissipate her fears. 'Love is as strong as death,' a Biblical quote opportunely reminded her. And if it was that strong, wouldn't it overcome obstacles much weaker than death?

On the deaths of others, those who were dear to Zygmunt, Clara had already shown she was capable of consoling him. It was in her music that he found comfort after the death of Dembowski; it was in her arms that he had come to cry, the following year, when imperial authorities executed the insurgent Teofil Wisniowski.

'He was perhaps the only man in the world who was like a brother to me,' Zygmunt sighed that evening, stricken, pressing his head between Clara's breasts. 'The only one, and he's gone. He was one of those rare men who, like me, saw the necessity of also emancipating the Ruthenians, and more—he saw that, limited to itself, a struggle for national liberation would end up only in new oppression. In the end, at least those are the opinions I think he had, given his actions . . .'

'He is a martyr,' Clara said softly. 'Cry for him, you're right, I am sure he was a worthy man. But isn't he also a martyr to his illusions? The Ruthenians aren't at all grateful for what he did for them—they see you Poles as their enemies, and, indeed, they proved this during the riots last year . . .'

'Here you are, my sweet, ready to fall in behind Friedrich Engels who, in my opinion, is too blinded by his hatred for Russia and everything that resembles it. Why set up divisions between peoples, why support some and reject the similar hopes of others? Aren't the conflicts between classes more important than the differences between nations? And yet you live here. You know as I do that, in our region inhabited by Ruthenian peasants, the riots have been limited to material destruction and denouncements. It is in the west that there have been so many deaths—in the west, where only Polish serfs live.'

'That's true,' Clara said, continuing to caress his hair. 'You're right, but . . .'

'But you want to forget that, don't you? Polish serfs are lending a hand to the soldiers of the Emperor out of hatred for their masters! That truth appears too monstrous to you, as it appears to those very ones who forge the categories that enable us to understand it. Do you know? At this moment I see circulating among the democrats of Europe reports that the Ruthenians alone were involved in the violence of last year, encouraged in their national resentment by a Metternich who divided in order to conquer. Such a distortion of the truth strikes me with the prejudice it reveals. Is it the emancipation of people that we want, or simply that of Poles? Tacitly supported by Metternich, aren't the Ruthenians as justified as we are in wanting their freedom?

'But they hate you, Zygmunt. If they received the slightest power they would use it, I'm sure of it, to oppress you in turn.'

'Perhaps, no doubt. So what? You're right, power corrupts the purest hopes, the most natural ones in man, which are to live in peace, to be fed by one's work, to speak and to transmit one's language. Masters of their state, the Ruthenians no doubt would attempt to expel us, forbid our language, persecute the Roman Catholics. Forget the social injustice that would have justified their struggle for independence, or remember it only to hone their national myths and re-establish that injustice in other forms.'

'So you do see!'

'But their claims are nonetheless just, Clara, and for that we must support them, or risk instilling in our claims a poison that will pervert them. Who are we to thus choose between two injustices, to decree that one is odious and the other nothing at all?'

'Oh, Zygmunt, you're frightening me . . .'

'I'm frightening you?' he smiled. And then realized that, carried away by his subject, he had spoken too loudly. 'Why do reason and justice frighten you?' he continued in a whisper, 'You who are so compassionate towards human suffering, my good goddess, you who carry in you enough love to spread over all of us?'

'It's not what you say that frightens me, my dear, it is what you are, I'm afraid for you. My poor love, to what isolation are you condemning yourself! What men think as you do, where are your companions in arms? I see you so alone on the paths of life, hated, cursed, surrounded by enemies . . .'

'My love, my very precious love,' he whispered and hugged her tightly, as if this contact were the remedy to the fate she predicted. And she, held like that, thought: My God, why am I speaking to him of paths of life, why am I pushing him away already? My God, make him not understand me. And she hugged the young man, feeling his heart beating as strongly as her own.

But soon, in this second autumn since the riots, other concerns came to darken her soul.

Urszula, settled in Lemberg with her husband, seemed very happy with her new existence. She went to the theatre, to concerts, discovered that she was indeed suited to living in town. As for Maria, she described the difficulties of her clandestine life, regretted not having better followed Madame Denisot's sewing lessons—repairing her skirts and Jan's suits now occupied a good part of her days; and she was learning to cook. But each detail she offered exuded the joy of living, the verve of a woman who loves and knows she is loved; she proved to be made of the stuff that made good wives of exiles and of soldiers on campaign.

How suited they are to each other, Clara thought while rereading the letters. They are afraid of nothing; she married, along with him, his cause and his enthusiasms, and she will follow him to the end of the earth— the end of the earth, for now, being a small town in the Carpathians where, from what they said, a national movement was also beginning to foment. My little Maria, my child of sin, no longer needs me.

The one who worried her was Wioletta. For several months already, Wioletta seemed even more sombre and more withdrawn than usual. Nothing cheered her—not balls, not dinners, not invitations to neighbouring estates. Clara had even suggested, to distract her, that she spend a few weeks in Lemberg with her sister but the young girl had rejected that proposal.

'*Oh non, Maman*, I'm better here, I don't want to leave,' she had whimpered; and Clara, already imagining her sent off to Urszula who would spread out in front of her all her new happiness and her new dignity as a wife, gave up that idea when she saw the beautiful almond eyes fill with tears and the lips tremble.

Asked for his advice, Zygmunt didn't know how to respond. He had also noticed the decline of his student. She no longer painted nor wanted to read; she spent hours in the classroom daydreaming darkly. Even on the physical level, her condition was deteriorating. Her skin had grown sallow, her pretty eyes were surrounded with bluish circles, at the table she ate almost nothing; yet the chamber maid discovered in the drawer of her bedside table a stock of sour apples, anise stars and rock salt which she must have been eating in secret. Were these the first symptoms of a nervous condition?

One Thursday, Clara kept Salomon Weinberg after lunch and told him of her concerns.

'Would you like me to examine your daughter, dear friend?'

'My goodness, yes . . . that is, without pushing her. Perhaps, in the form of friendly questions, you could . . . Or, as a doctor, prescribe her a bit more exercise? I find her both pale and as if she were congested . . .'

'Leave it to me,' he smiled. I have never pushed anyone, and I will show all necessary tact. What I fear is that her condition is not related to the realm of medicine . . . a distress, a secret pain . . .'

'Do you think? In that case, I'll go with you—as her mother, my presence . . .'

'Let me see her,' he repeated softly; and he spent a half-hour with the young girl in the first-floor boudoir, while Clara, uncertain, paced the hallway with slow and troubled steps.

When he came back out, his face was no longer the same. His smile had gone away, and he nervously wiped his pince-nez while his short-sighted eyes looked for a spot on the wall he could focus on.

'So, doctor?'

He led Clara into the bay of a window.

'I am very sorry to tell you, madame, that your daughter is with child.'

'With child!'

'Without a doubt—at three or four months.'

The shock this news provoked in me made the windows shake imperceptibly in their frames. How could I have missed such a thing!

'But that's impossible. Who, when . . .'

'I couldn't get her to tell me anything. She was unaware of her condition, which I had to explain to her in veiled terms—the innocence of girls is a virtue which, alas, has its disadvantages. All I can tell you is that she isn't ill. The little malaises she is suffering are only the effects of a pregnancy that, for the moment, seems to be going very well.'

This is all we need, Clara surprised herself in thinking, as she gradually measured the enormity of the catastrophe.

While she is seeing the doctor out, then going back up to see her daughter, on whose face the resolution not to say anything is already set, I remain there stunned and almost as unhappy as Clara at my negligence. Of course, I can't prevent anything; but from that reality to not seeing anything, there is an abyss that I indeed naively crossed. I listen to the mother who is questioning and the daughter who is silent, I look at her features without being able to penetrate her memory, her thoughts; and I feel, for the first time in my life, unbelievably stupid.

4

Clara's first reaction was stupefaction. If she didn't have every confidence in Salomon Weinberg as a physician, she wouldn't have believed him. And yet, looking at her daughter more closely, she is shocked she hasn't seen it earlier. That sickly mask, those strange foods, that swollen stomach—she is obviously pregnant.

Pregnant at twenty, and without any declared affection, without the slightest prospect for marriage. At her age and in her condition, it is just about the worst thing that could happen. My God! What will Jozef say?

Clara puts off the terrifying task of informing him. Perhaps we can still act, take care of things? Wioletta knows so little of life, she is perhaps inventing obstacles that come only from her pessimism and her sombre imagination. For hours, her mother questions her. Who is it? Who is responsible? If only she will tell her, Clara will see if there is a solution, a recourse. But Wioletta puts up an unmoveable resistance. She will admit nothing, even if she is tortured. She shakes her head with the patience of a martyr—she has become a Blandine herself.

After a few days, a horrible suspicion takes shape in Clara's mind. She doesn't dare admit it openly to her daughter and so takes a roundabout approach. 'My child, you don't want to tell me the name of the father. I understand your discretion. But perhaps there is also shame involved? No doubt this man is in fact your inferior, no doubt he is a man who . . . a man who is not . . . of our standing?'

Poor mother, poor lover! I alone know how much it cost her to ask that question.

But Wioletta remains impassive; at most, she raises her shoulders imperceptibly, and holds her mother's gaze with a spark of pride: 'No, Mama. The *man* is my equal, and I'm ashamed of nothing. But you will understand that I keep silent because there's nothing to be done—he's a married man.'

I admit that I felt the same relief as Clara at that—it would have been very upsetting to discover that Zygmunt was a duplicitous lover and a seducer of virgins. But I am no more advanced than she at this half-confidence. For the time being, Wioletta remains as opaque to me as she does to her mother, and I realize that she has been just as opaque to me for close to two years without my being aware of it. Because there was a time when I could see through her like the others, when I entered easily into her secret dreams. She must have employed all her strength (women in these times often appear as victims, weak playthings in the hands of males. It is true, but it is also true that their strength, which doesn't have the opportunity to translate into actions, unfolds entirely within, making them champions of passive resistance, indeed of self-destruction) to keep her secret to herself.

And for the time being, the fear of the scandal and of the coming birth manage to freeze her, to make her a block of stone against which I stop short. It is only once her destiny is sealed that she will soften inside, allow feelings and memories to rise to the surface, and that I am able to see everything.

So it was a married man. Reassured on one point, Clara despairs on all others. For what more can she do than hope that a prompt widowhood will allow the seducer to atone for his sin?

She agonizes, despairs. Since the resurrection of Jan, she thought she was rid of her guilt but now remorse floods back with the rage of the irreparable. She knows, this time, that it truly is her punishment that is striking her, a cruel blow from a vengeful and perverse God. Because in the end it is she, Clara, who has sinned, and it is her daughter who is carrying the burden of that sin. Pregnant! Who deserved that stigmatization, if not she, she who, with the discernment and experience of adulthood, had thus forgotten herself?

'I'm being punished, punished,' she cries, sitting on her bed in front of Zygmunt who is looking desolately at her dishevelled hair, her enflamed cheeks—dishevelment and redness in which, this, time, love plays no part. He is still the only one in the house who knows. She senses that she shouldn't tell him, that he is not only her friend but also her lover, and could thus be wounded by this remorse and these scruples of which he is the cause. But it is stronger than she. He is the only one in the world to whom she can unburden herself.

'Punished, why? For what? Rid yourself of these foolish superstitions, my beloved. What evil are you paying for? You have dared to love, you have made me the happiest of men—I see only bravery and generosity in that.'

'But I have neglected my daughter, don't you see? If I had concentrated on my duty as a mother, I would have watched her more carefully, I could have foreseen it, guessed it . . .'

'You speak of her like a chick that a buzzard has eaten. Wioletta is quick, intelligent, determined—she knew what she was doing.'

'As if a young girl knows these things!'

'Come now, Clara! Without knowing everything, a young girl of your class knows very well which words she can hear from a man, what gestures she can allow.'

'Oh, be quiet . . .'

He raises his hand to caress her cheek, and she pushes it away.

'You don't want me to touch you any more?'

'Forgive me. Oh, my dear, you are too young to understand the soul of a mother, you are so far from me . . .'

'Far from you!' he murmurs with a movement of recoil. 'How hard you can be . . . and unfair too! What makes you think I don't understand you?'

'Nothing, everything, oh, I don't know any more . . .'

He lets a silence fall, his shoulders low and his eyes heavy with pain.

'What I understand is that you have regrets. The cause of them doesn't matter. It's your daughter, but it could be something else, the result would be the same—you regret loving me.'

Now she is sobbing, wringing her hands, and he pities her.

'My sweet, awake from this bad dream,' he whispers, sitting next to her on the bed. 'Come to me, nothing has changed. You love me, and you are everything to me: so chase away these chimaeras, don't let them separate us . . .'

She gives in to the sweetness of his murmuring, allows his young man's arm to rest on her shoulders, hold her tenderly. He still loves her, yes, he was right to be angry—such scruples are a crime against love.

Still, when at lunch she sees her husband eat without suspecting anything, Elvire Denisot who always sets an example of the best table manners, Zosia and Jadwiga who chatter on without a worry in the world (will they still be able to find decent husbands after such a disgrace in their family?), it seems to her that her heart, out of terror, is breaking.

Already Wioletta, after the second course, must furtively loosen her dress . . . Oh, if only she could suspend the march of time, or even slow it down! But the days, the weeks go on, and a ferocious clock eats away at the grace period, the crumbs of happiness that Clara has left.

Christmas comes and goes, as does New Year Day. Eighteen forty-eight begins, and Jozef still doesn't suspect anything. Perhaps because he has better things to do than measure his daughters' waistlines. He struggles with his expansion projects, grows irritated because the cold interrupts work on the factory. The foundations are covered with snow, it is ugly, and a little depressing, let spring arrive soon! If Jozef could, he would move the hands of the clock forward and get rid of this useless winter.

And then one day everything explodes. It is a Thursday, the doctor is there (they are grateful, a few minutes later, to have an extra man as a barrier between the unfortunate girl whose father threatens to kill her, then and there). They get up from the table, and Jozef, somewhat relaxed at the end of the meal, remains seated, watching his third daughter go back and forth between him and the window. Wioletta, the unknown favourite, the swan among the ducks. And yet . . . how she has lost her beauty recently! He is shocked to notice. Till then she at least has remained spared from the bloating, has kept the grace of her movements, a lightness of step. Indeed, nothing of beauty endures here on earth, he reflects with melancholy. But suddenly his eyes widen, he drops the glass of wine from which he was savouring the last drops and his shrieks stun everyone present. 'But . . . that child is pregnant!'

His wife's terrified face and the doctor's look of consternation confirm his suspicions. He stands up, enraged; he demands explanations. Wioletta faints, Zygmunt grabs her in time to prevent her from banging her head on the corner of the mantle, there are cries, the bellowing of a man in fury . . . It is a horrible storm; then the head of the family is slowly calmed down; he goes into his library and comes out only hours later to announce to no one in particular that he doesn't want to see that whore until she gives birth, or he will strangle her without hesitation.

And they think he is perfectly capable of doing that; and, moreover, that his anger will never weaken. At the very most he is able to stifle it, to find a modus vivendi with it. Strangling the guilty one would be just but brief; it would at the same time strangle his anger but he loves it too much to wring its neck. So he composes himself, he negotiates. Clara spends her days as mediator between poor Wioletta, whose condition begins to require attention, and the patriarch in fury who is exasperated at knowing so little.

'Oh, she doesn't want to tell who! A married man, eh? She is right to protect him. If I knew his name, I wouldn't hesitate to demand satisfaction and to strike him dead with the first bullet—assuming that this kind sir is one of those with whom a man of position can indeed fight. Because the idiot girl is quite capable of getting herself pregnant by one of our peasants or by the pope, who knows! In these times, nothing surprises me.'

But he ultimately consents to do what is necessary to save what they can—appearances. The expectant daughter will be sent away a few weeks before she delivers and for a few months afterwards. At least the scandal, in this way, will be shrouded in cloudy discretion. As to the future . . . What future? Wioletta, it seems, has chosen her life—she will not marry, will never escape the paternal rule. Even her child, if he lives, will be subject to that. It will be sent who knows where, there is still time to determine that. One thing is clear. Jozef does not want the bastard in his house.

This is the context in which at the end of February the news of the French revolution and of the agitation fomenting in several other countries arrives; and Jozef gradually emerges from his anger and becomes interested in the news. Soon, he is seen almost smiling—a letter from Adam informs him that Lamartine, in Paris, is supporting the Poles, is even encouraging emigrants to return to their homes—it is up to them to win their liberty. Adam is getting ready, Adam is going to come! They can expect to see him before the month of April.

Jozef then hurries to organize poor Wioletta's exile. For nothing in the world does he want her, in her condition, to meet her uncle from Paris. Salomon Weinberg knows a midwife in a little town in a neighbouring district who takes in lodgers and doesn't ask too many questions. Very good, very good! Jozef doesn't want to know more. No details, especially not the details he detests. Leave those women's affairs to women. He will pick up the baton when measures must be taken, futures decided; but he does not want to know when the water is to be put on to boil.

And so Wioletta sets off one day with only a servant in the know as an escort. It will be, if I remember correctly, her only trip, her only escape. Does she foresee this? Oh, seeing her climb into the briska with her ungainly stomach and her luggage heaped around her, I feel bad for her, I would like to shout out to her: Flee! Make your life! However mediocre and unhappy it might be, it will be better than the one that awaits you within these walls. I breathe, in the nape of Efraim's neck, a little wind of madness to awaken the wild and impulsive philanderer sleeping inside him. Behind him is the most beautiful girl in the district, a little spring chicken, fresh, tender, fattened by her pregnancy. Let him take advantage of a deserted road, toss the servant into a ditch and run away with his passenger! She is already a pariah—they won't go looking very far for her if she were to disappear with him into the wild. Oh, let him be tempted!

But Efraim knew her when she was little, that Wioletta who then brought bits of sugar to his horses, and who, if he didn't prevent her, would have even given them Pastilles de la Vierge to munch. The bad thoughts I send to him bounce off his back. He starts off carefully, so as not to shake up the young lady, and he doesn't sing, because his heart is heavy.

As for Wioletta, she grits her teeth and clutches her handkerchief, terrified to leave her mother, her sisters, her childhood *dwor*. All that she hopes is that they will one day let her come back here to live. The wide world frightens her, the city must be full of noise, dangers, looks; her imminent delivery horrifies her. She will no doubt die of it— wouldn't it be better for everyone, anyway?

When the briska sets off, she continues to look straight ahead so she doesn't see her mother and Mr Borowski waving goodbye.

5

With the departure of this third daughter, who is leaving so ignominiously, it seems to Clara that for her the time of joy has passed, that the hour of reckoning has come. The inevitable is here and she must confront it.

Isn't it inevitable that the year 1848 cuts history in two, like a knife, the old world behind with its jails, its tyrants, its darkness, and the new world ahead? What! Each life henceforth cut into two, the before and the after, the past and the future, and she alone, Clara von Kotz, continuing on her path? She knows this isn't possible, so she too waits for the stroke of the blade.

While all of Europe is fomenting, while Louis-Philippe is tumbling off his throne, while Berlin is raising barricades, while the rulers of Italy are hastily granting constitutions to their peoples; while strikes in Vienna are forcing the old Metternich to flee piteously in the carriage of a laundress; while, drop by drop through the Prussian border, a flood of émigrés are coming back to fight for the independence of their Poland; while Prince Dubinski is increasing his trips to town and returning with cockades and *konfederatkas* which he then distributes to whoever wants them—soon he will leave as a delegate to Vienna—Clara waits. What she is waiting for she doesn't yet know but will soon learn. Time, henceforth, passes so quickly!

And nature enters into the fray and gets carried away. Spring this year proves to be extraordinarily early, a tender grass is already turning the hillsides green when we learn, through a discreet courier, that Wioletta has given birth to a male child who appears hale and hearty.

Before Clara's eyes Zygmunt is transformed. He blossoms, speaks more firmly, gives the impression of having grown taller. He exults at every word, even the birth of the little Feliks enchants him, as if it were not really a calamity.

'You see? Wioletta has pulled through, in spite of the delicacy of her constitution. Your bad dreams, your gloomy predictions were for naught. Smile, at least, Clara!'

Smile, thinks the new grandmother. How different we are, although he doesn't want to see it! From what would I derive any joy? He tells me that what the world thinks is meaningless, that every human life is a gift, that this new little man, however questionable his conception, is happy to have seen the day at the same time as the free world, that his mother has named him well. How can he be so blind to what society is, to what appearances are, to its constraints? Because he, himself, is happy, because the way things are unfolding is following the path of his desires, for him every event must necessarily be a joy.

But she keeps all that to herself, and with a great effort, smiles at him.

'You are right, I am very relieved. I've caused you to worry with my fears, my poor love, I see that now.'

And suddenly she has an inspiration, she knows what she must do. She continues, in a voice that she tries very hard to make steady and serene: 'You know? Now that I am free of that concern, you should take care of yourself. Why don't you go away for a week or two? I am sure that you've been dreaming of going to Kraków where so many things are happening now, where you have so many friends . . .'

Zygmunt looks at her, uncertain, his eyes full of sadness.

'Leave you, my sweet?'

'Oh, just for a little while . . .'

'It's true, a week goes by so quickly . . . But it's impossible. My responsibility lies here.'

'Nonsense! Zosia and Jadwiga will be fine without your instruction. If you wish, I will ask my husband for you. He won't refuse—you have never been absent in four years of service here.'

'No, no, it's impossible,' he repeats. And yet, dreaming, he spends an hour telling her what he would do there for those few days, the people he would see—émigrés of the old generation who are coming back, insurgents of 1846 who have just been freed and are returning, with blinking eyes, from prisons in Spielberg and Kufstein. 'But I won't leave,' he concludes firmly, kissing one after the other his lover's fingers.

Clara doesn't insist. It is enough to let the temptation germinate in him. And in three days, it is decided.

She faces it without bitterness. After all, it is what she wants. And what bitterness wouldn't have melted before the proofs of love that Zygmunt gives her at the perspective of this separation? The day before his departure he picks her up in his arms as if to take her with him, covers her with kisses, whispers feverishly all his thoughts, all his hopes; he tells her what he thinks will happen, lets his enthusiasm speak—he is radiant, that is clear.

'Go on, my dear,' Clara murmurs to him, her cheek pressed against his to hide her eyes. 'It's good that you're leaving, they need you. Your place is there, your place right now . . .'

And since he is pulling his head back with a little afterthought, a suspicion—those who are in love have such clairvoyance—she kisses his hair and adds: 'I would so love to go with you . . . You'll tell me everything, won't you?'

During the days he was away, a small event indeed occurred to distract Clara. One evening, a carriage stops in front of the gate; an old man gets out, preceded by a valet and an extraordinary moustache.

'Hello! Ho!' he shouts, for no one comes to the door (because an altercation between two maids has just attracted all the servants to the kitchen). Finally, a lackey arrives, running, to be of service.

'You may announce, my good fellow, Captain Zemka-Ponarski,' the new arrival declares in a tone of dignity through which pierces an intense jubilation. 'Zemka-Ponarski. And you can unhitch the horses. I will not be leaving any time soon!'

Adam is finally home, on his promised land, the former estate of his ancestors that he has never seen! I watch him with a great deal of curiosity, his military demeanour as he crosses the courtyard and climbs the steps. And in the foyer, while they are taking his coat, I am finally able to examine in the light this person of whom I have heard so much.

What a noble bearing, what ardent eyes under the great receding hairline! It's true, Jan resembles him. He is a Jan with august wrinkles, with bushy eyebrows. He looks around at the paintings, the furnishings; but now he turns with a shout. Jozef, his younger brother, has just entered, and the two men look at each other with an emotion infused with a great deal of stupor. They haven't seen each other for close to forty years!

How old he is! thinks Jozef, who remembers an emotional adolescent, whose still smooth cheeks reddened with fervour each time Bonaparte's name was uttered. How old he is! thinks Adam who remembers a shy school boy, as pretty as a Saxe porcelain figure. Then they fall into each other's arms and chase away the unease with a flood of words.

'Come in, sit down! How was your trip?'

'Excellent, yes, tiring but excellent, like every trip that brings you back to your motherland . . . Oh, Jozef, I am happy, happy!'

'I understand.'

'I'm not sure you do. *You* don't know anything about exile . . . It looks like your business is going well?'

Jozef feels rejuvenated by this tone of a condescending older brother, but irritatingly so. He straightens up, squares his shoulders: 'I'm not complaining, of course . . . Actually, you know, managing such an estate is not a sinecure, it is a lot of work, a lot of worry . . . Tomorrow, I'll take you to see the grain fields, the roads that I've had built, I've invested a lot, you know . . . And the work site of the new sugar factory . . .'

'Yes, yes, I will see all that, I'm delighted! Oh, but here is your wife, I presume,' Adam murmurs in a softer voice.

Clara, in fact, is walking towards him, smiling, intimidated at having to be introduced to this unknown man who is such an illustrious member of the family. Adam does not share her discomfort. Without knowing her, he has always imagined this Austrian woman as a sort of Marie-Antoinette, a superficial and imperious woman whom his brother married only for a good cause—her dowry. It was a diplomatic marriage, and the soldier in his soul judges with a certain disdain these chancellery arrangements.

'Madame,' he utters stiffly. And then, not very politely, he turns back to his brother in such a way, he believes, that will indicate to his sister-in-law that she is not wanted among them.

'Oh, Jozef, if you had heard Mickiewicz's lectures at the Collège de France! Such a flame, such elevation! Just listening to him, said one of my old friends, a man could die without having seen his native Poland again. It is moreover what happened to him that poor Erazm . . .'

But with this Madame Denisot appears. Discovering in the salon a man she doesn't know, she stands still, her eyes lowered, next to her mistress as if to ask for her protection and support.

'Oh! And this is the Duchess of Polignac, no doubt!' Adam whispers to his brother.

What is he talking about? I don't understand anything he's telling me, thinks Jozef, whom the entire scene is greatly irritating. Because in the end Clara is his wife and, though he does not love her, he would all the same prefer that what remained of his family treat her with the respect she was owed. That he, Jozef, mistreat his other half seems to go without saying; but for someone else to insult her in front of him shocks him. And suddenly, belatedly—much too late, in fact, even if he doesn't know it yet—he realizes that such treatment is indeed unjust. To turn his Clara, so right and so good, into an occupier, an enemy!

He also senses that this lack of courtesy shown his wife reflects the small esteem in which Adam holds him. And those reflections on the state of his fortune! Isn't he insinuating that Jozef is a sly one, a profiteer and an opportunist? What ingratitude! As if Jozef hasn't supported his brother for almost twenty years!

In short, as often happens, these so-hoped-for reunions leave everyone with an aftertaste of disappointment. The two men find they are strangers to each other, of different minds, character, habits. Jozef, who was used to lyrical letters from his brother, doesn't find their author in this old lesson-giving veteran. As for Adam . . . for the time being he blames his impression of discomfort on the fatigue of the trip. That evening, and the following days, he attempts to quell those feelings with the endless recounting of childhood memories, the only terrain the two men are sure to have in common.

'Oh, I see that you have kept this silhouette of Mother . . . Do you remember, Jozef, the day when the artist came to our house with his lamp, his screen and his scissors? "Don't move," he said, "your profile is charming." And Mother who didn't move, who no longer moves, until they noticed that she was asleep—sitting up with her eyes open. How we laughed!'

'I remember too,' adds Jozef, whom these memories have softened more than they should have, 'I remember our apprentice, the one who was in love with Mother . . . Each time he came to our house on an errand and Mother said to him, "Come in Bogumil, don't stay there at the door, come kiss my hand," he grew pale, and trembled and knocked over the candy dish . . .'

'And that gingerbread?—in the shape of a heart that he made for her feast day, do you remember?'

'Father wasn't happy. "You've wasted honey, little fool, for a vulgar sweet, a peasant cake, you'll end up an animal trainer at a fair, you don't deserve any better!" '

'Mother laughed.'

'She always laughed.'

'When she wasn't singing. "L'Amour qui règne dans votre âme, Berger, a de quoi nous charmer. Par votre généreuse flame, Vous montrez comment il faut aimer" . . . The first time I heard that tune sung in Paris, I thought I was going to die of nostalgia. That was all the French Mother knew, all that grandmother Ponarska herself had retained . . . Oh, Jozef,' he sighed, his big voice strangling, 'so many things past!'

Jozef also feels sad, feels the need of a male diversion. So he takes the émigré to the four corners of the estate, on horseback or on foot or in the briska when the weather is bad. Adam listens with great seriousness to his explanations, nods his head at the waterlogged worksite, studies the harvests, the grain, the issues of returns.

'Don't you have an overseer who takes care of all this?' he finally asks one day as Jozef keeps him for a half-hour next to three pigs and a pile of manure. He must confess that he is slightly bored. These fields, these hills, these thickets, everything that is in between the towns speaks to Adam only as battlefields. The countryside in times of peace seems to him naked and sad, smelly. How can one retreat to this life, to these rustic occupations?

What he dares not see but which is hurting my eyes is that he has, old Adam, lived much too long in exile—he is no longer able to live any other way. He has dreamt of this since 1831, of this return, and since he became a widower has wished only to finish his days on the former estate of the Ponarskis, surrounded by his Polish family. But he needed only two weeks to understand that he couldn't abide it. He has to leave, and quickly! Find other battles, other destinations! Soon, rather ill at ease, he tells Jozef about his new plans. He misses his Jan, it has been more than two years since he's seen him, he hasn't even met his charming daughter-in-law. In short, Hungary is calling him. Who knows—he might find there, in that region where national consciousness is beginning to awaken, the opportunity to put his military experience, his strategic talents to use. How could he spend peaceful days here, how could he enjoy this golden retirement when before his eyes people are crying out for justice, rattling their chains, calling to arms all the proud soldiers of freedom?

Jozef protests only for form's sake—deep down, this cohabitation is exasperating him, and he wouldn't survive three months, either. Let him go dive back into the smoke of heroism! The pure air, obviously, doesn't suit him.

'Above all, send us your news!' he says with sincere emotion to his brother, however, when they are saying goodbye. His old Adam is going away; he can finally start loving him again.

6

Zygmunt left, Zygmunt returned. The two weeks turned into four, but his masters couldn't hold that against him. Who could have predicted that the agitation in Kraków would degenerate into an open conflict with the Austrian army, that the population would take up arms and then be bombarded? Zygmunt had to witness the new capitulation of his dear city; then military law was declared and that delayed his return considerably. Finally he returned, unscathed. And, of course, he told Clara everything.

But as he tells her he discovers that his tale doesn't have the savour he had promised himself at the moment of their goodbyes. It seems flat compared to his experiences. It seems that when she hears it, Clara will tell him, What? That's all? Is that why we were separated for four weeks?

She wasn't there—for her, all revolutionary days are blended into one huge mass. For him, each day had its texture, its meaning, its consequences. He tries to reconstruct them, be precise, complete, adds details; he grows annoyed that he can't do it better. Or he tries to get Clara to feel what it is like when a city is being bombed, describing the gripping images in his memory: a gutted house, the wallpaper of its rooms exposed to the air, a naked child sitting on the rubble, mute with terror—all this translated into words, into weak and hollow words. Maybe he doesn't know how to speak of such things? And yet she listens, his beautiful Clara, his good, loyal Clara; she is interested in what he says and sympathizes with what he deplores; nevertheless, he has the impression that she doesn't really understand. It's not surprising—she wasn't there.

And so he makes do with a realm more familiar to them and in which they can understand each other better—the realm of ideas and analysis. He speaks to her of factions, oppositions between men. He speaks to her of that 'Ruthenian council' which, he has heard, has just been created in Drohobycz, and he reveals to her what he believes he thinks about it. He considers it a perfectly serious institution, unlike Jozef who thinks it the most grotesque of farces. ('*Rada Ruska*, really! It's wonderful, this bunch of puppets led by a Uniate bishop! What next?

Slovenians, Slovaks and other obscure tribes who will come to the front of the stage and claim they are peoples! I laugh, but I should be appalled at such insanity.') Zygmunt speaks about it with calm interest, wonders about the importance that should be given to this national movement and to others. Will they be a driving force of revolution, or, on the contrary, a brake, a source of possible divisions? Who knows; maybe we'll find out at the Slavic congress that will be held in Prague the following month.

Clara is even more surprised when he speaks of the Jews. Of course, she doesn't share her husband's prejudice. She even knows a Jew, her doctor, and another, their groom. But Zygmunt speaks of the Jews as he does the Ruthenians, Czechs, Croatians or Hutsuls—as a collective entity that should be emancipated all together. Up to now, those whom she had heard speak of the 'Jews' as a group were their servants or their serfs; the leader, for example, when she visited him for her works and he complained of the bad weather, the sleet or drought, suggested there was a Moschko behind it. Zygmunt simply sees them as a minority in the empire, he sees them theoretically. The question stimulates him like a good school problem: How can one treat with justice a minority that cannot be connected to any specific region?

'Alas, I fear, my sweet, that this issue will not go away any time soon, because it causes much discord, including among those concerned. It also, to my great regret, arouses much foolishness. Some among our allies literally lose their heads as soon as one brings up the subject, forgetting everything they are, all that they think, to speak words that your husband or Princess Dubinska wouldn't disavow.'

Clara shudders a bit at that connection but, upon reflection, sees it is correct. Yes, correct, like everything Zygmunt says. Zygmunt is so astute, so right; no prejudice affects his thoughts, no emotion undermines him.

'My pure spirit,' she murmurs to him, and she raises her hand to brush the cheek of the young man. He thinks she is only teasing him, and turns his head to chew on the fingers whose rings Clara had placed on her bedside table. No, he is not a pure spirit, he wants to prove it to her, and they begin to laugh and love each other as in the early days of their love. He came back—this time he came back, Clara says to herself.

She was the one who wanted him to leave; but he returned and, not without shame, she is delighted.

But Clara knows—one never truly returns. The man she is holding to her bosom is not the same man who left. She already feels in him a fluttering, a difference; obscurely, he must also know that he is not the same man, that one doesn't bathe twice in the same water.

They are each intimately convinced of this one day in mid-June when they are listening to Jadwiga play the piano in the salon. Music isn't her strong suit. Her only ambition is to one day play the organ during Sunday services; and, while waiting for that, she practises bleating hymns and lugubrious chorales on the Bösendorfer. Today she has asked to play in front of a small audience, and everyone is delighted to accommodate such a devout request. Madame Denisot has taken her place on the striped sofa, her hands folded, her head slightly leaning; Jadwiga is her favourite, and a smile of approval can be seen on her thin lips.

Standing up in the opening of a window, Jozef is chomping at the bit. He is listening, of course, he is listening, but he has other things to do and he would like this concert to finish soon, especially since he doesn't like religious music. Waiting, he observes the group formed by the pianist and her little sister turning the pages for her. He still has to find husbands for those two, he thinks with discouragement. Zosia is very cute with her braid hanging down her back—thirteen, but already quite nice. In other times she would have already been placed in the bed of an honest man and no one would have had objected; in the Middle Ages, princesses were married younger than that. Jadwiga, however, is right to study music; because, if she is counting on her sheep-like profile and her protruding shoulder blades to snag a husband, we'll have a long time to wait. (He has a fleeting thought for his only daughter who is truly beautiful, the one missing, the scandalous one, the deplorable Wioletta; and a surge of fury brings blood to his cheeks. What a brilliant marriage he could have arranged for her!)

Then his gaze wanders to his wife, seated on the sofa at some distance from Elvire Denisot. He watches her for a moment, then shrugs his shoulders—leave it to Clara to be so moved by these flat church songs. She has, while listening, dropped her needlework and not picked it up again. She is looking intently at the backs of her two daughters and her eyes are filled with tears.

. . . Yes, Clara is crying; these Sunday melodies, performed without soul and badly, ring in her ears like the funeral march of her love. Because here they all are, gathered in the salon, each in his or her place, each in his or her function: the wife seated, the husband standing, the young girls in front of them, to the left their governess, to the right their tutor. This is the order of the world, and everything else is madness, sweet and beautiful madness. Their love was only imaginary, a chimaera, everything fought against it—their positions, her status as a wife, a mother and then her age too; they kept it alive by sheer will alone. But what is the power of will against the order of the world?

Love is not as strong as death, she murmurs to her lover in her thoughts, not looking at him—because her duty, at this moment, is to look at her daughters. Love is weak, it is a little trembling flame in the tempest of the world, and only very young lovers, or those who have just found each other, can believe that it will take only their four hands cupping it to prevent it from going out. We are not the strongest, do you understand? We will give in, it is hopeless, it is only a matter of time.

This is what this woman of little faith repeats to herself to justify herself, or to justify Zygmunt (she doesn't know any more). It is her final sincere speech to the man who has loved her, who has understood her, who has been closest of all to her—her final sincere speech but one which she doesn't deliver.

Zygmunt is also sad, without knowing why. Doesn't he have every reason to hope, to delight in life? What he saw in Kraków and the identical fate that has just befallen Prague have obviously affected him, but the brutality of the state will have to give in against the strength of numbers. Men can't be held in slavery for ever; an explosive power is growing and sooner or later will burst forth and break the chains. The Stadions, the Windischgratzes, those bombers of cities and crushers of peoples, in the end, are only children determined to defend a sandcastle against the rising tide. They will also fail—it is only a matter of time.

Then why this sadness, why is his heart so heavy? How can things so dear to him, his love for Clara, take on such a melancholic tint, suddenly appear grey and faded, like old memories? He can see only his lover's profile and her low chignon. He wishes intensely that she would turn towards him, but she doesn't. Once she would have done it, he thinks; but it is not true pain that comes from that thought; it is an indefinable feeling of unease and instability. And he remembers that day when she had played for him for the first time. It was the day when Dr Weinberg had informed them of the death of Dembowski, the fall of the popular government. Two years already. Only two years! He corrects himself, and his unease grows.

When Wioletta returns from town, she isn't the same, either, as might be expected.

The sinner's return is indeed sombre. One afternoon at the end of June she returns in the briska driven by Efraim, who lets her out in front of the gate; she looks around her; her cheeks are hollow. And as she timidly moves forward behind the servant who accompanied her, the window to the library opens, her father appears and, coldly, signals to them to take the service entrance. Everything is said in that gesture— the main entrance is for honest women.

And so Wioletta begins her true adult life through the service door. Nothing has changed in her room, where she will henceforth spend a much greater amount of time. Drawings are still lying around, paints, dried brushes. She picks one up, brushes it against her palm. Perhaps she will be able to save it, perhaps it is not quite ready to be thrown away?

Of course it is, she concludes; and with a shudder she sees it as a reflection of herself.

After the brief joy at being home again she feels only desolation. What will she be from now on? A girl-mother without a status, without a future; a prisoner with a life sentence. And they took away her son, she won't see him again, God only knows what fate her father has in store for him. Her son! Oh! She falls onto the chair in front of the dressing table; it seems that the pain is too strong for her body, that she won't survive it. And I hold my breath so as not to disperse the bits of images she has gathered in her mind—because I want to see the child I want to see what he looks like, and, above all, whom he resembles. Maybe I'll have a better idea then.

But to my disappointment and her despair, she is incapable of bringing back his features. She is only able to find certain details, sensations: the unbelievable smallness of the being that was put into her arms right after he was born, the ear that was so soft and fine that it seemed made of tissue, the honeyed odour of the little body, the tiny hand clutching one of her fingers when she held it out to him. And then the sweetness of the fine hair (Feliks was born with a full head of hair) when she caressed him from his cheek to the top of his head. But his features, his face—where are they, what were they? She knows they are buried somewhere in her memory, she knows that she would recognize him immediately if she saw him again; but the image doesn't come. Why, why wouldn't they let her keep even a picture of her little boy?

She throws away the brush, takes a pencil and begins to sketch furiously, a forehead, a mouth. That's not it, it's not him, I can feel it, this drawing isn't alive. So she throws it away and begins another just as furiously, then a third—before falling onto her bed and bursting into sobs.

I am sad for her, very sad; at this moment I suffer terribly at not being able to take her by her shoulders and pull her to me. What a pity to be what I am! And so I do what I can to diffuse something peaceful into the air, I ask the big armoire to assume, more than ever, the presence of a big, loving mother under its caramel-coloured varnish; the clock to tick like the rocking of a cradle . . . A modest victory, Wioletta finally falls asleep on her bed to the rhythm of her weeping.

Indeed, the lives of my guests are not always happy, and I am no longer sure I am envious of them. How sad, this girl whom they will not allow to keep the little that she has (her child), something that would have done very little harm to anyone. How sad, this mother who, on the other side of the house is torn between her happiness and what she believes to be her duty, between a sweet cowardice and a bitter heroism.

And what is saddest of all are the conventions, the cultural schemas that prevent these two sad states from combining and thus cancelling each other out. Without those conventions, these women who at this moment are separated only by the length of a hallway, would ally their courage: Wioletta would find peace and a semblance of dignity under her mother's protection; and her mother would find a reason to live, however sad she might be. But these two creatures, so close, and deep down, so similar, have never understood each other and will never understand each other. For Wioletta, her mother incarnates renunciation and endures her life with a docility that turns her blood cold. A woman capable of smiling, playing the piano, approving menus, peacefully being able to have new dresses made season after season, whereas the world is so ugly, evil and sad—that paragon wearing the inscription 'model mother, devoted spouse' around her neck would be incapable of sympathizing with her daughter's suffering.

And Clara sees in Wioletta the materialization of her failure and her insufficiencies. She concludes that she has not been up to the task; that she has been a good mother, a good influence, in appearance only. Her modesty, her reserve have stifled confidence, bridled spontaneity, all around her. Didn't she think she should bury her own youthful error under a surplus of rigour? Out of that, out of her first sin, came everything else. And to that first sin, she has added another which has taken her even further on the path of dissimulation. Before her daughter Clara thus feels both guilty and powerless; and, because of that, she is.

And so these two unhappy women repel each other like magnets placed in opposite directions, whereas a flick of fate would have brought them together. A hallway separates them—it isn't very much, but it takes no more than that for, out of a single misunderstanding, two tragedies to unfold.

7

That December morning when Dr Weinberg, bag in his hand, went into Madame Zemka's room, he was struck, even more than by the change in her features, by the stupefaction he could see in her eyes. Because she herself had not foreseen that things would turn out this way.

And yet, she was responsible for everything; everything had been desired and arranged by her—she who had decided to be *wise for two*. She did it with a courage that forced me to admire her. Yes, I admire her, that Clara who, for the greatest part of her life had soothed herself with chimaera and naive illusions, let herself be duped and scorned while still saying thank you; and who, later, attained the foresight and the will necessary to accomplish such a thing.

That courage did not come out of a sense of decorum—it had been a long time, although she didn't admit it, since she had freed herself of that. It came, profoundly, from her love—it is because she loved Zygmunt (and loved him for what he was) that she realized she had to let him go. Ultimately, it was with him, her lover, that she truly achieved her work as a mother. But at what a price!

Because he resisted.

By pushing him into the first separation, she had poured into his heart the poison of yearning, and then observed within him its slow progress. But he was sincerely attached to Clara, had a sense of honour and loyalty. The poison was enough to make him understand that the life here, among his masters, in this remote corner of the world, no longer satisfied him; it was enough to make him unhappy, but not to lead him to decide to leave.

Zygmunt grew sombre, tense; his teaching tasks now weighed heavily on him. 'What!' a hateful voice uttered to him every day, 'Were you born to teach sums to two young girls? Europe is burning, impatient masses are waiting for their marching orders, goals, and you spend your time correcting handwriting, dictating grammatical examples?' The voice was speaking the truth, but he silenced it. How could he leave Clara, his benefactress? How could he respond to such love with such a selfish act? He couldn't.

When she noticed this in him Clara decided to go further, to make him doubt her love for him. Oh, it was easy—she had only to make him see reason.

'What's the matter,' he murmured to her, one night when he felt her strangely inert in his arms.

'Oh,' she said, 'I'm just thinking . . .'

'What?'

'Of us, that is, of you . . .'

There was something new in her voice that made him sit up to hear her better.

'. . . I'm thinking of events . . . I'm thinking that you don't have the position you would like.'

He couldn't deny it. His thoughts were going round and round this truth, seeking a path to escape it; and finally finding only anger.

'Why are you telling me this?'

'Because it is what I think.'

'That's not true, there is something else. Some thoughts you have you don't necessarily say out loud, when you truly love. Do you believe that I don't think?'

She wisely kept silent, to allow time for the meaning of the things he had just said to sink in.

And the meaning displeased him. He continued, his voice a bit thicker: 'So here we are. Telling each other coldly what we have in our hearts, weighing interests, opportunities . . .'

'Why are you using such words? I am thinking only of your own good, your happiness. I can see, my dear, that you're no longer happy.'

'What do you know about it! Happiness is not always seen, it is not incompatible with concerns, worries . . .'

'Come now,' she said, in a conciliatory tone. And she placed her hand on his neck, but he turned away. After a few minutes, he got up and, without looking at her, muttered that he was going upstairs to sleep in his own room.

That was the month of August.

That spat was a more effective poison. Because their combined will could have ended it as so many lovers' quarrels end; but Clara's will here pulled with all its might in the opposite direction. She was able to summon treasures of awkwardness and stiffness within her with which to poison him further. She was able not to find the words that would have brought him back to her bed the next night or the one after; and, when he finally took the first step and asked her forgiveness for his burst of temper, she was heroic enough to respond: 'Of course I pardon you, my dear. Isn't it my job to pardon you, to understand you? I have lived so many years more than you.'

He kissed her hand to thank her for her indulgence but didn't sense enough encouragement to resume his nocturnal visits; and Clara, at that moment, decided to bring back her spiritual advisor.

Shut in her room with the old Jesuit, she didn't really tell him anything true. She mentioned a long crisis of faith, doubts that had, those two years, if not made her give up the practice of religion, at least deprived her from its comfort. She admitted to lapses, dissected in herself imaginary scruples in which he diagnosed a minor illness that could be cured with patience and prayer. She listened as he described, his head gravely bowed, his programme of regeneration, while her eyes went from his bald head to the clock on the mantle—she meant to keep him here for an hour, and then to assume the appearance of having an appeased conscience and of having chosen virtue.

Is that the woman who loved me? Zygmunt was shocked when he saw her come from the gate and, when they met, offer him a smile full of chaste solicitude. I thought I knew that heart, I thought I recognized a heart like mine; but I was blinded. It was only the storm of passion in her. That passion is gone, and here she is again, the Clara who was once my twin and the mirror of my soul, caught up once again in the ways of her class, the habits of her class. I don't recognize her any more.

His eye wasn't experienced enough to detect the details that contributed to that impression: her hair, which Clara no longer coloured and which at the roots was beginning to show the grey; the dresses she had ordered that discretely emphasized the signs of her age—her bust took on a ponderous heaviness in her new blouses; the decorations added to her skirts, like lampshades, thickened her figure.

How strange it is, Zygmunt, sad and troubled, said to himself. Her noble stature, which I so loved, seems now to weigh on me, to repel me, I can't even conceive through what audacity I could have, just a month ago, rifled her clothes, disturbed the order of her curls, her chignon. Am I becoming estranged from her? Or she from me?

And yet, there remained the same understanding, the same intimacy between them; that is, Zygmunt still spoke to her with an open heart and with her, tried to penetrate the meaning of the most recent events— the debates at the Reichstag, the parties, the interests at play. But now a tension hovered over these conversations. They spoke to each other tenderly, as if nothing had changed, but each one thought intensely of the radical change that had brought an end to their physical love, abandoned without a word being said on the subject.

Zygmunt's rectitude suffered. Shouldn't I at least bring the subject up, explain myself? But what could I say that wouldn't hurt her? That body which she now seems to refuse me, doesn't attract me any more. How can I tell her? At her age, how would she take it? No, no, let's let things be. We don't need to tell each other such things to understand.

And he truly believed that.

On the December morning when Salomon Weinberg, as so many times before, approached Clara von Kotz's bed he immediately saw that her condition was serious, but he couldn't explain it. He knew his patient was in good health, her constitution was strong. And the Thursday before he had found her completely herself, maybe even more cheerful than she had been for several weeks.

'We should resume our literary conversations, doctor. I realize I've been missing them,' she had said to him. And without waiting, to indulge her, he had launched into a debate on the relative talents of the pastor Mörike and the poor Nikolaus Lenau, two poets whom she faulted, in spite of their talent, for being too elegiac. 'Existence here on earth is really not so sombre, what do you think?'

He had laughed at that affirmation, had responded that in his opinion existence was much more so, and no doubt less harmonious than their beautiful verses, but he was delighted to see her so gay; she hadn't been so recently, it seemed to him. And that evening, he left very content, as if brought back to the days when as a young mother, Madame Zemka sometimes found a few minutes to speak with him on subjects that had nothing to do with her daughters or their health or the concerns of her marriage.

It was true, Clara was indeed happy that Thursday, or at least felt her soul at peace. It had been two months, to the day, since Zygmunt's departure—she had mentally fixed that date as the limit after which she would no longer risk seeing him return.

Because the young man didn't leave easily, it was difficult for him to make the decision. To leave was to mark the failure of that connection which he had thought was so beautiful, the end of his illusions. It was to admit that those two years of love had been an error in his life, an error he would soon be ashamed of; a thousand connections, a thousand sweet memories kept him.

Clara watched him go through this agony with pity. How he is suffering, my Lord! she noted with dismay and a bit of involuntary joy. He is suffering as much as I am, how cruel to be forced to torment him this way . . .

And so it was out of compassion that she undertook to destroy Zygmunt's regrets. She started to talk to him about religion and morality; to launch into considerations on destiny, the order of the world, the organic laws of human societies. Where did she get such eloquence? Let's remember that Clara, without being any more educated than the average wife of an estate owner, had, in her youth, read a lot, had been impassioned by many things. Her sensitivity took the place of true culture, made up for her lack of intellectualism. Hadn't she as an adolescent shivered at reading Augustine's *Confessions*? Perhaps from that she had drawn bits of the feverish penitence, of the palaeo-Christian fervour at which Zygmunt was so disagreeably surprised. Her tirades, her eyes raised to the mouldings of the ceiling, that tone of conservative muse made him shudder. So this was the true face of his mistress, these were the depths of her soul when physical passion no longer animated her!

'Would it be an organic law of human societies that force you, dear Clara, to tell me such things?' he interrupted her, exasperated.

'What do you mean, my dear?' she murmured, leaning over her needlework.

'Oh, I'm just noticing the ease with which you dive into these visions, into these systems of thought that must be those of your milieu, to extract yourself from a . . . from an involvement that you no doubt regret.'

'That I regret?' she repeated, letting her needle fall for a moment. 'You don't understand me. I know, on the contrary, that regret is a vain attitude, the expedient of weak souls. And I feel full of strength. To want good, the salvation of my soul, of yours, that is the new task that strengthens me and exalts me—it is the very opposite of the weakness of regret.'

He watched her work for a few minutes, looking at her in the light. It came to him suddenly, like a obvious fact. 'Do you think, my pious friend, that the salvation of my soul and of yours requires my departure from this house?'

Here we are, thought Clara, with a feeling of victory that broke her heart, while her face remained impassive.

'That decision,' she said in a slow voice that she knew how to modulate and make hesitant as if following the curve of her doubts, and which spoke not a word that was sincere, 'that decision, if you make it, would cause me great pain, my friend. But it is not up to me to influence your choices. And it might well be for the best. Out of great pain sometimes unexpected consolation comes, and the paths of . . .' she interrupted herself, glancing at him with a look of ironic indulgence, 'the paths of our lives are quite impenetrable.'

At that she willed herself to be silent, and, just as slowly, smiling, raised the silk thread to her mouth and cut it with her teeth.

Five days later, Zygmunt informed Mr Zemka that family obligations forced him to end his functions prematurely. Jozef was not duped by his troubled look, his fleeting glances—those 'family obligations' seemed very much like those that, in the region, drained hundreds of hotheads towards the insurgent towns and the regions of the empire where the masses smitten with independence were taking up arms. He even agreed to reduce the term of his notice to fifteen days. To be honest, he didn't regret that departure. For many months this young Borowski had ceased being agreeable to him. Too discreet, too taciturn; Jozef wouldn't have appreciated some obscure tutor acting like one of the family and chatting with him on an equal footing, but even so—after a certain point, such reserve verged on impertinence.

I did the right thing, Clara said to herself, while her lover was busy getting ready to leave, his face sombre but already eager and impatient for his new life.

I did the right thing, she said to herself again the day before his departure, after he came to say goodbye to her in private. She maintained her role valiantly, expressed her wishes for success and happiness without revealing the slightest emotion. She even abstained, pretending indifference, from asking him where he thought he would go in the near future. Didn't she know? Wherever they were loosening paving stones to throw he would go; wherever the people were being shot at, he would go; wherever there was danger, action, he would go; and she would stay here.

And this was good, it was in the order of things.

It was in this frame of mind that she, hidden behind her curtains, watched him leave the next day on foot towards Grünau. His bag wasn't heavy, he walked quickly and didn't turn around, even at the thicket of willow trees. He left angry, and if he had one regret, it was clearly that of having lost two years of his life in loving a woman who had remained his superior and his class enemy. Perhaps one day he would understand? No, he didn't have to understand—because then he would return.

Please don't let him return, oh, don't let him see me as I will be then, she begged as she moved away from the window and sat down at her dressing table. And there, in the mirror, she saw herself as she really was—a poor old woman with falling cheeks, dull eyes, her mouth framed by two lines of pain.

She had done the right thing. For several weeks, that thought carried her.

The news from Vienna was alarming. The people, the students, the democrats were rising up, the army had intervened, they mentioned many dead, the leaders shot down. Was Zygmunt one of them?

She vaguely waited for a letter, a message of hope or of definitive loss. But she well knew that was a final indulgence she was granting herself. For peace of mind, she had to stop waiting for that final letter, that letter which, of course, would never come.

And she was successful.

A day came when Clara stopped hoping and fearing. She found peace, spoke of literature with her doctor, was able, for the first time in close to three years, to confess without a single lie, without a single omission.

So, I did the right thing, I am going to get on with my life, my life of before, the one I had been content with for ever, she said to herself; but the satisfaction of a job well done gradually disappeared and in its place came nothing. Had she really been content with that life? She asked herself while dreaming, standing at a window. She looked at the path to the sugar factory, the roofs of the farms, a bit of Grünau, and the sight of the thicket of willows now pinched her heart. The horizon was clear, the gaze travelled far, at least when the weather was good; but there was so little to see!

And then one night, one of those December nights when she wasn't sleeping and watching the embers in the fireplace in her room go out, her courage suddenly left her. Her world was a desert—she didn't want to spend one more day in it.

The next day, when little Salek from the town of Pogwizdow, where his father had had a porcelain shop, sat at the bedside of that daughter of barons, who had almost married the Counselor Menzel but had become only a wife of a landowner, and his friend—he sensed disaster. Her breathing was weak, choppy, her pulse nonexistent, her lips pulled into a rictus grin over pale gums. 'No, no!' he cried to himself feeling his hands shaking and a sweat of anguish dampen his shirt, 'I mustn't lose my head, I'm here as a doctor, I must save her!'

But there was nothing more to do, he was well aware. And when he was left alone with his patient and she brought out an empty vial from under her blankets and put it in his hand, he didn't even open it, and, without a word, slipped it into his bag.

She was still moving, though, opened her mouth, tried to ask him something; he leant towards her but the words didn't come.

'Go in peace,' he finally murmured, without being able to stifle the trembling of his voice. 'Go in peace, I won't say anything, no one will ever know.'

And so she let herself go with a sigh onto her pillow, and he thought that it was all over. But a few moments later she opened her eyes and, with difficulty, said, 'I did the right thing.'

He thought he heard, 'Didn't I?' but it already seemed like a death rattle or a whistling rather than speech, and he was silent. Anyway, it was too serious a question, too intimate, for him to respond with one of those encouraging phrases that he offered to everyone. The only sincere response worthy of the circumstances would have been: No, you did the wrong thing. I am angry with you, and I don't understand! You were the noblest, the loftiest person I've ever met, the most wonderful woman alongside whom I could ever have hoped to live! You have struck me cruelly in disappearing from my world, and I wish I mattered enough to be able turn you away from this, Clara, Your Grace, Clara, my old friend!

But he was a reserved and reticent man, content to hold her hand and then to close her eyes.

8

In the end, that would have been Clara's first and last act of will. When she was young, she had forcefully refused what she didn't want, and, while loving, twice, had forcefully decided to give in to her passion. But her end was the only plan that she herself had conceived, executed and brought to term.

And Jozef is not duped. His unexpected widowhood has left him stunned and troubled. Clara, dying before him and with no warning? Clara, who was made to endure her mourning and to whom he had even foreseen saying before taking his last breath: 'My poor, dear girl, I have caused you so much pain!'

Fatal fever, the doctor said; but Jozef was not convinced by his explanations. And why was he kept outside her room until she was gone? Didn't Jozef have a place at his dying wife's bedside? There is a mystery there that is eating at him but he doesn't insist on knowing more. If there were an investigation, questions would give rise to gossip, and he instinctively feels that this would not be in his best interests. What is no doubt most important is that his wife, so pious, can be buried in consecrated ground. And then, if what he suspects is true, another scandal for his family! A man can have his reasons for ending his life: gambling debts, public shame or another point of honour. But a woman, a mother, a Catholic wife—what abyss, what perdition such an action would suggest! No, none of that resembles his good Clara, he must be mistaken, he surely is mistaken.

And yet . . . Who was his wife, really? He thought he knew her, knew her only too well. Then why does her end remain so inexplicable? Was there something else in her other than that humble devotion which was able, so often, to get on his nerves? This enigma would always remain unsolved for him, and it would, moreover, be the turning point in his life. From then on he is a wounded man, and the curve of his destiny ceases to be ascendant.

On the surface, though, he continues to be what he has always been: practical, anticipatory, efficient. He pulls himself together, does what is necessary for the tomb and the memory of his wife. He writes many letters, receives many, and it seems to him that life has already resumed its rhythm.

Doesn't life always have the last word? Life is the little baby that Maria, in Hungary, has just brought into the world, and whose birth we have just learnt of here, at the same time as the baptism. Mathilde Lubina *Clara* Zemka-Ponarska—in that string of names, Jozef, sadly amused, sees the result of multiple negotiations. It is of course Adam who imposed 'Mathilde' on the parents, a not-too-obvious homage to the Bonapartes. Jan would have then honoured the memory of his late mother; and what tenacity Maria must have shown to have her mother's name added, as well!

Poor Jan, poor Maria! Adam, now living with them, must certainly be a burden. His letter of condolence had been a bad joke: five lines of haphazard regrets, followed by three pages devoted to a situation that he obviously felt was much more serious—the destruction of the Piedmont army by the infamous Radetzky, an army in which several Poles whom Adam knew in Paris had served. The letter that he sends to his brother to congratulate him along with himself on the birth that made them both grandfathers was not much better:

> What a sweet little child, Jozef! She already looks just like my poor wife. We've had to take a wet nurse because Maria is recovering nicely, but doesn't have enough milk. My goodness, so much the better! We will only see the next child that much sooner. Oh! Rest assured that I'm keeping an eye on them—it won't be long. And it will be a son this time, I'm certain of it. I know my Jan, I know what he's made of—he will give us a son, don't worry about that.

And as if that weren't enough, Adam is taking up his old hobbies again, and really envisions going back into the army.

> The urge for freedom is swelling here, dear Jozef, and I foresee that the storm is coming soon. I'm not asking you to join us, I know that at your age you don't launch into a military life about which you know nothing. But I, with the experience and know-how that I've acquired, I think I know where my future lies. I've exchanged a few letters with our great general Bem, who

has retired here after the battles in Vienna, and he seems very enthusiastic at the idea that I'm lending him my support. As for Jan, he will follow me, of course, it's already settled—your Mariszka is already sewing our uniforms.

Don't let him kill Jan a second time! shudders Jozef, who grows angrier at each line of this missive. Because he has no doubt, either—Jan will follow his father and, if necessary, even go without him to support the Hungarians, as he would support all people subjected by the state that he abhorred and which, by force of arms, had just dissolved the Reichstag. How could Jozef have believed that the prospect of being his heir would stifle in his nephew the flame that characterizes that branch of the family? Jan will never change, no more than that old pig-headed Adam. On the contrary, they even seem to have contaminated his daughter (Mariszka!), who by nature was as much moved by heroism as a bath rug.

No, really, that revolution has no importance for him. If everything were quickly transformed and for the better, his wishes would be granted. But it has been more than twelve months that they've been living in turmoil, that every street urchin has begun to shout, that Councils have been cropping up everywhere, that Parliaments where they tear one another apart convene without anyone being able to take things in hand . . . As for what concerns him, Jozef has lost a lot (his workers) and has gained nothing. Because in the end, good for the Piedmonters and the Magyars if they come out ahead—but where is that free Poland that Jan had practically promised him?

. . . Yes, for Jozef, life has definitely resumed its course.

For Wioletta, however, the death of her mother was a more physical and immediate shock. I saw her grow pale, in her room, when Lubienka came to announce the terrible news. Then Zosia and Jadwiga arrived, throwing themselves at her, crying; but a moment later they were bundled out by Madame Denisot whose primary task, from now on, seems to be to prevent those two pure doves from being infected through contact with their fallen sister. Scarcely had she been told than Wioletta found herself alone with her pain. They allowed her to see the body (she still shudders at the memory of those convulsed features). Then there was a veritable ballet of visitors, priest, neighbours, leader of the peasant community, and she wandered here and there, from one end of the hallway to the opening of a door. Wherever she went she was always in the way.

A single person stopped beside her—Dr Weinberg, who put his hand on her shoulder and even squeezed it. Then he took off his pince-nez, rubbed it thoughtfully with a corner of his handkerchief before murmuring, 'I offer you my sincere condolences, miss. This is another hard trial for you. Your mother did not have a very cheerful life. Console yourself, if you can, with the thought that she has no doubt now found peace.'

She nodded her head, and only later wondered what he could have meant. Her mother had a sad life? It was a new and disturbing idea. Her mother was her mother! Why go any further?

It took her several months to see the meaning of those words. Not that she conceived suspicions as precise as Jozef did, her ideas are vague but in a way closer to the truth. No, her mother wasn't happy, her mother was sacrificed—to whom? To what? To the ways of the world, perhaps, to customs, to social constraints. Wioletta begins to measure what must have been her existence with such a husband, deprived of friends, of well-meaning and sensitive interlocutors. The doctor seemed to have had her confidence and Wioletta would like to question him now. But he no longer comes by—his protectress is dead; and Jozef is finally able to act on the aversion he always had for him and changed doctors.

But I'm racing ahead, and I see that I have omitted to tell of a scene that is, however, crucial.

It is four days since Clara's death, and this morning we are waiting for Urszula and her husband to arrive from Lemberg for the funeral. It is their first visit here since their marriage—the first six months, Urszula, in short letters, took the liberty of letting it be known that for the time being she had better things to do than think of her family, and, a fortiori, of coming back to see them. Furnishing her home, finding her place in the good Polish society of Lemberg, showing herself in the afternoon under the chestnut trees of the Walys, required all her time and all her energy; she begged their pardon. Then there were the troubles of 1848 that dissuaded them, she and her dear Agenor, from undertaking the journey—although it is but a day in a carriage; but the roads are so unsafe!

Finally, here they are, in the first days of 1849. Their coach stops in front of the gate, Urszula gets out. She is wearing her black cape and mantilla with a certain flair, and her face, if it remains unattractive, radiates importance. Isn't her return home in the gratifying role of Married Daughter (the young Hungarians obviously weren't able to make the journey), come to bring her poor father and her young sisters the support of her tears, of her new domestic abilities, a victory?

'Oh, Papa! What a terrible tragedy!' she cries, throwing herself on the chest of the one concerned who is a bit surprised by these new mannerisms. 'My dear,' she then sighs at Jadwiga with a pained smile on which she quickly places a nice handkerchief hemmed in black, as if to wipe it. And little Zosia is graced with a few maternal gestures: a gloved hand caresses her hair and a finger rights the collar of her blouse (I don't know what Zosia thinks of this attention—she bursts into tears and runs to seek refuge inside while Urszula, obviously perfect, shrugs her shoulders with exquisite indulgence). A simple nod to Wioletta. Initiated through married life, the young Madame Karlowiczowa has now understood the strange rumours that have been going around about her sister and, so as not to be damaged by them, felt herself obliged to publicly condemn, that is in front of three dowagers, such a lapse. Wioletta is no longer her sister. It is indeed unfortunate, but her behaviour should not condemn all the women of the family to live as pariahs, should it?

Meanwhile *dear* Agenor has also stepped down. He, too, looks well. His black suit is almost elegant, his thick hair is staying in place. One senses here that a conjugal authority has taken things in hand and influenced his choice of wardrobe, his hair cream, his nail polish. Goodness! Poor Agenor; I think we can have a bit of pity for him.

But I think this only for a moment. Because after he has solemnly greeted Mr Zemka and his fourth daughter with a few appropriate words, he approaches Wioletta who has remained in the background, and leans over her hand to kiss it; and suddenly, as if she has received an electric shock, Wioletta pulls back her hand, trembles and turns away, a flood of pain fills her chest, with memories, images, regrets. And then I understand everything. It was he.

9

I understand, but I can't reconcile it. Such a sacrifice, such a renunciation of any life worthy of that name for a short-legged boy with a nasal voice, who, during their first real encounter had nothing better to say than that his feet hurt! Wioletta, please explain: What did you see in him?

Thinking back to that ball when Wioletta was debuting in the world, I begin to see, however, what she might have seen in Agenor—he didn't frighten her.

But really, how from that could she have gone to love, passion, the gift of her body—when Agenor pleased her precisely because he seemed to remain like a brother, indifferent to her body?

I wonder.

What I am reading in her now doesn't enlighten me much. She is remembering stormy discussions, phrases from him expressing doubts that devastate her; and finally an obscure bodily contact that, if I see correctly, seems to have been consummated one summer afternoon, when it was very hot, in a badly lit place that I am unable to identify. Was it here, in an outbuilding, was it in some uninhabited hut on the estate? What deviousness, in any case, what impudent hiding!

Here I am losing my temper like a vulgar Jozef Zemka. Let's keep a clear head. It was not deviousness that pushed her to that embrace, no more than it was blindness. In her memory as I read it, it was an act of despair, an all-or-nothing that she was playing out while overcoming her fears, her modesty—*because she could no longer do otherwise.* What is awakening in her, at the moment when the infamous one who got out of the carriage is bending over her hand to place his lips upon it, is a memory of abstract pleasure—the feeling of that other body, inhabited by a soul that didn't want her, nevertheless giving in to the attraction of her, of seeking it out, wedding it; of being able to wrap her arms around that fugitive being, and of seeing him, with minimal gratitude, place his mouth in the curve of a motionless palm that, a few minutes earlier, had been clutched in a gesture of beseeching persuasion.

My beautiful Wioletta, to beg this big boy to take you! It is too much for me—the idea is revolting.

A rapid calculation tells me that little Feliks must have been conceived scarcely a few days before Agenor's and Urszula's marriage. It was no doubt during that encounter, scraps of which I perceive; because I can't discern any others in Wioletta's memory.

The unfortunate girl must have believed that this last card she could play might have still changed the course of events, that the pact of her blood could have been stronger than the engagement that had already been announced. It was a losing card; after that, she held no other.

What torture that wedding must have been! And she still didn't know the worst at that time—that her all-or-nothing indeed had consequences, the most dramatic consequences that she would have to face. (He was also unaware of this at that moment, I must at least give him that.) And how I now regret not having observed her better during the blessing in the chapel! I was looking only at Clara who was crying. I thought that she, and Urszula, of course, were the central figures in the scene, Clara the sad and obvious heroine of the day. I had only glanced at Wioletta although even then I had found her not looking well. But I had attributed that to emotion. Such a fragile flower, I thought at the time, shrivelling up at the slightest bit of wind; it took only this ceremony to torture her simply because she was part of the family and people were looking at her. I had even shrugged (metaphorically) before going back to the mother, because so much prudery was somewhat annoying.

And I had been wrong about her.

And I now see the cruelty of the brief dialogue to which I had not paid much attention at the time. It was—let's see, was it before or after the engagement? It doesn't matter; it was the preceding spring when Agenor had returned from the waters. Urszula was sitting on a bench on the grounds and, with her folded parasol was sullenly drawing circles in the dust. Out of the corner of her eye she was watching, at a distance, her fiancé or intended who was kneeling down to remove a burr from Wioletta's dress—speaking to her, but not smiling—a sign, I now recognize, that was rather suspicious, because it indicated the intimacy of a serious discussion, even a quarrel. That had lasted some time; Agenor then stood up, they exchanged a few more words, then Wioletta walked away quickly towards the gate of the grounds. And Agenor, looking upset, had returned to the bench.

Urszula had played a bit more with her parasol before saying, 'There you are. I was getting worried.' A silence—a little inner debate between jealousy and pride. 'Sometimes I almost have the impression that you prefer my sister over me.'

He had not taken her hand then (no, they weren't yet engaged). He had only looked at her with his placid brown eyes, with an affection that, I would swear, wasn't forced. Of that I am sure—he was, he is sincerely attached to Urszula. I won't say that this attachment rests on something as burning and corrosive as love; rather on an intuition, a conviction that there was something in her similar to him, something positive, ambitious, that she was a true partner on the path that he had chosen without yet appearing to have come close to it. And he had responded, 'My dear, your sister Wioletta is lovely, but she frightens me a bit. She is a tragic heroine. A wise man, you know, stays well away from tragic heroines.'

But—again, according to my calculations—he was courting Wioletta then, that Wioletta who frightened him a bit. At least there was already the beginning of a connection between them, he must have foreseen putting his rifle on the other shoulder and choosing the third sister rather than the second, even if he had to wait a few years more to marry her. What must she have done, poor Wioletta, for Agenor Karlowicz to prefer her homely sister with the bad character over her? How could she have managed to *frighten* such a level-headed person?

Deep down, I can imagine it.

It had begun with friendship, with confidence. She saw him every day sharpening their pencils, laughing with them, bringing them fashion magazines, agreeing to sing duets with them. How nice it was, how pleasant to be so distracted from her phantasmagoria, those phantoms that had haunted her for ever! How they had fun together, Agenor and the sisters! And how they had missed him in the dark days of 1846 when everything outside their house was frightening and threatening, confirming the dark idea that she had created of the human world!

She had missed him, had thought of him during his long stay in Karlsbad. Urszula was lucky; he would be a good companion if he married her, someone with whom life would be easy and joyful. But would he marry her? It wasn't certain. When Wioletta remembered those months of his attention, she didn't see anything, or only the expectations of her family, which indicated that Urszula had been the chosen one. Upon reflection it was rather she, Wioletta, whose presence he had sought out; and more than once she had caught him looking at her admiringly.

Of course, she was more beautiful than her sister, and no one would have been surprised at his preference—except Urszula. Urszula was counting on him, and Urszula was first in line, due to her birth order, and due to the physical disadvantages that nature had given her. Wioletta would have committed an evil deed by entering the battle with the more powerful weapons of her almond-shaped eyes, her heavy hair, her figure (she was aware, even though she was very little drawn to that sort of examination), thin and supple like a reed, and made for . . . made for . . . she didn't really want to know what for but was beginning to sense that flexibility and suppleness could be, in a mysterious realm, advantageous qualities.

When they danced, for example . . .

Those memories of balls were not good memories—when a man's arm squeezed her around her waist, they were like opaque allusions to something else that made her sick to think about. However, it seemed to her that if Agenor had invited her to dance, his arm would not have caused her the same discomfort. It would have been the arm of a brother, of the big brother who would explain to you how it was done, no more nor less than if he was teaching you how to play croquet. It is true that Agenor didn't dance very well, and, in fact, didn't really like to dance. But . . . it was a shame that they had never waltzed together. Urszula had seen to that!

Her mind began to rebel against the dogma that had ruled their upbringing. Urszula was ugly, and, what is more, she did not have an assigned place among the sisters. She wasn't the eldest, nor the youngest, not pious nor an artist—she was simply the one who would be difficult to marry off. But how could you not see that this handicap, in the end, had become a privilege? That through a reverse injustice it was to her that henceforth all the encouragement, all the preferential treatment, the enviable suitor, their father's eagerness to pad her dowry, would go?

Even the seamstress who devoted infinitely more time to her than to any other woman in the family, determining with their mother which folds would best enhance her figure, what shades would make her complexion stand out. Lubienka killed herself to puff out bands that would hide the pock marks on her cheeks; and when Urszula was ready to appear in the salon, starched, curled, decked out like a reliquary, the other girls and their father were called into the hallway and everyone exclaimed before the beautiful work.

When at the fabric merchant's shop Wioletta timidly asked for some satin or a ribbon whose colour she thought would suit her, her mother only shrugged her shoulders and whispered softly to her, 'Now, my daughter, this navy blue will be fine for you . . .'

And one day when, overcoming the terror he inspired in her, she had asked for her father's support about some dress matter, he had looked her up and down with an air that seemed to say, 'Bah! Make do with what you have.'

She understood, but it wasn't fair. Was it even right? A family, sisters, could give in more or less willingly to this forced distribution of advantages. But why would others, outsiders, consent to the same sacrifice? If Agenor preferred her—and it increasingly seemed that this was the case—why would he fight, in the name of interests that didn't concern him at all, against his natural inclination?

And so she gathered her courage. And she understood better the long absence of the young man—he was hesitating. It was certainly not a small matter to disappoint the one who was already his titular love and to disappoint at the same time the entire household.

(I believe on that point Wioletta was right. I can see no other explanation for Agenor's manoeuvres, and I remember that, in the final weeks before the Galician riots and his flight to Karlsbad, he seemed ill at ease and silent in front of Wioletta; it should have intrigued me, so contrary was that to his usual joviality).

When he returned, she had decided not to do anything. She would do nothing to encourage him, because that would have been to betray her sister and to demean herself. But nor would she do anything to discourage him if he proved to be more explicit towards her. Urszula's misfortune should not condemn to despair two beings who were in love.

And so she didn't hide her pleasure at his return, and stopped remaining in the background as she had in the past. Of course, Urszula was always there, slipping into a conversation, or coming to take, *manu militari*, the arm of the young man at the moment he was about to slip it under Wioletta's elbow. And so she put down her weapons; but several times she noticed a glimmer of regret in Agenor's eyes.

How complicated life was, and how heavy was decorum! These discreet overtures were not enough. Agenor, too, was no doubt held back by his feelings of honour; maybe he was shy, like she was. She gradually fell in love with him, with the qualities in him that, under the circumstances, were an obstacle to her desires but which pleased her in the absolute (and in which—this time I can affirm, because I know what happened—he was entirely lacking. It was here that she began to go astray, and all her misfortunes arose out of this error in judgement). She melted with love when he observed her silently, then lowered his eyes, as if to say, '*That one* is not for me—why would I find favour in her eyes?' Oh yes, she was for him. How she wished she could disabuse him of his error!

I remember another conversation, with Zygmunt this time. He was teaching the girls about the American Revolution and the outline of the US Constitution, and, at the end of the lesson, Wioletta lingered to ask him some questions. 'And do you think it is legitimate to pursue one's happiness, Mr Borowski?'

'Well, of course,' he had answered, flustered by a question that awakened many intimate thoughts in him. And, to hide them from her, he had launched into considerations of political philosophy that she had listened to thoughtfully, frowning.

'. . . It is curious, though, that such a religious nation inscribed in its principles the right to pursue happiness, a right that is fundamentally opposed to the spirit of revealed religions. At most, those religions make happiness the reward for those who fear God and respect His laws, but still. If one might sum up what they think of happiness here on earth, it would come to one sentence, an eleventh commandment: You will be happy with your unhappiness. But . . .'

'Yes?'

'Well,' Zygmunt, who had forgotten his pupil, jumped, 'that shows that the United States of America is a curious laboratory, and that they no doubt still have many surprises ahead for us. I'll take this opportunity to ask you, Wioletta, to be careful with your cursive—the circles recently have not been well formed.'

For what followed, for the interval that occurred between Wioletta's discussion with her tutor and the little dialogue between the almost engaged, I am reduced to suppositions. How could the liaison have occurred? A mystery.

Wioletta must have stood before Agenor with her beauty, her sensitivity, her love that had already become ardent through waiting, and her scruples. She put all of this naively before him and, with the optimism of her age, believed that this would be enough, because he loved her and because nothing was yet settled with Urszula.

But that wasn't enough, my poor girl. It was too much, much too much, for the soul of an Agenor. But how could that innocent girl have understood a soul such as his?

10

They didn't read Russian novels in the Zemka home, and it was a pity. Wioletta would have been more wary of Agenor Karlowicz if she could have understood that he was, in his own way, 'a hero of our time'. Oh! There were no great deeds or phlegmatic bravura in that level-headed being; but he belonged to a human type that flourished in that era and which must have caused other comparable dramas in other homes.

Agenor was one of those young men who had entered into adulthood with the sad and crushing idea that they had been born too late, that they belonged to a race of eternal descendants. Or that they would never be anything but descendants. Their grandfathers had known the Napoleonic wars, had distinguished themselves in those conflicts; they had been born after the Congress of Vienna. Their fathers, still young, had valiantly sacrificed themselves for their freedom—the Russians by rebelling in vain against a despotic tsar, the French by overthrowing the last king of the Restoration, the Poles themselves by launching into a struggle for independence that had been ferociously crushed; at that time Agenor's generation was still swaddled or playing with hoops. They had been only spectators, and that position had become the key to their lives. They observed. A number of their contemporaries were heated by the causes of their elders, hoped, like Jan Zemka or Zygmunt Borowski, to take up their struggles, aware that history was always stammering and waiting, with more or less patience; that it will once again open its mouth. Agenor's kind considered that ability to wait with an astonishment mixed with irony. They would have really liked to believe in it too. But weren't they convinced that history was coming to an end, that that stammering was only the drivel of old age, that it was approaching the last degree of senility?

This taste for sceptical observation often made them intelligent men; which Jan had indeed seen the first time he met his future brother-in-law. Under the mask of nonchalance, Agenor was listening to everything, knew how to detect in the most superficial dialogue those inflections that betrayed a position, an intellectual or moral type. And nothing delighted him more than to discover in those conditions a hybrid, a rarity, one that he was quick to add to his catalogue of the spirit of the time. Whence that political finesse that would earn him the career we know of.

His talents were at first exercised only in the social world. How interesting they were, those workings of the soul, the feelings and the appetites that one could observe in the social world! The political dramas that were played out in Lemberg seemed much less captivating than the salon debates, the little exchange of replies that, starting with the soup course of an elegant dinner, signalled to whoever wanted to listen that such and such a lover had just been replaced by her rival. That was when he wanted to clap his hands and cry 'Bravo!'

He liked the muted, the unsaid, which was more attractive to his talent for analysis; outbursts frightened his blasé nature. What! All this noise for such interesting things, of course, but that are as intangible as the honour of a woman, a divergence of interpretation of worldly events? Did that really call for us to shout out, to kill one another in a field outside town? I often heard, right here, people praise his measured character that, in such affairs, had enabled him to be a mediator and prevent blood from being shed unnecessarily.

But, after some time, the social world of Lemberg had no doubt tired him—he knew it by heart. What new perspectives could be offered by the inner-workings of a country squirearchy! And then, he really should get married. That's what one did. It was even an obligatory passage if one didn't have one's own fortune or a powerful family. It would be fun too, to have a permanent subject of observation beside him, and to finally become, himself, an object of observation for another.

Because that is his flaw. That entomologist suffers from solitude among all those little beasts whose behaviour he is studying. Sometimes he would like to have someone with whom he could be surprised, laugh and exchange views.

More profoundly (but he doesn't admit this; I can only deduce it from the sharp remarks he addressed to Wioletta when they were together and which, in that moment, bubbled up in her memory while Agenor, flustered, went to take the arm of his new wife as they climbed the front steps), he has an open sore in him—his nonchalance, his coolness are a moral infirmity of which he is secretly ashamed. Woe be to the one who perceives this and, worse, forces him to admit it!

I believe Wioletta was that one.

He must have, he absolutely must have been interested in her—so pretty, so alive, so tormented. So proud! How piquant it would be to observe that collision between two so very different sisters who, apparently, were both interested in him. Did he immediately set out to make them rivals? I don't think he was that perverse; at least, if one sees perversity as the pure pleasure of causing pain. But if one sees it as the impulse that in part lies to itself, is covered with uncertainty, is in love with that which it destroys—then yes, absolutely, Agenor was a great pervert.

Such a conciliatory man (his role in the compromise that, in 1867, would give birth to the double monarchy would earn him, I remember, the affectionate nickname of 'Karlowicz the matchmaker') would not on his own have sought out the quarrels to which his liaison with Wioletta was reduced, would not spontaneously have acted with such harshness. For that, he really had to lose control of himself, act outside himself—for that he had, however briefly, to have been in love.

In love, the placid Agenor!

And that new condition was not in his plan.

He truly desired that beautiful girl. He really wanted her to love him enough to give herself to him. But already that desire was destabilizing and becoming, for him, a source of anxiety. Desire something? Had he ever desired anything in his life? It wasn't pleasant. It made your heart beat, woke you up at night. A little victory (the hand you touched while playing a game, for example, and which wasn't withdrawn) made you happy only for five minutes; afterwards, you needed more. A lack of satisfaction became your way of life; you were never content, never at peace. You didn't belong to yourself—you were delivered up, body and soul, to the whim of another.

And what other!

I look back in detail at the couple they formed in the garden in the spring, the day when Wioletta had caught the bottom of her navy blue dress (which didn't suit her at all, and whose little white collar made her look like a governess in a school play) on a thorn bush. What were they saying to each other that day that made them separate, one in tears, the other irritated enough to go and sit in Urszula's company?

'. . . I can't go on like this, Agenor, this situation is torturing me. When are you going to tell her? I can't look her in the face any more since you told me you love me.'

'This makes me think, my dear, that I should never have told you such a thing. Up to then you seemed happy, your eyes shone when they looked upon my humble self. Since then, you seem agitated, torn, suffering . . . Believe me, I feel guilty.'

'How silly, Agenor! I suffer only for having to lie to my sister, and to hide from her, uselessly, something she will have to learn sooner or later. What's the use of waiting, why let her keep her illusions any longer? It's cruel for her, and for me . . .'

'Shh, you terrible little selfish one,' said Agenor in a scandalized tone that was corrected, or, rather, complicated by a caress given apparently inadvertently on the ankle he was freeing. 'You have already taken her place in my heart. Does your victory in addition have to be thrown in her face? Give her a bit more time, and me as well. We sensitive souls, we need to store up our courage when it's a matter of hurting—what am I saying, hurting—I mean, striking to the death.'

'Oh, don't say that, it's horrible . . .'

He squeezed his hand on the white cotton stocking—a gesture that she should have known (Zygmunt had said so) she couldn't allow him and which, henceforth, placed her already on the fatal decline; because that hand squeezing the top of her boot, alas, no longer frightened her. What was that shaking in her body, that delicious warmth that was climbing to her knees? Surely, it was bad to feel such happiness when the hour was so serious, when her sister was suffering, alone on her bench over there, and was going to suffer a great deal more . . .

'It's horrible, yes, but it is your work, dear love. Here are our beautiful merciless ladies—they plunge their dagger into innocent hearts, and faint at the sight of the blood that flows!'

'Why are you making fun of me?' stammered Wioletta, her eyes filling with tears. 'I am nothing like a merciless beautiful lady. I suffer too, and perhaps as much as she, because I love you with all my heart and you are only saying mean things to me.'

Agenor pulled back when he heard that naively sincere speech. Something buried, a sensitivity that had been repressed for ever, was whispering to him, 'So admire her, see what courage she has to say that to you, to you who were mocking her! This is how those who are in love act—disarmed, begging, unspeakably weak. But in that weakness what strength, what audacity!'

Immediately, however, he pulled himself together. No, he didn't want to hear that. What did she hope to do in telling him such things? Delve into his heart, take his fortress, put her finger on his infirmity and, while she's at it, cure him of it? She should leave him alone with her wringing hands, her moist eyes and her declarations!

The little stifled voice, however, was still arguing, 'But this sincerity, this emotion should not be feared. It is only love, and love for you— you have everything to gain, let yourself go, don't be afraid . . .'

Afraid? I'm not afraid, his mind replied coldly, a mind that was ironic but rather vulnerable too, if one looked at it closely. (And Agenor, at that moment, let go of the dress, the ankle and stood up, rubbing his knees.) I'm absolutely not afraid; but I know what I want and what I don't want. What would my life be like alongside such an exalted, such an inflammable creature?

'An adventure; a beautiful adventure, constantly renewed . . .'

No thank you—not my cup of tea. A constantly renewed adventure, indeed! Leave me alone— I don't want to hear talk like that.

He hated her at that moment, the ardent Wioletta (that hatred was no doubt indissociable from his love. Today, as she has just rejected his greeting, he sees that, no longer loving her, he doesn't hate her, either, and experiences a bit of remorse for what he did to her—although he immediately decides not to lose too much time pitying her, a feeling that, as experience has taught him, is completely useless). He hated her for what she had more of than he, and for showing him in so such an obvious way. And that is why he then went away to join Urszula on her bench, not without adding over his shoulder, 'My dear, that martyred tone doesn't suit you. Please, find that proud reserve that is one of your greatest charms. Advice from a friend.'

Such rebuffs probably only made Wioletta go even further—on a forward flight dictated by a sure instinct of what would hurt her. Yes,

Wioletta also had her flaw—words that should not be said, gestures that should not be made attracted her as irresistibly as a moth to a flame. She threw herself into it, burnt her wings, did all she could to make things irreparable. It was no doubt out of a taste for the absolute; perhaps also from a desire (stifled) to act on her destiny. If the only possible action for her was to ruin herself, well, she would ruin herself; nothing could be more horrible than to wait, to languish, to be passively suspended by the decision of others.

A bad calculation, because it led her straight into complete subjugation. The more she gave of herself to Agenor in the hope that her audacity would cause the little voice of sensitivity to triumph in him (because Wioletta heard it too, but unfortunately heard only it), the more he retreated, afraid; until the day when, having given him everything and, hence, having definitely closed her heart, she could only return powerless to the paternal bosom and submit herself to its law.

How restful the company of her sister should have been for Agenor! Urszula held no tiresome surprises; the key to her feelings for him were gratitude, and a peaceful feeling of ownership. Nothing moving, nothing dizzying, nothing unforeseeable—this is how he conceived of life as it should be.

And to all outward appearances that union was a success. In the first years it is obvious that Urszula has blossomed. She can give free reign to her taste for authority which has not been seen before; she manages her home with an iron hand, gains the assurance that, later, would allow her to turn her salon into a pole, a place where it is useful to show oneself and where many things are decided. In short, she is a formidable asset for her husband, and the indispensable cement of a couple, the gratitude between them not flowing in a single direction.

He is truly attached to her. And, I am sure, he doesn't have other lovers, except perhaps the maid but only in passing. First, because a liaison outside the home always carries some risk, and there have been high officials who have fallen for less than that. Then, he isn't so stupid—he needs his wife and her devotion too much.

To satisfy his perverse nature, he has only to think of the mire upon which their union was built, of that secret that his wife still doesn't know.

With Wioletta, it was an adultery in anticipation, once and for all; he doesn't need more. He lives with a crime, he lives in the crime—that seduced and abandoned sister-in-law, that son he has somewhere and for whom, God willing, he would never be brought to account. It is a stimulating thought. Without it he would be bored, would seek another abyss to narrowly escape, would commit imprudent acts. Deep down he has his little share of shivers, above him his sword of Damocles whose blade sparkles but which he knows is safely stowed away.

And it is good this way. The most powerful cities were founded on the blood of a dead person; the most lasting buildings, somewhere deep in their walls, have skeletons. For the Karlowicz family, Wioletta was that Remus killed in front of the walls of Rome, that living cat that one walls up as a propitiatory offering.

11

There was nothing like that under my cellars or in my walls. Count Fryderyk was a rational spirit, a friend of philosophers and a strong adversary of the superstition of the people. He would have forbidden it.

This is what made me think at that time that I would perhaps not be as enduring as all that. It showed me that I was also a bit superstitious. The fact is that existence here was beginning to weigh on me; and whoever no longer likes his life assumes it will be short.

I had lost my self-assurance in discovering that I didn't know everything, that I could be wrong and miss—let's say it—what was essential. Wioletta, in her room on the second floor, had become a thorn in my side. I watched her, she never left my eyes; but what was there to see now? It was a duty I had assigned myself, one that was as pious as it was lacking in utility.

A certain sadness, a certain pessimism did indeed begin to slip into my perception of the world. It seemed that in me there was the moral equivalent of those mushrooms that attack the woods and day after day poison the atmosphere and anyone who breathes it in. I couldn't do anything about it but I felt it—I had something in me that was poisonous, a leavening of misfortune, and it was just beginning.

And then there were all those departures. First, my poor Clara. Although I told myself that her end had been a good end, an act of belated but complete emancipation, and observed with a sense of revenge the effects that act had on her brutal husband, her disappearance left a huge emptiness in me. What would I be without Clara? Hadn't she been my discreet and loving magnet, my musical angel, even when she didn't play? Remember, I knew her, as did Doctor Weinberg (another whom we no longer saw), since her late adolescence—she had been the first human whose fate I was truly interested in.

And Zygmunt! He was one of my rare male inhabitants whom I began to like (aside from him I had conceived, about the virile part of humanity, a rather low opinion: predation, authoritarianism, abuse of power . . . I could go on and on); and he left without looking back, wounded by his first love, his heart full of reproaches that he didn't know were unjust. Gone, in short, never to return. Was this the life of people? To be connected to others, grow attached to them, put one's hopes in them—and to be cruelly stricken by their departure or their death? I regretted not having stayed in my place, having wanted to escape the common lot of houses, passive, without affect and consequently without pain.

I often thought of Zygmunt, I wondered what he might be doing at a certain moment, and where. I assumed he had one of those unsettled lives, going from exile to exile, in which only ideas form an element of stability and coherence. Given his little concern for danger, one might fear that his life would be short. But that is not certain, because once, in 1864, I believe there was news of him.

I was asleep at that time, as I will explain later. But a door slammed, I partially awoke and my sleep-filled eye fell on one of Jozef's newspapers lying open on the footstool. A correspondent in London was describing a meeting that had been held to discuss the creation of an international worker's movement and it cited several Polish names among those in attendance. Was that he, that 'S. Borowski' who was mentioned? The first initial wasn't the same; moreover, it would have been surprising for Zygmunt, that essential subversive, not to see fit to assume a pseudonym. I would have continued to read to see whether, further on, S. Borowski might have said something to clarify things. But at that moment Jozef came into the room, took the paper, skimmed the page with a frown and, growling, balled it up and threw it into the fireplace.

Yes, whatever became of Zygmunt? Did he ever understand what had played out within my walls that he had left in so much anger, bitterness and pain? I think he threw himself into the flow of collective action and, my goodness, never came out of it again. That youthful love must have remained in him like a burning ulcer, the thought of which he suppressed as much as he could. For in the life of a conspirator there is no room for weakness, for the outpouring of emotion, for sentimental regrets. Furthermore, what would he have regretted? The circumstances of his departure did not encourage regret. Clara's suicide could have opened his eyes; but did he ever learn of it? At best, he could have learnt of her death and be surprised that it came so soon after his departure. However, since even those close to Clara only had suspicions and did all they could not to have them spread, he would have necessarily accepted the explanation of the 'fatal fever'.

(. . . While he was young. I'm not ruling out that later, when he was in turn at a more advanced age, he might have gradually guessed what a terrible sacrifice had been made for him. Clara had pushed him away so he could live and follow his path. I sincerely hope that at such a moment of understanding he was able to think that his path had been worth it; and, I don't know why, I have confidence in him on this.)

And there were other departures, other holes in this canvas whose multiple threads connected me, in a certain sense, to the history of the world.

The active Adam had finally found the death he had hoped for—on horseback, facing the enemy, in a struggle for independence that he supported through pure solidarity and which was thus all the more sacred in his eyes. He had been given military honours and his officer's soul must have rested in peace. In addition, he was lucky enough to die in time not to see the defeat of those Hungarians, his brothers, whom the empire had shamefully crushed thanks to the support of the tsar; so as not to learn that many of his comrades in arms, Bem, Wysocki and his son Jan, with his wife and little Mathilde, would be forced into an exile even more extreme than his own—to the Ottoman Empire, among the Turks, who had received them with open arms and given more than one officer a place in the armies of the Sublime Porte.

And so Jozef had lost his brother only seven or eight months after he lost his wife. (This is why, on the afternoon of 1850 that I mentioned earlier, the tea and mocha cake was served by Elvire Denisot who was still in half mourning.) To the extent that the first loss had disturbed him, the second seemed to be inscribed harmoniously in the order of things. His pain, under these circumstances, had been clearer, purer; nothing here to be hidden from the neighbours. *Pan* Zemka had lost his brother, an ardent patriot, the bold Zemka-Ponarski who had attempted (at his age!) a counter-offensive with a handful of men, just before the defeat of Temesvár. It was almost epic. Yes, one could definitely mourn with pride.

But now Jozef was alone, completely alone. No more good national consciousness observing him at a distance from the City of Lights, no more double heroics doing for him what he didn't have the time or desire to undertake. It was a relief; but it was also a challenge, and Jozef knew that it was a challenge he would never attempt to face.

And Jadwiga, as well, would leave a few months later. It took these shake-ups, these deaths, these tragedies for the bold decision to germinate and take root in her—she would devote her soul to God. Her mother taken by a sudden illness; her eldest sister gone to Constantinople among the Muslims; Wioletta fallen into disgrace, the causes for which her younger sister did not truly understand, and henceforth leading a sequestered life under the cloud of scandal—it was too much for Jadwiga. In her Benedictine convent, she wanted quickly to find the calm, the rest, and above all the certainty she sought. At least God would not die, would not go live on the banks of the Bosphorus, would not be subject to the nasty gossip of Madame Denisot.

What changes there were, then, and changes for the worse! How cold the climate had become in the last two or three years, how far away were 'those good old days' of apparent tranquility I, like Jozef, was yearning for!

There was no one left to add a bit of life to the place except little Zosia. And yet, at close to sixteen, even this sprite, under the blows of recent events, was tending (temporarily) to settle down. There was no more mischievousness, no more impulsive remarks; she folded in on herself, taught herself by delving into the books left behind by Mr Borowski, and, without knowing it, was gathering her strength for the great event that would soon propel her a thousand leagues from our world.

As for distractions, I don't even count the visits of her sister from Lemberg who, now a mother, came regularly to show us the little face and the hesitant steps of her little Andrzej. Elvire was delighted; Wioletta stayed in her room; Zosia played distractedly with her nephew, who destroyed her dress and screamed shouts of joy in the garden, while wondering if she really wanted to start a family. Jozef never failed to say to Urszula, 'And when will we have the pleasure of seeing dear Agenor?' then, after a weak response (Agenor avoided setting foot here as much as he could), went to take refuge in his factory. He rejoiced at finally having a male descendant but the little fellow shrieked louder than a girl!

The factory—that was another new thing that shook my daily existence.

It now stood behind me, to the right of the hamlet. The poplars that, today, in part hide it from me, had just been planted along one of the banks of the diverted river. Through them, I could distinctly see its tile roof, its arched windows and the entrance flanked by a white colonnade that made it a miniature replica of me.

(At the beginning, Jozef had wanted it made entirely of brick, that's true. But when the work was finished, seeing that reddish cube which ruined the view of the bucolic landscape, he changed his mind: 'Good heavens! We aren't in Manchester, are we?'

So they added the little façade, the very Galician colonnade, and put white badigeon on everything, which had the advantage of hiding the inscription 'Zemka Brothers', now sadly out of date.)

The smoke that escaped almost constantly from the three large smokestacks added a modern and industrial flavour to our fields, to the best effect. Aware of their status, they looked from on high at the greyish exhalations furtively emerging from the roofs of the cottages. They had no rivals; *Pan* Zemka's factory remained a rather frightening anomaly, one that could be pointed out from a distance. I had to get used to no longer being the focal point of the region. My little twin sister had taken my place.

I was no longer the centre of the world, or at least of a small world, except for my inhabitants and for a few others who were more or less at a distance: Jan and Maria in Constantinople; perhaps Salomon Weinberg. For some unfortunates, the centre of the world is precisely the place where they never set foot; in this category I must also include Vasyl Doroshenko, the now adult son of Jozef, who began to nourish a despondent obsession for the estate and sometimes wandered around its edges. And finally, for some twenty or so others, suppliers and game-keepers whose existence still depended directly on me.

For the others I was now only the symbol, and not the seat, of economic power. In Grünau, they spoke less about me. The sugar factory—I heard said in the kitchen—was the focus of all hopes. Every notable hoped to see his investments grow, every poor family dreamt of placing its excess offspring there. That might happen in time; for the time being, only some hundred fortunate souls worked there, chosen by Jozef and Gavryl from among the most deserving of the former serfs. Every morning I saw them converge upon the factory, watched by brothers, cousins, grandfathers nodding their heads. In the evening, as they were leaving, they caused less envy. Of course, they weren't very dirty, and didn't have to endure the biting cold or the burning sun, but they couldn't hide their bent backs, their sunken chests and hacking coughs. But they were still lucky. At Christmas, they received as a gift an entire box of Pastilles de la Vierge, offered them to their neighbours, then left the empty box lingering negligently on the table; they might even use it to hold some meagre savings.

And three times a day, carts stopped behind the screen of poplars, received their loads, then approached me—because the road leading directly from the factory to the town had not yet been constructed. I saw these comings and goings of worker ants, that laborious agitation of which I was no longer the soul; and I happened to think that I was now a beautiful, useless thing, a declining coquette who held forth on everything without really knowing anything.

12

Most of the time, what remained of the family gathered in the little blue salon to listen to a letter that the Zemkas in Turkey had sent to them by some traveller crossing the Black Sea and going up the Dniester. It also happened that the letter would come through Paris where many old émigrés had settled. They were proud that one of these letters had passed, by way of an entire chain of benevolent postmen, through the hands of Mickiewicz, the great Mickiewicz himself, whose bust, on the mantle, Jozef henceforth contemplated with a bit more familiar veneration. He had touched with his fingers a letter from his son-in-law; hadn't he become part of the family?

As for the tenor of these missives—they left more to be desired. Jozef found his nephew quite discreet on the future of the national movement, on the chances for support from the Ottomans. Caution dictated this, no doubt. But, deep down, Jozef felt humiliated that Jan had withdrawn his confidence in him, had inherited the views of his soldier father, and, to be perfectly frank, no longer counted on him. Why? he wondered. What did I do wrong? Aren't I what I have always been?

While he was ruminating on this last question, to which I will refrain from answering, Madame Denisot was complaining in a weak voice that they know so little about little Mathilde. 'She is growing,' wrote the mother. At the very least! Was she walking, talking? Did she go to Mass with her mother? Were there even any churches in that part of the world, and could an honest woman go into the streets without the risk of being kidnapped by a janissary and locked up in a sultan's seraglio?

'A seraglio, Madame Denisot! It seems you have forgotten you are speaking in front of a young girl!' scolded Jozef.

'Oh, my goodness,' stammered the French woman, blushing deeply and lamenting, once again, the death of Madame Zemka which had diverted onto her the teasing of the master of the house.

These letters from Constantinople left them wanting more. One sensed that their authors were busy with other things, implanted in another world, converted to a culture of exile about which they knew nothing. One also sensed a sort of fatigue, material concerns. In Maria's tone one guessed the always pleasant face of a cherished wife but on which the uncertainty of the following day and the exile in general had perhaps traced some precocious lines.

And Zosia wasn't happy. There was not much point in having a sister in Constantinople if she said nothing about the city, the country, its customs, its inhabitants! 'It's really humid in the winter, and Jan is coughing again'—apart from a remark on the many dogs wandering around that barked at night and awakened Mathilde, that was the extent of the information Maria ever gave on her surroundings. But what about the sofas, the hookahs, the fezes, the Golden Horn? What did they see in the bazaars, what were the smells of the Orient?

Wioletta also found these letters too short. Because once they were read, her father folded them and stared at his daughter with an eloquent look—it was the moment for her to get up and leave the salon where they tolerated her only in exceptional circumstances.

She then went up the stairs, walking slowly on purpose to be able to hear some final words of the conversation. Not that they were of great interest; she was looking for a certain family normalcy, that static social dance that is conversation, where each person, speaking in turn, seemed to advance a step, greet the circle, then move back in silence. These fantastic visions began to occupy more space in her mind which had been left empty through inactivity and the loss of those, man and son, whom she had loved. They appealed to her too when, banished to her room, she withdrew to her brushes, her pencils, her paints, and stifled her boredom by reproducing scenes from her everyday life: a hare killed in a hunt, bleeding from the nose into a dish next to a basket of prunes, and which was as sad as the Descent from the Cross; a corner of the garden in the spring which, in spite of its luxuriance and the burst of light, expressed the mysterious dereliction of a world devoid of people. Or she would paint my rooms, an angle of the salon, a winter sun falling through a window, and give the sculpted foot of a table, the round cheeks of a teapot, something humanoid that disturbed me a bit because I felt it was too close to my own gaze. She began to paint things the way I saw them—inhabited, almost animate; and it seemed to me that, for the young woman that she was, it was not very healthy.

I was relieved to see her stop working and walk over to the window to look outside and her thoughts once again become what they should have been. Grünau didn't interest her, or not yet. She was looking much further away. She looked for a long time in the direction of Lemberg, as if that scrutiny could, in time, make the inaccessible city appear on the horizon and bring it closer. Then her pupils deviated a bit, wandered to the east, and she took a deep breath—somewhere over there lived her son Feliks, raised by unknowns to whom he was nothing, burdened with the double misfortune of being both illegitimate and Polish in a region where his compatriots were treated very badly.

Because she was aware that her father also received letters from Russia. In reading them he had a certain way of avoiding his daughter's look, and after glancing at the front of the letter, then the back, if there was one, he would murmur, 'Perfect.'

What did he mean by 'perfect'? She wondered with alarm. Coming from her father's mouth shouldn't she deduce that her son was wasting away, was only an annoyance on the way to being resolved?

That wasn't the case, I would have reassured her if I could have. Jozef, through one of his business relationships, had merely had the baby placed with a wet nurse in a remote town in Podolia, estimating that by placing a border between it and them he would more surely prevent any undesirable contact. Every three months a notary informed Jozef that the modest payment had been made to the foster parents, informed him of some extra expenses, and that really was all.

But Wioletta's imagination pulled on its chains, beat its wings like a captive bird. Each letter from Russia alarmed her; at the same time, she prayed it would not be the last, so her father would not look at her in the eyes and, this time, say more, 'Perfect. Well I regret to inform you, miss, that your bastard has died of the croup.'

So much pain and apprehension created a fuel in her that radiated into a suffering beauty. Her almond-shaped eyes were even bigger, her sunken cheeks made her cheekbones stand out; in her lips, always trembling a bit, there was something fragile and desperate that would have forced the love of an objective observer.

'How pretty you are today, Wioletta,' Zosia told her as she caught up with her on her walk after getting away from Madame Denisot. 'But you seem so sad! Come on, let's sit on the bench. What do you think of my skirt? It's my first long skirt, Papa said I could wear it!'

'It looks very good on you. You're lovely . . .'

'Oh, I'll never be as beautiful as you.'

Wioletta didn't respond to that naive statement. No, may her sister never be as beautiful as she, because beauty, what she knew of it, brought only misfortune. May Zosia remain as happy, as lovely, may she be preserved from moral ugliness and from ill will . . . But how could she say that to her sister without saddening her and turning her into a cynic?

'I'm so bored here since Mama died,' the young girl sighed. 'I really wish Mr Borowski hadn't left. He always taught us something. But I feel as if I've forgotten everything.'

'That's only an impression, Zosia. Pick up your old notebooks, you will see that you have retained the essential, even that you understand things better.'

'Do you think so? You might be right, but I . . .'

'Quiet! Go quickly! Our father is watching us.'

Zosia got up quickly—indeed, their father was watching them from the window of the library. He disapproved of these meetings, had essentially forbidden them and assigned the governess the duty of enforcing the prohibition. But Zosia was becoming less docile. Why should she be forbidden from talking to her sister, the only one she had left? After these exchanges, Wioletta was visibly less sad. And why would something that obviously did her good be something bad?

When Zosia turned seventeen, to maintain order Jozef decided to send her to spend a few months with the Karlowicz family. She would be distracted there, would debut in the world, would return a bit less of a girl; and above all she would be removed from the influence of Feliks' mother.

13

So it has been five years since Wioletta received the seed of her misery from Agenor, five years that she hasn't spoken to him. What would she say? Everything has been said between them. And, assuming she has something left to say, the opportunities to do so are almost non-existent.

One might be surprised that such a situation didn't arouse any revolt in her. That would be not to know her very well. Wioletta bears her burden without a word of complaint because she assumes complete responsibility for it. To admit that she is a victim is to admit weakness, blindness, being influenced—no, it is better for her to think that she had gambled and lost.

And so she bends, languishes, lowers her head under the blows she receives every day. She is the dead hare that loses its last drops of blood in the dish; she is the undergrowth full of birds haunted by a cosmic absence. But a tenacious strength burns inside her—her secret, and her determination not to betray it.

That determination continuously fuels Jozef's resentment. Regrets, a tearful confession, would finally give him the sense that he is still the master. But her ability to suffer in silence while only shuddering at innuendos, at looks, maddeningly reminds him of his dead wife—but worse. Because Clara provided Jozef with convenient reasons to scorn her: her religious passion, her awkwardness, her lack of physical grace. But what are Wioletta's faults? She has none. Pain makes her even more beautiful, and the dark dresses that she is now forced to wear only highlight her queen's bearing and her lofty distinction.

Worse still, she is intelligent, with that critical intelligence that he so detests in a woman. He has adopted the routine, after lunch, of reading out newspaper articles that interest him—for the sole pleasure of hearing himself speak these technical or abstruse words to the little group of females around him. (He would not, however, dare to impose the smoke of his cigars on them, but this takes the place of that.) Madame Denisot consistently maintains an air of deep consternation; Zosia takes a little volume from beneath her sash and turns her back halfway to her father to read under the table something she is interested in—travel tales, poems, sentimental novels. But Wioletta really listens, even understands. He can see this in the expressions that pass across her face, in the line of attention between her eyebrows, in the shadow of a smile, which he watches, so it seems, only for the pleasure of being irritated by them.

She had smiled that way last year at the news of the *coup d'état* in France by Louis Napoléon. (How he would have loved to have had his Jan with him then! What an event, what memories, hopes, diplomatic perspectives!) She had smiled, her eyes lowered on her dessert plate; and raised them only during the brief silence that had followed.

'Why are you smiling?'

'Oh,' Wioletta had responded, in the scratchy voice of someone who no longer speaks very often, 'it went through my mind that the United States of America is indeed a strange laboratory . . .'

'And what, may I ask you, do the United States of America have to do with this?'

'But, Father, didn't you read us a short biography of the candidate Bonaparte last year when it was time for the French to elect their president? I remember there was mention that he had travelled to the New World in his youth, and it seemed to me that . . .'

'Spare us, please, what it seemed to you,' Jozef growled, opening up his newspaper with a dry crack. '*The candidate Bonaparte*, really!'

And so Wioletta puts up resistance, in her own way. Everything undermines her but nothing breaks her; one might even say that the blows only strengthen her more.

But ever since it has become a question of sending her young sister to stay in Lemberg, a breach has opened in her armour. It is her first true trial since her fall. Zosia, her only ally, will temporarily disappear from her world, as well—a temporary destined to change into a definitive. For it is indeed a matter of proclaiming to the world her status as a marriageable girl, and it is not out of the question that she will return from her stay engaged. Wioletta is delighted for her. But she would not be a woman, she would not be human if a note of bitterness were not mixed with that joy. Her youngest sister is to be married off—it is thus established, her own unmarriageability is thus sealed.

The trunks that are filled to prepare for the departure, the new long skirts that are quickly made ('but three are enough,' cautions the governess, 'as are only two hats. Madame Karlowiczowa will no doubt take care to take you to better stylists, the best seamstresses in the city. You won't use your outfits from Grünau for very long—I wager that in a week they will already appear frightfully rustic to you'), advice with which the debutante is flooded—don't say 'at home', say, 'on our land', don't ask naive questions, smile at what you don't understand—all of this saddens Wioletta who will never be the focus of such activity.

And there is something else. Zosia will be in daily contact with . . . with their brother-in-law. Zosia who has just slipped into her sister's room to say farewell, fearing that she wouldn't be able to tomorrow at the moment of goodbyes—Zosia will speak to Agenor every day, will take his arm to get out of the carriage, will perhaps serve him tea . . . Lucky, lucky Zosia!

No, on second thoughts, Wioletta would be mad to envy her that. Agenor is a cad with a heart of stone—his absolute silence all those years is sufficient proof for her. Not a word, not a look of compassion the only time he came back to bury their mother! He is a bad man, she affirms in her heart, even if she is the only one in the world to think so.

(Because throughout the region one can't stop talking about the miracle of the love that has transformed this wonderful weak-willed boy into a very esteemed counsellor of the governor Goluchowski, a good husband, even a good father—Countess Wytocka still tenderly tells how one evening, in town, among mutual friends, he had left before dessert when a messenger sent by his wife had informed him that his son Andrzej, then an infant, had fallen ill.)

Wioletta has always been indignant at that silence; but today, it seems that she should, rather, have been surprised at it. Shouldn't the cunning that she attributed to Agenor have made him capable of maintaining the role of brother-in-law towards her? Of course, she is a fallen woman to whom a respectable man need not be polite. The rare ones who are put a gallant nuance in their friendliness that proclaims her fallen status. Is it to spare her that humiliation that her former lover abstains from those niceties? Would she really have wanted, during his single visit, for him to have sat next to her to enquire familiarly about her health and to whisper in her ear, 'You are lovely, my dear, in your mourning attire'?

At least he respects her enough not to have done that.

And so he respects her a little. Perhaps he even feels guilty for the hurt—without having known it at that time—that he caused her.

She wanted to be sure. Existence would be easier for her if there weren't those zones of shadow, of the unspoken, between them. A simple word from him would appease her soul!

Would she dare?

Yes. A fever of activity takes hold of her. It is already late and her candle is going out, but she sits down at her little table, takes a piece of paper, a pen, and writes: 'My dear brother.'

Those words break her heart but she has courage, much courage today. She thinks for a moment, then quickly continues:

> I fear I would inconvenience my sister Urszula by asking her directly for this. And so it is to you that I take the liberty of sending this neck chain that belongs to me. Would you be so kind as to sell it for me and to use the proceeds for a gift for my little nephew? I am very grateful in advance for your consent, as well as your discretion.
>
> Your affectionate sister,
> Wioletta Zemka

Is it enough? Of course it is. The fact that she is writing to him says enough in itself.

She leaves her room, knocks on Zosia's door, gives her the letter, and Zosia looks at her sister with surprise.

'For our brother-in-law?'

'Yes. Oh, you can read it. I haven't sealed it. But it is essential that our father not know about it.'

That his unmarried daughter would have sold a piece of jewellery on her own, no matter how inexpensive it is, would indeed seem outrageous to Jozef.

Zosia nods, titillated by this little mystery. There is no doubt that, as soon as she is alone, she will read the letter . . . and will get nothing for her efforts.

It is with a beating heart and, after a long time, with cheeks reddened through expectation, that the next day Wioletta watches Efraim hitch the briska. From her window she responds to the complicit wave of her sister; then the carriage disappears under the November sky, and she closes her window.

How long they seem, the two days that separate her from Efraim's return! She braves the cold and the disapproval of her two jailers to go into the garden to dissipate her fever of impatience. The dead leaves roll under her feet, the air whitens with her breath, she can't stand still, dreams, can eat nothing.

Finally Efraim returns, joyful, as he does each time he goes into the city. And he has, for the young lady, a note from Zosia.

'All is well, I presume?' asks Jozef, offhandedly, who is waiting for the carriage to go to the sugar factory and, from there, to town.

'It couldn't be better, Father. Zosia is enchanted with everything. She went to the theatre the same evening she arrived, against the advice of my sister and her maid who found her green dress too mediocre. And it seems that our Zosia was right, because Prince Dubinski, whom they met at the intermission, complimented her on her dress and then went to a great deal of trouble to get refreshments for them.'

'Ho, ho!' Jozef adds with false indifference. 'This is very much like our accommodating friend.'

But while getting into the carriage he repeats, 'Ho, ho,' before taking the reins from Efraim to drive himself, something he does on his good days.

As soon as he is out of sight, Wioletta shuts herself in her room and with shaking hands opens the letter from Agenor that Zosia had slipped into her note.

My dear sister, it would be a pleasure for me to do this for you.
I will inform you as soon as possible of its progress.

Your very devoted,
Agenor Karlowicz

It is only a few words. But Wioletta reads them and rereads them to extract their quintessence. He replied—that is the great message of those two lines. He took the time to write them, just as he will take the time to go to a jeweller and, unbeknownst to his wife, honour his sister-in-law's request. Then there is the 'very devoted, it would be a pleasure'—formulae that, given their former connection, should probably be taken literally.

But, after all, they are only a few words. He who loved her, he whose child she had carried, produced only two lines when the occasion offered him the opportunity to write volumes after five years of silence. That is the great message that outweighs the first. And the gold chain that his erstwhile mistress used to wear under her clothes—he will sell it without even indicating that he recognized it, without expressing the slightest sadness, the slightest regret!

Wioletta places the note on her table and blushes with shame. She only got what she deserved. This letter—if you could call it a letter—she will keep it to reread when the temptation to forget arises again.

She gets up and walks to the little desk that once belonged to Clara and which her father had allowed her to keep in her room. One day she discovered a hidden drawer; she opened it and found an old ivory dance card, a leaf turning to dust, a glove . . . Poor Mama, she sighed, if that was the only use she could make of a secret drawer!

Poor Wioletta, ignoring the degree to which she is so like that mother; poor latecomers who, lacking imagination or modesty, believe themselves to be so different and so much better than those who preceded them. Close your drawer, Wioletta, on the first of your treasures. Others will come. One day, far in the future, another hand will discover them and you will be the one pitied for having placed such value on such insignificant things.

14

But I haven't described all the consequences of Zosia's departure. While my human guests, following the rhythm of the letters from the young girl, dream of balls, encounters, strolls and shopping, the inanimate objects, less sensitive to suggestion, feel only the deficit of life caused by that absence. Let's not even mention Zosia's room—for her neat bedspread that no longer has a wrinkle, for her books that are becoming covered in dust, for her clock whose chiming no one hears any more, it was a pure and simple hibernation.

But elsewhere too, there is vegetating, boredom. There is less noise, less movement, less commotion; because it still happened that that young girl, in her exuberance, didn't keep her elbows close enough to her body for the taste of her governess and for the safety of the knickknacks.

The most morose are the curtains in the little salon which are no longer percale—could I have forgotten that novelty? Yes, eighteen months ago Jozef, on a whim, decided that the little blue salon would henceforth be the little green salon. Everything changed: the wallpaper, the paint of the panels, the curtains, of course, which Caroline von Kotz had chosen with such love—*sic transit gloria mundi*. No *toile de jouy* to take their place. Having been delivered by Adam's death from his promise of a gift, Jozef was finally able to formulate his true opinion on the question—*toile de jouy* was a little bit vulgar.

And so today it is white damask curtains that observe the consumption of chocolate in the evening and the post-lunch conversations. They are young fools who protest a lot and still know very little about life. Where is our Zosia? Why aren't the people here laughing any more? Let her come back quickly! This is the extent of their complaints. They have no idea that laughter in the salon is not a given, that there are houses where there is never laughter—and that if Zosia returns, it will certainly not be for ever.

Those innocents don't even understand the threat that lurks in the letters that are read out loud. What is the meaning, to them, of the fact that Madame Karlowiczowa writes to her father:

The prince, dear Papa, came to my 'at home' again, and this time he stayed for three hours! I can only hope. Obviously, there are still obstacles you are well aware of. Princess Dubinska will arrive next week to settle in her winter quarters in her Waly Hetmanskie house. We will pay her our usual visit, and, if she visits us, I believe we will be able to consider things on the right path.

I don't share that optimism. The princess has been looking for twenty years for a match worthy of her son, that is, worthy of her. By what miracle would she suddenly feel that the Zemkas' youngest daughter, from a family of doubtful extraction and whose respectability is not without blots ('One of the sisters, well! you know . . .'), would correspond to that criterion? No, really, that is building castles in Spain, and I'm not the only one to think so. I see the green velvet ottoman, that Jozef bought at the same time as a rug from Trebizond and a dagger from Alep to give the room an Oriental cachet that reminded him of his nephew, smiling under the window. The other furniture chosen on that occasion, 'antiques'—the word is just beginning to come into fashion; in the time of the Ponarskis they would have been called old things—aren't duped, either. Because they have seen ambitions stifled, marriage plans go up in smoke! They exchange knowing winks and I can guess what they're thinking, 'Come now! Let's be realistic!'

We are thus all taken aback the day Jozef, opening a new letter from Lemberg, drops the pince-nez that he now needs to read and begins pacing the room repeating, 'Oh, my god, my god!'

It is out of joy, rest assured. His joy swells, overflows, he has to tell someone. Madame Denisot almost faints when, opening the door, she is almost picked up off the ground by Jozef who kisses her on each cheek, 'Dear Denisot, do you know what Urszula has told me? The princess died last Thursday from congested lungs!'

'My goodness, the poor woman,' says Elvire breathing a sigh of relief. Then she crosses herself, 'May she rest in peace.'

'Rest in peace, yes, yes! Oh, I wasn't expecting this. Right, start lunch without me—I'm going to write my condolences to the prince so he will receive them by return mail. This isn't the moment to tarry.'

The result of his efforts would be something to add to the annals of society. That society which, until then, might have considered Jozef

Zemka a lout entirely lacking in tact or finesse, would be shocked. When Jozef wants he can, beyond all probability, be caressing and ingenious with his words. Because really, in this case, who in the world regrets the demise of this mummified shrew besides her big clod of a son? Jozef nevertheless produces three long pages full of eloquence, recalls her 'so very aristocratic verve' which previously he had called only vicious ill will, laments a 'tragic loss for all us Poles' and outdoes himself in his peroration—aware that in matters of flattery, one never goes too far:

> Imagine, my poor friend, the peace the princess in her final moments must have found, the certainty she was leaving behind her such a valorous patriot and such a benefactor of humankind. Imagine that she left us with the thought that she had, in your person, contributed to the edification of all. We will mourn her, but for what she has given us we will be eternally grateful—you are her most beautiful work.

The postman of Lemberg leaves with this pack of lies, and Jozef then gives full reign to his scheming. Of course, he must strike while the iron is hot; but for the time being, he has done all that he can. The prince would return home for the funeral (which, moreover, it will be *absolutely* essential to attend), and propriety would prevent him from returning to town that winter. He would no longer be seen at the theatre or at Urszula's 'at homes'. . . The ideal would be to have Zosia return and to increase visits of condolences and small family gatherings. But to have Zosia return when all of Lemberg knows that she is supposed to stay with the Karlowiczs until the beginning of the summer? The manoeuvre would be too obvious. No kinship with the deceased would explain such a return. It would even cause tongues to wag, it would be said in town that the Zemkas must really want the match for the young girl for her to run that way behind her potential husband. No, no, that would compromise her. Let her stay there—she will finish her training, she will perhaps have other suitors which will raise the ante and make her more desirable.

And so Zosia remains there, and one can't say she isn't happy. The absence of her admirer doesn't ruin her pleasure—in truth, she never says anything about it. It is even a bit annoying, Jozef thinks. And in his letters he orders Urszula to occasionally sing the praises of the prince to her younger sister, to remind her of his attentions, to repeat them, inflate them, mention all the nice things he would have said about her to a third party.

As for Jozef—he isn't idle, either. The prince has returned home, stricken—for him and him alone it is a sincere mourning. He eats more than ever, lets himself go, sees almost no one, and Jozef, as his neighbour, allows himself to attempt to distract him. He takes him hunting, is ostensibly interested in the prince's charitable works, in the functioning of his model farms, all of that without, however, mentioning his daughter. It is obvious the prince isn't thinking at all about that right now.

He also visits the school that Dubinski has founded to educate and teach Polish culture to his former Ruthenian serfs, and returns thoughtful. The following days I hear him with Gavryl examining the accounts to see if it would be possible to do the same thing here.

After some reflection, he decides, no, we are not rolling in gold, that is, without being poor, we are living off an industry with revenue that is less certain than that of landed property, an industry which is just being developed. It is not the time to devote funds that would be better used for investing to the maintenance of a school.

And so Jozef invests. He acquires two more hydraulic presses and a large quantity of railroad stock. They are talking about finally linking Kraków with Vienna. Won't contributing to this great project serve the entire province, or at least be the first steps in that direction?

But, to seduce the prince he must still agree to a more immediate generosity which, however, will not be a continual burden on his budget. Thus he sponsors three orphan girls, helps sick indigents, gives a scholarship to a grandson of the Pavlyks who is too scrawny to work in the fields but who, with a bit of training, would find his place in the lower Uniate clergy.

In the environs there is stupefaction. Has hell frozen over?

Old Ulianna sums up everyone's thoughts. One day, after dropping off a basket of eggs in the kitchen she meets Jozef who is getting into his carriage, 'So, master, it appears that you love us now?'

(For Ulianna, masters remain masters. It doesn't matter to her that serfdom has been abolished and socage a thing of the past. As far as she is concerned, she gets up just as early to milk her two goats and, even though it's planted on a bit of land she now owns, the rye of her black bread doesn't taste any better.)

Jozef senses the sarcastic look in her little wrinkled eyes but he is not a man to get upset for so little.

'Come now, Ulianna my beauty, you know that I have always loved you!'

'That's true!' laughs the old woman, showing what remains of her teeth. 'When are we getting married?'

'Tomorrow, if I could. But you see, we are too old, you and I. Our children would laugh at us.'

'Oh, you're right, master, we are no longer in the days when I was still reaping and you a pink blond *sugar pie*. And then, what would I look like in front of the pope, poor sinner that I am, next to the saintly man you have become?'

Wench, thinks Jozef, a bit annoyed. And from up on his seat he throws her a handful of kreutzers, and a kiss just for fun.

It is indeed a saintly man who doesn't proclaim his saintliness from the rooftops. He counts on the gossip in the inn, on the suppliers from Grünau to whom one always serves a little glass of vodka and gossip in the kitchen, on the mysterious propensity of rumours to travel through the thickest woods, the most swampy fields and then to spread over the four corners of the district. Patience, patience—the facts will ultimately speak for themselves.

He would nonetheless like his unmarried daughter to accompany him on his charitable visits. That would be killing two birds with one stone. In some homes without a man, the appearance of *Pan* Jozef bearing offerings of money is a bit ambiguous without the presence of a female from his family. And Wioletta would thereby correct her bad reputation by displaying her piety a bit. It would be to help her sisters, in particular the one who is still waiting for a husband. Jozef is even surprised that the so-called painter hasn't thought of it herself.

But, great surprise, the dabbler protests.

'Oh, Father, don't ask that of me. These visits are awful, I won't know what to say to those poor people. I already pray for them, every day, when I am alone . . .'

'What, you refuse?'

Wioletta's shoulders shake with her own audacity but she holds her ground. There is even a glimmer of irony in her eye—this philanthropic display doesn't fool her.

'Oh, very well. I will leave you to your devotions in your room. And if by chance you examine your conscience, I hope it will torment you at least a little, because your ill will is hurting your entire family. I have always thought so—you're hard-hearted, you're selfish and you deserve the disgrace that has befallen you.'

With that he leaves, slamming the door, but he soon finds the opportunity to soften up—his efforts will be repaid a hundredfold. The prince, invited for a long time, finally agrees to come hunting in the little forest that separates us from the Wytockis' land. And following the lunch that honours his arrival, In the library where the two men go to smoke cigars, Dubinski places his hands on Jozef's shoulders and, with moist eyes, murmurs, 'My dear fellow, my generous friend! I have heard of all you have done for our neighbours—yes, yes, don't deny it, your magnanimity has gone beyond your discretion, I know everything. Oh, Jozef! Excuse me, I didn't really know you . . .'

'Jozef'! Our Zemka is overwhelmed beyond all hope. He grows pale, is forced to pour himself a little glass of cognac. Never as much as today has he had the sensation of finally reaching a goal; all the past humiliations are washed away by that prenuptial 'Jozef' in the mouth of the magnate. What! His grandchildren will bear the name of the Dubinskis, and, if Poland becomes free again and has a real king, they will most likely be welcomed at court!

It is too much. With a shaky voice he changes the subject and (marking more points in the prince's esteem, who sees only delicate modesty) throws himself wholly into considerations of international politics. His visitor, ill at ease on these complex subjects, responds only in monosyllables and widens his upset eyes, but Jozef is prepared to forgive him all his weaknesses. The prince has such a noble heart, deep down! How sweet it will be to respond to his goodness with human warmth which he must have always lacked from his nasty old mother! How everyone here will cherish this son-in-law who has fallen from heaven! And Jozef, softened, remembers his letter of condolences and now realizes that he believes every word of it.

15

Six weeks later he is still in that frame of mind when, returning from the sugar factory, he is surprised to find Zosia, who wasn't expected for another month. She has arrived in the Karlowiczs' carriage, chaperoned by a stern-looking servant woman. Jozef wonders what this premature return means, but in the end he is delighted: they will finally be able to advance the matter through more direct means. And then—his eye, which has become more forgiving through his ambition, detects—how that stay in town has benefitted Zosia! He was unfair to have seen as her sole attractions only spirit and good health. She is adorable, truly adorable! Her hands are not as red, she is holding herself straighter, her virginal braid has taken on something feminine and coquettish. What a handsome couple they will make! The difference in age will only be an additional charm.

'So, my daughter, all is well in Lemberg? I hope our little Andrzej hasn't fallen ill, for your sister to have sent you back before the end of the season.'

Oh, no, Papa, Andrzej is doing very well. And if you could see how well he speaks now! But the first heat has arrived in the city, and Urszula was afraid, not being used to it, that I wouldn't do very well . . .'

'Fine, fine,' interrupts Jozef jollily. 'Go have fun, find your books: it is good to have you back, we missed you so!'

But imagine his alarm when the chaperone hands him a letter and, opening the seal, he reads the following lines!

My dear Papa,

Forgive this initiative that I've taken without consulting you, but I felt there was a true danger.

Here is the matter. Last month, one day when we were walking in the gardens of the chateau (where there were a lot of people, because the view of the city is very beautiful from there), a young man greeted Agenor who thought he was obligated to exchange a few words with him. You see, he is the editor of a gazette in which Agenor publishes from time to time, one of those sons of Zion who have recently converted, in whom, without inviting into our homes, we can however recognize certain abilities. Agenor did not therefore truly introduce us, and that Mr Elfenbein, who is very handsome, by the way, was content to tip his hat and to politely bow in our direction.

But ten days later we happened to meet him again in front of the cathedral. I pretended not to see him and went into a glove store where I thought we were safe. Well, imagine that, he followed us! And, while a salesman was showing me his most beautiful suede gloves, I saw the individual smiling at Zosia with an air of recognition and entering into a conversation. After five minutes, very alarmed, I told the salesman that he had nothing I wanted and quickly left with Zosia.

I was going to scold her severely but do you know what she said to me? 'Oh, Urszula, I hope you won't be angry, I asked Mr Elfenbein to pay us a visit. He is charming, isn't he? And I thought I understood that my brother said a great deal about his talents with the pen . . .'

Here Jozef jumps and, looking the chaperone up and down, goes into the library to read the rest in seclusion.

'You fool,' I answered her, 'since when does a young girl extend such an invitation, and to a man who, in addition, has not even been introduced to her? Where is your reserve, where are your manners?' In short, I made her understand that it was out of the question that we receive that visit. I was forced, for a week, to give my porter draconian orders and to limit our outings to the strict necessities. Twice, that Elfenbein was turned away from our door, after which I would have thought he would understand. But Zosia who, you know, has her little character, did not see things this way and did not spare me her tears and foot-stamping.

Last week I thought I was done with this annoying situation. Well, no. It happens that at the theatre, where there was a rather remarkable singer from Dresden, by the way (I permit myself to observe, dear Papa, that your prejudice against anything German is of another age—I know many Poles in Lemberg who do not hesitate to go to the German theatre) . . .

'Oh, blast it all!' cursed Jozef, whose face became even redder. 'Now I'm of another age!'

So in the theatre, I saw our Elfenbein in the lobby. I pointed him out to Agenor who said to me: 'There's nothing surprising, my dear, Emil is also a critic.' 'So what were you thinking of, sir, bringing my sister here, where it was certain that we would encounter this undesirable?' Oh, men, men, my dear Papa! Poor Agenor was upset by this lapse, and to remedy it we joined the company of the countess Wytocka (you see, she herself doesn't hesitate to frequent this establishment whose musical programme meets her expectations), counting well that the young man wouldn't dare to follow us. We weren't mistaken. He watched us walk away without making a move but with an expression of regret that was extremely . . . extremely . . . well, dear Papa, I think I've already told you he is a very handsome man.

If only I had held on to Zosia's arm! After a moment, noting she was gone, I turned and found that the scallywag had gone to find him, that they were talking, that she was explaining and I guess telling him that it wasn't her fault that he was not invited into our home. Of course, she denied this and pretended they had simply spoken of Donizetti's opera that we had just heard. But I didn't believe her, and I felt that if, not content to be unruly, she was becoming deceitful, I could no longer be held accountable for her actions. That is why, with the agreement of Agenor, of course, I put an end to her stay here, counting on your authority to bring her to heel. So she will be deprived of a few final parties that she would have enjoyed. This little disappointment will perhaps make her reflect, and with God's help, I hope we will no longer have anything to fear.

Your affectionate daughter,

Urszula Karlowiczowa

'Oh no, no, no!' shouts Jozef, throwing down the letter. His first reflex is to go down and slap his youngest daughter before condemning her to dried bread and water. But he thinks better of it. In a week Urszula must have had the time to express all her disapproval to her sister, and, if he knows her, the admonitions must have been as good, on a moral level, as a pair of paternal slaps. His role is therefore limited to adding an official reprimand—it would be fruitless to give the incident a weight it didn't have.

And so he goes downstairs to find Zosia on the first floor speaking to Wioletta, and, when he appears, she steps away from her furtively. Wonderful, he thinks sarcastically, this is already better than the disengaged tone in which she had had the nerve to allege the first heat in the city. The first heat—really!

'Your sister has told me of your escapades, miss. No more of that in the future, please.'

'No, Father.'

'You have acted like a featherbrain, and proved that you are not yet old enough to appear in the world. Think of that, and know, that as long as you don't show a bit more decorum, there will be no question of another stay in town.'

'Yes, Father.'

He turns on his heels, cuts short any questions by Madame Denisot who is lurking, sensing a little scandal she could savour, and reminds her severely that this is not the time for her to lower her guard because the behaviour of her last pupil still leaves much to be desired. And, having called for Efraim, he orders him to hitch the horses in order to immediately see Prince Dubinski. The counter-offensive has begun.

'Life is so heavy for us girls,' groans Zosia as soon as the storm has passed. 'Oh, Wioletta, I don't understand how you can stand it. Look at these walls, look at those colours, that *Hunting Scene*, that *View of Kraków* that haven't moved an inch since we were born! It seems to me that, out of boredom, I will become mad, that I will grow claws and tear all that up . . .'

'Now, now, you're exaggerating,' whispers Wioletta. 'What do these engravings and hall decor have to do with anything?'

'But don't you see we're like they are? We are prisoners here, condemned to silence, to immobility, and time is passing over us and covering us with dust . . . You yourself, my beautiful Wioletta, you are fading, you are growing pale and sad like the paper on these walls . . . Oh, no, I don't want to become like you, I want to get out of here!'

At those words, I listen carefully, because I had the impression . . . yes, I briefly had the impression that through my objects, for the first time in my existence, a human was appealing to me.

'You are going to leave, you know,' says Wioletta, frightened by this nascent hysteria and a bit hurt. 'You're going to get married, another life is going to begin for you . . .'

'Get married . . . Yes, you're right, I'll be married,' sniffs the girl and quickly runs to her room to cry alone.

Wioletta, her head bent, then opens a note from Agenor that her sister had been handing over to her before their father arrived. She hasn't yet had time to wonder what it says; she unfolds it, her head empty; and immediately she is flooded with joy.

My very dear sister,

I am taking advantage of Zosia's return to tell you that I have been able to do what you requested. Our Andrzej is henceforth the owner of a holy medal that he likes very much, and thanks to which your protection will accompany him, I hope, throughout his life. I am infinitely happy and touched by this thought you have had, happy to know that you love him and are thinking of his happiness and his future life. Believe in my sincere gratitude as his father, and to my unfailing support as a man, of he who is and will always remain

Your servant and brother,

Agenor Karlowicz

Oh! Well played. Did Agenor, after a few months, calculate the threat represented in the discreet awakening of his tragic heroine? A woman capable, after what he had done to her, of begging for a few words of affection from him, wouldn't she go so far as to reveal everything and finish herself off while dragging him into her fall? So here is a little bone for her to chew, along with an adroit reminder that any revelations would destroy for ever her sister and her young nephew.

How he loves his little boy, Wioletta indeed thinks, moved and agitated. Yes, Andrzej's happiness comes before all else. Because he is guilty of no sin, nor is Urszula. We have sinned, we regret it, but those two innocents must for ever remain spared from our crime. We must protect them, watch over them—that is henceforth our common duty.

(It is a sad feeling, but more gratifying than that of having been defiled and deceived. Wioletta's heart softens more.)

Our common duty, I will fulfil it without fail, as will Agenor. What does it matter what separates us? Fate did not want us to be together. But without seeing each other, without speaking, at a distance we will work together. And that alliance, perhaps, will be stronger than all the visible links recognized by the world . . .

And so Wioletta re-embroiders the canvas of her existence and, gradually, succeeds in making it bearable. The second letter from Agenor has joined the first in the desk drawer. With a third, Wioletta will be able to tell herself that they are maintaining a correspondence. She is no longer a poor, wounded woman, a chained captive. If nothing has apparently changed in her existence, she henceforth possesses a distant ally, the other half of herself. And that distance, instead of being painful, is a source of energy for her; their tutelary task exalts her, and their double sacrifice has finally assumed meaning in the divine plan.

16

And so it is a new Wioletta, stronger, more active, whom I discover the next day. 'So, I'm fading, am I!' she exclaims each morning when she looks in the mirror—she sees there a woman with serene features, already reflecting cheerfully on what she will do with her day.

Most often, she paints until eleven o'clock, either in her room or, if the weather permits, in the garden. After lunch, it is time for a stroll with her sister. But Madame Denisot is always between them, discouraging private conversations and confidences. To speak alone they must walk quickly or pretend to lose themselves looking for blackberries or mushrooms.

'Phew! She doesn't see us. How do you feel today, sister?'

'Not well, I hardly slept at all, the clock in my room nibbled at the seconds and it seemed—oh, Wioletta, it seemed that my youth was ticking away too . . .'

'Come now, you silly girl, you're not even eighteen! Don't despair— this winter will no doubt be the last you will spend with us.'

But that prediction only darkens the girl more.

'The clock is already striking three o'clock . . . the prince won't be long, we should go back. What a pity, it was so nice out and we were finding so many blackberries!'

At three-thirty, indeed, the prince arrives, awkward and huge in his mourning attire. His visit consists in listening to Jozef comment on the events of public life, and in looking at Zosia.

'What do you think, Wladislaw, of the demands made by the tsar on Turkey? He is demanding rights for the orthodox subjects of the sultan, and things are heating up. If you ask me, he is looking for a war.'

'Oh, really?'

'I'm convinced of it. But, believe me, he will be dealing with a strong opponent. Because Napoleon III will be ready to fight with England to support the Turks. And my nephew Zemka-Ponarski, I'm telling you this in confidence, wrote to me recently that, in the entourage of Abdülmacid . . .'

How good she smells, how pink are her cheeks, thinks Wladislaw. Oh, if only she would look at me a little!

But she doesn't look at him, and in the smoking room Jozef must lavish the bashful lover with hyperbolic encouragement.

'She truly likes you, Wladislaw. I heard her just yesterday confiding in her sister (behind their bindings, Herodotus and Titus-Livy silently listen to this wild lie). But what can you expect! She is still very young . . .'

'Yes, yes, I understand . . .'

Don't let him understand too much, Jozef thinks, since the prince's lack of initiative is upsetting him and his plans. What to do? The way things are going, in ten years they will still be in the same place!

When the prince finally leaves, Jozef's smile instantly disappears, and Zosia is dragged over the coals.

'Were you asleep, miss? Once again, you didn't say a word to him. You are so sour that the poor prince hasn't even attempted to offer me the hint of a request for your hand.'

'A request? Oh, Papa, I don't want to encourage that poor man . . .'

'And why not?'

'But he's old! He's almost your age.'

'Humph!'

'. . . and he's an ass, you've always said so!'

Jozef grows pale. Did he really say, think such things? He can't remember. On the contrary, it seems to him that he has always seen the prince as a friend, simple but agreeable, his only fault being that until last year he was afflicted with such an odious mother.

'Hold your tongue, you little fool. An ass! Who are you to judge a man who is so above you? The prince is the best match in the province, his attentions for you are an unhoped-for piece of luck . . .'

'I will never marry that fat fool!' shouts Zosia, tears filling her eyes.

Never, with the exception perhaps of learning of the sin of his third daughter, has Jozef felt the temptation so strongly to break with his own hands a being issued from him, as custom and the law would give him the right to do. A murderous glimmer flashes in his eyes, his hands clench, but with a huge effort he is content simply to say, 'We will see.'

One morning in November, while he is lingering in the library (again! one must observe that at this time Jozef, preoccupied by his family projects, is neglecting the sugar factory a bit. It is the beginning of a fatal decline. A few months later, the crisis past, he will discover that his presence is not as indispensable to the good working of the business as he thought, since things are going as well as before. He grows used to delegating, to leaving it to others. Without being aware, it is old age that is watching him at the end of the path, old age and, in terms of money, decadence. But let's not get ahead of ourselves)—one day while he is reading in the library, someone knocks on the door. Without a doubt, it is Gavryl—only he can pound like that on a door as if he hoped to have plums fall off it.

'Come in, you animal!' he shouts impatiently from his table.

Gavryl enters, his cap in his hands.

'Master, there is a fellow downstairs who is asking for you.'

'A fellow? Well, have him come up.'

Gavryl clears his throat and shifts from one foot to the other.

'The thing is, master, he is, as you would say, in his Sunday clothes, in black with nice gloves and a nice hat. So I decided to put him in the salon.'

Dressed in black with nice gloves?

'You did the right thing, you did the right thing! Go back down and tell him I'll be there right away.'

Jozef runs to the mirror and with a trembling hand smoothes his hair and the back of his jacket. 'A fellow' indeed! Gavryl will never amount to anything as a major-domo, he'll have to find something else for him to do, now that he is too old to work the fields and the woods with his master . . .

These chaotic thoughts are suspended when Jozef enters the little salon. A young man in a suit stands up to greet him, asking if he is indeed Mr Jozef Zemka.

'At your service,' responds Jozef. Could this be an agent of the prince?

'Emil Elfenbein,' says the other, cutting those unspoken questions short.

Jozef grabs a chair and falls into it; his visitor, after a second of hesitation, draws up a chair in turn and sits down, his top hat placed on his lap.

He coughs, waits for some encouragement that doesn't come, and speaks. 'Mr Zemka, I have come to you with a request that you would be right to consider rash, perhaps even unseemly. At the outset, I excuse myself. Mr Zemka, I haven't had the honour of being introduced to you or to your daughter but, as extraordinary as this might seem, I have come to ask for her hand.'

Jozef's cheeks turn bright red.

'Mr . . . Elfenbein!' he barks when he can catch his breath. But his mind is in disorder and nothing else comes to him.

'I know what you think,' the young man murmurs with a slight smile that makes him even more attractive. 'I am well aware of the prejudice that my name and my origins might arouse in you. And so I have brought you, sir, my baptismal certificate . . . here.'

Jozef, flabbergasted, takes the document and looks at it without reading.

'I won't hide from you, either, dear sir,' the other continues, not at all discouraged, 'that I am not a rich man. My father is a wine merchant in Hungary, I have two sisters who still must be provided for, and my most tangible fortune, at present, is a doctoral degree in law. I could not promise, without dishonesty, that your daughter will have the lifestyle she is used to. But I can make up for that, in the beginning, with the strength of the feelings I have for her . . .'

'Good God,' Jozef growls, 'you've only seen her three times!'

'If you please,' the young man corrects him without losing his polite manner. '*She* has seen me three times. But I, sir, have seen her every day in town after a lucky chance encounter allowed me to see her in the store where I buy my gloves. Without daring to approach her, I followed her on each of her outings, I've seen her on the arm of her sister, I've seen her smile at others, nibble on a roll from the balcony of her room . . .'

'What! You've dared to spy on her at Madame Karlowiczowa's home?

'Dear sir, no imperial law prohibits a man from sitting as long as he likes on a bench in Lemberg and looking up,' the journalist observes confidently. 'This is what I did, every morning and every evening, as long as your daughter was in town. This is what I did for a week after her departure, in the hope that it would not be definitive. But I learnt that it was. Oh! Understand that the news affected me and that the months since then have not assuaged the loss.'

With the groaning that greets his words, Emil Elfenbein leans forward and continues, in an even stronger voice, 'Mr Zemka, don't be less receptive than is reasonable. You are yourself, as I've learnt, of . . . bourgeois origins and that is what gives me the hope of convincing you, in spite of everything, and of touching your heart. You see, I am not yet rich or famous, I am obscure socially, but I am very, very stubborn and— excuse a young man this lack of modesty—believe me, I will go far.'

'You will go to the devil!' Jozef finally explodes, having reached his boiling point. 'Not one more word, Mr Elfenbein. My daughter is not for you. My daughter is already contracted to someone else. Good day, sir.'

He has already got up; he clicks his heels, and his entire air indicates to his visitor that it is time to leave. But the young man doesn't understand, or doesn't want to understand. He stays seated, his eyes a bit wider, and for the first time since his arrival is unable to smile.

'Excuse me, but I'm not sure I have . . . your daughter is already engaged?'

'She is as good as engaged.'

'Engaged . . .' says the other in an almost inaudible voice, 'so quickly. I had thought . . . Excuse me, sir, for having troubled you. I will leave.'

But then a closet door flies open and Zosia appears, distraught, her cheeks red, 'No, no! It's not true! I am not engaged!'

In a flash Jozef regains his presence of mind, becoming a man of action. He walks to the closet, gives his daughter a look that silences her, closes the door and turns the key. Then he goes back to his visitor, 'You were just leaving, sir?'

'That is . . .'

'I suggest that you do so. You have heard me—the answer is no.'

Standing, Emil Elfenbein puts his baptismal certificate back in his pocket, examines the lining of his hat. And, while his host is indicating the door to the hallway, he raises his head, 'Sir, most men, faced with such a reception, would quickly forget that they wanted anything to do with your family and, like Aesop's fox, would say—these grapes are too green and aren't worth the trouble to have them. You must understand that I am different. For, while promising you that you will never see me again, I can assure you, sir, that I will regret this for a long time.'

He turns towards the cupboard and repeats, 'For a very long time.'

A minute later, I see him crossing the entryway, going through the gate and climbing up into the carriage that he must have rented in Grünau. And, before disappearing on the road to town, he looks back at us with a final look of anger and wounded love.

17

And now Zosia truly is on bread and water—her sudden appearance did not please her father at all. She has been told to stay in her room and to think about the error of her ways by studying Psalms, the only reading she is now allowed. If she wants this punishment to come to an end, it is very simple—she has only to agree to a meeting with the prince, to smile at him, speak to him, in short, provide him the encouragement to make his declaration.

Jozef has entered into a war of wills; but he didn't think it would last so long.

Because the days go by and Zosia, losing weight, still won't budge. And the prince, after a week or two, begins to worry. He has been told that she has a minor, but still worrisome, illness, and has been imposed a strict confinement. Zosia is doing a bit better, without being entirely well . . .

'Jozef, you're not telling me everything! Is her life in danger?'

'Not at all, that is . . .'

Overwhelmed, the prince forgets his reserve. He demands that he be allowed a few minutes at his young friend's bedside, raises his voice, almost shouts; an opportunity that Jozef is not too stupid to let slip by.

'Wladislaw,' he murmurs, taking his hand. 'I understand your concern but I can't allow such a request.'

'Why not?'

'My friend, you know the malice of others. I am a father and I know, alas, how the reputation of a young girl is a fragile thing. What would people think of your presence at the bedside of a child who is not related to you? Already, I've been told, evil tongues are wagging at your repeated visits—a man of your quality, single, in a home where . . .'

'Oh, Jozef, if only it were up to me!'

And to whom else? Jozef silently grumbles. But he stifles that bad thought and sanctimoniously asks, 'What do you mean, my friend?'

'That if I had the least assurance of being seen by your daughter with a . . . kindly eye, I . . . well . . . a fiancé has the right to do such things, doesn't he? When the one he loves is suffering!'

Jozef isn't concerned about the informality of this first marriage request. He falls into the arms of the prince and promises that he will discover the feelings of this little invalid as soon as she is better.

'. . . As for myself, Wladislaw, I would be only too happy and honoured to have you as a son-in-law. But, you must understand, I will not put my happiness before that of my daughter.'

'Of course, of course!' cries the prince, red with emotion.

But he must still wait six long days, during which he is told of a relapse, a possible contagion, severe instructions from the family doctor. Finally, one morning, pale, emaciated, with reddened eyes, Zosia asks the maid to bring her some warm water, 'Lubienka, tell my father that I agree to speak to the prince.'

For a few hours there are sounds of commotion. Jozef, who goes upstairs to congratulate his daughter, finds her looking terrible. True, she is supposed to be recovering from an illness. But with that face, she would be capable of ruining everything.

Her hair is quickly curled, her eyes are washed with rose water. Her prettiest winter dress has become too big, two seamstresses quickly take it in; she is ready, however, when Wladislaw arrives for his daily visit. And luckily, emotion has put some colour into the recluse's cheeks.

Jozef greets the prince, tells him the happy news—Zosia is out of bed, he can see her, speak to her! The convalescent is brought into the little green salon. Blushing, eyes lowered on both sides, the conversation stalls, they struggle to find something to say. The master of the house proposes a stroll in the garden, since the sun is shining and the paths have just been cleared of their coating of snow.

'And above all,' he whispers into his daughter's ear, 'put on your ermine cap and muff, since they look very good on you. Go on, go on!'

Outside, he lets himself be outdistanced by the two lovebirds, lights a cigar; and only smiles when, heading back, he encounters Madame Denisot who says to him, shocked, 'My goodness, Monsieur Zemka, look behind you! Zosia and the prince are all alone near the little bench. I'm going to go over.'

'You are going to remain here, dear Denisot, and do nothing.'

'But, oh! they are sitting next to each other and . . . good heavens! She has taken his hand. Zosia! Zosia! Come here immediately . . .'

'Leave them alone, I told you.'

He cannot help looking around, however, to savour the sight— Zosia, adorable in so much white fur, has indeed extracted her little hand from her muff, and placed it on the prince's wrist. She is speaking to him, he is answering heatedly, leaning his head to kiss her fingers . . . It's taking a long time! Isn't Zosia doing a bit much in their first meeting?

He is beginning to regret that he wasn't wearing his fur coat when the prince, very upset, stands up and quickly comes towards them. But instead of stopping beside them, he tips his hat, smiles at them weakly, and without a word disappears inside.

At first stupefied, Jozef quickly follows him, crosses the main floor, rushes down the front steps and finds the prince ready to get on his horse.

'But Prince, you're leaving already?'

'Yes, my friend. Prolonging my visit would be too cruel.'

'What could that little guttersnipe have told you? I'm going to call her over and demand that . . .'

'Don't do anything of the sort, my friend—I have heard enough. I don't want any more than you to have my happiness go before hers.'

'But see here, these are childish reactions! A moment of modesty, the flirtatiousness of a girl who won't say yes without being begged a bit first! Wladislaw, think. Wladislaw, come back tomorrow!'

But Wladislaw has jumped onto the saddle, and, from above, he says the most perceptive words of his existence.

'My dear Jozef, I'm forty-five years old. And, for my domestic peace as well as for my conjugal honour, I will not marry by force a girl of eighteen whose heart is already taken. Adieu.'

It is an earthquake; and like many earthquakes, it unleashes a storm.

Jozef begins by turning back towards me, the only witness of his defeat, and I feel uneasy. But it's not my fault, is it? Or, to be honest, not much! From under the plaster of my frieze, I force myself to send him the smooth image of the jewel of his ancestors but he just shrugs his shoulders and turns his back to me.

'Efraim!' he shouts.

Efraim comes running. He has a few bits of straw in his hair, and I suspect he has just been pulled from a nice nap.

'Harness the horses and get some blankets. Be ready at the gate, and don't move.'

Then the master returns to the vestibule, shouts more orders that make the windows shake on various floors. I have the impression that he is making a big mistake—but it will serve him right! Come what may.

What happens is that after an hour Lubienka and two helpers bring down trunks by the service stairs and put them in the carriage, as well as some furs and hatboxes.

Then Zosia, whom they finally found, pale from the cold and from fear, behind the trunk of a cedar, arrives; and, pushed by the maids, she joins the pile of baggage on the seat of the carriage.

She cries a little in front of Efraim who moves the boxes to make room for her. She cries more when her sister appears, out of breath, and holds her hand over the rigging.

'Don't cry, forget us!' Wioletta has time to whisper before her father, terrifying, pulls her away. Then he holds a letter out to Efraim and adds, through clenched teeth.

'Take this person to town, to the offices of *Phoenix of Lemberg*, and hand her over, with this letter, to its recipient. Go!'

(Here it is, the letter he has just furiously written in the library, and which he will soon regret:

Sir,

A few weeks ago you were kind enough to ask for my daughter. Here she is, now emancipated through this letter and given into your care. Given the ardour of the feelings you have for her, you will not be inconvenienced, I trust, to take her as her mother made her, without a dowry, trousseau or hopes of an inheritance. Yours sincerely, etc.)

Efraim, who is used to not asking questions, clicks his tongue, and the carriage takes off in what has become bitter cold.

The bells that are fading ring in a silence of the dead; the faces are full of reproach but no one dares say a word. However, when Jozef returns to the vestibule, he is greeted by Madame Denisot whom I have never seen prey to such indignation.

'Monsieur Zemka! Never in all the houses where I have been a governess have I ever seen such a thing. You have not behaved as a gentleman, and I will not stay one more day under your roof!'

Bless you, Elvire, for that act of courage. At the time, however, it only earns you a venomous look, and this sardonic response, 'Mother Denisot, it so happens that I no longer need your services. So do pack your bags. But, in order to be taken where you want to go, you'll have to wait for the carriage to return.'

While the governess spends the next two days filling her own trunks, not without praying for the salvation of her pupil and her own future, Jozef's anger dissipates. He won't admit it to anyone but he has pushed things too far. Let them come back soon! And with nothing worse than a bit of fright, a salutary humiliation, and perhaps a bad cold.

But, on the third day, Efraim comes back alone. Standing up like a charioteer, he is singing a happy song in the deep voice of a now forty-year-old. He is singing for himself, for his horse, for the sky, for the fields, and, even from afar, it is visible that he is not standing up very straight.

Finally the carriage stops in front of the gate. All the servants surround it, murmuring; but the murmurs stop when Jozef appears.

'So?'

'Oh,' says Efraim, jumping to the ground, 'the road was good, not much ice, no fog. Only, on the way, I had to stop in a barn because there wasn't any moonlight. I wrapped the little one up well with the blankets, and she slept like a baby.'

'But what then, you fool, what then?'

'Then? Well, we arrived in town, and we followed your directions. The young mistress was crying because she was afraid we wouldn't find her love. But I told her: Don't cry, miss, I'm ready to go around the town three times . . .'

'Ok, get to it!' cuts off Jozef who isn't smiling at all.

'Well, we finally found him, at the newspaper, as expected. He read your note, became very red, then white . . . It's true, he's a handsome boy.'

He stops to catch his breath; and Jozef says, 'Do you mean, you good-for-nothing, that you left them alone there?'

'Oh, not at all. First the young master shook my hand, and said to me—listen well—that I had brought him the best news he had ever received in his life. Then he climbed up next to me on the seat and had me take him to the mother of one of his friends. But he turned around all the time, because the young mistress was behind him and he was afraid she would be cold, that she would be shaken up . . . As if I shake my passengers!'

'Yes, fine!'

'The lady was very surprised but she took the young lady into her house, warmed her up and settled her in a room, and in the end she must have made the young master leave, if you please, because he didn't want to go any more. So he left to see to his business and to publish the banns, and in my opinion, in fifteen days the affair will be settled, because you can see he's a boy who knows what he wants.'

Silence.

'So that's all,' Jozef continues.

'My goodness, yes. Except that before leaving Mr Emil shook my hand again and gave me ten florins to drink to their health. Ten florins, master! Can you imagine!'

Personally, I imagine that he doesn't have many left. But Jozef doesn't answer. He is defeated, stricken, furious. His last hopes have just been dashed; furthermore, he is about to lose face in front of all his servants on whose faces contemptuous smiles are now visible.

'Oh, that's perfect,' he finally declares, his chin raised. 'Long live the Elfenbein family. As for me, I wash my hands of them.'

18

Was it the after-effects of this over-abundance of affect, hope and disappointment? Was it the relief of having seen, in Zosia, at least one person escape my unintentional curse? The fact remains that after learning, through whispering in the kitchen, that Miss Zemka and Mr Elfenbein had indeed been married one February morning in 1854, a sweet torpor settled over me. I stopped my surveillance, stopped being on guard. I felt relaxed and, yes, fatigued.

After all, I had been watching for more than a century.

I became indolent, lost a chip of plaster here and there, a roof tile. It wasn't unpleasant, and the voices around me began to melt into a soothing brouhaha.

'Hey, watch out in front!' cried the carters passing under my windows with their crates of sugar. I thought I recognized in one of them the voice of my friend Gavryl. But come now, after all, they must have found him a quasi-sinecure to finish up his days, I suppose. But I didn't have the strength to open my eyes to find out.

'Yes, yes, sell,' Jozef said to a young unknown man who must have been his new overseer, 'go ahead and sell, this little wood doesn't earn us anything any more. The values are high, and in the end it seems we will not be going to war with our Russian neighbours . . .'

What war? I wondered. But since we weren't going to go to it, I didn't have the strength to get interested.

A bit later, in the kitchen, there was a female chorus whose fervour again managed to pierce my envelope of indifference.

'. . . They say she's the most beautiful woman in the world,' the cook whispered, seated, as she almost always was now—because, having developed gout, she didn't stand up any more except to stir a sauce at a critical moment. 'My niece from Przemysl has a brother-in-law who lives in Vienna and who saw her. Well, it seems that she is beautiful beyond imagination.'

'They say,' added the blonde Ruthenian, halting her chopping for a moment, 'that our young emperor is madly in love with her, that in the Church of the Augustinians his hand trembled when he put the ring on her finger. Then Elizabeth raised her eyes and smiled at him.'

'To see her smile,' Leokadia continued, 'it seems it is like seeing a rain of roses, her skin is so lovely. And her figure! Do you know she is so delicate that she can put her hands around her waist, and that a ten-year-old child can't fit into her clothes?'

'And her hair,' sighed Lubienka, dreamily. 'They say it is so long, so thick, that it takes three hours each morning to dress it . . . three hours . . . can you imagine?'

'A handsome couple, yes, a handsome couple; Oh! It's a blessing for the entire monarchy.'

I thought I saw a brush pass over and over an interminable head of hair, I thought I saw a torrent of pearly petals fall from the top of a church. A blessing, a blessing, I repeated over and over; and I was already asleep again.

The clocks ticked in my rooms, the mice nibbled, the time passed over people and things, but I was no longer there.

Sometimes I turned over with a sigh, and there was a crackling in my framing that alarmed the household and caused the overseer to ask an expert. Without results—I may have some defects but I have never had termites. I also happened to let escape through one of my chimneys the billowing of a dream which I would have a hard time remembering. What do houses dream of? Colours, conditions, tiny sensations. That must be what little fellows dream of in their mothers' wombs.

There were periods, however, some of which were rather long, when I was awake. But what I saw in those moments did not have the texture of usual events. It was an abbreviated history, without substance or meaning, like a serial story of which one had missed too many episodes. And when I began to come to myself again, to grasp who was who and what was in question, the torpor fell over me again and maliciously breathed into me. The next episode will be in the next issue.

And so while I was still in my very first sleep, one day I thought I heard the voice of Urszula; but it was an unknown Urszula, an Urszula with the vibrant tone of authentic pain.

'Poor Jan, poor Maria,' she sobbed. 'I can't believe it. Oh, what misfortune, my God!'

They were all there in the small green salon: Jozef, Wioletta, Urszula, her young son, even her husband.

'My dear,' he muttered, in mourning attire like the four others. 'Come, come, my dear . . .'

And attentive, solicitous, he held out his handkerchief to her, because she had already soaked her own.

Wioletta, sombre, remained silent; nor did Jozef utter a word. But in his heart there was only revolt against the cruelty of fate! Maria, his first child, whom he had taken from the hands of the midwife with such mixed emotions but of whom he had ultimately been so proud . . . Maria as a little girl, perched on the back of their gentle mare; Maria engaged, radiant, Maria the wife of Jan, the heir to his name!

Then a flood of sorrow shook the master, because Jan was also dead, Jan who was practically his son. The only one whose opinion he had ever listened to with curiosity, even respect, Jan who had led him to believe that, sometimes, the young did better, thought more clearly than their elders . . . Jan, who once brought him (against his better judgement) into the world of tomorrow! What would he do now?

Jozef had already mourned his death once. But how far away that time, scarcely nine years ago, now seemed to him! Struck down by an Austrian bullet, Jan in February 1846 had died a martyr. The wound to Jozef's heart had been deep then, but clear—he felt no bitterness.

Today, there was something putrid in his pain that, later, contaminated the past. To die of cholera, even if one shared that misfortune with the great Mickiewicz, had no glory to it; it was a lamentable, sordid end. Jozef saw it as an epilogue to an entire patriotic epic. Good God!— so much heroism, so much effort, so many young lives sacrificed, to end up fighting in an unhealthy war, for unclear ends? Jan had certainly explained it to him, in his last letter, that the game of chess around the Black Sea could shake things up and should thus receive the support of all the refugee Poles in Turkey; but Jozef didn't believe it any more. The truth was that Jan, like the others, had lost sight of the national objectives and henceforth fought only for geopolitical calculations—to support a sultan who, perhaps, would support them one day in order to crush a Russia that had always harmed them. Where was freedom, idealism, in all of that? Before the walls of Silistre, Sebastopol, in the bitter cold that crippled men and killed horses, heroism lost all meaning. Jan had sacrificed his life for nothing, not even while fighting. What was worse, he had dragged his wife into it. Why in the world had that foolish woman decided to follow him to the Crimea!

'And what is to become of their daughter?' asked Agenor, who was looking ahead.

'Oh,' the hollow voice of his father-in-law finally spoke, 'she is in good hands. A year ago, her parents placed her with the wife of one of their colonel friends. The couple, who don't have any children, adore her, and are now trying to adopt her . . .'

His granddaughter Mathilde would thus become the adoptive daughter of a Hungarian colonel converted to Islam under the name of Anvar Bey, he realized, again in silence. Life was strange. Life, for several years, seemed to be a crazy dream. And he now looked at Urszula: Who would have believed that this graceless daughter would become the refuge of his hopes, his only promise for the future?

To tell the truth, his Urszula had changed a great deal. She had become capable of compassion and love. Through their tears, her eyes fell on her husband, her solid rock, she glanced at Wioletta without much harshness (after all, whom did she have left to envy?), at her father with understanding. The breaking of glass suddenly shook the adults out of their dark thoughts—having found the ball-and-cup game in a drawer, Andrzej, with an unlucky shot, had just knocked over a glass lampshade and it had shattered.

'Enough!' shouted his grandfather, 'go play somewhere else, we're in no mood to put up with your foolishness. We are in mourning, after all!'

'Now, now, Papa, don't be so harsh,' Andrzej's mother intervened. 'This poor dear is as affected as we are, but sorrow always makes the child a bit wild. And then, you must be fair, he listened to a long Mass, he only got up three times, and if he knocked over a chair, it was not really his fault, was it? The chairs in the chapel are so unstable!'

Andrzej, who was waiting for that encouragement, resumed his game of destruction before the ball hit his fingers and he burst into tears.

They hovered around him, cajoled him, they rang for the maid to take him out. I saw the stricken face of a young woman under a white cap, the cries and sobs dwindled in the direction of the grounds, and calm returned.

But before going back to sleep, I still had time to discover, an hour later, Wioletta and Agenor talking together in a nook in the hallway. He was holding her shoulders, looking her in the eyes and murmuring very softly, 'My dear sister, let me, without witnesses, assure you of my deep compassion. I would like to tell you that . . .'

'Oh, I know, I know, don't say anything,' Wioletta whispered. 'We both know, don't we?'

'Yes, we know,' murmured Agenor tightening his grip on the shoulders covered in black cloth. 'Oh, Wioletta, that sin of youth, I feel as if I will pay for it, regret it, my entire life . . .'

'No, you mustn't! Agenor, don't be sad. Think of Urszula who loves you, think of your Andrzej, of your public life where you are thriving . . .'

'Oh,' said Agenor with a doubtful pout.

'Yes, Agenor. Believe in yourself the way I believe in you. From here I pray for your happiness, for your success . . . Oh, Agenor, don't give in to sadness—I want to be proud of you.'

So God does look out for children, fools, drunks and rogues, I marvelled, while Wioletta, filled with emotion, quickly ran away, her heavy braid dancing on her back.

Agenor watched her leave. Really, she was still attractive at almost thirty years of age, he thought. Her hair was still magnificent, her ankles sculptural; even if, close up, her face was no longer exactly what it had been. And what was more, she still loved him and wished him no ill. Indeed, he wasn't so disappointed with his day.

Later, when he would inherit the property (for he would now that Maria and Jan are dead), he would, however, have to make her understand that such cohabitation was impossible, indecent. Anyway, as Romantic and exalted as she was, she would feel the same. To enter the orders, at the age she would be then, would probably be the only reasonable solution. Didn't she already have a Benedictine sister?

He expected a lot from that inheritance. By living here part of the year, he could deploy his local ownership, something that was indispensable in politics if one didn't wish to look like a bohemian, a plotter. A landowner, he would have more influence than a mere director of a textile factory. He would be a man with a place, a man of land; yes, he would wed this property as he had wed Urszula.

There would also be expenses, many expenses, he was well aware of that. This county *dwor* would be an asset for his career, but he would have to watch out that it not also become a sinkhole. The roof, for example, needed to be replaced. A few more years and the damage would be irreversible. As for the cellars, there must certainly be something that could be done to avoid the humidity on the ground floor that could, in time, become deleterious. Should he mention it to old Zemka? No, it was premature, it wouldn't be very elegant. Maybe Urszula could during her next visit . . .

Shark, I thought. And I fell back asleep, this time for a long time. Because there now reigned a calm over the house that was conducive to sleep. They probably did hammer in poles, shoot at rabbits, close to my walls; and the servants, the day-workers, the merchants from our countryside, never did speak in soft voices. But those noises were in some sense a part of me, and I was no more disturbed by them than Jozef was at night by his own snoring.

One summer I was in fact disturbed by the sounds of my roof being replaced. It was a disagreeable period—I was upset, I didn't like the drafts or the agitation that had dispersed my nesting birds and swept away the dust. And the spectacle, down below, was not distracting.

Here was a Jozef, now in his sixties, who had once again let his sideburns grow. But they were no longer those proud locks that had once framed his temples like those of a Napoleonic marshal. They were grey and droopy and swelled at mouth-level like grey jowls. A fashion, no doubt, as the attorney from Grünau was also sporting them. Jozef, once every day, took all that hair out on a walk to the sugar factory, but he didn't stay very long. He seemed to feel he had spent enough time working and his proxy was doing very well without him.

In the end his only *raison d'être*, along with his hunting and reading the Lvov Gazette, resided within these walls. And if I believed my eyes, it or, rather, she was not doing very well.

She (I mean Wioletta) had, however, climbed in status since the departures of all her sisters and Madame Denisot—she now had the honour of running her father's household.

It was not very difficult, at least in theory. It was no longer a matter of managing a family of some ten people, of organizing receptions, seeing over the education of minor girls, as her mother Clara had done in her time. She simply had to assure the comfort of the master and supervise the servants, whose numbers were, moreover, vastly reduced; because those that left were not replaced unless Jozef felt they were truly indispensable. It had been necessary, of course, to have another cook, but Wioletta could very well dress herself and fix her own hair without the help of a new Lubienka.

In fact, however, the task was thankless and exhausting. Jozef was simultaneously always there to criticize his daughter's work and never there to respond to her requests for clarification. Wioletta spent her time running around the hallways looking for him, a set of keys at her waist like a portress nun.

'Father, the overseer is looking for you, he needs you to . . .'

'Go take care of it. The roofer wants me to go up and look at the roof. Take care of it, will you, I can't do everything!'

When she had settled, as well as she could, a problem concerning an invoice to pay and an indispensable accounting matter with Mr Bialy, she was called to the kitchen—the cook Bozena, an unhelpful type who didn't hide the fact that she had worked in better houses, reminded her that it was already ten o'clock and, that if she weren't told the lunch menu, *Pan* Jozef would have to be content with cold meat.

'What! You haven't prepared anything yet?'

'Of course not, I was waiting for my orders. Mistress didn't say anything to me yesterday, and I wouldn't presume . . .'

'Make . . . a rice soup, a timbale, and uh, a sautéed chicken, something that doesn't take very long . . .'

'For dessert?'

'Let's see, are there any of the peaches that the countess Wytocka sent over from her greenhouses?'

'So mistress doesn't require another course,' the woman concluded with a disapproving sniff in the face of so much incompetence, and, with a scorn, transcended class inequality for a mistress who wasn't married and never would be.

'No, wait, yes . . . Listen, I give you carte blanche.'

'As you wish, mistress.'

The mistress was already running down the stairs to settle a dispute between two leaseholders, one Polish, the other Ruthenian, who were fighting about the use of a pond and the carp that could be fished there. She went back up to consult her father, who sent her away so she was forced to find the overseer to ask him to go inquire at the land registry. A few strands of hair were now escaping from her braid, and she was red and winded from these comings and goings. It was time for her to wash up a bit before sitting down at the table, or she would be viewed with a critical eye by her commensal father in a silence that would say: '*Négligé*, my dear, is no longer becoming at your age.'

Her hair combed, her face washed, she looked much better. Her features had softened with the beginning of maturity, her periwinkle eyes were still gorgeous, even if they might be considered a bit too large for a face that the bloom of youth had abandoned; or her mouth that was a bit too mobile, constantly grimacing with explanations and excuses that she dared not utter.

That day was a good day, however; her father restricted himself to glancing at her and acknowledging her with a little nod. But things quickly deteriorated.

'Rice soup! But you know I can't abide this.'

'Really?' Wioletta stammered. 'My goodness, I'm very sorry, I had forgotten.'

'Forgotten!' Jozef continued, stopping with a gesture the lackey who was about to serve him. 'It's true you've never had a very good head.'

Wioletta allowed that unfair, but prophetic, statement to pass. And once the lunch was over, she slipped away to her room in an attempt to find a bit of calm. She finished a gouache, began a sketch, and I noted that her style had changed. The stroke was more solid, the colours deeper. And her subjects were no longer the landscapes from around here, the details of my rooms—to my surprise, I discovered under the brush of this sedentary woman mountains, valleys, sea cliffs battered by waves, or palaces and the gold of dying empires. It was . . . it was beautiful, yes, beautiful, but a bit ghostly. If one were to consider these as reflections of her soul, her soul had become something quite rocky and labyrinthine.

After an hour or two, her father shouted from the stairwell: 'Wioletta! You're taking your time, it seems. Have you forgotten that I have four letters to dictate to you? Hurry up, please, the postman from Lemberg will be by shortly.'

Sometimes it was a document that he couldn't find in the library, a visitor who needed to be entertained with tea or coffee with cream; or a letter from Podolia which he didn't want her to read but which he insisted on reading silently in her presence.

'Perfect,' he would then mutter. (It was out of habit; because recently the little rascal had begun to worry his guardians. The notary had found him a position as an errand boy with a colleague, and the young Feliks Zemka apparently stood out only through his lack of discipline). 'Perfect. Wait, not so quickly, my dear, I still need you to cut pages.'

The truth was that he couldn't do without her, without her bewildered eyes, her trembling mouth. She was like a beautiful harp in his hands that the slightest word caused to vibrate and tremble. But a harp is a fragile instrument, whereas Wioletta was indestructible; only time, it seemed to him, had left its traces on her.

I didn't agree with that. I recognized a double blindness in this, the blindness of love, that jealous and destructive love for her which he had never admitted to himself; and that of tyranny which is always mistaken about the ability of its victims to endure and to survive. Oh, yes, Wioletta kept traces other than just the lines on her forehead and at the corners of her lips. Like the arabesques of a blind calligrapher, they overlapped on the walls of her psyche. This sight didn't please me at all; and at the end of the summer of 1859, it was a relief when, under my new roof tiles, I closed my eyes again.

19

They left me alone—perhaps a bit too alone. In a cloud of confusion, I sensed that the world around me was changing, that either very close by or far away slow metamorphoses were occurring. New names, new phrases struck my ears through the screen that protected my senses, 'Maximilian', 'Sadowa', 'zemstvos', 'Austria-Hungary'. . . I wanted to say: Will you wake me up if something happens—you'll wake me won't you?' But you can be sure, when you ask that, that they won't wake you until everything is already over.

Every time I peeked out, other figures, about whom I knew nothing, were there: a man with a pince-nez, for example, whose nasal and Germanic accent could be heard throughout the house; a young cross-eyed servant girl named Nikolaïa; a fat man with a moustache who always carried a whip and seemed to have taken Efraim's place. Or they were known but I didn't recognize them, so greatly had they changed.

It took me several moments before I understood that the heavyset woman with the disenchanted pout was the blonde girl I had heard talking about the imperial marriage one day. 'Oh, you Poles . . .' she said, perfidiously, to Bozena. But a little man in dolman sleeves made his way into the kitchen and was requesting, sweetly, for a drop of port to dip a cookie in, and I blinked my eyes, amazed, because the two women forgot their earlier quarrel to hover around '*Pan* Andrzej'. . .

I closed my eyes again and when I opened them I saw the same boy, who had grown five inches, with the shiny eyes of pubescent curiosity.

Another time I sensed an atmosphere of anguish that seemed to belong to another time. 'I must be dreaming, I think I am still in the spring of 1846,' I reassured myself. But, shaking myself awake, I indeed saw my grey-haired Jozef of the 1860s and a Wioletta who no longer had anything in common, alas, with the willowy tragic heroine of 'the good old days'.

They were sitting across from each other in the library, that old father and that ageing daughter, and the air around them was crackling with the same electrical tension that had been discharged seventeen years earlier in uprisings and riots. History, again, was starting up; but there was no more Jan, no more Zygmunt to gather its message of hope. It started up somewhere else, beyond the border. And perhaps there, in Russia, other young Poles in turn thought they were on the threshold of an era of justice and freedom. Here, in any case, there reigned only fear. What had happened to Jozef that he saw this new insurrection as only the affair of other people, and as only a danger for him? Did the fear of popular excess overwhelm his patriotic soul?

'Father, I read in your paper that the repression against our compatriots in Podolia has been terrible, that in several places serfs have risen up against them . . . Father, I beg you, if you know something of my son, please tell me.'

'And what would I tell you? In fact, well before the intervention of the army, your Feliks disappeared and no one has heard from him since. I will point out, in passing, the ingratitude of his actions. A modest but honourable placement was found for your bastard, a means to finally insure his livelihood without depending on us . . . And then, this. Disappeared. I do wonder exactly where he went, by the way, but at fifteen, without an education and without a penny in his pocket, I can say with some certainty that wherever he is he is doing nothing good.'

Wioletta was crying now.

'Disappeared? Oh, Father, and you never allowed me to write to him, to tell him that I loved him, that I was thinking of him!'

'My girl,' Jozef threw in with satisfied irritation (because she rarely gave him the opportunity for such a settling of accounts), 'it has always been up to you. If you had only told me who your lover was, when and where you had committed your sinful acts, I would have agreed . . .'

'I will never tell you,' Wioletta gasped, her head lowered as if to offer less resistance to a force that was, henceforth, without strength. And I thought I saw a closed oyster between the hands of a brutal little boy who, enraged, considers throwing it onto a stone in order to see inside it at last.

These snippets were glimpsed in a barely awake state; they had the evanescence of a magic lantern show. Others, however, were clear and precise but so precise that I came to doubt their reality.

Thus one summer day there is a little party in the garden; parasols, a ground cloth, a wasp sucking on some pâté, a ringed hand (belonging to Urszula, wearing a diamond of her late mother's) moving to shoo it away; and then heads that, all at once, turn towards the gate.

Behind it stand a poorly dressed man and a little boy. They are looking at the chateau-dwellers with such intensity that the latter, one after the other, put their glasses, as well as their dishes of sorbet that they were eating in little spoonfuls, down on the cloth.

'What is this!' Jozef finally mutters, and, getting up with difficulty from his garden chair, leaning on his cane, starts towards the gate.

Vasyl? he thinks, incredulous, when he recognizes that the man is the son he had once had and with whom he had definitively broken some fifteen years earlier.

But Vasyl, without looking at him, grips the arm of the boy, and his voice slices through his father as if he didn't exist.

'Do you see them, Oleh? Look at them, look at their hats, their nice clothes, their porcelain and their crystal glasses! All that is from the sweat of our brows, all that was stolen from the Ruthenian people. Look at them well, Oleh, and never forget!'

Then Agenor gets up; the young Andrzej prudently hides behind a low shrub, leaving his mother and his mother's friends (Wioletta isn't present, as is usual when her visiting Lemberg family is entertaining guests) to their frightened murmuring and their hands clutching their throats.

'Come now, Vasyl, that's enough,' says Jozef in a low voice, because his son-in-law has got up and is approaching them. 'Now, wait a minute . . .' He digs into his vest pocket to find a few coins, doesn't find any, is sweating; too late, Agenor is there and takes things in hand.

'Allow me, Father,' he murmurs; and then says, in a very dry tone, 'You are on private property, and you are disturbing the ladies. I advise you to depart before our overseer releases the dogs.'

Vasyl, the grandson of the old Doroshenkos, takes a step backwards; and his hand, still gripping the child's shoulder, becomes white at the joints.

'Do you hear how they speak to us, Oleh? Yet they are on our property. This land is ours, look at them, the thieves, the parasites . . .'

The child, mute with attention, stares first at the old man who is sweating, at the short fat man who has just spoken meanly to them, at the women who are still sitting down and the adolescent boy with long hair whose head is showing above the shrub; and each one of them shudders under the gaze of the child who still doesn't understand everything but who already knows how to hate. In the distance, they hear the barking of the dogs.

'Oh, but you will pay,' shouts Vasyl, his fist raised, 'one day you will pay, and the Ruthenian people will take back what is theirs . . .'

They leave, walking briskly, the father pulling on the hand of his son who is still looking behind him; and in my memory all the picnickers stay there, petrified, as if the wand of a fairy has turned them into figures in a lugubrious *tableau vivant*.

This image pursues me for a very long time. It settles into my dreams, I would like to rid myself of it but am unable to. Thus it is with relief, much later, that I hear someone pounding against a wooden panel.

'Finally,' I say to myself vaguely, 'they are striking the three blows, the curtain is going to rise and I will see something else.' And I expect, in half sleep, to see Mary, Joseph and the baby Jesus or Herod, because I no longer really know whether my inhabitants are puppets manipulated by a Moravian troupe and their tribulations a Christmas pageant being rehearsed.

But the pounding continues and I wake up—no, we are not at the theatre, and what I hear is only the striking of a hand against a door panel in the second-floor hallway.

The hand isn't striking hard, and I am somewhat surprised that I am able to hear it. To whom does it belong? It is dark in the hallway but a bit of moonlight comes in through the window and casts its light upon the glass of a pince-nez. Oh, it is that man with the nasal voice that so likes technical vocabulary. A new overseer? But why is he knocking on Wioletta's door in the middle of the night?

She finally hears him. A match is lit, slippers swish on the floor, the key turns in the lock, the door opens.

'Herr Jäger?'

'Oh, you were asleep. I beg your pardon, I thought . . .'

'It doesn't matter,' Wioletta murmurs, adjusting an old cashmere shawl over her shoulders and taking a step backwards. I see her better—she has just got out of bed but I guess, with a heavy heart, that those dark shadows, those folds have henceforth settled onto her ageing face.

'What can I do for you, Herr Jäger? Is someone ill?'

'Not at all, rest assured . . .'

Rudolf Jäger has the annoying habit of clicking his heels each time he answers a direct question. It even seems that this military gesture sums up his response and that his convoluted phrases are there only to add a bit more, a sonorous ornamentation. 'Excuse this unpardonable liberty . . . An attraction impossible to fight, and so understandable . . . Two lonely hearts, wounded by life . . .'

Wioletta listens mutely to this flood of stupidities. What does he want with her, what has he come here for? She doesn't understand. But her mouth becomes pinched, her forehead is creased with a horizontal line when, in conclusion, he utters these astounding words, 'Dear, dear Wioletta!'

She stares at the intruder, looks from his feet shod with impeccable boots to the false collar covering a large Adam's apple. She looks further up and observes the mouth that is showing a bold smile, the pince-nez shining with libidinous flashes.

Dear Wioletta!

She then takes hold of the door and bursts out laughing. The laugh, from a woman who has probably not laughed in fifteen or twenty years, is not pleasant to hear. There is nothing gay about it—there is a discordant note in it like the sound of a cracked bell. It fades, then starts up again. Herr Jäger is no longer smiling and retreats into the hallway. It's a good thing, because a moment later Wioletta shuts the door in his face. She can still be heard laughing behind the door; the overseer remains there, uncertain, humiliated, then takes off his pince-nez and rubs it nervously with the bottom of his jacket.

They're going to pay for this.

They would indeed pay, because two weeks after that failed attempt at seduction the thief makes off with the safe, a few pieces of jewellery and railroad stock from the Lemberg–Czernowitz line—taking at the source what he had hoped to obtain by way of alcove encounters and a possible marriage. Wioletta is thus directly implicated in this drain on the Zemkas' fortune. But, luckily, no one but I will ever know anything.

When anyone speaks of Rudolf Jäger in front of her, she laughs, with the same cracked-bell laugh as that first night. I don't know what to think of that laugh. The bitterness of a woman who measures her decline by the only suitor that fate, belatedly, saw fit to send her? Tell me who courts you and I will tell you how far you have fallen . . . Or— a more disturbing hypothesis—it is a laugh of scorn, comparative perhaps. Wioletta, give in to the advances of that clown? She has had much better than that. She already belongs to a sort of Celestial Spouse, and, though their union will no longer be consummated, it presides mysteriously over the harmony of the world. (For this is how she sees things; and from her vantage point, she is not completely wrong.)

That laugh upsets me, it reveals something disturbing that has been occurring, perhaps for years, under the shell of that unhappy woman. Her huge eyes carry a mystical spark in them that is not good; her mouth, when she isn't laughing, is shaken by tics. No, this interval of courtship did not cheer me up. It was grotesque without being funny; and when I go back to sleep afterwards, it is almost with the hope that I never wake up again.

20

I sometimes wonder what would have happened if, in fact, I hadn't woken up again. Probably nothing other than what did happen, in fact. In one hundred and twenty years of existence, my walls and everything that makes up my body had been filled with images, memories, words and odours so that it went on influencing the actions of my inhabitants. Saturated, my body began to exude all that it had been previously filled with, without it needing my conscience or will for that. Like slices of cucumber on which one has poured salt (rock-salt, the good salt from the state salt reserves of Galicia), they slowly formed the pearly drops of nectar that men would call—depending on their frame of mind—necessity, destiny or atavism. The pragmatic Agenor saw them as drops of humidity. That is not entirely false but it is indeed reductive.

Everything would thus have occurred in pretty much the same way if I had not been there to see it. New birds' nests would have been constructed, year after year, under my redone roof, and new generations of cats would have slipped through the gaps in the air vents to wreak havoc. New generations of worms would have eaten through the hard pulp of the furniture and made pathways in it, the Ringstraße and the worker quarters of a miniature Vienna. New generations of cooks would have chopped, plucked, boned and whipped to feed new generations of masters. Children would have been born, grown and given birth to others before growing old and leaving their places to them; men would have died, and trees, as well.

And what would have become of me, the sleeper resolved never to wake up again? I like to believe that I would have left my corporal envelope there prematurely to join the mineral substrate common to all houses. 'For dust you are and to dust you will return'—that phrase read in the big book that has so occupied Wioletta for a few years seems to me to have been written for us, much more than for men. Because, really, let's be serious! Everyone knows that men leave a lot more than a bit of dust. They leave their names, their descendants, their memory, the trace of their actions or their works. So let them spare us such self-pity, such anthropocentric whining—we houses know better than they what it is like to disappear from the face of the earth.

So I would have sunk into my last sleep, and I don't think about it without some curiosity. First, I would enter into the good rich earth that is waiting under my cellars, fertile coolness, filled with vegetal memories, earthworms and insects. That layer would still tell me things about the human world—here and there I would have discovered an old ploughshare, a broken pipe, a belt buckle, a coin with the effigy of Maria Theresa or even a Jagiellon king . . .

I would have gone down farther, struck new objects at which I would be seized with doubt. Shards of pottery or fossilized mud? Arrowhead or a vulgar stone chipped in a landslide? Had that bone of an aurochs or of another extinct species, been pierced with a little hole by design or by chance?

But soon I would have forgotten even these enigmas—no more men here, no more camps or families or primitive graves, nothing but the lace of a fern printed on the rock or a scarab prisoner of his resin gangue to remind me of the world above. And there, so far from the daylight, I would perhaps have fallen on a layer of coal or a layer of oil, waiting for all eternity for someone to discover them.

And then I would have known what Night truly was. Not that pleasant interval that is called night on earth, so relative, in the end, with its moon, its lamps, its stars and its fireplace fires. So alive, really, so sensual, so rich in events for those who aren't sleeping. I have already spoken about a night of that kind. But the night I am speaking of, that of these huge rocky depths that extend beneath us, where not the slightest breath of air or life moves, has nothing in common with those few nocturnal hours of August 1846, nor with the darkest night of the darkest winter of the darkest period Poland had ever known. It is absolute Night, at the thought of which we are instinctively filled with terror and attraction.

Wasn't it out of that terror that Zygmunt Borowski, for example, wished so ardently the dawns, the days to come, the spring blazes? And isn't it out of fascination with that Night that we are so eager to penetrate the bottom of things, the dark plots, the depths of our soul, and disappointed that we must illuminate them in order to do so?

I, too, have my dark zones where the rays of the sun will never reach. And I am not transparent even to my own gaze. I feel the Night in me, I feel it, like all of us—men, animals, plants or buildings—in the heart of our world. And the battle it wages against logical clarity, the warmth of blood, the flights of hope and the solar joys is much more uncertain than the pendulum struggle of day and night, happy Sisyphuses, in the end, with their complementarity and handshaking, in the morning and at night, like two loyal partners. Because in that battle there are true losses, true victims, things that pass and never come back; beings, ideas, states doomed to extinction without any hope of dawn or revival. It is that battle that accounts for the fact that there are things irretrievable in our world and—as a corollary—things absolutely new.

No, the march of time and genealogy are only clear and rectilinear in appearance, and if the new descends from the old, it is just as mysteriously as the daughter of Anvar Bey descending from Tadeusz Zemka or Oleh Doroshenko from the counts Ponarski. The Night, I am convinced, presides over these curved filiations, over these historical shipwrecks of which nothing is foretold and that everything, in the end, nonetheless explains.

And I who am always there, even when I sleep; I who never move while everything fluctuates. Isn't it natural that I sense better than anyone else, through my foundations, the push of those chthonian forces, the rising cold of that which makes things fade, overthrows empires, warps heredity?

III
SOME LEAVE, OTHERS RETURN

1

The shouting of children awakened me from my sleep once and for all.

It must have been spring, April perhaps; a timid sunshine played on my windowpanes, on the other side of which tender leaves on a young branch were swaying.

And, if my ears weren't deceiving me, there were children playing outside.

'Give it to me! Give it to me!' shrieked a shrill voice in German. In response, a mocking laugh ran away, zigzagging, and I heard something like the rustling of leaves and broken branches.

Who were those children?

I put my nose to the window and saw three shapes chasing one another. And, good gracious, how tall the trees on the grounds had become!

The little band had gone beyond my field of vision and, resigned to learning nothing more for the time being, I looked around me.

On the roof of the first cottage, the smoke hole had gradually grown bigger and sunk, so that the thatch seemed to have been eaten by a huge cow. The wooden church was still standing, but the effects of the weather had caused it to lose even more of its colour and it seemed that the entire building had gradually become lopsided.

But, my goodness, where had the sugar factory gone? Through a curtain of adult poplars I was finally able to see its three smoking chimneys; even if, looking more closely, only two out of three of them were smoking. My little sister had thus not gone away.

Now the children were coming back towards me, and I saw them better. The tall girl who was walking in front, sternly dragging someone else by the ear, was a maid, very young, in a black dress, her waist cinched by a white-bibbed apron, her face determined under a cap of fluted lace.

'That's enough, Kazimierz! Leave your sister alone or I'm really going to get angry. And when I really get angry, you know I become very, very mean!'

A final shaking of the guilty ear, and its owner was thrown within my line of vision. Kazimierz, then. No doubt, this Kazimierz was one of the family. He looked surprisingly like the young Andrzej, a few years younger than the latter, the last time I had seen him. He looked like him but had red hair. And in the lower part of his face I saw something of Zosia.

With a final sniffle, the youngest one arrived with an air of sombre victory, hugging a doll to her chest. Hey! It was our good old Cordelia, in fact, wearing a crinoline dress that Madame Denisot had made for her back in 1842. But the years since then had inflicted a great deal of damage on her. Her arms, which had lost almost all their colour, were unusually long and thin, as if she had in the meantime suffered from cachexia; and on her wax face the red of her cheeks and the black of her eyebrows were almost gone.

But the little girl holding her seemed blind to those defects. She kissed the frizzy wig, rocked the long thin body, enjoying her spoils of war; and Kazimierz, his head lowered, shot vindictive looks her way.

Force has never established a lasting peace. A moment later, having finished rubbing his ear, the scamp pulled hard on Cordelia's wig and ran away with it, laughing.

'Mitzi! Mitzi! Catch him!' shrieked the little girl; and the maid, with a sigh that raised the pretty curves of her bust, ran off in pursuit of the scalper of dolls.

But now the window of the green salon was opening and I saw the face, then the shoulders of Urszula appear.

'Tessa, what is all this noise?'

'Oh, grandmother, Kazimierz is taking all the toys that I found upstairs! And he breaks them! Look what he did to my doll!'

Urszula, wearing a silk dress whose cut seemed unusual to me, gave Cordelia the shocked look that was expected, then murmured with a gesture, 'That is very mean of him. Now go look for them, my dear, I need to speak with your father.'

Urszula a grandmother! And those two rascals, the children of Andrzej, no doubt! It was disconcerting. In the space of a minute, I felt the panic of an old person who begins to lose her marbles but still has enough to be aware of that fact.

Let's see, has so much time really gone by? What year were we? Had I slept longer than I thought?

Observing Madame Karlowiczowa more closely, I was, however, reassured. No, my internal clock had not deceived me—we were not much later than 1877 or 1878, 1879 at most. I had before me a solid woman in her fifties; and since she had conceived her son in 1850, he must in turn have become a father at a young age.

That was interesting. I could see an entire saga here, adolescent passion, perhaps, or a duly legalized elopement such as that of the Zemkas in Turkey—in short, an incredibly romantic story that would have taken me back to the time in this century that I knew better. But while following Urszula inside the green salon, I was disabused. The young man—no, the still young man who was seated there had never lost his head nor upset two families to marry his sweetheart. He had frequented the race tracks, lost a lot of money playing cards, looked at his already wrinkled eyelids in the mirrors of houses of ill repute in which he had, if one were to believe the blasé fold of his lips, exhausted the blonde and brunette pleasures a long time ago. But I couldn't see a trace of any other passions in him; and the tone in which Urszula spoke to him was that of a mother confident that she did not have a rival.

'And so I suggest, Andrzej, that you stay here another week or two before leaving. Your children hardly know your grandfather or my poor sister . . . they don't know this house or this countryside . . .'

'Oh, Mother, I don't know it any more than they.'

'Nonsense, my boy. You spent almost all your summers here before we moved to Vienna.'

Well! There certainly had been some changes. Agenor's career had apparently taken off, and the Poles of Galicia had given up playing the disgruntled sons of the empire, if I understood correctly. This somewhat overripe reveller was thus a bit Viennese; and what had struck me in his mother's elegance was not only the change in fashion but also the mark of a metropolitan stylist.

'And then, my dear Andrzej, it wouldn't be a bad idea if you began to learn how the factory works, to study the accounting and be introduced to the staff. It takes a lot of tact, you see, a lot of subtlety to manage these people. They are Ruthenians, and . . .'

'I know.'

At Andrzej's dry tone it seemed to me that the little scene caused by the Doroshenko boy had left a bad taste in his mouth. It even seemed that I saw on his face a fugitive expression of fear and repugnance that made me think that no, he had not enjoyed those summers here, at least since that day. If Urszula managed to get him to stay two weeks, she would certainly be a masterful woman.

Now he was listening sullenly, and she was looking at him in a way that spoke volumes. That boy had made mistakes. They must have rescued him from some dilemma, a gambling debt, some sort of fraud or compromising liaison, and in return they must have demanded that he now toe the line. Perhaps this precocious marriage and parenthood were the cell of sobriety into which they had hastened to throw him before things really turned bad?

'. . . Because, don't forget, my son, that we are grooming you to direct the sugar factory. And such things cannot be improvised. One day, your grandfather won't be enough. He is declining—you must have noticed that yourself. And the business, I've understood, is declining too. For your own interest, I can't encourage you enough to go see what is wrong and suggest some reforms to your grandfather. He is an old man, you know . . .'

'I'll do it, Mother, you can count on me.'

'I knew I could. Oh, I am happy, very happy, very proud of my boy.'

There was a silence, contemplated with amusement by the Alep dagger hanging motionless on the wall, and by the discreet Trebizond rug. Indeed, in Andrzej Karlowicz we had a repentant sinner who had been taken in hand to be reformed. And I also noted that Urszula's satisfied smile fit, at both corners of her mouth, in between already old lines, like a foot slides into a slipper that through long use has been shaped to the foot. I guessed that it had already been many years that they had counted on Andrzej, that they had been proud of Andrzej, in short, that they had been very busy keeping him on the right path.

'What a pity, all the same, that your wife isn't here! She would have been a great help to us. On this land, a man without a wife does not inspire confidence. And then, for your children, to settle them in, her presence would have been very beneficial.'

'Mother, you well know that Gertrud doesn't endure travelling, and . . .'

'Bother, in eighteen months she went to Salzburg, Karlsbad and then Lake Garda.'

'For her health, Mother. She was only following our doctor's advice. Those trips are a trial on her nerves and her constitution, but the benefit once she is there is evident. Whereas here, with the humidity of these rooms, the sometimes unhealthy air when there isn't any wind, the mosquitoes when it's hot . . .'

'Yes, yes,' Urszula conceded sharply, 'Let's not exaggerate. The air here is not that unhealthy, and the house, God knows, is no more humid than any other. To hear you talk, one might be surprised that we survived it, my sisters and I, for more than twenty years.'

A wave of sadness passed over her face at the memory of her two sisters whom she had lost in the meantime, one a long time ago, and the other more recently; and her eye lingered on a painting that I hadn't seen before, the portrait of a Benedictine nun with a calm face, her hands peacefully folded on her rosary—Jadwiga, who had obviously enjoyed the peace of the Lord well before leaving the world below.

Andrzej, who had seen that look, lowered his bare forehead over his mother's hand, and murmured with a smile, 'That's true. But you, Mother, are made of steel.'

Flattered, Urszula smiled in turn and sat back in her chair.

'Thank God, I have nothing to complain about with my health. But I believe your wife could have assumed her responsibilities, made a little effort. Because I am forced to take care of your children and organize their stay here at a time when the situation in Vienna is very uncertain and when people still don't know who will succeed Prince Auersperg. Your father doesn't yet predict the future cabinet, but one thing is certain—he must take advantage of the opportunity to leave his unjustly obscure role and finally reap the fruit of his talent.'

Andrzej maintains a hostile silence. I sensed the old bitterness of a son who must have had to fight against the adored husband for the attentions of his mother and only succeeded by making himself noticed in negative ways; of a son who, I would have sworn, had not found the same indulgence in his father, had disappointed him, and knew it.

'Let us think of it no more,' said Urszula, getting up. 'In fact, I think I will serve the tea, since Wioletta isn't coming down.'

I left them, and went off wandering through the rooms, noting here and there a new wallpaper, a dent in the door of a buffet. The large salon was ghostly—all the furniture was draped with dust covers, the windows were not very clean, and the huge pendulum clock must not have been wound for ages, because its weights were grey with dust. Evidently, there had been no balls or parties here during my long sleep; and, in their gilt frames, Kosciuszko and Bonaparte exchanged looks filled with unfathomable boredom.

A floorboard creaked and I turned around—emboldened by my invisible presence, Mitzi had just come in and was engaged in the same inspection as I. I read on her little face with her sensuously opened eyes, 'Not bad! It would be pretty nice, if they took the trouble to clean it up a bit.'

She pinched the two edges of her apron, hummed the first bars of The Blue Danube and then began spinning while the wooden flowers of the parquet floor whispered to one another, 'Did you see? Someone is dancing, the time of disgrace has ended!'

Naive. Nikolaïa was already sticking her head through the doorway, shocked to see it was open, saw the dancer and coughed loudly to bring her back to order.

'What?' said the girl over her shoulder. But Nikolaïa remained impassible, her fists on her hips with an imperious look, and the intruder had to leave.

What a place, Mitzi thought, climbing the stairs to look for the two children whom she had temporarily abandoned to their fate. Oh! It was going to be fun. No young man anywhere near here, and for fellow-workers fat cows with red hands who garbled German. To go to Grünau you have to trudge a half-hour on bad roads. And their Grünau, let's not talk of that! Only one dressmaker, not even a promenade or a music kiosk, nothing of interest to see except their fat brick *ratusz* and bunches of Jews with forelocks and caftans. How boring! (She moved out of the way when Wiolctta, a pale ghost in a brown dress, passed by without seeing her, her mouth clenched the way it was every time she had to play mistress of the house.)

That one! Madame Urszula was a pill, but that one, the sister, she gave you the shivers. An entire summer running into her in this huge house where the furniture creaks at night . . . brr! Not to mention the food. You had to see what they eat in the kitchen! This morning, she came down to have her coffee and a little cake. There was the footman there in front of a platter of potatoes, chopped eggs, fried onions and God knows what else. Fried onions at seven in the morning! These Galicians!

'Tessa, Kazimierz, where are you, my darlings?'

The problem with this house is that it was full of doors that all looked alike. In two days, try to find your way around. Where was that nursery? She turned a doorknob at random, pushed her head inside the room.

'What! What is it!' growled old Jozef who was dozing with an open book on his lap.

'Excuse me,' mumbled the maid in broken Polish but with a smile that would have melted the heart of an Ataman. 'Mistake . . . wrong door . . .'

'Mistake! Mistake! You're not in a maze, here. Who are you, anyway?'

'Mitzi, sir,' said the young girl with a curtsey, before reverting to her native language and finding her chattiness again. 'You saw me yesterday. I am your great-grandchildren's maid.'

Jozef had adjusted his glasses to look carefully at the one who dared respond to him in a language other than his own.

'You don't speak Polish?'

'Not well, sir. I am from Meidling, you know.'

'Well, my girl, you must start learning it. In this house we speak Polish. In the entire province, we speak Polish. We have fought for the right to do so.'

'Of course, sir, but . . .'

'Be quiet. Polish has been the official language of this province for almost ten years. Perhaps you didn't know that?'

'No, sir. But I will be staying here only three months and . . .'

'Now, now, now, no explanations, no excuses. In this house we speak Polish,' he repeated. Then he sank into a meditative silence while his sideburns, now as white as snow, moved nervously on either side of his mouth.

Mitzi tiptoed back towards the door.

'Now there, don't leave,' muttered the old man with a little jump. 'Come here, come here, come closer to the light. What did you say your name is?'

'Mitzi, sir,' she said with another curtsey while he looked her over with a more indulgent gaze.

'A strange name, that, Mitzi. A strange name, eh?'

'My baptismal name is Marie, sir, if you prefer.'

'Marie, Maria, Mariszka . . . No, Mitzi is fine, I'll get used to it. One gets used to anything, right?'

'Oh, yes, sir,' she said with a smile that made the tip of her nose wiggle.

'Ah ha! I sense you are a bit of a flirt, Mitzi, a famous little flirt from Meidling!'

'Not at all, sir, I am the most serious girl in the world.'

'Flirt!' Joseph said triumphantly, pinching her waist. 'Go on, get to work now, and I must also get busy. We'll speak again.'

She left and, pensive, shut the door behind her. They were certainly hot-blooded in this family. She already had to deal with Herr Andrzej and occasionally with Herr Agenor. Will she also have to put up with this pompous old fool whose sideburns look so much like those of the emperor that it is comical?

Oh well, he's right, one does get used to anything, she concluded with an amused shrug of her shoulders.

She was already less bored.

2

While waiting for the dinner hour, I continued my exploration. Nothing remarkable in Urszula's room, formerly that of her mother, by the way. A few books, some magazines, some creams and lotions on her dressing table—Madame Karlowiczowa took care of both her physical and moral appearance. I should give her credit, moreover, that for her age, she wasn't bad at all; and I thought again with a little shudder of pity of that Wioletta whom I had seen on the stairs and who, despite being three years younger, now seemed much older than her sister.

Her room looked entirely different. Over time it had amassed a disturbing collection of useless objects that she must have gathered because they reminded her of the people she had lost or of her youth: an old pink satin parasol, a reticule dating from the late 1840s, the footstool from the old blue salon, which had lost a leg and had to be propped up against the wall. I could also make out a few of her paintings, those, no doubt, that had been considered not fit to hang in the rooms where they entertained. And I understood why. What visitor would not have shuddered at those monks dragging a young, naked girl towards the gallows, those monsters crouching in the cyclopean ruins, those scenes of Gothic drama and of Final Judgement?

Poor, poor Wioletta, I thought. And I went to look in her secret drawer which never held any secrets for me, to see if I would find any new letters there.

Oh, but yes. Her correspondence with Agenor had indeed expanded—it now formed a little packet tied with a mauve ribbon. I slid into it, saw the dates—they came, more or less, at a rhythm of one or two per year. There were always the same phrases with double meanings that denoted either very formal politeness or an unavowed love. 'My very dear sister . . . The great concern I had over your problems of health . . . Those whom we love, you and I, and whose happiness is so dear to us . . .'

One of them, dating from 1863, was, however, written with a more troubled hand; one could sense that it was written with urgency, even panic.

. . . It goes without saying that I share your concerns; but what you ask of me is completely impossible, don't you see? What do you think a mere deputy can do to find a Russian national outside our territory? And, my dear friend, the governor of Galicia can't do anything, either. The fate of the Poles of Russia is not within his jurisdiction, especially in these troubled times; not to mention the fact that Feliks seems to have left his job and his home voluntarily, and that his official guardian does not wish to try to find him.

Allow me, dear sister, to speak to you as a friend. Providence has not wanted you to see your son again, and his fate is no longer in your hands. Accept this as a trial but also as a sign of His grace. Accept what He has given you, and, once and for all, forget that child.

I don't know how Wioletta had taken this friendly advice; but afterwards the letters became more spaced apart, and were then rare. The last one was from 1871.

All of this made me rather sad, and I was happy to hear the dinner bell ring. The family meal would perhaps be more cheerful.

Already, in front of the door to the dining room, Tessa and Kazimierz were fighting about who would go first. Mitzi brought order with two impartial slaps, fixed Kazimierz's bow tie, rubbed a little spot off Tessa's cheek and, somewhat nervously, allowed them to go in in front of her.

'Well, you are late!' said Jozef who presided at the head of the table where a lackey was tying a napkin around his neck. 'I don't like people to be late. Punctuality, rigour . . . *la politesse des rois*, as my Uncle Krzysztof used to say . . . Did you know, Countess, my uncle, Krzysztof Ponarski?'

'Well, I don't believe I do,' muttered his neighbour (one of the Wytocki's daughters-in-law) with a large embarrassed smile. 'I seem to remember that he had been dead some seventeen or eighteen years before I was married. He was . . . a very cheerful, exuberant man, my in-laws have mentioned, a sort of unique person, wasn't he?'

The ground started to slide. Urszula quickly tried to divert the conversation.

'Come now, Kazimierz, sit down, unfold your napkin, and don't start eating bread right away, please. And you, Tessa my dear, say goodnight to everyone before you leave us.'

The little girl opened her mouth, then turned towards her maid, 'I'm not eating with them?'

'Of course not, dear. At five, one doesn't yet eat with the grown-ups. We're going to have supper in the nursery, like last night.'

'But there are guests tonight! I want to see them! And I want a roll too, like Kazimierz, and a pretty napkin!'

'You will have all of that upstairs. Now curtsey, dear, and come with me.'

The sweetness of the voice did not hide a certain firmness. Tessa curtsied, Mitzi did the same and they both disappeared.

'Your Tessa is a dear. And her maid is quite charming too,' Countess Wytocka observed, turning vaguely towards Andrzej, then towards his mother, not knowing which one of the two should be congratulated. 'What a nice person. But isn't she a bit young to take care of two big children?'

From under his red eyelashes Kazimierz gave her a sharp look. How stupid she seemed! He hated adults who always appeared to be excusing themselves for something. They said they were *good*; the very word made him sick, it made him think of an oily piece of pastry. When he is an adult . . .

'Not at all,' replied Urszula, in a peremptory tone from which I deduced that she had been personally responsible for hiring the maid, as she had, perhaps, all of her son's domestic staff. 'Mitzi is a very capable, intelligent girl who has a lot of initiative. Oh no, Mitzi is very good.'

'Very good,' stressed Andrzej, without lifting his eyes from his bowl of soup.

Disturbed by this double response, the poor Countess blushed and launched into the tale of the troubles her own daughter had had in Lvov with an Armenian nurse who had not been sufficiently trained.

'. . . But of course, it isn't the same, I do see that your young girl, she . . .'

'Naturally, it isn't the same,' Urszula cut her off. 'You see, Countess, Lvov is a city that I did not leave without regrets. But, as far as the training of servants is concerned, and may I say in passing, on the level of social life, Vienna is incontestably superior.'

It was strange for me to hear Lvov and Grynow mentioned casually like that as they were before 1772, in my earliest childhood. Since then, Jozef or Jan had certainly spoken of our county seats using their Polish names but it had never been in this tone of calm nonchalance—rather, it had always been with a little militant and vengeful shiver in their voices.

In Lvov, then, objected the Countess, who wouldn't yet admit that she had been beaten, there was still a lot to do, a lot to see. And since they had installed gas lights, it was undeniable that the streets had become much more . . .

'No doubt,' said Urszula, with a condescending smile. 'But, Countess, how can you compare those improvements, which are, in fact, quite old, to those we have in Vienna right now? The new Reichsrat, the university, the Hofburg theatre they are building . . .'

I observed Wioletta who had not yet joined in the conversation. Slowly, she emptied her bowl which the lackey, moreover, had not entirely filled, took a few sips of wine and didn't move on her chair except to indicate, over her shoulder, that the dishes should be removed.

At the other end of the table was an insignificant-looking man who seemed to be the new overseer, conversing over Kazimierz's head with another man who must have been the Uniate pope and who was honouring the meal by eating a great deal. But Jozef wasn't happy—his daughter and his grandson, now, were speaking softly, or at least too softly to be heard.

'What are you talking about?' he finally said, tapping on his glass with his knife. 'No secret conversations at table, please, I want to know what is being discussed.'

'Father, Andrzej was only telling me that before he left he had learnt that the Elfenbeins had just moved to Vienna, and . . .'

'Who?'

'Now father, Zosia and her . . . her husband.'

'I don't know them.'

There was a strained silence which Wioletta broke by muttering, without looking at anyone, 'Her sons must be big now.'

Another electrified silence. The Countess placed her hand on the patriarch's arm and muttered something about a saint's feast for which she was looking for an appropriate venue—perhaps their barn?

'Sh, sh,' Jozef stopped her impatiently, pushing away her hand and giving Wioletta a burning look. 'What sons are you speaking of?'

'I'm talking about my sister's twins,' said Wioletta with a trembling voice. 'They must be close to eighteen, if I'm calculating correctly.'

'I don't want to know. I don't know those scoundrels, nor their father, nor their mother. And they will not be mentioned here.'

Wioletta lowered her eyes but her older sister, less impressionable, intervened.

'Father, dear, allow me to tell you that the subject deserves to be mentioned. Professor Elfenbein has just been knighted, and two of his sisters have married very well. I know several honourable families who entertain . . . Israelites. Let me add that the professor converted a very long time ago. Agenor in fact was telling me that such contacts can be useful, indeed, precious. In Vienna, you know, we don't always see things the same way.'

'The Viennese are welcome to cajole their Jews if they want to!' shouted Jozef, whose face was getting red. 'Here, we pick our guests more carefully.'

He looked around the table at the diners,, beginning with the pope and the overseer who were politely silent, at Andrzej who, leaning on an elbow, stared at him thoughtfully, and finally at his two daughters who, in the middle of the table, were seated opposite each other.

'And I forbid you, do you hear me? I forbid you from associating with . . . those whom you know! To speak their names in front of me! Or I will disinherit you, as well! I will disinherit all of you!'

He punctuated his words with pounding on the table, spraying the tablecloth with little drops of sauce, his cheeks now scarlet below his trembling sideburns.

'Oh my goodness,' the Countess uttered, not knowing what to do.

It was too much for Kazimierz who had been silent since the beginning of the scene. With his mouth closed, he chuckled.

'Kazimierz!' shouted his grandmother before turning towards Andrzej.

'It is intolerable,' he said calmly. 'Aunt Wioletta, call Mitzi. This child is going to leave the table and I will see that he is punished severely.'

Wioletta gestured to a lackey who disappeared; the door opened again, the maid entered and listened calmly to her instructions while the guilty party, without lowering his eyes, nonetheless grew pale under his freckles.

'Come now,' intervened the countess, 'I'm sure he wasn't thinking of anything bad. Isn't that right, my little friend?'

Her little friend, who was getting up, gave her an ambiguous smile and followed his maid with an air that exuded rebellion; and old Zemka, whose face was still very red, muttered, following him with his eyes, 'You'll never make anything of that boy.'

A bit later, Tessa, awakened by a fracas in the nursery, stuck her head through the communicating door and was terrified to see a nonetheless familiar scene—her brother in his nightshirt, fleeing before the whip, fighting with fists and elbows and ending up helpless, writhing under the blows being administered, without pleasure or fear, by the efficient Mitzi.

3

Thus begins the Karlowicz children's stay which will last much longer than three months. Without their knowing it at the time, this Galician vacation is ringing in a new life for them.

Mitzi would have probably taken flight on the first day, if they had told her that she was going to lose the bloom of her youth here. But who could have guessed? And when Herr Andrzej left at the end of four weeks (four weeks! hats off, by the way, to his mother), she will have already found enough male distractions here to be like a fish in water.

In the kitchen it is said that Mitzi has 'the beauty of the devil'—an expression that I have never understood, because the only devil that I know, on a fresco in the chapel, looks like a monkey, with bent legs and cloven feet with which he tramples a carpet of red burning coal without feeling any pain. Nothing could describe Mitzi any less. I, who see her every day getting washed, can certify that her feet are adorable and that her thighs are satiny, although they are still lacking a bit of flesh. Her bust, on the other hand, is already entirely pleasing—that is, at least, the opinion of those who look at it daily and assess it through the fabric of her apron.

Because Mitzi attracts the eye like a pretty wild animal; and any eye she doesn't attract, she seeks out with a throaty little laugh or a movement of her hindquarters. Her eyelashes come together almost to the point of touching when she listens or when she laughs, and in that thin slit men imagine a paradise of promising pleasures. She promises a lot, Mitzi, but she gives only when she wishes, or when she must. It is not by choice, for example, that she endures the particular embraces of Herr Andrzej but because Frau Urszula subtly asks her to. That wise mother prefers for her son to be amused at home rather than visit those 'houses', a practice that would perhaps attract more gossip.

Herr Agenor is something else. Herr Agenor is Mitzi's little personal initiative. Because Mitzi is not a cowering girl; and although she accepts to do what they want her to do, she doesn't stop herself from doing what *she* wants to do. And he doesn't displease her, Herr Karlowicz, with his slow glance, his portly body and his political prestige. She senses that he pulls against the conjugal yoke and she likes the way he brushes against her in the hallways in Vienna when he comes to have dinner at his son's house. She derives at least some moral pleasure from it—that flirting helps her in enduring the oppressive orders and infinite demands of his wife who is always at their house. (As for Frau Gertrud, she is a laughable mistress. Besides the fact that she is almost never there, one senses that at twenty-seven she has ceased to consider her marriage the main focus of her life, that she is little concerned with knowing whether their servants are stealing from them or if her husband is cavorting in the servants' rooms.)

From Mitzi, then, an erotic perfume subtly exudes within my walls. In contrast, the rooms she passes through seem darker, dustier, the objects more worn, the local customs ancient and outdated; I can even say that her arrival triggered more upheaval here than the year 1848. The peasant women from the hamlet follow her with their eyes when she goes to town, once a week, for her afternoon off; the pope and the overseer too, but for different reasons.

Her seduction is most powerful when she isn't trying to use it— when she is dreaming, her eyes to the heavens, or absorbed reading a story in a journal. The sight of her filing her nails, casually leaning on a windowpane with her lips partially open, is enough to awaken the dead.

And the dead are awakened.

Jozef stirs on his pillow when Wioletta, escorted by a servant, comes to bid him good morning and bring him breakfast in bed because he isn't feeling very well.

'No, no, go away, I don't need you this morning . . . Where is that girl, you know, with that funny name . . .'

'Mitzi?'

'Yes, Mitzi. Go get her, she knows better than you how to look after a sick man. And she is more cheerful too, not to criticize you, of course.'

Wioletta has nothing to say. Of course Mitzi is more cheerful, younger, fresher, who could deny that? She leaves the platter and goes out, humiliated perhaps but relieved too. The weight on her shoulders has lightened since the arrival of this pretty young girl who knows how to humour her father, and of those two children whose noise bothers him but who directs his animosity away from Wioletta.

And then Mitzi enters, a smile on her lips, her hands on her hips, 'What do I hear, *Pan* Jozef? You don't want to finish your eggnog? Oh, we can't have that, can we? Give me that spoon and open wide . . .'

'Pan Jozef' was all the Polish that Mitzi ever learnt. But old Zemka no longer even protests. He likes to hear that animated chatter that causes suggestive dimples to form in Mitzi's cheeks, and if she must speak German for that to happen, then by God, he has nothing against it. Mitzi has the gift of erasing his oldest resentments, of making him forget his most sacred dogmas.

'But that's very good. Eat another piece of toast, *Schatz*, and I'll be very happy with you.'

With Mitzi, there is no overly subtle . . . discrimination. Everyone is her *Schatz*, and, in the attractive parade of her memory, I see that word associated with the most diverse objects: a baby she takes for a walk to the Prater in a carriage with big wheels; a canary in its cage; the large red member of the Croatian sergeant who is getting ready to penetrate her on the iron bed of an attic; or even the old blind lady whom she helps—because Mitzi has a good heart—to cross a street where speeding carriages are going by.

Mitzi thus lives surrounded by treasures, like the guardian of a grotto in the *Thousand and One Nights*. It is also because her happy nature and her powerful seduction turns that which was lead into gold; this means that, turning men who approach her into predators with beating hearts, she creates around her the excitement she needs to feel at ease and, within a few days, she feels at ease everywhere.

In Jozef she is almost able to resuscitate the seducer of serf women that he had been in the past. Once he is feeling better, he eagerly breathes upon her neck or squeezes her waist, knowing that he doesn't risk any other rebuke than a mocking smile and a tap on the arm. The overseer wouldn't dare indulge in such liberties, but he assails her with his eyes and she is convinced that at night he thinks of her a lot beneath his duvet.

As for the coachman, whom everyone here very respectfully calls Master Semien—although she can't really understand why he earned that respect; perhaps simply due to his being very, very fat, and having a moustache without rival in the canton—she begins to find him less rustic ever since he has started looking at her. Anyway, he isn't really that fat . . . powerful, yes, powerful is the word. And so we see Mitzi more often in the kitchen. The cook isn't duped but her sharp remarks slide over the Viennese girl who, untroubled by those remarks, takes a second full serving of gruel and accepts a little glass of vodka 'to help it go down,' as Master Semien says. Finally, that food he eats is not so bad, when one gets used to it. And he has such a funny way of applauding and saying 'Oh! oh!' when Mitzi drinks her vodka in one gulp!

(I've never been able to find out what happened to Efraim. All I was able to learn is that one fine day he disappeared and that Jozef, very angry, had to get old Gavryl, still alive, to urgently hitch the cart. What notion had taken hold of him, then, that morning in December, 1857? Did he want, belatedly, to have a home, a wife and children? Did he flee to Lemberg to become a jack of all trades in the Elfenbein home? Did he return to Wadowice, his pockets as empty as when he left, like the vagabond he was, to find his horse-trading father, his brothers, his sisters and a slew of nephews and nieces? I prefer to believe that, bitten by the wandering bug, he flew off that morning on the back of a stork, a ram or some other flying mount and, a *Luftmensch* for good, never came down again.)

Mitzi has thus found her bearings; this is less true of the two children.

Of course they have her, and despite her faults and her lapses in behaviour she is, I quickly realize, their most solid anchor. She dresses them, feeds them, consoles them and disciplines them, makes sure, for various reasons, that they go to bed early. As the months pass, and the date of their return is pushed back *sine die*, it is even she who notices that Kazimierz might indeed need to resume his catechism, math and German lessons, and recommends a young man in Grünau whom she knows a bit.

But, in the end, Mitzi is too young and too flighty to serve as their mother, and Wioletta is too old, too withdrawn. Their great-aunt actually frightens them with her curious manias, the hours she spends in her room painting who knows what, the empty looks she sometimes gives them without a muscle in her face moving. Sometimes she even bursts out laughing, just like that, out of the blue. When she isn't around, Kazimierz has fun imitating that laugh but Tessa doesn't find it amusing at all.

The younger child grows used to wandering around the cottages, because there are chickens, pigs, a huge turkey that frightens her (though less than Aunt Wioletta). The Pavlyks' daughter-in-law tolerates her under her feet with a pity mixed with annoyance because she already has five children, and would indeed be happy not to have a sixth—a girl who is a nuisance, moreover, since she has twice spoilt good grain by giving it to the animals and gathered eggs for the kitchen that were already hatching.

'Don't go into the stable, little mistress, you're going to get your pretty dress dirty,' she says to her in the little Polish she knows; and she shrugs her shoulders when she sees Tessa returning from a walk carrying a large bouquet of flowers. Rather than the flowers with which the fields are filled, the little girl should be offering her some kreutzers for the damage she has caused and the time she has made her lose. But she is young, after all, she doesn't know, and it's very nice when she calls you 'Nanny'. And in the end, it is she, Oksana, who gives Tessa gifts, a little wooden cart, wooden shoes to walk in the fields; because those satin shoes would never survive.

Kazimierz, who now must study for three hours every day, looks at his sister with envy when she goes to play with the little peasants, climbing the trees to look for birds' nests; and when she comes back, he apes the new manners she has acquired and mockingly repeats the Ruthenian words she has learnt.

He hasn't yet found his place in this country home. That is, he wishes he could at least enjoy it too. But by virtue of a distinction that for the moment weighs upon him, that of being a male, thereby being expected to face all sorts of obligations and demands, he cannot. He must learn how to read, to write, to count, and he is already expected to know how to behave—it would not at all do for the great-grandson of the master to climb trees to find eggs or to awkwardly milk the cow of old Savjuk. He has already been beaten for doing what his sister does every day; he is also beaten when he hasn't learnt his lessons, responds insolently to his tutor or behaves badly at table.

Ah, those meals! They are a nightmare for Kazimierz. The rest of the time *Pan* Jozef leaves him alone, absorbed as he is by his business or his memories. But at table Kazimierz becomes his obsession. Here he is, finally, the son he was unable to have, the son to take in hand, to make just like him. He is still just a little whippersnapper of eight but Jozef doesn't despair that he will one day be a man, a true man. Because, when he thinks about it, neither Agenor nor Andrzej correspond to that definition. Agenor does pretty well, makes decisions in several ministries; it is thanks to his intervention that the road from the sugar factory to the town was surfaced courtesy of the district administration, and that one day the train will come through here. But really, he isn't cut out to be a man of state, that is obvious, and he will never leave his role as *éminence grise*. Also, he is so under the thumb of his wife that Jozef sometimes feels sorry for him.

As for Andrzej, his prematurely decrepit face promises nothing good. Where in the family have they seen a man become bald before he is thirty? Contaminated blood, from Agenor's side, no doubt; too soft an upbringing, caprices of an only child who was allowed everything, and here is the result.

To make a man out of Kazimierz he will have to be raised harshly. Jozef can easily see him as an officer because the Zemkas are a military family, at least in their hearts. And a future officer must know how to endure hardships and discipline with a firm soul, without the nervous swooning of Andrzej when he was little. If Jozef deals harshly with Kazimierz, it is thus because he loves him and has ambitions for him. For Tessa, whose future matters little to him, he reserves riddles, tapping on her cheek, the right to delve after lunch into his personal reserves of Délices de Sissi.

Oh, but I've left out a crucial development. The Délices de Sissi are the fruit of Andrzej Karlowicz's expertise, the stone that, in four weeks, he placed upon the teetering foundation of our factory.

He had to persevere to get his grandfather to allow him to enter the holy of holies. I suspect Jozef fell ill on purpose to delay the moment of that passing over of power. But it was only a little chill, quickly cured, quickly overcome; five days later, I saw the two men, Karlowicz and Zemka, their canes in their hands, walking towards the sugar factory.

What was wrong at the sugar factory?

Of course, there was the crash of 1873 that had precipitated many Austro-Hungarian banks, factories and stores into the abyss, among them the shawl factory in Jaslo that Agenor had inherited from his uncle. The sugar factory had weathered the storm but just barely—they had to let go close to one hundred workers, take back the raises they had just given the others and sell two hydraulic presses—at low cost, because potential buyers found them obsolete.

But really, that was six years earlier; since then, things were still stagnating. Jozef saw business around him picking up, businesses climbing back up, and, for some, taking off. Why was the sugar factory lagging behind? Why were they selling fewer Pastilles de la Vierge?

It was a reality that he still didn't want to face—that Tadeusz Zemka's candy was no longer very popular. The shopkeepers in nearby towns were ordering fewer and fewer, taking ever more time to replenish their stock. Andrzej hadn't dared to tell his grandfather but, more than once, when he mentioned them to Poles in Vienna, he would get nostalgic smiles and this remark, 'Oh, the Pastilles de la Vierge!'

Someone would evoke his childhood in another Galician *dwor* and trips to the main town to get stocks of coffee, cocoa, nice fabrics and Pastilles; another would speak of his great-grandfather who, a soldier in 1831, left for Warsaw with a full box of that candy which was as pious as it was patriotic. But they were all amazed that it was still being produced.

This is what Andrzej, not without some diplomacy, had to make his grandfather understand.

'Do you know what we need?' he said to him in the library after that first factory inspection (which he had found quite long, by the way, not liking the proximity of the Ruthenian workers who followed them with hateful eyes; and, from what he could tell, they must not wash very often). 'We should do for our times what your father did for his—find something that represents the spirit of the current time . . .'

'I hope, my boy, that you are not expecting me to go into licorice,' Jozef had interrupted, in a huff.

'Not that. In truth, I hadn't thought so much about changing the composition of our pastilles, which have proven themselves, than about giving them a new name, something more cheerful, more modern. A name, for example, that would evoke the pomp of the imperial court. The people adore the imperial family . . .'

'The people! The people! I'm not making candy for the people. Why not sell spice cake in the markets while you're at it?'

Andrzej had coughed.

'Now, Grandfather, don't get upset. It's just a matter of taking advantage of that love that rises up to our sovereigns. The people won't eat our pastilles but they will know of them, will want them and will thus make them famous. Listen: What do you think of Délices de Sissi?

On that day, Jozef had dismissed the idea out of hand. But he was still lucid enough to calculate that that idea, a priori unpleasant, was no doubt their only means of salvation.

And so he got on board, decreed that he would rework the formula all the same. They did away with orange flower and chose roses, opted for a longer shape, a smoother texture and an incarnadine tint that, Andrzej assured him, would by itself praise the beauty of the Empress. It was now a matter of sending a sample to the court to get their consent for the use of the name.

'That's not it, that's not it,' Jozef muttered, standing at the window, when Andrzej had just read his fourth draft of a letter to accompany the candy. 'It's too obsequious, too servile. Don't forget, my boy, that I am a descendant of the Ponarski counts, after all!'

His grandson picked up his pen, crossed out some words and proposed something else.

'No, no, that won't do. My poor Andrzej, you know nothing of form, you know nothing about the aristocracy . . .'

And then he finally was quiet, absorbed in contemplating the large fields on the estate and the medley of the peasants' plots which, year after year, became more numerous and narrower; because our Ruthenians were not yet emigrating but still had as many children.

Andrzej had in the end written a letter in his grandfather's name and, without a word, taken it upon himself to send it.

4

But I still have to explain why the little Karlowiczes, instead of three months, stayed here twelve years. To simplify things I might say that they were simply forgotten; but that would be a bit unfair to their legal guardians.

Their mother, for example, did not forget them right away. The following October, she even braved the long trip by train to Lvov, the awful crossing of the countryside and, finally, the unhealthy air of our fields to come get them.

She's a tiny little woman, adorably blonde, exquisitely gloved, that Gertrud Karlowiczowa who gets out of the carriage while her maid and Master Semien unload a large number of suitcases which, for anyone else, would indicate a six-week stay. Her feet step gingerly onto the muddy ground which seems quite dangerous for her boots, her fingers latch on to the arm of Master Semien, next to whom she seems reduced to the proportions of a fragile doll. One shudders a bit imagining this twig pregnant or giving birth; and I understand better what Mitzi means when she suggests to the other servants that if it is up to Frau Gertrude, the young Karlowiczes will have no more siblings.

But now they arrive, with their maid, to greet her, those children she nonetheless has had. Her face lights up, her eyes fill with tears, she goes towards them, but that move is halted by the need to raise the bottom of her skirts because the ground of the courtyard is also soaking wet.

'My dears! My loves! My goodness, Tessa, how you have grown! And you, big boy, how healthy you look! Come tell me everything and—yes, Jenny, be careful with the trunk—what do you think of my new hat, Kazimierz?'

It is the beginning of a monologue that stops at bedtime only to begin again all the more vigorously the next morning. The children look at her, smile at her, come close to her, try to touch her, to get on her lap, to rub their cheeks against her shoulder or her hip; but they are pushed away by that flood of tender words that, little by little, seem to be a sort of invisible shield.

Only Mitzi is able sometimes to silence her in order to give her information about the children's progress, their illnesses, the small decisions she has had to make in Gertrud's absence.

'That is very good, *Kind*, you've done well, I know that I can rely on you,' she responds with a ravishing smile; and, a philosopher, Mitzi doesn't even bother to consult Frau G about the plan for the next day.

They set a date for the return, they prepare for it, they even pay several goodbye visits as a family. At the same time, a contrary wind seems mysteriously to blow over the plans, a wind blowing out of the mouth of Gertrud. There are considerations about the length of the trip for these two poor children, renewed exclamations about their healthy glow and the appetites they've developed during this stay. An exchange of letters with her husband has not entirely reassured her about health conditions in the capital. Andrzej writes that to his knowledge there is currently no talk of an epidemic of diphtheria or measles. That is indeed not very encouraging—as if one couldn't fall ill in such a large city of diseases other than measles or diphtheria!

Finally, at the last minute, a sleight of hand produces a completely different set of plans. Gertrud will join a group of friends in the mountain town of Zakopane—'very close to you, my darlings'—where she will spend the winter before returning to get them in April or May.

And so Gertrud leaves, her eyes just as teary as when she arrived.

'I will write to you, my darlings!' she cries while leaving; but before receiving her letter, they had time to wait, to be concerned and then to worry. Even the imperial court, despite the delays of protocol, was quicker in giving signs of life.

(As relatively prompt as it was, the response to Andrzej's letter was disappointing. Her Imperial and Royal Majesty, a court functionary wrote to them, thanked the candy-maker Zemka for his gracious honour and agreed that he could use her name; but nothing indicated that she had liked, or even tasted, the pastilles. It even seemed that no, considering the allusions to her failing health, her lessening taste for the pleasures of the secular world (more or less)—everything was made to suggest that Her Majesty the Empress was not quite in the mood for eating candy. Jozef had to erase the prestigious mention 'Suppliers to the Court,' even if the new boxes were selling well enough for business to be picking up and justify the rehiring, at least during the Christmas holidays, of some twenty workers.)

In June, Gertrud did indeed return, and her stay, like all those that occurred in the next three years, followed the same model as the first: tears upon arriving, a flood of adoring names, alarmed cries as soon as she set foot outside—there is too much dew, mud or dust when it isn't the ants or, worse, spiders—and finally a departure filled with sobbing and promises that were never kept.

In the beginning we would also see Andrzej make a few appearances but they didn't last. Andrzej, it is obvious, likes neither this place nor his tyrannical grandfather, nor that accursed factory that is supposed to become his livelihood and which he has decided to manage from a distance. Furthermore, with the launch of the 'Délices de Sissi', it seems to him that, for the time being, he has done enough. His children's fate concerns him more than it does his wife, and he listens attentively to Mitzi's reports. But he gives the impression of being overwhelmed, tired, and the information he receives about the conditions of their life here, and the schools in the region, leads him to the conclusion as well, but for different reasons, that it is preferable that they not go back to Vienna.

What about Urszula and Agenor?

As I've said, Agenor rarely comes here. Unless there is a death or another important event, he comes only every other year to see that the estate, and your humble servant, are not deteriorating too much. Wioletta's presence repels him; moreover, I believe that he is struggling, at this time, not to be politically put out to pasture. The end of the liberal era and the renewal of the governing class seemed to him to be an opportunity to forge ahead but, no matter how cautious he was, he is aware that he is henceforth associated with the era of the Auerspergs and the Andrassys. And so he frequents the salons of the capital, conspires, does a thousand favours; and Urszula, who entertains at a wild pace, really doesn't have time to come play the grandmother here.

Agenor and Urszula don't wish anyone's death, obviously. But it would be an opportune moment for them to finally become owners of the estate. Thanks to the income it generates, they could relax a bit, spend a few months here every year, establish a sort of provincial base for the Polish Club of Vienna where there could be lectures and hunting parties. But Jozef holds his own; he has kept his sight and doesn't seem in a hurry to leave this world. Agenor even finds him more youthful than ever when, in 1881, he comes to pay his biennial visit.

This is because there is nothing to keep an old man youthful like the presence of youth, and, even better, the excitation of his senses. And with Mitzi around, those senses are constantly aroused, even though things, as one can imagine, haven't gone any further than a nuzzling of the neck or an examination of a ribbon on her garter. Mitzi knows that it is appropriate, at this stage of life, to place limits. She even has the art of doing so without offending, and the old gallant blushes, is flattered, when she leaves him murmuring, 'Now, *Pan* Jozef, leave me alone now, you're going to make me lose my head.'

And so Jozef seems to get younger, as much as a man of eighty-four can get younger. He gets dressed every day, has the newspaper read to him, still brushes his thick sideburns carefully. In a word, he keeps his looks and even his drive, and it is with some fear that Agenor, one day at lunch—the first lunch at which Tessa is allowed at the grown-ups' table—hears him click his tongue after tasting his wine, then say, while looking at his great-granddaughter, 'Heh, heh! I had an old liquor keg filled with this wine when this little one was born. And we will drink it, oh yes! We will drink it all together on her wedding day.'

Her wedding! Tessa, who still plays with dolls and is only just learning her letters, bursts out laughing; but Agenor doesn't laugh. And he experiences an obscure relief in learning the following year that, through an inexplicable misfortune, a rat got into and drowned in the nuptial keg and the entire contents had to be thrown away.

On that visit Andrzej has not accompanied his father as he usually does. I am surprised by this until the day I happen upon a long conversation between Zemka and his son-in-law just outside the house. I make out phrases like 'sickly asthenia' and 'cerebral lesions' and 'a progression at best that might be delayed'. Jozef shakes his head with the affliction that stifles the triumph of still vital old men who are informed that people younger than they are faring much worse. 'That doesn't surprise me,' I even read in his eyes. 'I thought so, it was bound to happen!'

What was bound to happen? It takes another four months for me to learn because Andrzej's illness is not one of those that are discussed in the salon. But as he declines and has to stay more frequently in institutions carefully called 'rest homes' in the suburbs of Vienna, I learn that his illness is the consequence of the excesses of his youth, that it makes excusable and even desirable the physical separation that has been established between him and his wife. I also see that Jozef is not at peace, that he seeks to question his son-in-law and daughter through letters on the chronology of this infection whose name, like that of the Elfenbein's, will not be uttered in his home. He often gives his great-grandchildren a suspicious look; a somewhat strident laugh from Kazimierz, a sudden paleness in Tessa, alarm him as potential fore-signs of a decline.

His fears are not justified—the two young Karlowiczs are beaming with health and show no signs of congenital syphilis. Kazimierz has something shifty and haughty in his expression which is not pleasant, but he seems quite sturdy and, in the sun, his carrot-coloured hair shines like the helmet of an ancient warrior. Tessa is still only a small, lisping, chubby little girl. She is rather spoilt, as a child whom no one watches can be. The cook gives her all the cake she wants to get rid of her; Oksana, marked by centuries of servitude, would never dare scold the child of the masters; the lackeys still prefer her antics to Jozef's shouting; and the latter, perhaps to make Kazimierz understand better what it is to be a man, ostensibly allows his sister to get away with the most outlandish behaviour.

As for Wioletta, what she thinks of these two little Viennese children does not show on her face. Does she love them? Why would she love them? Why would one automatically expect a mature woman, especially an unmarried one, to adore any child that crossed her path? When he was a child, she could extend to Andrzej the love she had for his father and, from afar, cherish him. But one cannot decently ask her to cherish Agenor's descendants for centuries and centuries. She pities Kazimierz a bit when she hears him crying when he is beaten, she would like to have enough authority to put a stop to it. But she is nothing in this house, and what she thinks interests no one. Furthermore, Kazimierz is in fact a brat whose brutality and hard heart repel her. And Tessa is hardly any better with her tantrums, her teasing, her eyes devoutly lowered when they spank her brother.

No, those two children do not play a large role in her life. And when Tessa begins to go to the Polish school in the district, when Kazimierz, at eleven, is a boarding student with the Jesuit fathers, their great-aunt scarcely notices their absence.

5

What, then, plays a role in Wioletta's life? How does she spend her days? Well, she manages the house. Each meal occurs under her mute direction, each hallway receives her daily visit. Sometimes she goes to Grynow to buy something, to return books to the lending library, to attend vespers there with the poor Catholics in town whom she mysteriously seems to prefer to her closer surroundings. Except for those outings, she doesn't leave here.

And, except for the two children who are somewhat afraid of her, no one sees her. Her father glances over her as if she were transparent. She gives directions to the servants in a voiceless murmur which in time they have learnt to decipher but which is not enough to make her presence more palpable. In fact, it is rare that anyone wonders where she is, what she is doing; she could disappear and no one would notice before a week or two, and that too only when the reserves in the pantry would begin to dwindle.

She reads more and more. She reads all the new books that can be found in Grynow, all the classics from my shelves, including those that Count Fryderyk and Baron von Kotz had not intended for female eyes. Philosophy, natural history, epics, flow through her hands, as well as the Church Fathers that her mother liked to read. They fill her mind with a jumble comparable to that in her room; there are treatises on botany and memoirs of insurgents, apocalypses and anatomy plates, half-gods, the Garden of Eden and the battles of Titans.

And on this hilly plain of human history, she places herself within the lineage of miraculous mothers of mythology. Not immaculate (at that blasphemous thought she crosses herself quickly and murmurs a prayer), but not a part of the usual laws of generation either. Didn't she, like Io or Leda, descend almost to the rank of the beast to conceive a divine son, a son who didn't have a father among men? Because no, Feliks did not have a true father among men. Feliks is the son of a spouse with whom the portly sixty-something Agenor has only a distant connection. Wioletta agreed to abjection so that perhaps a redemptive miracle would occur.

These thoughts do not prevent her from knowing who she is, in what year we are, at what date she should arrange the great spring cleaning and remind the overseer to see to the stove. All the same, it happens that she loses ground and allows her extravagant ideas free reign. Such as the day when she thoughtfully declares to her father that she wants to live in Lvov for a few months and take some courses at the university.

Jozef, as expected, bursts out in a booming laugh that ends in a fit of coughing.

'Courses?' he is finally able to say. 'But my poor girl, the University of Lvov is not a hospice for old maids with no prospects. What would you do there, I wonder?'

'Well, I think I would enjoy studying theology . . . or law.'

This time Jozef doesn't laugh. This opinionated delirium is beginning to really worry him.

'I can in fact see you as a judge or an archdeacon. Have you lost your mind?'

But Wioletta simply passes her tongue over her lips and calmly argues, 'I don't want to become either a judge or an archdeacon but only educate myself. Those subjects interest me. Furthermore, I expect I won't be the only female auditor at the university. If one were to look at the novels of Madame Orzeszkowa . . .'

'Madame Orzeszkowa, like all the young featherbrains who indulge themselves in writing today, seems to have taken a vow to exhibit what is ugliest and most unhealthy in our current Poland and curiously to find motives for hope in it. Her heroines are mad women, her heroes are imbeciles or rogues. Don't say another word about Madame Orzeszkowa, and even less about playing a *student* in town! If you don't have anything to do here, I have something for you—we are finally selling my father's house in Grynow and there is a huge mess there to get rid of. Take care of it. At least you'll be doing something useful!'

Whoever could say whether Wioletta was affected by this flat refusal of her request would be quite clever. Apparently, she swallows her pride and, the next day, leaves for Grynow with a servant and a handcart, wearing a grey smock to cover her clothes.

In the evening she returns at the head of a true procession. The handcart disappears under cartons and, behind it, two carriages shudder under a pile of furniture.

'We gave away or sold all that we could,' she explains to her father who is alarmed, 'but no one wanted what was in the attic.'

'Hmm! In truth, I understand . . . but yes, there's the sofa where my mother, Elzbieta, spent most of her days. And the chairs from our dining room, and . . . my goodness, that is the little rosewood desk Mother kept from the Ponarskis! It was already rickety when Adam and I did our homework on it . . .'

He goes up to it, moves an embroidered panel, opens a drawer that stays in his hands and spills the contents onto the ground.

'Good heavens! They left all our school pens, glue, my mother-of-pearl-handled knife in it . . . And the paper? Poetry! I wrote poetry? No, it was Adam. "To Madame *** . . ." The fool! He really was in love with her, the entire summer of 1807. She was the organist's wife. She was considered the most beautiful woman in Grynow and she would have been perfect, in fact, but for a somewhat lazy eye and a slight limp . . . How stupid young people are!'

He picks up a stool, opens an armoire out of which escapes a pile of rags and a toxic cloud and—my goodness, it looks like his eyes are moist.

'Should we keep some things?' his daughter suggests.

'No,' Jozef replies, turning his head. 'Get all of this out of my sight and, tonight have it burnt in a big bonfire.'

But the overseer knows only too well the price of heating wood. In come the axes and saws, and my furnaces have enough to eat for the next four months—four months during which, through my twenty chimneys, all the remnants of Jozef's childhood softly fly away.

All of them? No. Wioletta could not bring herself to throw the books and other papers into the fire before reading them. So she turned the pages where, written in a brownish ink on paper that had aged over almost a century, she decoded an 'Ode to Dombrowski' and a 'Tomb of Kosciuszko' written by the young Adam, devoured the novels that

Elzbieta Ponarska never finished, no matter how enticing the plots, because she always ended up finding the type too small for her eyes and the binding too heavy for her hand. Then, at the bottom of a chest, she discovered the four volumes of Tadeusz Zemka's journal.

Her critical mind—because she still had one—was first surprised that one could waste so much time noting down such minutiae. 2 August 1798: 'Our son Jozef has cut his first tooth.' Twenty-fifth December 1801: 'Blessed are You, Lord, who sent Your son to earth to save the human race. Amen.' Twenty-first February 1817: 'The rooster in our farmyard died, I'm going to quickly buy another. As my sainted mother, Anna Scholastyka, said: *It isn't good for chickens not to have a cock.*'

Marriages, deaths, historical dates, the boys' baptisms and solemn communions—these events, of course, duly appeared in the almost daily notations of the candy-maker. But also someone's cold, someone else's whitlow, a few lines on the saint of the day, the acquisition of new gaiters, the detail of what Tadeusz and his little family had eaten and drunk. Fifteenth July 1806: 'Last night we stayed awake; then at midnight we had some vodka with jam and we hugged one another.'

And all of this was padded with sometimes pious proverbs, most often grotesque, that the journal-writer never failed to attribute to his 'saintly mother Anna Scholastyka'. *Never wake a sleeping dog. Who knows if it will bite you?—When you have crossed the water, turn back towards it but don't lean out over it for fear of getting wet*—etc. One did strike Wioletta: *Two trees between which flows a river will not bear fruit unless the wind rises.* That one has a certain beauty—it makes Wioletta shiver, and she begins to think: The wind, yes! Please let the wind blow.

But ultimately those two lines do not carry a lot of weight alongside the thousand pages filled, day after day, by the father of her father. And this mass even fascinates her in its monstrosity. Ten times she has rejected with a sigh one of the open volumes, ten times she has returned to that psychological enigma—the need Tadeusz Zemka, a simple man with a banal existence, had to leave to posterity the minute details of his passage on earth.

'Did you know Anna Scholastyka, Father?' she one day has the courage to ask.

'Who? Oh, yes, my grandmother Zemka. No, I think she died when I was two or three years old.'

And her husband, what was he? Your father never mentions him.'

'What was he?' mutters Jozef, who has never been very interested in the common branch of his family. 'Bah, a candy-maker too, no doubt. To tell the truth, I don't know anything about him, I only know that he died young, at the time when our Poland still existed.'

He adjusts his pince-nez, 'My poor child, why don't you study the history of the Ponarskis instead?'

But Wioletta is stubborn. She dives back into Tadeusz's journals, lingers in town when she takes her great-niece there, wanders the streets, the churches and the cemetery. I know this through Mitzi who flirts, among others conquests, with the young secretary of the town hall—he says that he now sees Miss Zemka look at the houses as if she is looking for who knows what evidence, wander into the back courtyards, sketch this or that in her notebook. (Soon she will paint *The Old Quarter in the Rain* and *The Drapers' House*, but for the moment the little green salon displays only the first painting of this fatal series.)

Yes, Wioletta has finally found a field of study, and too bad if it is modest and petty—it is the only one she has been given. It would indeed have been better for Jozef if she had been able to become a judge or an archdeacon and, however old he is, he will still have time to regret this.

He doesn't see the storm coming. He is content to shrug his shoulders when, timidly, she asks, 'Why, Father, did you celebrate every 14 July with drinking vodka, eating jam and then embracing?'

'Good heavens, you're the only one who can ask such questions! Are you unaware of the importance that the great French Revolution, especially the storming of the Bastille, had for us? I don't remember but, indeed, we celebrated that day when I was a child. How far away all that is!'

He hunches down in his chair, becomes absorbed in meditating on the passing of time which makes you such a stranger to the things in which you once saw the essence of your life. Yes, 1789 was their big date, France the country from which would come their national salvation, political hopes. All of that, today, seems as hollow to him as the madrigals dedicated to Madame *** . . . by a beardless Adam.

And Wioletta, who watches him relax, leaves and, once again, opens her grandfather's notebooks. The storming of the Bastille? Come now. As far back as the journal goes, to 1782, 1783, *Pan* Tadeusz was already spending that night celebrating with his saintly mother.

6

Around this time the lamentable affair of the Grynow train station erupts. I say erupts because it has been simmering for many years, being one of those affairs in which regional quarrels, matrimonial intrigues and large sums of money are intertwined, and about which it is as futile to seek the origin as it is to wonder which came first—the chicken or the egg.

Within my field of experience, which depends essentially on kitchen gossip, there nonetheless emerges a sort of primary fact—a debt that our coachman Semien had once contracted with a Polish peasant whose land (tiny) abutted that (no bigger) of his parents. A debt of a few hundred florins but which, not having been paid back in time, had grown with interest and become a tidy sum.

Master Semien lived with his debt as others live with a goitre—it grew and bothered him more and more but had become a part of him. He had come to see it as a given in his existence, just like the fact that he had been born a mortal man. 'Oh, yes! I must pay back my debt some day . . .' he sometime sighed at the servants' table and that thought incited him to take another bowl of soup, a large tankard of beer which he then solemnly emptied, his face sad.

It was even said that on market days in town the debt pushed him to compulsively buy objects he didn't need, a scarf, a salt box or a woman's belt, which rid him of the little money he had managed to put aside—like the sinner haunted by the prospect of eternal flames who cannot prevent himself from sinning again and again in order to avoid thinking about the hell that awaits him.

This had been going on for ten years. In the meantime, however, a solution had been offered, a radical iodine cure for that growing goitre. Our servant Nikolaïa had an old aunt in town—a widow, without children, who would have been happy to marry off her niece before she died. Nikolaïa, at the time we're speaking of, is almost thirty-five, and the passing years have done nothing for her crossed eyes nor brought colour to her pallid complexion. (How could this pale fish be the great-granddaughter of the beautiful Ulianna? Here is another of those enigmas of kinship that I'm unable to solve.) In addition, she has a bad character and tends to look down upon her peasant entourage, she who, working in the *dwor*, no longer works the earth and no longer wears wooden clogs. But the aunt knows what she wants and, calling upon the pope, lets Master Semien know that she would assume the debt and its accumulated interest if he agrees to take her niece as his wife.

This has little to do with the train station, you might be thinking; but we're getting there . . .

We are only at the first stages of this transaction, because Semien is dragging his feet. It would be his salvation, no doubt. But when one's salvation is cross-eyed and bad-tempered to such a degree, what Christian wouldn't prefer prolonging his state of mortal sin? So Semien dithers and stalls while Nikolaïa, at the table, admires his nice build, his pink cheeks and his stentorian voice.

Since Mitzi has arrived, things are dragging even more. How could Nikolaïa not suffer from any comparison with this pretty girl who loves to laugh, knows how to drink and makes a man's mouth water when she simply gets up to get the bread? 'Oh, if only I didn't have to pay my debt . . .' thinks Master Semien following her with his eyes. And Mitzi, whom the situation amuses greatly, arches her waist and rubs against the coachman's wide back when she walks behind him.

In the hamlet tongues are wagging. Until now, this marriage project was laughable but now, with this little tease in the picture, there is rising indignation. To break the heart of a poor girl that way! To lead astray a good man who is resolved to repent! The Grynow aunt came one day to have a look at Mitzi and, at the end of her inspection, murmured murderous words to the cook which the Viennese girl didn't bother to have translated—what honest women said about her had for a long time ceased to affect her. She even held their gaze and insolently passed her tongue over her lips, electrifying the overseer who happened to be there.

The affair causes such a stir that the Uniate pope, in the little nave of our wooden church, goes so far as to curse the Whore of Babylon against whom everyone should rise up. But really, did these great words describe poor Mitzi? That Ukrainian zealot, avid for public action, was perhaps only against the Austrian monarchy which, it seems, wanted to force the Uniates to adopt the Gregorian calendar. It doesn't matter, because Mitzi wasn't there; and, if she had been, she would not have really cared. And the facts seem to be going in her favour the following week when, suddenly, the winds shift.

Semien's old parents come to learn that their patch of land is on the site of the future train station and, overnight, everything changes. They are to be paid, and handsomely; so they give the cold shoulder to Nikolaïa, whom I see one day returning on the road, her nose red from crying. She has learnt that her future in-laws, or those she thought would be, are saying many bad things about her. Do we need her money now? Soon the debt will only be a memory—she can hope all she wants, that not-pretty one, she who thought she could have their boy seized as if he had been, God pardon them, a plough or a chest!

In the servants' quarters at night I see Nikolaïa lying awake and worried sick. She loses weight, goes to Grynow every day to consult her aunt, tries to get the overseer, in whom she senses a possible ally, to come to her aid. (Clean-shaven and wan, the Zemka's overseer is indeed tortured by the same agony of forced chastity. He is angry with Mitzi for letting herself be courted by all the men in town, having her neck nuzzled by three generations of masters but pinching her lips with scorn whenever he looks at her. Because the only thing that repulses Mitzi in a man is sexual timidity, of which this forty-something virgin is the incarnation.)

It is at this moment that I begin to be worried for our children's maid. I am probably the only one. Doesn't she have her beauty, her youth, her city-bred self-assurance? Who would worry about this Amazon of twenty-three who, with the batting of her eyes, obtains what she wants from any man, whom old Jozef calls his fine little bird and his charming demon? There is even a question that he might leave her a little something when he dies, and that would be only right. Mitzi feeds him, tucks him in and dries him when he gets out of his bath with an enthusiasm that largely exceeds what is expected of her.

But it is precisely all this that worries me. The favours she enjoys causes her to be hated but her youth blinds her to the danger. Mitzi knows the life of a town working quarter, the quarrels that are resolved with insults or singing, not the dark quarrels of the countryside where peoples and classes cohabit without liking one another. Our land, in which she sees only a threat to the leather of her boots, our Galician land is soaked with old blood. Be careful, *süßes Mädel,* here it is with the throwing of stones or the blows of a scythe that accounts are usually settled . . . But Mitzi only laughs when someone whispers as she goes by the word 'whore' or when she finds a dead cat under her straw mattress, courtesy of Nikolaïa.

'If you think, my poor girl, that that will make you more beautiful!' she yells out with good humour before throwing the carcass into her rival's room.

She still laughs, but a bit less (because the hostility of males for her is a new and unsettling occurrence), the day when a son of Semien's Polish creditors meets her on the road to Grynow and spits in her direction. No doubt that good Catholic wants to show that he disapproves of the bad conduct of one of his own. But it is, above all, because the fate of his family depends entirely on the reimbursement of the debt and thus on the marriage in question. Karol, the father, intends to immigrate; and how can he do so before recovering what his Ruthenian neighbours owe him? A remnant of peasant solidarity has prevented him up to now from selling the debt to a Jew from Grynow ,but that could still happen.

(Yes, I haven't had the chance to talk about it yet, but all the other Polish families have left the area in the last six or seven years. Some have settled in Grynow and work at the sugar factory, or in the other factories that have appeared in the region, others in the western districts of our province, even in Prussian Poznania where the peasants also speak Polish. Still others have made the great leap to America—this is what Karol and his family, who are beginning to feel quite alone here, dream of. Paradoxically, I have never heard Polish spoken less beyond my gates than since it became the official language of education and administration in Galicia.)

Thus it is thanks to Mitzi that Karol's wife and Semien's mother no longer exchange the names of 'liar' and 'ursurer', of 'Uniate dog' and of 'Polish leech' over their common walls. They continue to borrow salt and kitchen utensils and, each time, together curse the 'German' who is causing them so much trouble.

What about Semien in all of this? Do not think that all this agitation leaves him indifferent. If he eats and drinks as always, sings louder and louder when he is hitching the carriage, it is to endure the torment of his guilt. Because of him, the meals in the kitchen are henceforth funereal—the cook, who once really liked him, scowls at him now; since she is related to Karol, she feels she has an interest in his cause and because the debt that isn't paid seems to be an injury done by the Ruthenians to all the Poles. Mitzi is bored and kneads balls of bread, while the overseer, tense, watches the movement of her little pink-tipped fingers. And Nikolaïa no longer speaks to anyone. 'Come on, have a drink and smile, cousin,' the guilty one murmurs kindly to the one whom he no longer dares call his fiancée, but she turns away. So Semien's eyes fill with tears. Oh, if only he had paid his debt when it was only at three or four hundred florins!

And then there is a cataclysm. Following the joint efforts of the Grynow aunt, who must have bribed an engineer, and the overseer, who must have convinced Agenor Karlowicz that the first location chosen for the station would be prejudicial to the expansion of the sugar factory, the train tracks, they learn, will be diverted by some five hundred metres.

For Semien's parents it is a catastrophe. Not only will their little plot not be bought but also the proximity of the tracks will make it impossible to be built upon, and thus impossible to sell. For Karol, on the other hand, whose land will be bought, it is a blessing—a blessing that, in all the farms of the area, causes angry grumbling.

'It's not fair!' I hear Pavlykowa angrily exclaim on the threshold of her cottage. 'It's not enough for those Poles to be here among us and squeeze us like lemons since the world came into being—they must still unite, get richer, and everything good has to be only for them!'

The neighbours come together, agree; the pope arrives and takes advantage of the gathering to give a little speech on the former Rus of Kiev and the era of glory when no one would have dared dispute their right to be a nation nor the enjoyment of their land.

Nikolaïa is as indignant as the others but is triumphant inside. Semien's parents give her a jar of honey from their hive and beg her to pardon them, because old Karol is beginning to have enough and is getting insistent. One of his cows died inexplicably and, one night, a fire destroyed his fennel. People are against him, it's clear, and he wants only one thing—to leave here as quickly as he can.

In the past Clara would have thought that this affair was her business as mistress, a Christian, and, more generally, as a friend to her neighbours. Whatever form her intervention might have taken, it is obvious to me—the wedding would have already occurred. But it has been twenty-five years since Clara has gone and no one has come to take her place. Wioletta knows nothing about what happens among the servants, wants to know nothing. And Jozef? He did in fact walk to his window the evening when the sky, to the north, was reddened with the glow of a fire. But in learning that it was Karol's fennel that was burning, he went back to bed. He has never forgiven Karol for having humiliated him in front of ten other serfs one day in March 1846, by asserting that the Poles were masters, those who know how to read and write. Let him make do now with his Ruthenian neighbours! He asked for it.

So it is up to our coachman, and to him alone, to act. What is he waiting for?

It would take only a word from him, an arm placed affectionately around the waist of our servant; he need only offer her the coral necklace that his parents, with the last of their money, bought for her, and to visit the Grynow aunt who, each day, puts on her best dress in expectation of that visit. He has no other choice—the time has finally come to pay back his debt.

But he doesn't do it.

Why? It would be impossible to say. And yet he is suffering, God knows how he is suffering, he suffers more than Jesus on his cross, in thus prolonging his state of damnation. At each meal he sticks his hand in the pocket that holds the necklace, opens his mouth, turns his eyes to Nikolaïa; then he sees, opposite him, Mitzi mischievously looking at him while biting into a raw carrot, and a weakness stops him. What a great sinner he is, oh God! How has he, a poor man, become such a great sinner? Was there a place for this abyss in the soul of this humble coachman? He trembles; and instead of talking to Nikolaïa, he lets go of the necklace and holds his glass out to the cook to be refilled.

Was our train line really worth all the unhappiness it caused? Honestly, I wonder. Of course, I know that thanks to it people will be able to go to Lvov from here in four hours and to Vienna in a bit less than thirty. But what difference does that make to me? Will I take that train? I have only a vague idea of what it's all about and, unless an earthquake one day flattens the bend in the land that hides the tracks from me, I will probably ever know only the plume of smoke that, three or four times a day, will wind round on my left.

From my perspective, the train was the cause. One morning in the woodshed Master Semien, who has set down his whip, discovers Mitzi who had hidden herself to adjust her stocking. She turns her head towards him; curls are shining on her neck. Semien closes the door, walks towards her and pushes her down on the logs. Her black skirt was already raised, he has only to push it up a bit more and tear away everything else that stands in his way: lace, ribbons, garters, and any other frills upon which city gentlemen linger and at which some, it is said, stop. Semien is a simple man, and goes right to the target.

'Ah!' he exclaims when he is done which is quite soon.

Mitzi has seen a lot since she was fifteen but, all the same, he has some nerve! Her corset has lost its hooks, she hit her head against a log, scratched her arm on a nail. As soon as Semien allows her some space, she sits up and assails him with a formidable slap and with the saltiest curses in the repertoire of this little flirt from Meidling.

Semien understands only the gist of them, but that's enough—he falls on his knees.

'Forgive me, forgive me,' he begs in his language (I get a little dizzy when I consider that I am the only one, in this scene, to understand everything that is said). 'Don't be angry, my little angel, I will marry you, I swear I will marry you—oh, my God, but I must pay my debt!' At this thought tears come to his eyes and, as compulsively as he buys scarves at the Grynow market, he gets up and defiles Mitzi a second time.

Mitzi's credo is to take life as it comes. So she leaves there furious but, in an hour, is already beginning to see the humour in the thing. That fat man crying while kissing her hands after having twice almost knocked her out! She quickly repairs her linen, passes some water over her face and on the gash on her arm, looks in the mirror above her basin and puts the coral necklace that Semien gave her to excuse him for his actions around her neck.

'You bet I'm going to wear it,' she murmurs, smiling at her reflection in the mirror. 'I certainly earned it!'

The gods . . . what do the gods do to those whom they want to see fall? I no longer know. But when I saw Mitzi come down the stairs for the noon meal wearing two strands of coral on the swell of her bust and sit down, provocatively, opposite Nikolaïa; when I saw the overseer choke on his soup, the cook shake her head and look at Semien who didn't dare say a word, my stone heart clinched. And it was still beating, too quickly, when night fell.

The next day is wash day. I usually like these days for their odour of ashes and soap, the warm steam that spreads over the first floor and dampens the wallpaper, the varnish on the wood. These are days when one doesn't invite guests, indeed, because of that odour and humidity, when Jozef stays in his robe until mealtime. There is an atmosphere of relaxation and vacation here, except, of course, for the servants and the laundress responsible for the work.

But this day I feel ill at ease and worried. All that steam oppresses me, and the clouds of soap almost make me ill. So I go to the little back garden to take refuge and to breathe a little out in the cold, because it is March.

Then I see Tessa coming, her cheeks reddened by her walk in the fresh air. She has slipped her hands into her sleeves like a skater and is having fun breathing out clouds of white, like *Pan* Jozef when he smokes cigars. She goes towards the service entrance, which she sometimes does although she has been forbidden from doing so, because it is the shortest path when she returns from the farms. She takes her last steps, knocks her feet against the stones of the threshold, puts her hand on the doorknob.

But just when she is about to turn the knob, the cook races up to her and, without a word, pulls her away.

'Not here, little mistress,' she whispers, picking the girl up in her arms. 'I'm going to the garden, come with me and help me pick some vegetables.'

And Tessa, raising her eyes, finds her so pale that she lets out a little cry but agrees; and soon the two disappear behind a shrub. Thus Mitzi doesn't see them when, three minutes later, she in turn goes through the little garden, crosses the threshold and pushes open the service door.

I hear the bell on the entrance door ringing when Mitzi opens it, ringing a second time when she closes the door—a system conceived to alert the servants of the presence of a supplier and, more generally, to prevent anyone from entering in the back without being noticed. Then the bell is silent; and suddenly, from inside, there is horrific shrieking.

In the blink of an eye the entire household runs to the ground floor, including Wioletta and her father who were in their rooms. Semien leaves the shed slowly, the overseer comes out of another door, I even see the inhabitants of the hamlet who, at the windows of their cottages, stick their heads out to see what has happened.

What has happened is that Mitzi entered the kitchen hallway at the moment when they were carrying a cask on the staircase overhead. Bad luck would have it that the cask then tipped over and the boiling soap spilt through the railings. No more is known at present but the town doctor arrives; in the back garden, the presently compact crowd breaks apart to let him in.

'I told them,' cries the laundress, wringing her hands, 'that cask has a loose handle, how many times did I say it needed to be fixed!'

An old man makes the sign of the cross. Three older women take away a pregnant woman, ordering her not to look. Semien stands petrified, his legs frozen, the whip he is holding on his shoulder trembling in his hand.

Later the doctor leaves, his face serious—he can't yet predict. Only the next day do we learn that Mitzi has lost an eye, that the other sees almost nothing, that her right hand will regain some mobility only in a few weeks; as for the rest of her face—it's better not to talk about it.

'Go dance now, my girl . . .' Except for these words murmured by Nikolaïa behind the doctor, I will never again hear the servants say a word about the accident.

Mitzi will not see the Grynow train station. She was sent back to her family in Meidling, with a small stipend that would enable her to live as the invalid she is.

Semien will not marry, will never repay his debt. The day after the tragedy, a bad wind blew him towards town where he got horribly drunk, picked a fight with a Hungarian horse-trader and, while they were trying to separate them, plunged his knife into a gendarme's stomach. In the county prison, he is now waiting for them to determine his fate. He spends his days on his knees, they say, singing psalms. Tears flow down his face but he smiles in ecstasy in the midst of his torment. Because he is a saint, yes a saint, he has finally understood. True sainthood involves enduring the suffering of a sinner, and the greater the sin, the greater the suffering and more certain the redemption. Oh! If only he could die already, as he is, his arms in a cross, in this tortuous beatitude!

And his parents, whose farm was seized, came to live with us. The old Tarass became a coachman in his son's place, old Oleksandra can still do some small tasks in the kitchen. Every day they see Nikolaïa, with whom they speak as little as possible. The only thing that consoles them is that she won't ever marry, either.

But the handle of the cask was repaired.

7

And so Mitzi will not see the Grynow train station. But, after all, what did all the hoopla over a little provincial station mean to her, as she had contemplated, with her still shining eye of youth, the much more impressive one in the imperial city?

When I think, however, that she would not even see the renovation of the large salon . . . What would you have said, Mitzi, about that reception room which not only has been cleaned but where the dark pink of the walls has been restored as has the stucco that covers them with a coat of new badigeon, the Empire furniture, restored, refinished! Kosciuszko, Bonaparte and the family portraits shine under many lights; the loveseat and the assorted chairs voluptuously wait for someone to sit on them. Each credenza has a vase filled with flowers that our overseer went to get in the carriage from the best florist in Lvov and brought back yesterday in boxes filled with a salt that keeps them fresh.

And in the monumental brown velvet armchair Jozef, a sphinx under each elbow, waits for the party to begin.

His dried-out body expresses satisfied rest, no more—Jozef is no longer at an age where one is joyful, even for a few hours. Joyful? How can he be when most of those he has known are dead, when the world he saw born exists only in the monographs of local historians? The only thread that connected Jozef to life broke with the accident of his little Viennese protégée. Now it seems that everything round him is pushing him into his grave; his favourite food which doesn't have the same flavour it used to, the international situation which he doesn't understand at all, the falling of the leaves in autumn, the sugar factory workers who grumble and demand to work one hour less . . . One hour less! As if Jozef, in his time, had counted the hours he spent going over his plans, bartering for parcels of land, fighting with the columns of numbers and issues of rent!

'A bad time, bad mentality,' he murmurs, shaking his head but with a shadow of a smile.

'What did you say, Father?' asks Wioletta, arranging some flowers in a vase that looked too stiff.

'Nothing, I was thinking of Gavryl,' he says before sinking back into silence. He is indeed superfluous in this world of the living—those winks to the past amuse no one but him. Does Wioletta even remember who Gavryl was? The overseer belonged to that masculine realm that a young girl, the young girl Wioletta was at the time, had no reason to frequent.

His faithful servant, grouchy and uncouth, how he misses him today! Efraim was amusing; but Gavryl was a *friend*, someone who had the same interests, and, without seeming to, could penetrate your soul.

A man like Gavryl, that's what they need at the sugar factory. A man who had known poverty, a man all the more capable of being firm with his subordinates. Moreover, what is that worker and peasant poverty that the socialists are waving like a flag these days? True poverty, Jozef saw it here when he was still young. It was scrawny children, grandparents who died from neglect, perhaps even from hunger, because, too old, they were no longer of any use. Today, many of his neighbours sometimes eat meat; and all, or almost all have a lithograph of the reigning emperor, whereas in Jozef's time the best off had only one or two little dusty icons hanging on their walls.

In Jozef's time? But yes, it is indeed our Zemka who is thinking in those terms. Jozef, after having fought so hard to stay in sync with the movement of things and not to be outdated, has finally seen the obvious—these times are no longer his. The clock of his life has stopped on a certain hour; and from now on, like a very old man, he only counts the strikes, always the same number, invariably.

But now five o'clock has just struck on the large clock, and two doors open. Through one enter several servants who have come to put the final touches on the buffet, and through the other Madame Urszula who, with a supporting arm, leads in her poor son.

'Papa, mais quelle splendeur! I haven't seen the great salon so beautiful since my last ball here.'

Wioletta starts. Wasn't Urszula's last ball here her first ball? She sighs, gathers herself, greets her sister and her nephew whom they seat in another armchair facing his grandfather, and who, in his cushions, is already pale with fatigue.

'A terrible trip,' Urszula states, as she in turn falls onto a seat. 'These roads in Galicia are a horror. I can't wait for the train to come here . . .'

Her mature face, adeptly powdered, artistically sporting a chignon, exudes the will to face up to—to the flood of illustrious visitors that evening, to the need to show her son to stop the rumours that are circulating about him. (I think I can already hear her in her Viennese circle: 'Andrzej? My goodness, yes, a bit worn out, no doubt, but that didn't prevent him from coming with us this summer to our property, he so wanted to come. The estate means so much to him!') Her face exudes determination but one begins to see the effort; and in the smile that reveals her still impeccable teeth, there is now a note of forced optimism. Who knows, perhaps Andrzej will survive them, after all? Medicine these days is progressing so rapidly.

But doors slam, voices sound on the ground floor, the flames of the candles tremble when the major-domo (rented for the occasion) opens the door wide and announces the first guests. It is our dear Countess Wytocka, escorted by a husband, a daughter and a young man who proves to be her nephew. Greetings, hand-kissing, a procession in front of old Zemka who clears his throat as a welcome and doesn't even pretend to rise from his seat. The happy privilege of age! Andrzej must pull himself from his cushions and endure the ritual of conversation.

He holds up honourably but I see Urszula watching him and, looking carefully, and never going very far from him. What is she afraid of?

I will find out later, because a second wave of guests pours into the great salon. There are politicians, other landowners, a journalist from Kraków and his wife . . . A journalist! I am shocked they are entertaining such riff-raff here and I observe Jozef to see what he thinks of this innovation.

Jozef doesn't notice—his animosity is concentrated on the countess' nephew. A good conversationalist, a handsome man, he speaks with ease, a glass in his hand, in the middle of a circle of older ladies and gentlemen. Just returned from a world tour that has taken him five or six years, he is regaling his audience with anecdotes from his travels: an unfortunate love affair in Valparaiso, a shipwreck in the Persian Gulf, adventures with a tribe of negroes who wanted him to be their king, a complex affair of honour in Sicily where he almost lost his young life.

'Insufferable blowhard!' Jozef exclaims. But since he speaks under his breath, the heads that turn towards him do not lose their smiles. The Countess even leans over his chair to whisper enthusiastically, 'His stories are fascinating, aren't they?'

There won't be any dancing this evening, for what's the use of a ball in a home with no young people? It is only a large reception that Urszula and Agenor hope to be the first of a long series. No diaphanous dresses, no ceremonial uniforms, no sparkling earrings or tiaras in the hair—only elegant evening attire of excellent cuts. But I have indeed decided to dance—I swore to, in memory of poor Mitzi. I will spin around their seats, I will waltz, invisible, on the parquet of brown flowers that was, the day before yesterday, impeccably waxed. And if they sometimes feel the brushing of my presence against their hips or on their backs, too bad—they will attribute it to the communicating heat of parties where the wine is flowing.

I weave, I fly, I intercept here and there bits of conversation: 'A lovely fur . . .', 'the future, have no doubt, depends on the zeal that we put into developing societies of credit . . .', 'Imagine that one day when I was hunting a tiger with a maharaja . . .' The voices swell and form a vapour of words that, gradually, filter through the cracks in the walls and the gaps in the floor and, to breathe a bit, I end up following them.

The kitchen is a battlefield overcrowded with steaming pots and pans, moulds being hastily washed, thirsty sauce dishes and empty platters dying of solitude. Mrs Glowiecka, (the new cook) is red and dishevelled, shouting orders in an already hoarse voice while Oleksandra runs around on her swollen legs between that erupting volcano and the iceberg that is the morose Nikolaïa underneath her white apron.

'Quickly, quickly,' cries Wioletta from the top of the service stairway, 'the *pâté en croute* is already gone . . . Lord, more people are arriving. Nikolaïa, take care of the buffet!'

I push through to the other side of the gallery where I thought I saw a little light. Oh, of course, they put Tessa and her big brother, who have been with us for a few weeks, there and they are obediently waiting for the moment they will perform a little musical duet for the guests before going to bed.

In the meantime, they have been forgotten, as usual, but they don't complain. That moment will be torture for them, an additional anguish for their great-aunt and, for the rest of the company, ten forced minutes when they will not be able to eat or speak or cough too loudly. Who is this farce for, then? wonders Kazimierz, whose critical mind has grown as fast as his preadolescent arms and legs. This is no doubt what they call 'form'—something that does nothing for anyone and bores everyone but is nevertheless sacred.

'Stop shaking,' he says to his sister who, nervous, is constantly wiping her palms with her little handkerchief. 'Those people know nothing of music. No matter how badly you play, they will find it *delicious* and *charming*.'

'But I'm afraid!'

Kazimierz shrugs his shoulders, bites into one of the pastries he has secretly taken while a platter was going by and murmurs, 'Idiot.' She turns her head but doesn't get angry. These two understand each other so well! They look surprisingly alike, she is like his little feminine replica, her hair long and less red, her cheeks a bit rounder. Of course he bullies her and speaks to her meanly, but it is their game, that game where they pretend to be distinct, even enemies, whereas they are a single soul divided into two bodies.

She still has no idea that they came from the same womb. But in her dreams about the origin of things, she sometimes imagines that he and she have hatched from the same egg like two miraculous birds. A Fabergé egg, like the one she saw in a picture in the illustrated journal: mysterious, infinitely precious, opening up onto strange and miniscule figurines, a complete world unto itself . . .

'Hey,' murmurs Kazimierz, 'come look out the window. Isn't that grandfather getting out of the carriage?'

Agenor Karlowicz must have been able to get away sooner than expected; he has come to attend the party celebrating the improved business of the sugar factory. What a surprise for his wife! A smile of anticipation grows on his lips. That smile, however, cannot erase the lines of worry, the puffiness of cynicism on his sixty-year-old face which does not know it is being observed. And the children, behind the window, are sort of repulsed by him. Their grandfather has arrived, so what? Tessa, who was going to tap on the window and wave at him doesn't move in the end, and pensively puts a fondant into her mouth. And Kazimierz, next to her, completes her thought by saying in a dull voice, 'Don't worry, they'll come get us when they want to see us . . .'

Those two are really darkening my mood! Quickly, some air, some space, above all, some voices, the voices of adults who perhaps don't always say what they think but at least they say it cheerfully and loudly!

In the great salon, Agenor has just entered to much fanfare. There are exclamations, Urszula runs to his side, the audience of the young globetrotter disperses and reforms around the newcomer. As for Wioletta . . . but whom is she speaking to? To whom belong those wide shoulders (I take a spin in their direction), to whom belong that big stomach and those sad dog's eyes? I'm right—it is our old friend, Prince Dubinski.

The bashful lover has thus forgotten his wounds. I'm delighted, and I'm even more delighted to note that the years have been kind to him. Apart from his increased girth and his completely grey hair, he is just as he was—gauche, likeable, discreetly considerate. I am so close that I can hear him one moment when he interrupts himself and whispers to Wioletta with a timid smile, 'What a pity, isn't it, that there isn't any dancing tonight!'

Wioletta smiles too; and fleetingly I imagine the possibility of an autumnal idyll between Wladislaw and the sister of the one who once had scorned him. But a more attentive eye dissipates that chimaera. No, the prince is one of those men who love only once; his fingers are wearing no wedding band or sign of attachment; on his pinkie, only a signet ring with his family seal (an eagle, greedily pulling a fish out of the water). And if he leans into Wioletta's ear, it is only to respond to an earlier question, 'The night of 14 July? Let's see, isn't that the feast day of Saint Nicodemus, of Saint Simon of Lipnica? Your date doesn't mean anything to me but I will look into it for you. These popular customs are so interesting!'

Let's leave him then to his pet hobby and go listen to what Agenor and the Countess' nephew are talking so softly about.

'. . . I've never had the pleasure of being introduced to your father-in-law,' compliments the young man. 'He's a fine figure of a man; a true sample of old Poland, isn't he?'

Agenor's evasive response doesn't discourage him and he moves his head closer in.

'Unless I'm mistaken, doesn't he have family in France, a distant branch?'

'Family? Oh no, not for a long time. His brother did in fact live in Paris in the entourage of Prince Czartoryski, but that was during the Great Emigration. Captain Zemka-Ponarski, you know, the one who fell at Temesvar . . .'

'Exactly. I'm reassured, and now I feel completely free to tell you my story.'

'Oh?' questions Agenor, and it seems there is a slight wave of concern that blows over his face.

'Yes. You'll see, it's rather strange.' (He dips his lips into his glass of cognac, takes a sip.) 'Imagine, one day in Franche-Comté—it was in 1878, at the very beginning of my voyage—bad weather led me to an inn where I was forced to spend the night. To say that I slept there would be a lie—it was one of those establishments that was infested with fleas, even though the proprietors, upon your arrival, give you their *word of honour* that that was not the case. I can still see him, a fat man with a moustache which one of our Ruthenian peasants would envy, swear to me that . . .'

'So, you were not sleeping.'

'Not at all. I didn't sleep a wink all night. And then at dawn I hear a terrible din in the house. Steel-tipped boots running up the stairs, a woman shouting, a young child crying . . . Resigned, I had my valet dress me and sent him to find out what was causing all the noise. And what did he tell me? It is a novel, sir, a true novel. A young man who had come to the inn was one of those rioters from the Commune of Paris condemned to banishment. And he had broken his territorial interdiction to meet his wife and little boy there. His wife, from what I could understand, was a person whom I had noticed the day before when I arrived—something like a schoolteacher, one of those creatures with a large mouth who make their own hats and give poor women lessons in hygiene, if you see the type I mean . . .'

'I can well imagine!' agreed Agenor, encouraging.

'The lady in question was being held by one of the gendarmes because she was holding on to her husband, it seemed, and screaming loud enough to hurt your ears: "Félix! Félix!" Resigning myself, I went down to the dining room to be served a restorative. The innkeeper, a woman with a kind heart, explained to me while wiping her eyes that the little boy was ill, quite ill, and that it was in order to see him that the exiled man took the risk of crossing the border . . . I'm telling you, a true novel.'

'Indeed!'

'But wait, that's not all. At that moment the gendarmes came down with the man who had broken the interdiction. Imagine, sir, a tall darkish fellow, a sharp nose and green eyes like yours but terribly piercing and moving. I assure you I would not have liked to meet him in a dark woods. He sat down between the two gendarmes who asked for a pen and began to write their *rapport*—paperwork, you see, is a passion for the French, our imperial and royal functionaries, next to them, are only poor amateurs in that. It even happened to me one day at customs . . .'

Agenor, at this promise of a new digression, cannot hold back a gesture of impatience.

'I'm too long-winded, my excuses,' the man said coyly.

'Not at all, on the contrary, I find your story fascinating . . .'

'And so I watched the gendarme who was scribbling on the paper under the dictation of the other one, and, at loose ends, I asked my valet to go get one of my books. Immediately our prisoner, who was listening to me, rose half way in his chair and said in our language: 'Sir, you are Polish?' Difficult to deny, eh? And then my curiosity, I admit, was not just a little piqued by this encounter. The prisoner obtained permission to come closer to my chair, introduced himself and in a few words told me of his adventures. He was one of our compatriots from Podolia who had taken part in the insurrection of 1863 by lying about his age, because at the time he was no more than fifteen or sixteen. Having had to leave the Russian empire, he took refuge, like so many others, in France. In Lyon he was a clerk in some bureau, then he joined the Polish Legion when the Franco-Prussian war broke out. He didn't tell me much about his exploits during the Parisian riots of 1871, as you can imagine. It remained that they earned him, the following year, a condemnation of ten years of banishment and of being sent to the Swiss border. What do you make of all that?'

'Indeed, it is a quite extraordinary account!'

'Not as unusual as you might think. There were many Polish émigrés, he told me, in the federate battalions, two of them were even made generals . . . Whatever the case, our man, for his headstrong actions, had risked four to five years of deportation in New Caledonia. And then he whispered to me: "Forgive my taking the liberty, but I have no other choice . . . sir, in the name of this chance encounter that put you in my path, in the name of our common fatherland, in the name of humanity which may make you take pity on the fate of three beings in the depths of distress, I beg of you: help this poor woman whom I must leave here and who is my companion, the mother of my child . . ." His companion! I thought. Those two, of course, were not even married. "If you could advance her a bit of money to take care of our son, she will pay you back, sir, even if she has to deprive herself, because she is a woman of honour . . ."—"I will do it, never fear," I hastened to assure him given his state of excitation. "I will help her as much as I can."—"Oh, you are a generous soul! You have lifted a terrible weight from my heart. Wait, she's coming over—I'm going to tell her she can count on you." And while his tall beanpole of a woman was clinging to his neck saying her goodbyes, I saw him murmuring in her ear and looking in my direction. Then the gendarmes, who had finished their report, got up and the little group finally set off. That, sir, is the last image I have of that famous Zemka who is not related to you.'

Agenor has grown very pale but, apart from that, his face reveals nothing. One doesn't have the career he does without being able to swallow this sort of news while continuing to smile. And it is while smiling, after having clinked his glass against that of his interlocutor, that he asks, 'Tell me, how did the affair end?'

'What? But my dear sir, I asked for my bill and to have my bags packed in order to, as the French say, "prendre la poudre d'escampette!"'—and get out of there as quickly as I could. You see, it has often happened in the course of my travels to fear for my life. I have found myself nose to nose with a lion of Atlas, and it was a miracle that I wasn't eaten by sharks when I was shipwrecked. But never, you understand (he coughs and smiles, already preparing his finale), never have I felt such fear as at the idea of being burdened by that adept of free love and her scrofulous son!'

He laughs and Agenor imitates him, while his thoughts—and mine—are in tumult. Wioletta, where are you? Alas, she is still talking to the prince and has her back turned. Jozef is dozing. So they know nothing? It's horrible!

Green eyes, piercing and moving, black hair, the build of a lumberjack, . . . I didn't imagine our little Feliks like that, born, as Zygmunt said, at the same time as the free world. If it is he, he is a streak in this dynasty of blonds. But it is he, I'm certain. In telling his tale, the globetrotter, with that art of mimicry which every good storyteller has, subtly assumed his tone of voice and physiognomy. And what did they remind me of, that face and that sharp nose? I am almost stunned when I grasp it—as if through three or four layers of gauze, or a prism that would show only features and would distort colours, I thought I saw, yes, the distant face of Count Fryderyk.

There is good reason to be troubled by the appearance of these two ghosts and, for a few moments, I don't know what to do. The candles have melted, the mountains of fruit have collapsed, the laughs start showing evidence of drunkenness and fatigue. Never have I felt so powerless. My eyes remain fixed on Agenor's neck, the only one who knows except me and who, I guess, will try to prevent the story from getting around. What a pity! How I would like to do more, to learn more! If only I had a body worthy of the name, a voice, hands that could address—what?—notices to the French press, a letter to the governor of Nouméa!

When I think that this story is already six years old, and that in the meantime Feliks Zemka has perhaps truly died, between a stunted palm tree and a fortress wall; when I think that I don't even know nor ever will know the name of his companion or his scrofulous son, despair overwhelms me. And I begin to understand what are, for humans, time and its irremediable flow. For me who allowed myself to live with the idea that everything is always there and can be recalled at leisure, I discover the human bitterness of opportunities missed.

Yes, Feliks' brief return on my captive's horizon marked a decisive turning point for me. That evening, I began waltzing again with complete abandon but my heart was full of rage. I didn't want to know what the Prince might have been murmuring into Wioletta's ear to make her look at her shrunken father with an indecipherable gaze. I did not smile when Urszula, finding that her sister had monopolized the Prince long enough, came over and took him away. I didn't even bat an eyelid when Andrzej, after a few glasses drunk behind his mother's back, abruptly took by the throat the journalist from Kraków, whom he accused of being a Serbian spy and of hiding snakes in his vest pocket.

It would have taken more to distract me.

I danced, danced till I was out of breath, then I went into the little green salon where the two children, after waiting so long, had fallen asleep. Tessa's head had slid onto her brother's shoulder and her handkerchief had fallen on the rug, underneath her open hand. Kazimierz, his eyes closed, had something delicate and vulnerable that wasn't seen when he was awake. I watched them for a long time while I caught my breath. And I said to myself that I would give everything, truly *everything*, to get away from here.

8

That evening something also happened to Wioletta, I don't yet know what but I am certain of it. She is carrying a little flame of joy, almost of malice, inside her—I noticed it three days later, when Agenor, just about to leave, was saying his goodbyes to her. He looked at her in silence, and I realize that on his forehead I saw the vague desire to tell her what he had learnt. He even opened his mouth; but then another thought appeared. Wioletta would try to find that son, the word would get out. Who knows if, through word of mouth, people would find out that Councillor Karlowicz had an illegitimate son somewhere in the world and, in addition, a former communard? Oh, no! That's all he needed. And then—it was this more charitable, more presentable thought, that he finally held on to—it would not help Wioletta, in the end. She has forgotten, or at least has resigned herself. Why awaken that old pain, put her on a path that, perhaps, will only lead her to more disappointment?

So he was content to brush her hand with his moustache while murmuring, 'I have been, my dear sister, delighted to see you again.'

'And I, as well,' Wioletta responded lightly. '*A sister without a brother*, right, *is like a boat without oars!*'

Agenor was stunned and I, metaphorically, burst out laughing. Hadn't she just replied with a proverb from Anna Scholastyka?

It seems to me, by the way, that her good spirits are linked to that genealogical research, and I now regret not having listened to what Prince Dubinski was whispering to her. The few snippets I heard leave me in the dark: '. . . Completely characteristic, and even repeated word for word in the manuscript that I will send you . . . A remarkable page in our history . . . Parish records . . . it would be easy to find out . . .'

I regret it all the more because Wioletta has recovered a condition that she hadn't had since she was pregnant—once again she is closed to me, excludes me from her inner depths. I am reduced to following her comings and goings in the house, watching her leave on the road to

Grynow, looking at her paintings. She has just painted *The Flour Scales at Dusk* and *The Old Quarter in the Rain,* but those works, I have the impression, are, unless I am mistaken, a pretext to get away rather than the reflection of her preoccupations.

When, after settling her father in the little green salon, or in the armchair of his room if he has arisen unwell from his nap, she lingers near him, rearranges a knick-knack, straightens a painting that is slightly askew, it is only Jozef whom I hear, depending on the case, dreaming or reflecting. She presents to me only an impenetrable face in which only the big blue eyes have a hidden spark.

'Father, have I ever asked you where the Zemkas came from? There is no one with that name in Grynow, or in the neighbouring cantons . . .'

I would like, Jozef thinks with annoyance, for her to stop digging into that, she'll end up telling me that we have descended from Ruthenian ragpickers. Where does that name come from? What do I know! I've never liked it. What bad luck for my mother to have had to agree to such a misalliance . . . Poor sacrificial lamb, said my Uncle Krzysztof. My good father adored her, I must admit, and never blamed her for having been married without the slightest dowry. On the contrary, he always spoke of the Ponarskis as his benefactors. It is certain that such a woman was an asset to him, which he would never have obtained without the ruin of her county family . . .

'Would you like me to adjust your blanket, Father?'

He lets her do it in spite of the mild weather, because his old bones are now cold no matter the season.

'There, you're all wrapped up. Do you need anything else?'

He looks up at his daughter. How tall she is, standing in front of him, and how little he feels, sunk in his armchair! No, he doesn't need anything, he would even prefer that she return to her easel. When she surrounds him with her care like a governess, he feels belittled and, in an obscure way, threatened. To get her away, he closes his eyes and pretends to doze off.

Who was Tadeusz Zemka?

A good imbecile, pious and hard working, like so many in those times. 'Today, my sons, we will go to the church to celebrate the death of our Lord Jesus who was sacrificed for the salvation of all men, and who promised to return to earth . . . Adam! don't pull on the buttons of your tunic or you'll pull them off!' A little, honest bourgeois without genius, doing his work throughout the year with strength, and thanking God . . . 'Don't ever change the formula!' May he rest in peace, I didn't listen to him, I even think that I don't remember it, his famous formula. '9. Aqua, 17. Sacchari' . . . All that is so long ago! 'One day you will understand, Jozef, why one must never change the formula . . .' No, I did not understand. It was he who didn't understand that tastes change, like the times, and that one must be aware of them . . . 'Never forget, my sons, that you must adore the Holy Trinity . . .' How simple beings are indecipherable, in the end, and difficult to define . . .

And suddenly something makes him open his eyes; a certain quality of the silence, perhaps, disturbed only by the noise of the pencil with which Wioletta, on her canvas, is sketching something.

'What are you drawing?'

'A view of Grynow,' murmurs his daughter without moving her head.

'Grynow, always Grynow!' A long moment goes by, but it seems to Jozef that something in the air remains in suspense.

'And what is the title?'

'I don't know yet,' Wioletta responds. Then she pivots on her stool and slowly smiles at him.

Above them, in the schoolroom, Tessa and her brother are reading across from each other, their hands on their heads. Her book is illustrated, she reads the text, in fact only to better understand the drawings—huge oceans wracked by cyclones, glaciers, herds of elephants . . . Sometimes she stumbles on a word she doesn't know, and timidly asks, 'What is a degree of longitude?'

And Kazimierz, under his breath, immediately throws out a definition before going back to his collection of poems.

They are so absorbed that they allow tea time to go by and are surprised that, on the fields, the shadows have lengthened, that the light has assumed dark purple shades.

Kazimierz's heart is heavy. At his school it is the hour when studies are over, when the students go into the courtyard with shouts of joy. That boisterousness dupes no one, or at least doesn't trick him. Its only goal is to mask the horrible feeling of solitude that takes hold of them as soon as their minds are not subjected to the need to listen as carefully as possible in order to avoid punishment. All the students who are shoving or fighting have, he knows, a great desire to be at home with their mothers, or simply (for those who don't have mothers) at home. 'Catch, Karlowicz!' shouts a Czech friend who throws a snowball at him. '*Knedlo*-eater, you're going to get it!' he responds, bending over in turn to make a snowball, hard, painful, one of those technological snowballs that, more than his musical talents and his ability to learn, makes Kazimierz the envy of his classmates.

At that hour at school there is fighting, boys' mouths seek (while looking out of the corner of their eyes to be sure that the priest who is watching them is not within earshot) the lowest insults, the most abominable accusations against the chastity of mothers and sisters, a word that will wound one's adversary—a companion in misery—at his most vulnerable point. They hurt one another but it is good—that makes them hard, a bit like the morning wash in icy water.

At the same time, here, there is calm in the fields, the sound of the birds that fly through the sky in flocks, from left to right, from right to left, as if they were wondering, the poor things, where the great light of day has gone. There is silence on the floors of the masters, the clock that, calmly, drones out the minutes, the soft steps of Nikolaïa who comes to bring them a lamp or light the fire. Down below, in the kitchens, there is a clattering of pots, a clinking of plates, laughter; but that animation is only a prelude, Kazimierz knows, to the darkness and the immobility of the night. And the thought doesn't tighten his throat any less than it does at school. It is even deeper here, because there is no remedy: Where would he want to be, since he is already at home?

He shivers, then listens. From very far, he can hear a choir of peasants who are returning from the fields. It is still only background noise, as impalpable as the mist that, now, is rising above the fields.

'Can you hear it?' Tessa whispers.

Of course he can hear it. That need people, including his sister, have to say what goes without saying, to put words onto that which can do without words! He can even hear that the choir is approaching and can now distinguish three voices, three voices that weave together like knotted fingers; he wants to cry. But in Kazimierz tears only fall inside, they are an emptiness, a vertigo, a hollow and a yearning, those tears that flow inside him without finding a way out . . .

A false note—he jumps. Thinking it will please him, Tessa, standing next to him, has just joined the choir. She knows the tune well, she even understands the Ruthenian words; it is a sad story of departure, regrets, and she does her best, utters the words of love, raises her voice on the final notes of the refrain, when it goes: 'Oh, my little flower . . .' His sister sings well, standing next to him. However, he looks at her meanly, and under his breath says, 'Be quiet, I'm listening.'

Let her listen too, instead of singing without understanding! At the beginning of each couplet there is a short, unstable chord that gives the sense of falling, then catching oneself. An impression that he would like to deepen; but Tessa prevents him, because, stubborn, she has started singing again.

'I told you to be quiet—can't you?'

That dissonance, he wanted to catch it in his hand like a little plant, put it in the earth. It would grow, would have leaves, would become a tree, a dissonant tree. He shakes his head. No, that's not it, that wouldn't be enough (he thinks, although he promises himself he will find it, tomorrow, at the piano). What he would like, in fact, is for everything that surrounds him to become dissonance, everything: the earth and its chequered fields, its trunks of birch, its zones of heather; the little pond over there, above which a hoopoe has just taken flight; the sky, its first stars and its pink stripes, on the side where the sun has now set . . .

In that world of discord, of movement, of rhythmic fractures, life, perhaps, would deserve to be lived. In that world—his thoughts are suspended a second to better penetrate the revelation he has just had— he would finally be *at home*.

And further above them, on the servants' floor (this isn't the same day, it is not even the same year, but for me, as I've said, everything blends into an immense present; and the singers might well be the mothers or the grandmothers of the ones that we've just heard, the song hasn't changed), Zygmunt, who was writing, has just put down his pen and opened the window. He sees them, those serf women who are walking in a group, some in front, others a bit behind because their feet have gone into a hole or knocked against a stone, but they hurry and, soon, they are the ones walking in front. And, young or old, in front or behind, they are all singing with joy because the day is done and the hour of rest is approaching.

What strength in them, thinks Zygmunt. What strength in even the servile, humiliated soul. Their cheeks are hollow and their shoulders stooped with fatigue, but they sing, all together, strong from the earth that they sow and harvest, that earth where their legs stand firm and which is theirs, whether they recognize it or not . . .

Then his eyes fall upon Clara who is standing under the trees on the grounds and listening, she too, soft with pleasure. She has seen him, she turns her head under her hood tied with a pink ribbon under her chin. And she is so beautiful like that, her upturned face, her eyes raised towards him without daring to smile, she is so beautiful, he loves her so that something seizes in his chest and, forgetting all caution, he throws her a kiss.

9

The death of old Zemka in 1885 was hardly an event in our region. At eighty-eight, you can scarcely expect more from your descendants than for them to say: 'May he rest in peace, he had a long and good life,' or: 'Now that was a man!' for the more eloquent. (Agenor Karlowicz said as much in his funeral oration.) And yet, in a sort of belated symmetry, Jozef's end, like that of his wife, was completely different from what it appeared to be.

For several weeks, Wioletta was glowing. She was glowing to the point of persuading me that in the end there was probably indeed the beginning of a little love affair between her and Prince Dubinski. She was so excited, so joyful, when she received one of his letters or sent one to him! The creases on her forehead and her mouth had softened, she was standing up straighter, her huge eyes were shining as in the past. She finally looked like what she was—a woman of fifty-eight who had been, in her youth, exceptionally beautiful.

But few of my inhabitants paid any attention to her. Do we ever really look at those we see every day? Tessa did indeed remark that her great-aunt didn't frighten her as much, but didn't wonder why; no more than Nikolaïa wondered why, lately, the mistress was so insupportable to her. Hadn't she heard her singing one morning while getting dressed? At her age, singing!

In fact, only one person saw that beauty—her father. He was disturbed by it, upset, and followed his daughter with his eyes as if to attempt to get to the bottom of it. What is happening with her? What is making her so cheerful? I heard him wondering. The silly woman was cooking something up, that was clear; even if she was still applying herself with as much calm to her brushes, mixing her colours with as much patience and concentration.

One day when he was watching her paint and noting that her fine and proud profile had essentially not changed since the time she was fifteen, sixteen—*in those days*, he thought with a sense of mourning, of irreparable loss—she turned towards him and, with a clear eye, asked, 'Do you remember Jakob Frank, Father, that Jewish heretic who, in the middle of the last century convinced thousands of his fellow Jews to embrace our faith? A remarkable page in our history, which you must be aware of.'

He looked at her, disagreeably surprised. Forty years earlier, he remembered, a journal from Warsaw had published a series of articles on this subject; it had been filled with so many illustrious names that the publication had been suspended after a few issues. Then there was a flurry of articles and pamphlets in which scholars and odd people outdid one another in analysing the reason for that wave of conversions that took place shortly before the end of Poland. Such an effervescence, such enjoyment in the grotesque and the doubtful, such discredit thrown on the most holy hours of the past and on the ascendancy of certain national glories, that was the thinking at the time. Those Forty-Eighters didn't respect anything. It even went so far as to implicate the great Mickiewicz, who nonetheless died a martyr, yet was also sullied by these insinuations . . .

'Yes, so?' he barked while a redness began dangerously to colour the cheeks underneath his white sideburns.

'So?' She dipped her brush, wiped it carefully on the edge of her pot and resumed, calmly, 'Well, imagine that Piotr and Anna Scholastyka, your grandparents, were two followers of that curious person.'

Slowly her words entered Jozef's mind and he said, 'What?'

'I repeat, Father, that your grandparents Zemka (whatever their name before that date might have been) were among those many Jews who, in 1759, became Christians upon the appeal of their leader, the famous Jakob Frank.'

He watched his daughter who was still painting, and suddenly he was afraid. A madwoman. I have always suspected as much, and this explains many things. I am being taken care of by a madwoman, and that madwoman is my daughter. For now she isn't looking at me. But when she turns her big blue eyes towards me with that delighted laugh that she has had for several days, I won't be able to endure it. Oh! If only I were strong enough to go pull the cord of the bell hanging over there on the wall . . .

'What's the matter, Father, you're very agitated? Do you need something?' said Wioletta, who had been watching him out of the corner of her eye and now seemed to be getting up.

'Nothing at all. Stay where you are,' he cut her off with a vigour that surprised him most of all.

He had to buy time. Cajole this delirious woman, make her talk and calm her with words—anything other than watching her smiling, attentive, getting close to my chair . . .

'Come now, my girl, how could you have got such a strange idea into your head? The Zemkas, Jews, now really! They were, quite to the contrary, pious Catholics who scrupulously observed religious holidays. How many times did our father annoy us with his processions, his pardons, the life of the saint of the day he made us read about early in the morning? Even my mother, Elzbieta, though she was very pious and raised by the nuns, grew weary of it, and found pretexts not to accompany him to church.'

'That doesn't refute anything that I told you, Father. A fastidious religiosity was precisely what the master demanded of his followers after their conversion. And he himself, I read . . .'

'You don't know what you're talking about—I knew my family better than you, I believe. My grandmother followed a true cult of the Virgin, I was told, and it was even in her memory that my late father baptized his pastilles in the name of the Mother of God.'

'Really?' said Wioletta, before pensively adding a touch of white to the corner of the canvas. 'Indeed, the cult of the Virgin was one of the Christian dogmas most dear to the heretic Frank. And those Pastilles de la Vierge, now that you mention it, would be another evidence of . . .'

'But you are delirious!' replied Jozef, beginning to lose patience. 'Come back to earth. My father hated the Jews who, already, were doing a great deal of damage to our business. There wasn't a day that he didn't curse, as he said, those "Talmudist dogs", whose disloyal competition and fraudulent cooperation made things so difficult for an honest Christian artisan (there were so few) to earn his living; and . . . and . . .'

He had lost the habit of speaking at such length, and he was out of breath.

'Those Talmudist dogs, you say?' Wioletta repeated with a little laugh. 'That tells me a lot. Don't you know that those mystics in fact professed to denounce the Talmud that their fathers revered and showed their attachment to our faith by ostentatiously speaking against it?'

'Be quiet!' interrupted Jozef, terrified by that irrefutable logic.

'There, there, you're getting overheated . . . Do you want me to ring for Nikolaïa to bring you your lemon water? Yes, now, be reasonable.' She got up and, very calmly, pulled on the rope twice. 'Your father detested the Jews? I'm not surprised. Do you think that the Believers, as Frank's disciples liked to call themselves, really appreciated their fellow Jews and their rabbis very much, those who had excommunicated them, disturbed their meetings, refused them housing and jobs, threw stones at them when they went through a town with their women and children?—Thank you, Nikolaïa. Please go get a glass of lemon water for my father—Yes, in that Tadeusz Zemka was a very typical Frankist . . .'

'Be quiet!' repeated Jozef in a wheezing voice, when Nikolaïa, surprised, turned around at the door before shutting it again. 'I forbid you from going into this type of madness in front of the staff. I forbid you . . .' He was getting hoarse. Make her be quiet. Lock her up? Oh, if only Agenor Karlowicz had been there at that moment . . .

'And where, my poor child, have you found this information?' he said, forcing himself to smile.

'From your friend Prince Dubinski who is very interested in our history, as you know, particularly in the last years of the Polish kingdom. He has developed a collection of old manuscripts, with a section he calls 'esoteric.' Do you know, Father, that he lent me one called *Sayings of the Master*? It's very striking. One finds word for word certain proverbs . . .'

Then Nikolaïa entered with a glass on a tray, helped the old man to drink, took the empty glass and, with a curtsey, went out. And all that time Wioletta remained silent, her eyes lowered with a sweet irony that said: Don't you see how good I am? Rest assured, I won't say a thing as long as she is here.

'From Prince Dubinski, then,' she resumed, when Nikolaïa's footsteps had faded in the hallway. 'And through his intermediary, Prince R***, who is enthralled with this subject and who is believed to have offered an enormous sum to acquire the skull of the master, buried in the German city of Offenbach, in order to put it under forensic examination . . .'

Prince Dubinski, Prince R***? Jozef thought he was dealing with *one* mad person; it now appeared that the entire world had gone mad. Or maybe it was he who was losing his mind? *The skull of the master*! . . . What had he done, but what had he done to deserve this?

'Oh, you've spit up your medicine! Take my handkerchief to wipe yourself and breathe deeply, I'm going to summon Nikolaïa again. Do you want me to send her to Grynow to get the doctor?'

In a few minutes the entire household knew that *Pan* Jozef had had a spell. The doctor came by, and was reassuring—general fatigue, rapid pulse, but a few days of rest would do the trick. From his bed Jozef listened, haggard, his temples throbbing. What had become of his familiar world, why was he surrounded only by witches and necromancers? That doctor from Grynow and his short little beard (a quack or an assassin), that daughter of his, moving around the room under the pretext of fluffing his pillows, that horrible Oleksandra with veiny legs who spoke only Ruthenian and shook her head like an ape while she swept the floor, all these people were lemurs, larvae come to torment him, his bed was a dissecting table, a torture chamber . . . Get up, he said to himself, get up from the sickbed and go sit in my chair in *my* little salon, whose furniture and green walls I have chosen! Seated in my chair, I'm not as afraid of them.

Clara, he thought again. Clara would know how to get rid of these evil spirits, Clara would have cured him, saved him . . . 'My poor, old girl, my ugly duckling,' he murmured in a half-sleep; and Tessa, who was brought every day to his bedside to kiss his hand, shivered in terror and recoiled while whispering to her great-aunt: 'He's talking about a duckling. Aunt Wioletta, can I go now?'

It was a relief for her as well as for her great-grandfather when, after four days, he could finally get up again. Settled in the salon in the chair that at his request had been brought nearer to the window, where the light was brighter, he was surprised at his recent agony. Had that absurd dialogue really taken place? Opposite him, Wioletta was still painting, even if she turned towards him more often to ask him how he was feeling

('Surround him with care,' the doctor had recommended during his last visit. 'Don't let him get excited, but don't let him live in his thoughts because I suspect he is in a state of melancholy. Try to distract him peacefully, dear lady, in short—attend to him.')

Wioletta did attend to him. Each time Jozef looked in her direction, he was sure to encounter her smile and the almond shape of her big blue eyes. She would then make a remark on the weather or the news of the region, even interrupt her work to read him the newspapers.

'Look at this engraving, Father. It is a new vehicle with wheels moved by the muscular force of the user. "A chain connecting the pedals to a driving wheel, set in a frame with a second wheel of equal diameter, whence the name 'bicycle'" . . .'

'Hmmmm,' grumbled the old man.

'Or, listen to this,' pursued Wioletta without getting discouraged. '"Last 17 June the French ship *Isère* landed in the port of New York with two hundred and fourteen crates containing the monumental statue of the sculptor Bartholdi: *Liberty lighting the world*. Once assembled, the work on its foundation will rise close to one hundred metres in height."'

'Liberty!' murmured Jozef, shrugging his shoulders.

Wioletta endured all those rebuffs with the patience of an angel; and the doctor and the servants, in the following months, could not stop talking about the devotion with which Mistress Zemka was accompanying her father in his final days.

'Do you know what I think?' said this devoted daughter to him after a few days, putting some varnish on her finished painting. 'I think that you didn't believe a word I told you before you fell ill.'

She smiled at him cheerfully and he thought: Wonderful, she has become herself again! But she had better apologize, and soon. And I maintain, yes, I maintain that this type of joke verges on mental illness.

She approached his chair, picked off a gray hair that had fallen on his shoulder and whispered in his ear, 'Isn't that right, you didn't believe me?'

'Of course not.'

'How stubborn you are, Papa!' she laughed. 'I thought so, and that's why I brought you this.'

Mute, he looked at the bundle of manuscripts that she had put on his lap.

'It is a registered copy of the list of anti-Talmudists converted in 1759, with some facts concerning them. You see, on 17 September in the cathedral of Lvov: Piotr Zemka, twenty-three, and his wife Anna Scholastyka, nineteen. From a village in Wallachia, thus Ottoman subjects. Ottoman subjects, yes, just as today Jan and my poor sister would be. Isn't it amazing that the history of families can, through the whims of fate, end up in the same place this way?'

Jozef looked at her with horror; he thought that something in his chest was about to explode. He breathed noisily, blinking his eyes.

'It's written here, right above my finger. Can't you read it?'

He nodded yes, then moved his head away so he couldn't see the paper any more. At his side he saw only the dagger from Alep whose blade was shining, he thought, evilly, then the Trebizond rug whose appearance he suddenly found treacherous, like a hunting trap in the depths of a forest.

'Are you going to believe me now, Papa?' Wioletta cheerfully insisted. Her index finger descended the paper a bit, 'And look here, it's strange. Do you know who your grandfather's godfather was? Look: Godfather, Fryderyk, Count Ponarski.'

It was the second time in a few months that chance reminded me of my noble founder, and this time I shuddered so much that the pendants on the chandelier started to clink.

'No!' Jozef was finally able to utter. 'Not another word, I don't want to hear that, do you understand? I forbid you to mix the Ponarskis up in this sordid affair.'

'*Mais mon pauvre* Papa, I fear that they mixed themselves up in it, and not just a little—I think I saw elsewhere the name of the Countess, his wife, who was the godmother of a five-year-old child. Wait, here it is—little Ignacy from Kamionka.'

'Silence! None of that is possible. What would the Ponarskis be doing among those illuminated beggars, tell me that?'

'Admit at least that they were in good company,' Wioletta tranquilly observed. 'You see, on the other pages, the names and positions of the godfathers and godmothers: Jan Kalinski, court churchwarden; Justyna Countess Pawlowska, Lady of Zytomierz; the Starosta Bratkowski . . . Our nobility has always wished to work for its church. And what a wonderful cause, wasn't it, to thus contribute to the salvation of lost souls and bring so many new believers into our faith?'

Jozef was panting.

'Yes,' continued Wioletta in a pensive tone, 'our nobility did a great deal to encourage those poor people to follow the right path, many of whom came with all that they had from the countryside in Podolia, Wallachia, and farther still, because Jakob Frank had spent his youth in Turkey and was still well-known there. Do you know that some great landowners offered their godsons a bit of land, even invited them into their homes or nearby to be sure they were duly catechized? That is no doubt what the count did for your young grandparents. And I'm no longer surprised that your father, in his journal, always calls the Ponarskis his benefactors.'

Once again something rose up in me—a memory, a very old, certainly unpleasant memory, but one that I would still like to remember, instead of feeling it flying around me and constantly hiding. The count . . . What did I remember about Count Fryderyk? Nothing, or very little—those years, all my first sixty years were lost for me in the clouds of youth; and what I knew of them came more from stories I heard, paintings I looked at, than from my own experience. Oh, I almost had it! No, the memory is gone, gone out of the window that Wioletta has just opened wide.

'Breathe in a bit of cool air, you seem congested . . . Do you know what I think? It was to repay that debt that your father married Elzbieta Ponarska. Because, in the end, what reason did a small artisan, even in love, have to marry a young girl without a penny and who, as you have already suggested, didn't know how to do anything with her ten fingers? The Ponarskis had nothing left, were nothing any more, and he took care of her. What a wonderful gesture on his part, what piety! Yes, in that your father proved to be truly worthy of the name of Christian and, my goodness, you need not be ashamed of his origins. What is important are actions, no? Much more than birth.'

An ocean was raging in Jozef's heart; he made a gesture of fury, and if his daughter had still been standing in front of him he would have seized her by the throat and shaken her with all the strength left in his old fingers. But she was moving back and forth behind his chair, and all he could see of her was the bottom of her grey skirt brushing the rug.

'You look quite red, quite agitated . . . Would you like me to move your chair closer to the window? No, it's not too heavy,' she said with a little laugh, 'you have forgotten that I am strong, *mon cher* Papa, and that you weigh very little.'

The she-devil no doubt thought that with that she had given him the *coup de grâce* but Jozef did not admit defeat. He looked out the window as if the sight of the branches swaying in the wind, a sparrow perched on a branch and jumping in a ray of sun, had mysteriously attracted all his attention. He stayed like that until Wioletta grew tired and left the room and, finally, he could close his eyes.

The next day a little party was held to celebrate *Pan* Jozef's recovery. The countess and her husband were invited; Agenor, on mission in the province, had announced he would be there; and, since the day was a holiday, they had even sent the carriage for Kazimierz who had arrived right at four o'clock in his student uniform.

Agenor was next; then came the Wytockis in their landau with their spaniel and a large basket of pears from their orchard, which they knew Jozef enjoyed. Everyone went into the little green salon where the patriarch was enthroned, came one after the other and, with voices lowered, paid their friendly respects. But he responded to these greetings with a stubborn and dark air; and even the good Countess, after a few minutes, gave up.

On the other side of the room, people were admiring Wioletta's latest painting. 'So realistic!—A bold subject . . . beautiful composition . . .' murmured the adults. Tessa, who really didn't like the smell of varnish, wrinkled her nose, while Kazimierz thought, it's not too bad, for once, it's true, it's not bad at all . . .

The Countess had just joined them, 'My goodness, it's beautiful. My dear Wioletta, you truly have talent, I assure you—real talent!'

'I agree,' coughed Agenor. 'Allow me to congratulate you, sister.'

Jozef, on the other side, was moving around in his chair.

'What's going on? I can't see very well.'

'What are we thinking!' murmured the countess. Couldn't we, Councillor Karlowicz, bring the easel closer to him? You will see, Jozef, it's lovely. Your daughter has outdone herself!'

And so they brought the painting closer to Jozef, who leant forward.

In the foreground, two little boys, seated on the ground, were playing jacks. One had just thrown them into the air and was sticking out his hand as if to catch them, while the other, his cheek covered with a lock of hair that had fallen in front of his ear from his dark hat, turned towards us, with laughing eyes, one side of his mouth raised. Farther, there were dogs going by, women with light-coloured scarves tied around their heads, one carrying a chicken, a child or a coal bucket. Only then did one distinguish the men, for their suits were black against the black of the pavement, the narrow facades and the entrances of the stores—it was *The Jewish Quarter Seen from St George Church*.

Everyone was now looking at the master of the house, waiting for his approval. Mouths were smiling, eyes sparkling, Agenor Karlowicz was whispering to the Count who was looking at the patriarch and responding in a low voice, Jozef felt a warmth rise in his chest, an infernal heat; he looked back at the painting, where a little pair of dark eyes looked back at him.

And what were those eyes saying?

That life was bitter, it ended up taking back all that it had given, and more—that life was a fistful of jacks that, however strong you were, however adept, however tenacious, always ended up sliding out of your fingers, like water, like sand . . .

Then Jozef Zemka felt the last, the greatest anger of all his existence, and from the depths of his body one word, a single word, burst out, 'Rubbish!'

He had time to sense that it wasn't that, that wasn't the word, it was too weak, completely inadequate for the tragedy that was his life; then a huge wave crashed inside his head and he no longer thought anything at all.

10

And so Jozef didn't get to see Grynow Station, either; and despite the promise he had made to himself, nor would he see the wedding of his great-granddaughter.

The stroke from which he died after forty-eight hours did, however, occur at an opportune moment because everyone, or almost everyone, was already there. Kazimierz prolonged his holiday for a week to stay with us, Agenor was able to help his poor sister-in-law arrange the formalities of the wake, and moreover, very quickly, Urszula arrived as a reinforcement and took things in hand.

Then the whirlwind gradually died down. Kazimierz left for Lvov, Urszula and Agenor, three weeks later, went back to Vienna where they couldn't leave Andrzej for long without visiting him at the rest home. The letters of condolence grew less frequent, and then stopped; and on the family vault of the Ponarskis, the name of Jozef Zemka seemed to have been engraved for all eternity.

But humans, as I've already pointed out, have that ability to live on among those close to them and in the things they leave behind. Wasn't I, myself, the legacy of old Jozef who had turned me into his . . . his jewel, the material reflection of his ambitions? And the sugar factory, now an orphan! In spite of the flow of workers who, from morning to night, went through its doors, I could see, thanks to my objective vision, that it had aged a lot recently. Its white badigeon coat now verged on ecru, its little front had wrinkles, and its chimneys, even though they smoked as much as ever, had asthmatic bursts in their exhalations about which I was amazed that no one besides I was worried about. No one, not even Agenor, the fortunate heir who, in his optimism, saw only figures, excellent ones—all the more excellent in that the few other sugar factories in the province had closed one after another so that we were now in a position of quasi-monopoly.

Wioletta had presented a scene of true emotional distress during the reading of the funeral oration by the Councillor Karlowicz. Since then, she had once again fallen silent and resumed her habit of humming all alone while rinsing her brushes. Moreover, apart from rinsing and rinsing them again, she no longer used them, and those around her were dismayed that, after the beautiful *Jewish Quarter*, she had definitively given up her art.

'Poor old woman!' murmured the visitors as they were leaving. 'Her father was her entire life in the end, and it's possible she will never recover from his death.'

She recovered, however, in only a few months. Following prostration there was sadness, then a state of melancholy that didn't keep her from taking an interest in others. And they knew she had recovered when she began to take very good care of her great-niece Tessa.

Because the poor child—Wioletta finally realized—was desperately in need of a female influence. Her mother, in the past three or four years, lived in Italy with one of her *friends* (and the divorce that followed had not even given the Karlowiczs the opportunity for a public indignation. How could they heap anathema onto Gertrud without revealing the reasons for her flight, Andrzej's illness, the decline of his mental health?). In the hamlet, *Pani* Pavlykowa, whom Tessa once called 'nanny' grew less familiar with her, began to treat her with the distant politeness that she showed to other inhabitants of the *dwor*. And on the New Year that followed Jozef's death, she abstained from offering the girl her sacrosanct pair of wooden clogs.

'Thank you for your kindness, Mistress Teresa,' she murmured with a curtsey upon receiving the purse containing her New Year gift; and, for the first time, that gift was not reciprocated. Tessa was very affected by this, I think she even cried a bit, then, in her great-aunt's apron, into which she had developed the habit of pouring out the troubles and memories that tormented her little soul: Gertrud climbing into the carriage waving a handkerchief soaked in tears but giving the driver the signal to hurry off; Mitzi shrieking, a hand on her face, her forearm scarlet underneath her black sleeve; finally, *Pan* Jozef, beating the air with his hands and shouting a bad word before suffocating . . .

And Wioletta, moved, softly caressed her long brown braid.

What luck for this poor little girl to have finally found a mother, they said in the environs. Love is such a dogma, among humans, that you will never hear them complain of one of theirs being loved by others.

But when I saw Wioletta's hand linger pensively on her grand-niece's neck, when I heard her read one of her bedside books to her, to suggest, if the weather was good, that they attend vespers in Grynow or visit her old friend Prince Dubinski, I admit I was ill at ease.

I wasn't at ease either when Tessa, for a change, transferred her sadness onto our Bsendorfer; and yet, it also liked her a great deal.

His entire life, this fickle lover had been in love with whoever touched him with even the slightest bit of sensibility. He had loved Clara, had a crush on Maria and Wioletta; not Jadwiga, no, that one really didn't understand anything . . . But the new little girl who had been tapping on his keys for several years, and especially the boy, her brother, who tried bold chromatics on him—those two he loved, both of them, with an impartial and hermaphroditic ardour.

Even if the boy was fickle and often preferred his violin; because then the children would play together, and it was nice, very nice, a true four-person idyll. *Mutatis mutandis*, it was like one of those families where two sisters marry two brothers and where everyone is doubly cousins. In those moments the piano exulted, put forth amazing vibrations, held its two candelabras out like ecstatic arms. Yes, yes, he sang, yes, adorable Tessa, strike me, strike me again . . . (I, who hadn't had the opportunity to see Master Semien in his prison cell, celebrating his mysticism as a sinner, I imagine him very much like our piano, in these moments. Am I wrong? Who will know! Anyway, he was hanged.)

And a strange sensation arose in Tessa. The ancient passions of her great-aunts and her great-grandmother rose up through her fingers and penetrated her flesh and she was seized by a fervour whose cause she didn't know, it seemed to her that life, in front of her, was opening up, that anything was possible . . . And when she had struck the last chord of the accompaniment, when Kazimierz, after a silence, raised his bow to look at her: 'You ruined the adagio again,' she bit her lip but her happiness did not diminish—on the contrary. Because she was thinking, One day we will do better.

No, I wasn't at ease at all.

I was relieved when the young girl, stubborn as ever, put on her smock and her clogs that were too little, crossed the little garden and ran to the cottages where, as she knew, however, she was no longer welcome—in fleeing my walls and all these influences, she was showing a true instinct for survival. Out there she promptly fell among her old playmates, babbled in Ruthenian, laughed out loud . . . Well done, I said to myself. And I kept an amused memory of the day when Danylo, the very young brother of the Pavlyk woman (until then a worker in the oil well, visiting here to find work a bit closer to his family), after watching Tessa play, had caught her by the end of her braid: 'Who are you, sprite, one of my nieces? I don't recognize you.'

Slyly, she shook her head no, while looking at his large cheekbones, his thick hair, the turned-up nose on the face that had not long ago left childhood.

'What farm are you from, then?'

And, either disturbed by the misunderstanding, or out of mischievousness, she made a vague gesture in my direction, muttering, 'Over there.'

Then he freed her with a tickle under her chin, promising that one day he would take her and his nephews fishing for tadpoles in the nearby pond. When Tessa had left, oh, how poor Danylo had been scolded!

'You idiot!' his sister yelled at him, her two hands on her hips. 'You don't know that's the masters' little girl? I can't believe you pulled on her braid!'

'Your children play with her, don't they?'

'She comes to play with them, a lot of good it does us! But you, no one asked you. I hope they didn't see you, at least. If you think you're going to get a position at the sugar factory!'

'Bah, for what they pay!'

'That's it, be choosy on top of everything. A position is still a position, and *it is a dirty bird . . .*'

'. . . *who shits in his nest.* Don't worry, I'll leave her alone, Your Highness. Now give me the boots, I have to go to Three Oaks to meet a friend.'

'Our boots? How am I going to do my shopping in town?'

Danylo, pushing his cap back, put a big kiss on his older sister's cheek.

'One day, sister, we will all have boots. Grandfathers, grandmothers, fathers and mothers, even the children. One pair each.'

'A pair each, eh! In America, yes.'

'No, here.'

'You and your ideas! You must have gone to the reading circle again. OK, take the boots. But go to Grynow before Three Oaks, and bring me back some thread and two flasks of oil. And don't come back in the dark!'

Danylo shrugged his shoulders and set off. But at the corner of the cottage he turned back to me and saw Tessa who, in fact, was going up the front stairs. The masters' daughter, eh? Good for her, and too bad for him.

Good for her—I wasn't so sure.

11

I suspect that those who are listening to me are beginning to wonder if, yes or no, someone has finally been able to see the Grynow train station completed. Oh yes, it will be completed; and its inauguration will propel it to a degree of fame that no one could have foreseen. But we are in Galicia and here everything happens much more slowly, at least when Jozef is no longer around to accelerate the movement. I remember, or it was said in front of me: Count Fryderyk was already complaining that his most spirited racehorses, as soon as he brought them to the *dwor*, became lazy and as sluggish as mules. And the trees grow very slowly. Even the raindrops fall slowly, as if they are saying to themselves on their journey: What if, rather, we went up?

There is nothing surprising, then, if at the end of eighteen months of shocks, comings and goings and activity on my left, we are only, it seems, at the first stones of the future building.

While waiting, what happens here? Not much that can be seen. They are preparing mentally for the installation of Councillor Karlowicz and his wife to that social renaissance which some anticipated with excitement and others dreaded. Tessa, almost twelve, is beginning to dream of balls and her debut in society, even if that seems as far away to her as a tale in the *Thousand and One Nights*. Tarass wonders whether, with his stiff leg and watery eye, they will still want him as the *dwor* coachman. Wioletta must have been worried: What would be her place in this home once Urszula will have taken the reins and she will have to, ten times a day, run into the former Celestial Spouse?

But perhaps she has understood that between the cup and the lips, between this moving project and the move itself, there was a formidable obstacle—Andrzej, who was not well enough to endure such a transplantation, but not ill enough, either, for his family in Vienna to be able to count on an imminent end to their burden.

Does Wioletta understand this? I think, above all, at that moment, in spite of the maternal attentions she bestows upon Tessa, and intermittently on her brother, her mind is elsewhere.

A few months ago she was doing research; now she is studying. A few months ago she was satisfied to have finally discovered the truth, or so she thought. Now, she is becoming aware that the truth is not something upon which one can put one's finger after having sought it, like a game of hunt-the-thimble. What one finds raises other questions, contradictions appear, one tells you white, the other black, which can you believe? What interest do they have in lying, how can they, on such a point, be wrong?

She copied by hand *The Sayings of the Master* in order to be able to return the manuscript to her friend the Prince, and was forced to admit that she didn't understand anything in it. Throughout it there are only terrible animals, furious admonitions, promises of cataclysms—all things that inspire Wioletta's imagination. But what are they talking about? For whom are they talking?

Taking into consideration the original text and the citations in Tadeusz's journal, she looked at the evidence— her paternal grandfather was not at all an initiate. He knew only the most insignificant of the *Sayings* and retained only a vague and concrete wisdom from them. When he reminded the reader *not to wake the sleeping dog*, for example, it led into the tale of his misadventure with the neighbour's dog which, that morning, had bit him on the arm. 'But,' he hastened to add, 'my good Elzbieta put some cream on it and the redness is disappearing.' We are relieved! As for *the water over which one should not lean once it has been crossed*, far from seeing the religious parable that was jumping out at Wioletta, poor Tadeusz thought very seriously that it was a rule to follow, in everyday life, if one didn't want to get wet.

He had no doubt only been the conveyor of a family tradition in which he saw no harm; and everything led her to believe that he didn't know he had descended from converts.

In time, Wioletta's principal source of information, Prince Dubinski and his cousin Prince R***, also proved to have limitations. Those collectors of curiosities were only interested in what tickled their taste for Baroque kitsch: the mysterious grotto in which Jakob Frank, during his captivity, was supposed to have hid his treasures and bury his closest initiates; the colossal sums he was able to extort, for thirty years, from his followers, his pomp of an Ottoman pasha, his personal guard of

Cossacks and haiduks; his repeated interviews with the great of this world. But when Wioletta asks Dubinski what in his opinion Joseph II and Maria Theresa of Austria, the prince of Offenbach, even the tsar Alexander I could have expected from an interview with this person or one of his descendants, he scratches his neck and can only respond, 'But, dear friend, think of the support that would have been for our faith, to convert those Israelites who inhabited so many towns and villages! To use Frank and his influence, wasn't that the duty of every Christian monarch?'

Yes, yes, no doubt, thinks Wioletta; but she isn't satisfied.

'I think,' the prince tells her one day, 'that you should meet a young scholar with whom my cousin is corresponding. He is something of an expert in this domain, collects all the information that can be found, has even gone to Offenbach where Frank and his followers finally found refuge after leaving Poland, in order to establish a potential oral tradition there. Believe me, dear friend, he is the man you are looking for. It even seems that you once knew his family, if I'm not mistaken.'

The Prince serves as an intermediary; and thus a short time later I see stopping in front of my gate a hackney carriage out of which climbs . . . my goodness! Salomon Weinberg!

Looking more closely, no, it's obviously not him. Moreover, I am aware that Salek passed away some twenty-five years ago, worn-out by his exhausting duties as a country doctor. This man is scarcely thirty, his hair is still quite black under his soft hat. All the same, what emotion fills me when I see him follow Nikolaïa into the large gallery and, in passing, examine our family portraits through his pince-nez! Even his slightly bent back reminds me of the man who, if I calculate well, should be his grandfather.

'Ludwik Wajnberg, Lecturer at the University of Lvov,' says the card that Nikolaïa, indifferent—and illiterate, moreover, unlike her peers in the coming generation—brings to Wioletta who was reading in her room. In passing I see that, as a sign of the times, this young university fellow has kept the Polish form of his name, whereas his grandfather, at the beginning of the century, had been so zealous in Germanizing his. When you will have children, Ludwik, I wager that you will speak Polish to them at home. Perhaps you will even read passages from the *Ancestors* to them at night? No, Poland is not lost, in spite of the apparent decline of its national movement. That day, seeing that card and the change of name, I have the idea against all likelihood that its resurrection, perhaps, may even be round the corner.

He is serious, young Ludwik Wajnberg. With his arms crossed behind his back, I guess that he is intimidated, in spite of the welcoming decor of the little green salon. Hesitant to take a seat before his hostess arrives, he walks around, inspects the 'Grynow series' on the wall and blinks his eyes with reserve before the *Street of the Jews Seen from the St George Church*; while the Bösendorfer, intrigued, wonders underneath its cover: Oh! Oh! Whom have we here? Has this nice stranger come to play on me with his beautiful fine hands?

Finally Wioletta makes her entrance, excusing herself for having taken so long. The two cough, exchange pleasantries, not knowing where to sit down. If I don't step in, this meeting between two shy people will be a fiasco. Fine! Since my curious presence seems to stifle them, I will leave them to tame each other and will return a bit later.

And so I pay a visit to the kitchen where Glowiecka is busy plucking a chicken, then go into the servants' quarters where only two or three mice are stirring at this hour. Hey, Nikolaïa is stealing bits of food from the kitchen—a cardboard box, under her bed, is hiding some macaroons and pieces of sugar. Nibble away, little mice, the cake is at the bottom!

I lean out over the edge of the little window and look from up there over the pond and its reeds. Another sign of the times (because such encroachment in Gavryl's time would have been unthinkable), Danylo is fishing for tadpoles there with an old pickle jar. The children are around him, he turns towards them and, with his finger raised, speaks to them. I wager he is forbidding them from wandering here without an adult and reminds them that others, before them, have drowned. Very good, very good! This young man with subversive reading materials has a head on his shoulders and the children with him are in good hands. I congratulate myself even more when I see that Tessa is with them and, like the others, is shouting with excitement. So Danylo has ignored his sister's instructions? I expected as much.

Finally I go back down, because it seems to me that I've been away long enough. I slip through the door to the little salon. And there, what is happening? *Pan* Wajnberg is red and talking loudly, I would say he is almost shouting; opposite him Wioletta is very pale, and trying to calm him.

'Yes, I understand, such excess was obviously not . . .'

'Excess!' exclaims Ludwik bitterly. 'But do you know, dear lady, what that Frank truly was? When he and his henchmen were placed under the protection of the archbishop of Lvov and other churchmen, do you know what they did? Do you? Not content to profess their new faith in Jesus, the New Testament, and the Holy Trinity, they had to attack the Talmud and publicly claim before an ecclesiastical tribunal that its hidden doctrine, for some rituals, required Christian blood. In a word, they resurrected the old accusation of ritual murder about whose dangers they could not have been unaware.

'But,' objects Wioletta, 'those poor people had to protect themselves from the persecution of their community, didn't they? It was a way to . . .'

'Persecution? Oh, you're speaking of excommunications and all that follows. Of course, but what were those persecutions next to the ones that, through that infamy, fell upon my people? Do you know that the year that followed the first large wave of conversions and accusations of that type, in the town near Wojslavice, gave rise to a trial and to particularly horrible sentences—I'll spare you the details, dear lady, out of respect for your sensibilities—against a few local Jews? Jakob Frank, with that little game, plunged Poland back into the darkness of the Middle Ages, that Poland which, for centuries, had been a haven of peace for many Jews . . .'

'Pardon me,' stammered Wioletta, 'I didn't mean . . .'

'It's quite simple,' pursued the visitor without stopping, 'in their distress (because in addition to those trials and physical attacks, in the Galician towns the Catholic clergy had all the available copies of the Talmud gathered up and burnt in a public square), my fellow-Jews went so far as to address, twice, a plea to the Roman curia to be formally washed of this accusation. And it did so, can you imagine? Two popes, in succession, sent a clear and precise denial to the Polish authorities, calling upon them to put an end to these atrocities. Without success, by the way. You must know of the magnitude of the violence that was unleashed upon my community a few years later, masked by the troubles of 1768 . . .'

1768? This time I understand! Bless you, Ludwik Wajnberg, for having just made me remember what I have been trying to think of for so many months. How could I have forgotten such a scene, or think that I knew of it only through local gossip? I know that I was then in what humans would call infancy, but that doesn't explain everything. It is even incredible—now that the memory has returned after one hundred and eighteen years, I see that it has indeed marked me in each of my fibres, that in short my entire being knew though I was unaware.

12

It's beautiful today; nice enough for Count Fryderyk to go out onto the grounds with a book he is reading, absorbed, slowly walking around.

He's reading—I get closer—Rousseau's *Emile*, in French, a language the Count has mastered almost better than his own. And the work makes him think, because from time to time I see his sharp nose lift under his powdered wig and a thoughtful line form on his forehead.

He doesn't seem to realize that his country is prey to a frightening political fomenting that will be the cause, in a few years, of its decline; that at a few hundred lieus from here, on the right bank of the Dniepr, the Ruthenian serfs have taken advantage of the turmoil to remove their yoke and kill their masters en masse as well as those who support them. He knows it, of course, but will not lower himself to be affected by it. Anyway, how peaceful it is here, even if the Potockis and others, over there, are seeing their terrestrial Eden turn into a Gehenna! How can you get upset when a crane is gliding peacefully above you, when no breath of wind disturbs the surface of the pool, and, above all, when you have a book in your hand, a good book, the book of a strong mind that elevates one's thoughts above common prejudices and the vicissitudes of history? Divine Jean-Jacques.

In his buckled shoes and white stockings, the Count heads towards the pool. I open my eyes wide—I had always thought that the pond, the tadpole pond, was only the last vestige of the swamp that had been drained before constructing me. That is no doubt true, but I was unaware that in the meantime it had been turned into a pleasure pool, flanked by a statue of Venus whose graceful forms were reflected in the water. Where did it disappear to since then? Broken, probably, and gradually buried in the ground around the water.

The Count arrives at the edge of the pool, breathes deeply and smiles.

But he doesn't smile for long. There is a noise on the grounds, a very unpleasant noise. Since when does one hear the shouting of peasants here, the metallic clanging of farm tools? He will have to summon the overseer to remedy the situation immediately. Could it be the felling of the great buffering beech tree, day before yesterday, that has made this sonorous pollution possible?

Displeased, the Count closes his book. Who could read in the midst of such a din!

Then he jumps—imperceptibly. It is not only noise that has invaded his refuge, there are now real people there—a dozen peasants carrying scythes and flails are coming towards him and, even more unbelievable, their wool caps still on their heads!

'Count!' shouts a voice behind him at the same moment. He turns and, seeing the young man running under the trees towards him, recognizes his faithful Piotr, his godson, protégé and figurehead in Grynow. What has he come here for, why the devil has everyone decided to invade his park, his sanctuary, without his permission?

'Run, Count, Run!' his friend Zemka seems to be shouting at him. The Count, nevertheless, does not run. He finally understands that he is in danger, but a Galician count does not run away like a hare chased by a pack of hounds. He faces the intruders and, his chin high, says, 'What is the meaning of this?'

In response, the blade of a scythe awkwardly strikes his hip and he staggers—out of surprise more than pain for now—while on the white silk of his trousers and his stockings drops of red begin to appear.

The one who has struck him is a large man in a tunic with a drooping moustache. I remember, I remember now! Last week, the Count was riding and passed by him on the road and, finding he was taking too long to get out of the way, struck him on the shoulders with his crop. But he didn't recognize him—all those Ruthenians have the same moustache, the same tunic, the same crucifix at their waist; unless they are overseers and one has daily contact with them, it is almost impossible to tell them apart or remember their names.

Piotr Zemka knows their names, though, at least two or three of them. He has just arrived at the group and grabs the flail of another Ruthenian who is raising it and is about to strike, 'Stop, Roman, stop, look at me!'

(I think I am dreaming. That huge fellow, still beardless, who was just called Roman, is unquestionably the one whom I have known at almost one hundred years old as the leader of the peasant community.

He probably became pious and submissive later on, like so many others; even the devil, one says, becomes meek. But for now . . . God keep the Ponarskis!)

A shove sends Piotr Zemka to the ground but he gets up and returns to battle. He has had time to count—only two men have scythes. If he manages to get the one from fat Kouzma, the battle, in spite of the strength of their numbers, would be less unequal.

In the meantime, all the same, Kouzma has again prepared to strike; but the Count has tried to cover himself, an arm in the air, to take the blow. Two fingers on his left hand are cleanly sliced off and now the blood is flowing with each movement he makes. Is it the loss of his physical integrity that has awakened the instinct for survival in him? Blast his dignity! As quickly as is possible for a man of his age, he runs away from the mob. Kouzma follows him, not without having time to see that, behind him, Piotr has grabbed the second scythe from the young fellow to whom they had imprudently given it and is wielding it to keep the others at bay.

The Count staggers, falls to the ground, tries to get back up. But is he still a count? He is nothing more than a hunted man, whose wigless head reveals thick blond-grey hair, whose silk suit and lace cuffs are soaked in blood and who, with his uninjured hand, clutches *Emile* to his chest like the final shield.

A useless defence—Kouzma falls upon him.

'He's too far away, your Piotr, he can't save you. And I know why he loves you so much, I know since yesterday,' he says in a low voice. 'Ah! Dirty dog, you treat your Jews better than you do us other poor Christians!'

Those were the last words that Fryderyk Ponarski would hear on this earth; because just then the scythe opens his throat, then rips open his chest and continues to strike him, again and again, until a bullet fired from the first floor of the house strikes Kouzma right in the heart.

Other bullets are fired, men fall, Piotr among them. The rest of the band disperses, leaving flails and scythes lying on the ground, and only their presence on the impeccable grass would signal to whoever didn't want to see the blood or the dead or the two cut-off fingers, that the order of things here has, for some time to come, been violently upset.

Eyewitnesses will explain the misunderstanding, and Piotr Zemka's honour will be belatedly restored. But what is the weight of that misunderstanding next to the tragedy, the scandal, the monstrous parricide that is the murder, by his serfs, of a Count Ponarski?

13

'. . . A few years later, masked by the troubles of 1768. All of that, dear lady, is the work of that Jakob Frank who fascinates you so.'

'But,' whispers Wioletta, 'why that lie, so heavy with consequences? What interest did Frank have . . .?'

His voice trembles, his features are taut, Ludwik Wajnberg takes off his pince-nez and rubs it with his handkerchief.

'Excuse me for getting carried away but these subjects lately have become relevant again . . . and notably in Russia . . .'

He puts his pince-nez on again, and after a silence resumes, 'What interest? In purely pragmatic terms, none. Even vengeance against a community that had execrated him is not enough to explain such infamy. Frank's goal went much further—to see our most holy collection of laws burnt in a public square did not just bring him a perverse joy but also the feeling of accomplishing a duty, an almost sacred task.'

'A sacred task!' cries Wioletta. 'But, dear sir, what do you mean?'

'I mean that in his horrible paradoxical mysticism (and he had theorized this point abundantly), the destruction of the Law and its abolition were, if you wish, the means to its supreme accomplishment.'

'Oh,' murmurs Wioletta, calmed down, smoothing a little fold in her skirt. 'I can understand your vehemence on this subject . . . But there is nothing in it that surprises or shocks me. Jakob Frank had become a Christian, and every good Christian admits that, with Christ's arrival on earth, the rule of the Law was abolished to open a new reign of love and grace. The former alliance was destroyed, the new alliance is the spirit that gives life. Didn't Saint Paul write: "The laws of the Jews are only the shadow of things to come, but the body is Christ?"'

Ludwik Wajnberg blinks his eyes. Apparently he didn't expect to have to undertake a theological debate with this old lady friend of Prince Dubinski. A light of interest shines in his eyes and he replies with a slight smile, 'Saint Paul? Ah! Indeed, all our Jewish heresies seem to have a common substratum.'

This is too much for Wioletta who gets up as if, suddenly, her seat had become too hot. "All our Jewish heresies . . ." Is it decent for her to hear such things? Should she laugh as if it were a joke, or get angry? Not knowing, she takes two steps towards the window, two back towards her guest, and, that movement not pulling her out of uncertainty, flatly says, 'I am very sorry, I didn't offer you anything to drink. Will you have some tea, a bit of port?'

Wioletta, I adore you! When you started talking with that little voice of an ill-at-ease hostess I really thought I was hearing your mother, Clara.

But her visitor declines. Like all shy people, nothing can stop him once he has started, he will not be distracted until he has told his interlocutrice, who is more astute than he expected, all that he has to say to her.

'I said that in jest, excuse me. But it's because, you see, your reading of the facts is . . . comical, there is no other word for it. A good Christian! In truth, mistress, I must disabuse you—the abolition of the Law as Frank intended had very little to do, I'm afraid, with Christian morality or even with any sort of morality. It did not consist only of having our law texts burnt, of carousing during our greatest fasts, of substituting for the commandments and rites of our fathers the ostentatious observance of Catholic rites and dogmas. There was also an entire undercurrent of depravity—the most unbridled polygamy, the consummation of unnatural unions . . . Do you imagine, for example, that it was to have them go over their catechism that the master, from time to time, gathered together in private those whom he called "sisters" and "brothers", took his clothes off in front of them and made them do the same?'

Wioletta watches him intently and he stops talking, his cheeks now so red that he looks much younger than he actually is.

'I beg your pardon,' he stammers, 'I should not have mentioned that sort of thing in front of an honest woman.'

A wave of emotion rises up in Wioletta. How long had it been since she had been called an honest woman? Her eyes linger on the face of her visitor, much more at ease since he, being troubled, isn't looking at her; in an instant she has the crazy notion of hugging that young scholar who has, in a word, rehabilitated her..

'I understand,' she finally says in a slow voice. *A sister without a brother is like a boat without oars.* Yes, I think I understand.'

Ludwik raises a sceptical eyebrow towards the old spinster and quickly continues, 'It is because crime, discord, the transgression of the commandments, for Frank came out of a messianic plan—by installing a reign of evil, he was attempting to hasten the end of the world. And do not believe that Christian symbols were beyond his profaning rage. It is said that, just before the first conversions, he obtained a huge cross in Kamieniec, not to adore it, as you might expect, as the symbol of Christian grace, but as that of moral confusion which leads, in his words, "here and there". . . A debauchery, dear lady, a true debauchery occurred during that night of 14 July 1759 . . .'

'On 14 July!'

'Yes. A debauchery with strong drinks, Turkish delights which Frank had enjoyed during his youth in the Ottoman empire and from which he derived many parables on salt and sugar, the bitterness that the inversion of ethical laws would transmute smoothly, the sin that would become redemption . . . But, above all, carnal debauchery, consummated all together with his closest disciples.'

There is silence. Then Wioletta whispers, horrified, 'My God, around a crucifix!'

She even starts to cross herself, then looks at her fingers warily and places them on her thigh before continuing in an almost pleading tone, 'But the cult of the Virgin? Can you deny that those thousands of Frankists believed in the divinity of Jesus and showed the devotion to His mother that she deserved?'

'Oh, oh! Frank's virgin,' says Ludwik with a laugh that ended in a cough. 'Dear lady, you are right on one point—most of these many followers who were converted, no doubt in good faith, did nothing more than transmit certain obscure hymns, certain secret rituals without understanding their true meaning. Those, indeed . . . But the Virgin Frank spoke of to his followers, believe me, had nothing in common with Jesus' mother. She was primarily a mystical figure vaguely inspired by the gnosis to which he later decided to give a tangible form. Thus he gave the role to his daughter whom the "brothers" and "sisters" had to serve and worship, as if she had been both a royal personage and a divinity. The girl was very beautiful, it was said, but a virgin, I think she no longer was when her father offered her to the emperor of Austria to obtain his protection and largesse . . .'

He falls silent, and this time for good. How could he, in front of this old lady whom he has known for less than an hour . . . The old lady, moreover, also seems to think they have gone too far. She stands up, rings to ask for tea, serves her visitor, then kindly asks him about his academic work. They are both very careful so that the conversation no longer diverges, and they end with banalities—'thank-you's for this very kind welcome, for such useful information, etc. I am almost certain they will do all they can never to see each other again; and the world being what it is, that will not be very difficult.

The awkward meeting is over.

Is it really? One might doubt as much, given the nightmare that Wioletta has a few nights later. A nightmare, no—a vision, rather a hallucination, so greatly does it borrow elements from her familiar surroundings.

She is comfortable in her bed, in the place she should be; she has just been awakened (she believes) by a little noise at her door. Yes, the door is ajar. And slowly someone or something is coming towards her. The cat? It does indeed seem to be coming low on the ground, because at the height of a person she sees nothing. But what can one see in this darkness? She tries to strike a match, her fingers are trembling and she is unable to do so. Then, giving in to terror—because the thing, she senses it, is now at the foot of her bed—she reaches her arm towards the curtain and pulls it so the light of the moon will shine through.

She cries out—the august head of Mickiewicz is staring at her with his eyes of stone. And, most frightening, it is held at the end of an interminable neck whose folds slither in through the opening of the door, losing itself in the hallway and (Wioletta guesses) in the stairway, then in the hall of the first floor and onto the mantle of the little salon on which the bust, probably, is still in place.

'So, you're awake?'

Mute with horror, Wioletta doesn't respond.

'Excuse me for frightening you but, you see, it was necessary that one day someone tell you . . .'

'What?'

'That the storming of the Bastille was just a Frankist festival. Ha! ha! ha! ha! ha!'

'No, no, that's impossible! Mr Mickiewicz, I beg you—go back where you came from.'

'Oh no, my lovely. Not before defiling you, the better to honour you . . .'

'Go away! Go away!' she shrieks, at least in her thoughts; because the statue, with a tongue as extensible as its neck, now appears to be slithering into her mouth as far as her throat. Luckily, Wioletta's temple bangs against the headboard of her bed and instantly the head disappears, followed by its neck that retracts amazingly quickly.

Wioletta, shuddering, sits up in her bed, rubs her wounded temple, and slowly the beating of her heart calms down. Then she lies back down in the milky light of the moon. What a horrible dream! She thinks, pulling her blanket up to her chin. And she remains a long time like that, her eyes open, before falling back asleep.

14

Behind me there are still the grounds, the fields; and on winter days, when a thick layer of snow undulates as far as the horizon, softening the hills, exalting its whiteness only to make the sky greyer and lower, one might believe that nothing has changed or will ever change here.

That is only an impression. How many things, on the contrary, are simmering under this grey sky in the winter of 1886–87! The sugar factory was the theatre of something astonishing, which must have—I haven't verified this—caused the remains of Jozef to turn in their grave in the Ponarski crypt. The workers, who obviously don't understand anything about the laws of competition (that of Russian sugar from Podolia is beginning to worry even the placid Agenor), and seem more emboldened than satisfied by the first legislations on salaried work, have got it into their heads to strike to obtain a slight raise in their pay.

It's a delicate situation for Agenor Karlowicz who knows his law (calling on the army, since strikes are not legal in those times) but who will restrain himself from resorting to a too-brutal management of the crisis, fearing the ruin of what remains of his political credit. And he is cautious enough not to set foot here as long as the strike lasts, to negotiate only through an intermediary. He quibbles, procrastinates, drags out the affair in torturous procedures in which the most enlightened get tangled; and, during that time, a few henchmen carry out discreet sabotage on the ground. It is quickly learnt, for example, that one of the strikers most opposed to a resumption of work, three years earlier, had had an illegitimate child that she placed with a nurse somewhere between here and Rzeszow.

'And that one dares to give orders with all of that!' groan the gossips on Sunday, after Mass, as they are tired of feeding their children clear broth, not having the two or three salaries they usually could depend upon.

Even in the strikers' camp discord has been spreading ever since one of the leaders, very resolute up to then, begins to utter lenient and pacifying words. And what a scandal when it is discovered that he received money to change his tune! Most of the troops, demoralized, talk of abandoning ship, and consider themselves lucky to get out with the bit of consolation that *Pan* Agenor offers them—a Christmas bonus, paid just this once. But some don't see things the same way; and Danylo Pavlyk, especially, has a hard time convincing them that they would lose a lot more than they would gain, the Christmas bonus representing only a week's salary whereas they've been striking for four weeks.

'What do you want? We always lose. You're not going to change the world!' respond, resigned, those who have a family. And one of them, annoyed, finally says to him dryly, 'You read too much.'

There are only about twenty strikers left, in the end, to keep the doors to the sugar factory closed; but twenty with hot heads and combative spirits. They won't win, they now know, just as they know that the silence of their peers around them is increasingly a silence of animosity. But to give in, to put their yoke back on now, after four weeks of hope, of lean years and sacrifices? No, a hundred times no! Before that they'll have to walk over their bodies

And that is what happens—when the overseer has been persuaded that the time is ripe and that an appeal to the forces of order will provoke less indignation than relief in the canton.

The unequal battle doesn't last long. There are, on the one hand, only good functionaries who see it simply as their duty and their daily task and, on the other, twenty enraged people who are fighting for what is most dear to them and doing so all the more ardently because their cause seems desperate. But what can a few clubs do against thirty bayonets? Only one gendarme is wounded, and just slightly; opposite, there are no fewer than two dead.

From the window in the classroom Tessa, very pale, has followed the confrontation. What are those shouts, those blows, what is happening behind the screen of poplars, what is the district commissioner shouting over the embankment? She only knows confusedly but guesses that all of that, in a certain way, is being done in her name. This is what paralyses her, her hands damp, behind the window. And she doesn't dare go downstairs until the tumult gives way to a forced silence.

She goes as far as the gate but she's afraid of what she will see. She is also afraid she'll be seen, afraid that the eyes of others will rest on her to ask her to account for what has just occurred in her name. She is thirteen—she is too old to be able to take refuge in childish ignorance, too young for her mind to develop the reasoning that would enable her to be indignant or, on the contrary, to agree with it. And so she is afraid, but doesn't retreat, she even pushes her forehead between two bars in the fence—an impulse, or perhaps authentic courage. Why wouldn't there be any in little things?

She needs even more courage when, in the middle of the gendarmes, the strikers that have just been arrested, including her friend Danylo, pass by. He is wounded, blood is flowing from a gash in his cheek. Nothing serious, however, she can tell by the way he is moving—he is walking calmly, his head raised, looking straight in front of him. And yet Tessa chooses, when he goes by, to raise her forearm and wave her hand a little. And that little movement attracts Danylo's eye, his head turns towards the gate, an indecipherable smile, vaguely ironic but not really mean, in the end, appears on his lips while with his bound hands he tips the visor of his cap.

And so in twenty-four hours calm returns and work, without transition, resumes. They are grateful to the overseer for refraining from any commentary when he receives the employees one by one in his office to pay them the little he owes them as well as their Christmas bonus. The dead? Of course they are missed. They even notice, now, that they were the best of their generation, the old-age crutch of their parents, the pearl that their ex-fiancées will never find again. They forget that, three days earlier, they were cursed for their intransigence; and people wipe their eyes and cry loudly at the cemetery when the pope, using a rhetorical slight-of-hand that first causes shock, but then fervent support, celebrates them as two martyrs of the Ukrainian nation.

Almost at the same time, with the ability that the everyday has to mix tragedy and jubilation, motifs of pride and desolation, a festive spirit arises, discreetly, and blows over Grynow. This is because the train line is finally in service and, soon, the station will be, as well.

Until then, the Grynowians were proud only of their market square with Renaissance facades, of the brick *Ratusz*, of my aristocratic splendour, things that in the end one finds pretty much everywhere.

Whereas a train station, and four trains every day! Henceforth, they looked down on their neighbours from nearby towns who were not as well off as they. Grynow, already, is more attractive; on market days, there is a true parade of carts and carriages that flow onto the roads before me. Agenor Karlowicz attempts to restore his image by reminding us that all of this is owed to him, to his pressure, to his consummate art of knocking on the right doors. Representing the fruit of this campaign, he is moreover invited to honour the inaugural ceremony with his presence.

And so the previous day he arrives here with his wife who hurries to put the household on battle footing, to constructively criticize the preparations of her sister for the private reception that is to follow, to put the finishing touches on her puce dress with black stitching, and, above all, to apply, on her eyelids and cheeks, the compresses without which her face would not have the desirable glow during this public appearance.

'We are no longer exactly what we once were, right, dear Wioletta?' she sighs, while smiling at her sister who surprises her as her hair is being dressed. And it is said with such conviction that, even in her innermost self, Wioletta does not formulate the sarcastic response that such a remark called for. Urszula, deep down, has always been able to disarm her ill will.

Finally comes the morning of the big day. Agenor, stuffed into a morning coat on which several decorations stand out on his chest, is the first to leave in the carriage that is to take him to the preceding station. Everyone knows he is staying here but, for the solemnity of the spectacle, it is better that he arrive in the train with his retinue and get out, *deus ex machina*, onto the platform of the station of which he is the demiurge. Then the ladies and the little miss are dressed; and Kazimierz, present for the occasion, is inspected head to toe by his grandmother who prescribes a bit more pomade for his hair and a little shaving of the hair that is growing on his upper lip.

'Perfect. Perfect!' she then approves in front of this group portrait. 'What a pity that Andrzej can't be with us . . .' On that sad thought she gives the signal to leave, and the whole group sets off.

The inhabitants of the hamlet fall in behind, as do our domestic staff. And so I stay here, rather angry at not being able to go with them, with only old Oleksandra—who clearly was suffering too much with her legs and was busy in the kitchen darning rags—as my only company. What time is it? Ten to eleven. I have never been so empty in my entire existence; and how this emptiness makes the time seem long!

But now I hear a noise, some shouting, the hissing of an approaching train . . . They're arriving, they're here! A brief silence and suddenly a burst of music—the Grynow band has just valiantly struck up a military march. And boom, and boom, and bam, and bam! If only I could share these somewhat vulgar pleasures that enchant everyone so! I even believe I perceive a smell of cake in the air . . . Come now, let's not think of it any more. Anyway, the band is quiet and, for me, silence returns.

I obviously couldn't count on Agenor's nasal voice to carry as far as here. (When I think of it, it is perhaps due to the lack of a nice baritone voice that his career did not take off the way it promised?) But it doesn't matter, because his speech, I know it—he repeated it twice yesterday in front of the mirror in his room. 'On this day, my dear fellow-citizens, when I have the distinct honour . . . To greet the efforts of our general leadership to develop our province and, I dare to predict, finally make it the pole that it has always deserved to be . . . Yes, people of Grynow, you knew before others . . .'

But what is this? One, two detonations, four or five more others, shouting . . . The final salvo, already, fired by our garrison? I don't think so. I observe Oleksandra, but, deaf as a stone, she is still dozing as peacefully as ever over her darning. Is someone finally going to tell me what is going on over there?

At the end of twenty long minutes a huge crowd makes its way towards me. Then I notice in the middle the carriage that Tarass, pale with emotion, is driving with difficulty and inside it are several forms that I can't make out. Yes, however—the seated silhouette is that of the doctor of Grynow. And those two bodies over which he is leaning? Something bad has happened, that's obvious—but to whom, to whom?

It's useless for me to delay any longer, because the rest is history. The next day, each child of Pest, each old person from Transylvania, each cowherd from Tyro,l will have learnt of the assassination that took the life, that April morning in 1887, of the Councillor Karlowicz and his wife, inopportunely present at his side on the podium of honour. For a week, all the Austro-Hungarian dailies would make it their headline; it was discussed within my walls by the groups of politicians, police and journalists who established their quarters here.

'A serious attempt to destabilize the state,' according to the *Neue Freie Presse* which, in passing, criticizes the role of the Uniate clergy in fomenting the Ruthenians while also insinuating that a foreign power, nearby, could only profit from this agitation. A more liberal daily publishes a few in-depth articles on the deplorable situation of the Ruthenian population and calls upon its representatives to create organisms and parties that will serve it better than this blind violence, prejudicial to the development of a true democracy. The *Arbeiter-Zeitung* salutes the disappearance of a class enemy and recalls the crushing of the factory strike but hesitates to congratulate this breakthrough, in Galicia, of the most retrograde elements of the oppressed classes. Because what can be made of this terrorist who, before being struck down, could only cry out: 'Death to the Poles, glory to the Ukranian people'? And to recall the counter-revolutionary role held by the Ruthenians in 1848.

'Boom, boom! The Slavs are killing one another off,' shouts another headline in a satirical Viennese publication; but my staff looks at it and only becomes indignant.

This sudden celebrity frightens me, I admit—it seems to me that my peaceful anonymity has been suddenly shattered. It is true that in the surrounding area the course of things has not always been idyllic. But this commotion, this upsurge of explanations, analyses, the taking of sides throughout all Austro-Hungary, does not bode well. And it is with relief, almost with gratitude, that I read the editorial of our local gazette, where the event, as bloody as it was, is reduced to the proportions of a family tragedy:

> Yesterday, during the inauguration of our new train station, a cowardly attack took the life of the Councillor Karlowicz, an honourable citizen of our town, as well as his wife, nee Zemka, the niece of the hero of Temesvar.
>
> Overcoming the vigilance of our guards and under the cover of the crowd, a gunman fired upon the couple before

being struck down by the forces of order. According to our preliminary information, the young man, named Oleh Doroshenko, was a cabinet-maker in a neighbouring village, single, without known acquaintances in subversive circles. We can only deplore this excessive murdering insanity and address to the family of the victims, in the name of the editorial staff and all citizens of Grynow, our most sincere condolences.

15

These condolences were well received—but I don't know of any condolences that have not been. I must mention, however, that the attitude of Mistress Zemka on this occasion was not at all what anyone expected. Of course, she attended the various memorials and cried abundantly during the speeches that accompanied them. Her great mourning, the vestiges of her beauty, the pathetic group that she now formed with, on one side, her great-niece and, on the other, *Pan* Kazimierz, gave spectators the uncharitable but quite human feeling that they were getting their money's worth. But . . . but what? Something was missing. One assumed, for example, that this frail person would finally be broken by so many losses in two years. It was assumed to such a degree that people were already making plans about the probable outcomes, pitying the two minors who were now essentially without support.

But, no. Wioletta returned to life, even seemed to become much more alive. She was seen standing up to the servants, taking initiatives in matters of oversight and planning, changing the curtains in the little green salon, coldly giving the municipality of Grynow the gift of a bust of Mickiewicz which, as everyone knew, had been the apple of her father's eye. She was seen showing interest in the accounts of the factory and sacking the overseer who, as the only one in charge, had profited from that to steal large sums of money. A supreme sign of vitality, pale Wioletta was in the process of making a few enemies. The former overseer, of course; but also the workers in the sugar factory, who suffered under her directives; Nikolaïa, who didn't like being spoken to in such a tone; suppliers, about whom Wioletta dared sometimes to say she wasn't satisfied; and even her needy neighbours to whom she had however started to pay charitable visits.

'God bless her,' grumbled Pavlykowa when the lady of good works left her house. 'God bless her, but I don't know why, she sends shivers up my back.'

And that statement pretty much summed up everyone's opinion.

For Tessa, on the other hand, the death of her two grandparents was a blow that wounded her for ever. She wandered in my rooms, her heart heavy with pain, walking up to the windows, contemplating the horizon that had become so familiar. Once, she remembered, there had been something else. A large apartment, lively streets, lights, a brouhaha of receptions and the voices of adults . . . And that almost mythical past, that Viennese existence from which she had been taken at the age of four, she knew, ever since the murder, that she would never see again.

She became even closer to her great-aunt. Wioletta seemed to have embraced solitude and resignation for a long time, and the girl, for whom that condition was new, mutely sought guidance alongside her.

As she grew older, she also started wondering about the destiny of this woman who was her surrogate mother. Why hadn't Wioletta ever married, she who, if one were to believe the old portraits and the public opinion, had been so beautiful? One day, in the little green salon, she asked her.

'An unfortunate love, my dear,' her great-aunt had responded, smiling.

Tessa added a few stitches to the handkerchief she was hemming before observing, 'That's sad!'

'Perhaps . . . and perhaps not,' murmured Wioletta who was embroidering. And, raising her eyes to look at her niece, she scrutinized the virginal part in the middle of her hair, the eyes of a moist brown, the lips that, in spite of all the balms, remained chapped summer and winter, and added, still smiling, 'And I have you.'

This was one of those statements that adults said to you without having taught you how to respond. Should she throw her arms around her great-aunt's neck, kiss her on her cheek? Or pretend not to have heard her and, under that affectionate gaze continue to sew while keeping, so to speak, her pose? It seemed to Tessa that the second idea was the right one, but after a few moments she couldn't keep it up and went over to play the piano. She played for five minutes; then, still feeling the weight of her great-aunt's gaze on her, spun around on the stool and said timidly, 'What is it?'

'Come here,' Wioletta said to her, beckoning her to come over. And when the young girl was in front of her chair she took her by the wrist, enveloped her with an intense look and breathed, in a voice that seemed to come from very far away, 'Whatever happens, listen to me: Never, ever allow yourself to be separated from your child!'

An awkward silence greeted those words. Tessa licked her lips, carefully released her wrist and, sensing it was better not to ask any questions, not to go any deeper, simply responded, 'Yes, Aunt Wioletta.'

And she never brought the subject up again.

That young girl and that old spinster, alone in this big house, made many tongues wag. It was felt that Wioletta was wrong in taking her great-niece's education upon herself, keeping her three or four hours a day in the classroom.

'She's stuffing her head, there's no other way to put it!' Nikolaïa assured the neighbours, who shook their heads.

From the point of view of clothing, as well, there was much to criticize about Wioletta's influence. The mistress of the *dwor* had never stood out in the way she dressed, far from it. But one would have thought that she now wanted to make up for it through her pupil, for whom she ordered brilliant silks, plunging necklines ('You still have so little chest that it isn't indecent!'), dresses that indicated she was available. The men who had known Tessa for ever, who had seen, without reacting, her uncovered calves running through the fields, now blushed before the little bit of ankle that was revealed underneath her long skirts.

The girl went along with everything, and in time even saw the attentions as a consolation. This wasn't how she had envisioned her adolescence—she had expected a few balls, a fiancé, then a new home where she would have soon become a mother. For the time being, that future was fading into the mist. But how rich with excitement was the indefinite present in which fate was holding her! What an adventure, each day, to be dressed by her great-aunt, to discover herself in the mirror dressed up as a woman, and then to go out, to Grynow with books or to the farms with alms—and everywhere, in every male eye, to confirm that there did indeed shine a spark of insistent surprise that gave her, for a moment, the feeling she existed!

She wasn't really beautiful. But cute, yes, cute and lively, as Zosia had been.

'Ah! My dear, I believe you did indeed turn his head, this time,' applauded Wioletta after a visit during which Prince Dubinski, moved by a certain resemblance, had lingered while kissing the young girl's hand. And she was delighted with the compliment, as if the entire goal of her life had been to turn the head of this doddering old man who, three years earlier, still bounced her on his knee.

When Kazimierz was there, however, and drove the carriage with his sister by his side, she felt much prouder than when she succeeded in attracting the eye of the coal vendor in Grynow, or that of the local pope. They must have been handsome, the two of them, so similar, she thought. People must have watched them, but Tessa noted that she was no longer looking for looks, that her happiness, for a time, was enough. And it seemed to her that she was anticipating something on an even more superior degree of maturity—to be a woman, she sensed, was to give up all the looks in order to shine under only one, to lose interest in all other men to love only one. Even if that one pushed you away, saw nothing in you, examined your long skirts only to say, 'You are grotesque, my poor girl. What is this get-up?'

'Aunt Wioletta chooses my dresses,' she responded with a rather crafty cowardice, still smiling, because to be a woman was that, as well.

And when they played music together . . . No, in those moments, in spite of Kazimierz's teasing and meanness, there was something else expressed—the complacency of a big brother for the child she still was. Because without that complacency he would never have agreed to play those sonatas full of lyrical excess, those moving pieces of bravura in which he excelled on the violin and which Tessa adored, although they were difficult to accompany.

His tastes were the opposite of hers. He hoped for . . . things that perhaps didn't yet exist, for unheard of dismemberments, for melodies broken into little pieces. He sometimes sat down at the piano to wildly explore these new atonal lands. 'Ah! It's terrible, but oh, it's exquisite,' exclaimed that polymorphous perversion of the Bösendorfer; and Tessa, frightened, shrunk back along the wall. Is this what Kazimierz loved, that destruction of all sweetness, of all sentimentality? She really wanted to leave the room, not to hear that. Because she felt that it was also her little girl's soul, her little romantic heart that he was trying to dismember and destroy. And her only victory was to stay to the end, without even protesting when Kazimierz, as a conclusion, said over his shoulder, 'You obviously don't understand any of it.'

Then the holidays were over, Kazimierz took the train at the Grynow station, and, on the return, Tessa felt calm and sad like a lover who has just been left behind. She lived for a few days with the memory of that chaste fraternal involvement; then it faded and she threw herself wildly back into her flirtatious games, her exercises of seducing all and sundry.

That young girl and that old spinster, alone in this big house . . . alone, they were however, far from it. In addition to Nikolaïa, the cook, Semien's parents and a few other assistants who didn't live here, there were others, more and more numerous and obvious in this autumn of the century, but whom none of my inhabitants could see—and I will always be surprised at that. When Tessa scratched the ball-and-cup with her nail or brushed her sleeve against an old fan, she didn't see the figure that, like a djinn, emerged from them: a pouting Urszula between her two ringlets or Maria smiling gaily at her cousin and fiancé. Wioletta almost, at times, sensed a funny odour in the air, she couldn't identify the liquored breath of her Great-Uncle Krzysztof whom she never knew.

And at night, what a gathering! Jozef's shadow wandered endlessly from the cellar to the attic, from the attic to the cellar, as if that relentless worker needed to win over the inactivity of death. Clara, too, wandered the hallways in her batiste nightgown, her greying brown hair loose down her back; but their routes, strangely, never crossed.

The most lively was Count Fryderyk whom my failing memory had so long relegated into limbo. Was it the joy of having returned from that forced exile, or the blooming of an exuberance that, while he was alive, he could not unleash? The fact is that this humourless cold fish had become, in the beyond, an expert in the most dubious practical jokes. I am persuaded that Wioletta's nightmare had been the first sampling of this. And since then, I stopped keeping a list. Sometimes the Count assumed his first appearance to beg Clara von Kotz (who else! he certainly wasn't going to offer his arm to a plebeian) to dance a minuet with him; but while dancing he couldn't prevent himself from acting the clown and regaling his audience with unbelievable grimaces. Sometimes he took a sly pleasure in wandering around with his open wounds, like a true ghost of a Scottish manor, and sprinkling all his dead relatives, while they were peacefully in their beds, with his blue blood. But the worst was when, arriving from behind, he put his chopped fingers over their eyes and shrieked wildly, 'Guess who!'

I have never believed that the presence of the dead was a danger in itself. It is quite natural, on the contrary, for me who knows that nothing or no one ever really passes, and that everything that ever lived in a place remains there for ever, in one form or another.

It is rather the ratio that became critical. How many shadows, henceforth, for four or five living souls! What weights on their shoulders, how many invisible gazes concentrating on them! I wasn't surprised when Tessa, around that time, started suffering from little ills, fainting spells, mood swings, in which the doctor from Grynow, not very clairvoyant, diagnosed only minor problems associated with puberty. And I was less surprised when she began locking the door to her room at night.

16

It wasn't Wioletta's management that sank the sugar factory, although in the region it was predicted that nothing better could have happened to a business led by a woman. Nor was it the modest demands of her employees, nor the boom in Russian sugar which remained expensive to import. What caused Jozef's wildly successful enterprise to fail was the decision of Archduke Rudolph, in January 1889, to end his days in his hunting lodge in Mayerling, with his very young mistress, the baroness Vetsera.

I learnt of this tragedy, as usual, in the kitchen. I arrived there one morning, eager for the daily gossip that smelt of the world of the living; and imagine my surprise in discovering our female staff sitting around the large table transformed into a group of wailers!

It was polishing day. The cook, her large shoulders shaking with sobs, was scrubbing one pot, then another, while Oleksandra and another girl were polishing the countless pieces of silver while dabbing at their eyes. Nikolaïa was putting away this, carrying that, hanging the shining pots back on the wall; and if her eyes were still fairly dry, her nose was red from having been wiped many times.

'What a pity,' sighed the cook. 'Oh, God preserve the emperor and our poor Elisabeth! To have lost their only son, their heir, that way in the flower of his youth . . .'

'I've always said,' declared Nikolaïa, 'that his marriage with Princess Stephanie would not be happy.'

'And it wasn't. And she, the young baroness—imagine, she wasn't yet eighteen!—it seems she loved him, her Rudolph, to distraction. For months she eyed him at the opera, at the Prater, during all his outings, until he noticed her . . . The sweetest, the most likeable of creatures, they say . . . What a pity, my God!'

'They are joined together in death,' said little Ulianna, in a small voice. 'What else could they do? Lord, grant them Your mercy, for they have suffered greatly . . .'

The three women sitting at the table began to pray.

But Nikolaïa had detected a dark spot on one of the pots. She put it in front of the cook, and with a fist on her hip, said, 'All the same, not all is clear in this story, and I wouldn't be surprised if . . .'

'If what?'

'Oh, I know. My aunt in Grynow, who has the newspapers read to her, says there are many mysteries, many facts that have been lied about. The pistol, for example . . .'

'Of course they lied,' sniffled the cook. 'Our poor sovereigns have done what they could. A double suicide! Perhaps you'd like our crown prince to be buried outside the walls like a dead dog?'

'The emperor didn't get along at all with his son, and for a long time,' whispered Nikolaïa. 'They say that one day they almost came to blows! Rudolph had ideas . . . ideas which were not to the taste of the old man, nor to those of many others. And I tell you that this affair isn't over, you're going to hear more about it.'

'You always see the bad in everything. If they first hid the body of the girl, what's surprising in that? He was an adulterer, you mustn't forget. Could they . . .'

'Have you read,' Ulianna interrupted, 'that they transported her body sitting up in a carriage so people wouldn't see that it was a corpse? And then they buried it in secret, in an unmarked grave. Unmarked!'

She shuddered and stood there, a fork in her hand, a rag in the other; and her eye was so fixed that the cook, worried, gave her a slap to shake her out of it. These young people were a bundle of nerves, they had all sorts of twisted ideas about love and the beyond. If one weren't careful, there would soon be an epidemic of suicides in the double monarchy.

The girl rubbed her cheek then, without transition, started crying.

'I'll light a candle for her, with my earnings . . .'

'That's right, you'll light a candle,' said Glowiecka softly, reassured. 'But for now, hurry up and finish the fish forks, you still have all the spoons and the sauce dish and the knife holders. To think that we have to keep all this silver clean, three-quarters of which is never used!'

'God save the emperor,' muttered old Oleksandra, sensing that she should put her two cents into this funereal gathering. Then, not knowing what else to say, she crossed herself on her forehead, her mouth and her heart, following the ritual of the Greek Catholic Church.

On the main floor no one was crying; and yet it was there that there was something to cry about. The two ladies didn't know it yet but it was, ultimately, the end of their fortune.

The Délices de Sissi? That name now sounded like a bad joke. As for the delights that the mother of the suicide had had, in twenty years: a brother-in-law, Maximilian, gunned down in Mexico; a sister-in-law, the widow of the former, who became mad with sorrow; a cousin, the extravagant Louis II of Bavaria, found drowned in unclear circumstances; not to mention other relatives and friends who, around her, were sunk in dementia or died horrible deaths. Mayerling was the ultimate tragedy. In the following week, couriers from shopkeepers were running here to cancel their orders, production had to be suspended, new boxes bearing the sober name of Incarnate Pastilles had to be made and placed hastily on shelves to make up for the loss in sales.

But the Incarnate Pastilles, although identical to the ones before, did not sell well. Was it the magic of the name that had been broken? Or was it on the contrary the old name that endured in peoples' minds and, like the first layer of a palimpsest, came back to the surface with the unease associated with a lugubrious memory? Even the sugar from the factory, as if through contagion, stopped selling. 'Zemka's sugar? Humph!' murmured the retailers—at least I imagine as much—before they settled on the Podolian competition. It was, however, an old brand, honourably known for sixty years for the quality of its product as well as for its very reasonable prices, a jewel, almost a monument of the province. And so?

Of course I had recently heard mention of a new deity called Economic Rationality. But what rationality can be expected in a domain where decisions are the realm of investors believing in Providence, of superstitious stockholders, of brokers capable of fighting a duel because one had said that the other was unlucky in business? If money, as I believe, is only the most complete expression of human credulity, why would its laws and its causalities be more tangible? The reasons, good and bad, don't really matter—the Galician merchants no longer bought their sugar from the house of Zemka, and that was that.

And our lifestyle very quickly began to decline.

Mistress Zemka continued to help the poor, Mistress Karlowiczowa to wear her dresses, her chignons, her jewellery which were too old for her. But my fence was covered with climbing vines, my walls needed a good coat of paint, and my roof, redone forty years earlier, was now disappearing under a layer of lichens and moss. Over there, behind the poplars, my sister the sugar factory looked pretty bad too, with her cracked exterior and her obstructed windows. An entire wing was abandoned; and what was the use of repairing windows in a workshop that was no longer used?

In Jozef's time, it was a point of honour to receive guests with a very aristocratic soberness, far from the avalanches of cream-filled cakes, tea sandwiches and pretentious little tarts that marked the teas of the nouveau riche. But increasingly, through the facade of aristocratic sobriety there pierced need, pure and simple. Kazimierz, when he was there, had to send distress signals when Count Wytocki's glass, sitting on the footstool, was getting low and the bottle next to him was already almost empty. Wioletta then went flying down to discover, 'What, Nikolaïa, there isn't any more cognac?'

'Of course there isn't. I told mistress that we needed to buy more.' Then she added, slyly, 'But I can go get some from Grynow right away, if mistress wishes.'

'Cognac from Grynow? Oh, no, good heavens! We'll do without,' Wioletta concluded with a burst of dignity. What man in the world would have agreed to put his lips into the concoction that was sold in Grynow under the name of cognac?

As for Tessa's dresses, in which a kindly eye might have seen the vestiges of a noble extravagance, people in the environs began to consider them as the impudent strategies of a procuress 'Well she *is* trying to marry her off! She's definitely trying . . .' whispered the cook to her helpers, when the young girl came down in the mornings. 'But to whom, that's what I want to know. After all, the girl won't have much of a dowry . . .'

And the day when Tessa left for Prince Dubinski's funeral in a black outfit clinging to her thin legs, a red rose on her shoulder, it was in a loud voice that the Pavlyk woman said, from the threshold of her cottage, 'Now I've seen everything!'

Yes, this family that was once free to beat its male serfs, rape its female serfs, pay its workers almost nothing, and in exchange received only a fearful admiration—this same family, or what remained of it, now that its fortune was drying up, inspired only a wary aversion in its neighbours.

'What is going on in there . . .' muttered onlookers on the road, pointing to me. And yet not much extraordinary was going on for now, apart from a few ballets of ghosts and the slow exhalation of old words with which for more than a century the furniture, the walls and objects had been stuffed. Now my only inhabitants were an old unmarried woman, a young coquette without a dowry, sometimes a student whose tuition was no longer paid regularly, and who soon, dreaming of studying composition, would nonetheless be forced to study law, that law which, they say, leads to everything . . . But there was the past, that is, me. And they couldn't be pardoned for trying to keep the cachet and the manners of that past which were now well beyond their means.

Kazimierz, for example, continued to treat our neighbours and servants with the arrogance of an owner, and it was because of him that Glowiecka decided to leave—he had managed to offend her while observing during a meal that she certainly had a heavy hand with the pastry. This had been reported in the kitchen by Nikolaïa, and, immediately afterwards, something I've never seen, Glowiecka came into the little salon where they now took their meals.

'I'm told the master isn't happy with my little pastries?'

Her eyes were shooting sparks, her cheeks were scarlet and her chest, in her indignation, was rising like a stormy sea. But Kazimierz, coldly, responded, 'That's right, I am not satisfied. To tell you the truth, I find them a bit—greasy.'

'Greasy? That's unbelievable! Me, who . . .'

She was no doubt going to remind the young master that her wages had not been paid in two months. But the young master, smoothing his growing moustache, interrupted her, 'Dear Glowiecka, I appreciate the trouble that you've gone to but your devotion should not make you inaccessible to any criticism, and . . .'

'Just a minute, you little runt!' she exploded. 'I was cooking here when you were still being whipped, and that is just what you deserve now, however much a *gentleman* you have become in the meantime!'

Kazimierz wasn't smiling any more.

'Glowiecka, you are speaking to me in a tone that is no longer appropriate. You will apologize to me immediately or I fear you will have to leave.'

And so Glowiecka left on her own volition, still shaking with fury, before evening fell. Since then, they made do with meals prepared by Oleksandra, which had the advantage of economizing considerably on the costs of their food because they could count on her to reduce the cream and not to prepare any more meat than was necessary. And Kazimierz could complain about the results as harshly as he wanted; the poor old lady wasn't of an age or a temperament to rebel.

In the end, with a bit of optimism, one could consider this change as progress. And optimism, these days, only increased among my guests. 'It will be better this way.' 'Good riddance!' 'In the end it was a waste of time, and I don't regret anything:' such statements flowed frequently from their mouths. When they had to sell off a parcel of land, then another, and when my fence was surrounded by bits of land that were no longer ours, Wioletta, a champion of optimism, congratulated herself out loud that from then on, we would no longer have to employ farm labourers. It was such a bother to pay them, especially to keep them, now that, at the slightest lack of surveillance they threw themselves into the arms of emigration agents! The Wytockis had to have some twenty of them caught by the gendarmes and give severe orders to the judge of their village so that he didn't deliver any certificate of morality without first asking their permission, because they knew what that meant. Good riddance to those concerns! We are better off without them.

And when the same Wytockis, knowing that their neighbours were incapable of reciprocating their invitations for lack of funds and personnel, had the delicacy not to invite them any more, it was, according to Wioletta, even greater progress. 'That poor countess was so silly, my goodness!' And Tessa, who quickly understood what was expected of her, made her great-aunt and brother laugh to tears in reporting that twice she had seen the Count, during a visit here, slip his little teaspoon into the pocket of his coat.

'A count, steal the silver! How shameful,' Wioletta concluded, wiping her eyes. 'You were right to tell me, my dear, and I'm not upset that the bridges have been burnt.'

Yes, we were definitely going from progress to progress.

17

Optimism wasn't pushed to the point of seeing progress in Andrzej's death. Wioletta, on the contrary, cried bitterly. Forgetting the last ten years in which her nephew, in her thoughts, had been only a distant little dark point, she remembered what Andrzej had once represented for her: the adored child of her Celestial Spouse, the innocent Dauphin for whose good she had sacrificed her happiness and the interests of her son.

The two orphans did not cry. Kazimierz, because he never cried; Tessa, because she had already mourned that perpetually absent figure, and because the tears to be shed had already been so in abundance, a long time ago. What had her father died of, anyway, what was that mysterious illness that, except for a short outing here after the attack at the train station, meant that they hadn't let him out for close to six years? 'You'll find out some day;' and her brother's explanations were left at that.

A great emptiness, a great coldness, that was all they felt. Not at the time—when they had to urgently pack their trunks, look into the train schedules and follow the telegraphed instruction of the executor, their guardian, to join him in Vienna—but on the return, when all of that was over.

'Come, my children,' Wioletta said to them seeing them seated among their baggage. 'It is a terrible trial, but be consoled in thinking that life goes on. Life, in the end, always goes on.'

Oh really? Not for old Tarass, at least, who chose to give up the ghost the following week, so that Mistress Zemka had to learn how to drive the carriage herself (and soon acquired an ease that scandalized the neighbours). But for the others, in fact, life did resume its course. Kazimierz stayed with us all summer, then left for Lvov where he would begin his first year at university, as well as a few young male distractions. And a new routine then settled in, somewhat painfully, in an almost total absence of events.

On the main floor, our last two servants wandered around without saying anything. Oleksandra had become too deaf to hold a conversation, and Nikolaïa, upon whom all the heavy work had now fallen, sighed with fatigue and thought of her future on this sinking ship. Oh, if she had been able to marry her Semien, if fate had not been so harsh on them!

In the big salon, it was worse. The walls were covered with mildew, you tripped on the warped parquet and only two empty spaces on the wall recalled *Bonaparte at the pont d'Arcole* and *Tadeusz Kosciuszko in the Uniform of Major General of the Polish Army* which had been sold (at a low price, because they were only badly executed copies).

And the little green salon? Ever since they started taking their meals there, there was a continuous odour of food; that room which was filled with books, newspapers, yarn and needles, saw its Ottoman splendour gradually turn into a Levantine dishevelment. When Kazimierz, arriving from Lvov, found the two women lying on cushions between their glasses of tea and their cups of jam, he wrinkled his brow.

'I'm going to have to impose some order here—I'm ashamed before our staff,' he observed severely. 'And you, Tessa, take that cloth off of the piano—I want to play.'

Tessa, from the sofa, looked at him sideways, then slowly got up. 'All right, all right!' And it was with rebellious slowness, a consummate art of female annoyance, that she passed in front of him, brushing the silk of her skirt against him, gathered her skeins of yarn one by one, a little smile on her lips, before leaving the room.

Christmas passed almost unobserved in that long torpor. Tessa was sixteen, Wioletta, the poor woman, began suffering from rheumatism, there was Lent, then Easter . . . How slow were the clocks, that year, in droning the time! Without my memories, without the wandering of my nocturnal ghosts, I would have died of boredom.

It was so boring that one day in April I went up to see what was going on in the space under the roof.

There, it was teeming with life. Crazed parents went back and forth to feed their offspring; other mothers, wings covering their eggs, were still awaiting the happy event; the air was filled with chirping and the rustling of feathers. Well, would you believe it? This spectacle did not cheer me up. It even pained me when, looking more closely, I saw what was underneath.

In one of the most beautiful nests (a model nest, a true poster for natalistic propaganda), I discovered among six or seven baby birds an unlucky one who must have hatched after the others. You mustn't hatch after the others. Tragically underserved by this delay, still tiny and without feathers, he opened his beak to the arriving food, but, pushed away, crushed, received nothing at all. Out of despair or exhaustion, he didn't cry any more, and, on the other side of the space, his already cloudy eye fixed on the white light of day. What did that circle of light represent for him who knew nothing of the world outside? An unfathomable enigma, a beyond that he would never know. Poor little bird, why were you born?

Then spring arrived for good. A green mist covered the trees, the earth sang, a softer breeze moved the branches of the willows and the aspens. Some days it rained, but it wasn't the sad rain of autumn that flows on things as if to rinse off any hope that remains. It was a vivifying rain that made our peasant neighbours smile and it spoke of fecund growth and dense harvests.

Tessa became a bit thinner during those months. Her childish cheeks became hollower under her cheekbones, just as her waist became thinner under her more feminine bust line. She spoke less, walked slowly along the fence of the grounds, looked sideways; and when the wind gently pushed the already tall wheat, or a ray of sun fell from a crack between two clouds to dry the rain, her eyes filled with tears. Perhaps it was all the recent tragedies; or perhaps the desire to finally set off on a path— but which one? She was, she thought vaguely, like a letter that is placed on a pile of mail marked 'For Reply', then covered with something else, and finally forgotten. Her daily existence was sad and always the same. Only Kazimierz's visits cheered her up, but Kazimierz, this year, came rarely; and when he was there, he seemed more distant to her than in the past. He no longer teased her, agreed to play Wieniawski with her without plying her with sarcasm, no longer criticized her dresses, her hair. And if he still sometimes improvised on the piano, he soon interrupted himself with a sigh of resignation. Studying law! Studying law and no longer thinking of anything else.

Tessa was waiting for the summer when her brother would finally spend close to two months at home. She waited for the nights to become milder, the days to become longer, waited for them, however, with a somewhat heavy heart, as if she already knew that what we wait for fervently is most often disappointing. Through the windows she observed her old Ruthenian friends who, now, wielded sickles and hoes, looked at one another, joyfully slaving away. Soon, some would be married. And, several times a day, she heard the train that brought and carried no one or anything dear to her.

Then suddenly summer was there, and so was Kazimierz.

It seemed to Tessa that a golden age had returned. She would have had great difficulty explaining that impression, since never before had she experienced such shimmering days, such simple pleasure in spending them together. Never had she and her brother explored the grounds in that way, run through the fields together nor talked for hours on the stone bench about poetry and the novels they read together. She had taken on wisdom, reserve, she was no longer the puppy with which one could have fun for a few minutes before easily pushing it away. Kazimierz, henceforth, treated her as his equal. And their great-aunt, whose rheumatism often caused her to stay inside, smiled from afar at their two figures which, in spite of the hips of the one and the shoulders of the other, had the same unbridled vigour, the same firm gestures. She smiled at them because they were all that remained on earth of the man, of the only man whom she had ever loved.

One afternoon Kazimierz and Tessa had a little fright. They had just discovered next to the pond the base of a statue and (through one of those temporary returns to childhood that are the charm of the beginning of adulthood) knelt down to try to unearth it with their bare hands; then they jumped, because behind them someone had coughed.

Yet, there was nothing frightening about the very old man who was . . . I can't say that he was watching them because his eyes, completely white, must not have seen them. He stood there in his threadbare coat, moved his mouth as if to find his words, and when he raised the rabbit-skin cap he was wearing in spite of the heat, probably because he had no other, I recognized him. But the two orphans would not have known who he was.

'What are you doing here?' said Kazimierz.

'Peace be with you, whoever you may be . . . Excuse me, am I indeed at the *dwor* of Grynow?'

'Not only are you there but you have entered our property. I'd like to know how, by the way!'

'Oh!' smiled the blind man, turning his palms towards the sky, as if to say that he didn't know himself. 'You are the new owner, is that it? God keep you, young master, God keep your health and wealth . . .'

That would have been the moment to give him something. But Tessa didn't have any money with her, and Kazimierz—irritated at having been afraid, or perhaps at having been spoken to familiarly by this old Jew in rags—didn't even pretend to search for something in his pockets. The blind man must have understood because after a moment, nodding his head, he asked in a weaker voice, 'Does the cook Bozena still work here?'

'Never heard of her,' cut in Kazimierz. 'Now, please leave.'

He pulled his sister, who hesitated, by the arm and dragged her towards me. 'Incredible nerve! These fleabags think they can do anything!' he muttered walking quickly. The apparition had disturbed him greatly, as if they had been caught in the middle of doing something bad. But having arrived in front of the door, he stood still, uncertain.

'Wait for me here, I'm going to lead him back to the entrance,' he said to his sister. 'That old beggar is likely to fall into the pond and drown.'

In fact, shaken with remorse or with a more obscure feeling of threat, he intended to take the opportunity to pass a few coins to the old man. But when he arrived near the pond, no one was there.

'Disappeared. The old fool! This fence is full of gaps that must be repaired,' he explained to Tessa when he got back. And they went in to have tea without saying another word about the incident.

18

That night there was a storm, and the following morning it became clear that there would be another one by the end of the day. The heat crushed the fields, made the horizon glimmer like the desert—at one o'clock in the afternoon, no one was outside. Even the birds had fallen silent. And as there rose from the glebe an odour of dust and, faintly, of cooking, the sky lost its blue and was covered with a matte grey.

The orphans were smart enough to go outside while it was still cool. Kazimierz had hitched the cart with our last old horse, Tessa had gone upstairs to ask her great-aunt if, really, she didn't want to go with them, and at her negative response, had gone back downstairs with a basket filled with two glasses and a bottle of lemonade.

And they left with the crack of the whip, both seated on the driver's bench but leaving, I noted, a little space between them. It even seemed to me, from the attitude of their two backs dressed in black, that they weren't speaking. Perhaps it was the scene from the day before, or the heaviness of the weather, that disturbed them.

After two hours they returned, just as taciturn but in an altered state of mourning—the dust of the road had tarnished the black of their clothing and their straw hats. Tessa was now seated in back under her open parasol, her eye fixed and her face a bit clenched; and the idea struck me that she must be a bit sick.

They picked at their lunch behind the closed shutters. Then Nikolaïa cleared the table, went back down to the kitchen to wash the dishes that Oleksandra slowly wiped. Some potatoes were already soaking in a pan for the evening meal.

In the little salon they didn't know what to do. A torrid breeze came in through the slits in the shutters as well as a noise of regular banging, like that of a mallet falling on wood. Someone had apparently braved the furnace outside to repair a cart or drive a stake but none of my guests had the strength to open the shutter to see who the courageous soul was. Wioletta proposed a game of cards; they sat down at the table, the game began, while each person thought: If only it would rain!

But the storm didn't erupt, not yet.

After a moment, Tessa and Kazimierz, who were drumming their fingers, waiting for their great-aunt to play, noticed that she had fallen asleep.

'She's sleeping,' Tessa whispered needlessly to mask her unease before the relaxed face, the open lips out of which soft snores were escaping.

Kazimierz looked over at his aunt's hand, shrugged his shoulders, 'In any case, she would have lost.'

Their eyes met and Tessa let out a nervous laugh. This isn't good, she scolded herself, I shouldn't laugh at my great-aunt while she's asleep; but she couldn't help it, and Kazimierz, also cheered up, pulled her into the hallway where the young girl gradually calmed down.

Finally, she let out a big sigh, went to the wall, and squinted her eyes, 'Oh, I've never noticed that it was a view of Kraków. The background is so dirty!'

'And next to it, there is a hunting scene,' Kazimierz murmured in her back.

'Yes, I knew that,' said Tessa, sullen once again. How could she have laughed like that? This heat put her nerves on end. She would have really liked to move but Kazimierz remained absorbed contemplating the stag that was beautifully dying, its stomach crushed, its muzzle turned towards the sky, while a hunter on horseback was getting ready to administer the fatal shot.

Then their great-aunt, in the salon, groaned and they retreated.

They wandered from room to room, without speaking, happy to call each other over with a gesture, occasionally to observe together— oh, very little: a fly strangely imprisoned by a glass globe; a tear in a panel showing old wallpaper underneath; notebooks covered with purplish writing belonging to . . . Jadwiga Zemka? Yes, their Benedictine great-aunt's books . . .

'Worcell, an original edition!' said Kazimierz, breaking the silence. 'I wonder how it got here. It really isn't the type of writing that customs allowed to get through in those times . . .'

But he fell silent because his words, he sensed, rang false— something in the air made him feel it was better not to speak.

They left the classroom and, after some hesitation, went into the service staircase. They had never been in there. When they were small,

Mitzi slept in a room between their two rooms; and when she moved to the floor with the other servants, they were too old to visit her.

The steps of the staircase creaked. And above, there was only an endless hallway bordered by doors that were all the same, and they were a bit disappointed. But they pushed one open, to see—it had only an iron bed, a wardrobe and a little table on which there was a spotted mirror.

The heat was terrible. Through the small window they saw the top of the trees, farther away the gold wheat where tiny figures, bent over, were seen once again; the hour must have struck. They should go back down, they thought, but then the staircase creaked and a quick step, that of Nikolaïa, approached in the hallway.

Tessa wanted to close the door but Kazimierz, an arm over her shoulders, signalled with a mute pressure that they just had to stay still. And in fact they heard Nikolaïa enter another room, rustle around, grumbling, open a window, and, after a few moments, go back down the staircase which creaked again. Only then did Kazimierz let his arm down.

Their hearts were thumping. They moved apart and, turning, saw themselves in the mirror. The silvering was greenish and both of them discovered in the face of the other irregularities that habit erased when they looked at each other face to face. He has one eye a bit smaller than the other, and his nose is not exactly symmetrical, observed Tessa. That's not handsome. Then she blushed when she realized that he must see her the same way.

It was time to go. They left the room, went back down the two flights and, still without a word, returned to the salon where Wioletta was still sleeping.

But she finally did wake up. 'Oh, yes, it's my turn,' she muttered, picking up her cards again. And after having lost, she cried gaily, 'Thank God, this afternoon went by more quickly than I feared. Don't worry, children, it will soon be time for dinner.'

At dinner no one was hungry, except her. During dessert the storm broke and outside there were cries of panic, shutters violently shut, the brouhaha of tools and the carts that had to be brought in before the rain. Then there was the rain itself, at first torrential, then steady, then fine and regular; and night, as if it were waiting only for this relaxation to arrive, fell suddenly.

'Why don't you play me a little sonata?' Wioletta proposed when Nikolaïa had brought the lamps. But Kazimierz didn't want to, and Tessa was tired, and their great-aunt, without insisting, began to knit, getting up from time to time to go watch the rain fall or to straighten the Trebizond rug, which was always wrinkled, with her foot.

They didn't stay up late. It was one of those moonless evenings, without the croaking of frogs, without the shrieking of owls, when one wants only to go to bed and read for a long time before blowing out the candle. This is what Tessa did; but she didn't fall asleep immediately. A smell of wet earth floated in her room, a breeze blew the page upon which she had stopped, she could have held out her arm to close the book but didn't have the will, because the air, by contrast, now seemed cold to her.

How many little noises there are at night! What was surprising was that in normal times they don't prevent you from sleeping. Water dripping from a gutter, a mouse or a rat stirring in the wardrobe, the frame of the window creaking. In the hallway too, the planks groaned as if under a human step, and behind the door . . .

Behind the door someone was breathing.

'Who is there?' she said softly.

Finally she wasn't sure there was anyone there. The wind, blowing under the door . . . *Your Grace* . . . what was the wind blowing? *Your Grace, open up, don't be so cruel . . .*

She got up shivering, put a shawl over her light nightgown, and put an ear to the door.

'Tessa, open up, it's me.'

Herr Jäger?

'Kazimierz? What's the matter?' she whispered, unlocking the door.

'I want to talk to you.'

'I'm cold.'

'Then get back in bed.'

'I can't find the matches.'

'Leave the matches, we don't need them.'

She got under the covers that were still warm, folded her legs and waited. She was beginning to get sleepy now, her eyelids were getting heavy; but Kazimierz, sitting close to her, was still not saying anything.

My dear sister . . .

'What are you doing!'

'Don't be a fool, lift up your hands.'

'I don't want to.'

She was breathing very quickly, and it seemed to her that the noise of her breathing could be heard through the room, where it was so dark. *Your Grace, Clara! Don't be so childish. Isn't that your greatest desire as well as mine?*

'But stop, stop, what are you doing?'

'Little sister, you didn't lift up your hands so that I would stop, did you? So be still.'

'I beg you . . .'

'Are you crying? You disappoint me. I thought we understood each other.'

It's true, Tessa was crying. *Because I love you with all my heart and you only say mean things to me . . .* It was like listening to those harmonic massacres on the piano—they hurt her, they hurt her, but it was still love, in a certain sense. And love, all the books said so, was the most noble thing in the world; she need not, for the comfort of her little ears, for the tranquility of her little soul, shy away from it.

'You know, you can give me your mouth now. We have come this far!'

Tessa was no longer crying, no longer fighting. No, she wasn't afraid, no, she would not disappoint the expectations he had of her, without telling her, without ever showing her—'Because in the end,' she thought in the middle of the chaos that was her thinking and all her physical perceptions, fear, pain and upheaval mixed together, 'I have more courage than he, who never admits anything . . .'

Buoyed by that certainty, she went to the end and even beyond, offered what she could offer and yet didn't know, an hour earlier, that she had. And when it was all over, when the silence had returned, interrupted by the dripping of the drops that fell from the top of the roof, what awakened in her was a feeling of fullness and not of emptiness; of accomplishment, and not of despoiling. *Didn't she have what she wanted?*

19

Love, the most noble thing in the world? How much damage has already been caused by that lovely illusion, especially within my walls! What cruelty, what baseness it can on the contrary make possible, I had just again had proof of this; what recklessness too, I saw the next day, when Tessa, with the falsest of smiles, assured her great-aunt that yes, she had slept rather well in spite of the storm, and valiantly planned her strategy to wash and dry the sheets, unseen by the three women of the house.

I admit I was stunned; and it seems to me that Kazimierz was, as well. When at the table, above the head of their great-aunt who was peacefully eating her soup, his sister went so far as to smile at him, yes, smile ('See how strong I am! You can count on me'), I saw him pale with shame and turn his eyes away.

What had he done, but what had he done? As he had wished, the entire earth had become chaos and dissonance, but he didn't feel the anticipated contentment. It was, on the contrary, a feeling of absolute dereliction, the feeling of no longer having a refuge anywhere. His only home, his only true family, and he had horrifically sullied it. And what was worst was that he already knew there could be only one remedy to this feeling—to resume, to continue, to lose himself in those arms . . . Perhaps she would then stop smiling that horrible smile, perhaps in her—so strong—he would find a consolation, even an absolution at the very depths of his sin?

It went without saying that things did not occur that way the following night. You were quite naive, Kazimierz, even for your nineteen years. Do you think your sister was that strong? Where would she have got the tender power to console and absolve? At her age and in this realm, she could only know what you had taught her. What more could you have expected?

Two days later, well before the anticipated date, the student left for Lvov. He had alleged a need to study, the possibility of earning a little money working in the library of a rich man—in short, he fled. And in the following months, we almost never saw him here again.

One single Saturday in October he returned, skinny, feverish, worrying his great-aunt with his appearance, at meals he sought a glance from his sister, which he found but couldn't decipher; and when he wanted to come to her that evening, she locked her door and wouldn't open it to him.

And so she had pulled herself together, they say in moral terms; but I'm not sure morality played a big role here. It was rather her instinct that had finally told her no, she was not that strong, and that it had to stop there. And the last image of her that Kazimierz carried away as he was leaving for the train station, where, claiming fatigue, she refused to accompany him, was that of a Tessa with an impassive smile, with her hands calmly clasped in front of her skirt, with an attitude of confidence, a sort of heaviness that he hadn't noticed in her before.

That calm, for her, didn't last long. After a few weeks she had to admit that something was wrong. She was less tired, even felt like walking, cleaning up, doing useful tasks; but her body seemed to be escaping her control and living its own life, inexplicable anomalies increased, food disgusted her, her skirts no longer closed.

She didn't remain ignorant for long; much less long, in any case, than did Wioletta in her time. Lingering around the farms, listening to what the woman whispered, comparing a cow before and after its birthing, shed a certain light on this matter. And one morning, she had to face the fact in looking in the mirror at her rounded stomach under the fabric of her nightgown, her breasts that had become heavy like those of a mature woman—she was expecting a child.

What am I going to do? she thought in terror. She could hardly put on the last dress that fit her, she had already let it out three times using what she could from the seams and the pleats. The fabric made folds over her stomach, the bottom of her skirt went up to the middle of her shins in the front. How is it that no one noticed? How could her great-aunt . . .

Today, looking at me, she will understand, thought Tessa; and fear knotted her throat.

That fear, however, was mixed with a bit of hope. Wioletta would be shocked, horrified, she would no doubt cry; but she would know what to do. She thus had to screw up her courage and go downstairs to confront the inevitable storm.

Her fingers trembled on the banister of the stairs. In the green salon she found her great-aunt who, lying on the sofa, was reading a book; she interrupted her reading to smile at her gently.

'Hello, my dear. Sit down, have some tea, eat something. You look pale this morning.'

Tessa didn't move, her arms hanging at her sides, her stomach protruding. Oh, if only great-aunt could see her better!

'What's the matter?'

Wioletta looked at her carefully now, but her smile was still just as radiant.

'Aunt Wioletta . . .'

'Yes?'

'I . . .'

'Tell me, child.'

'I think I'm pregnant.'

Wioletta closed her book and set it down by her side. 'But I know, my dear, that is, I suspected as much. It's wonderful, I'm so happy for you!'

Tessa gulped. An unprecedented horror was spreading in her, she even reflexively placed her hand under her ribs as if to protect the little being that, in his misfortune, was growing there. And—still holding on to the idea of a misunderstanding, of an absurd mistake—she took a deep breath to whisper, 'But Aunt Wioletta, it is the child of . . .'

'Yes, yes, I know,' repeated her aunt patiently before getting up and coming to her. And, gently taking her head in her hands: 'Don't worry, my dear. Don't worry about what people will say, of what the world thinks—you are holy. You are both holy.'

'Aunt, please don't talk like that, I'm afraid . . .'

'Afraid? Of what?' Wioletta murmured with a soft laugh. 'Oh, I know. "You will observe my laws and my commands and you will commit none of these abominations . . . Take care that the land doesn't vomit you out, if you soil it, as it will have vomited the nations before you . . ." but all of that is past, my dear. The law today is all spiritual, and you can let its letter fall away as the snake lets its old skin fall away . . .'

'Aunt, I beg you!'

'Don't be afraid, come now.' And more softly: 'It is the others that God vomits, do you understand? All will be well. We will raise your child together. The three of us will raise it, and it will also be holy, even holier than us.'

With this, Tessa pulled away with a shudder, left the room and went down to take refuge in the garden behind the house. She walked for a bit on the paths of the vegetable garden, and suddenly, at the sight of the neat rows of vegetables, the last vegetables remaining calmly to be picked and eaten, she burst into tears. 'Nanny,' she called, 'Nanny!'

But her voice was so low that Pavlykowa, in her house, couldn't hear her. Tessa then picked up her skirts, and, hiccupping, ran to the first cottage, opened the door and disappeared inside.

I don't know what was said there, but five minutes later I saw her come back out very pale, and Pavlykowa, on her heels, standing at the door as if to bar her access for ever.

And Tessa came back.

Twice that day she told her great-aunt that she didn't feel well enough to go downstairs to eat. Twice Wioletta, concerned, herself brought up a platter filled with nourishing food. And to avoid any questions, Tessa forced herself to drink a few mouthfuls of the bouillon and nibble on one or two pieces of toast.

She had to wait for the night. If she didn't wait for nightfall, she would be stopped from doing what she wanted to do and she would have to try again.

Perhaps she should pray too? On her lips the words seemed completely devoid of meaning, but this mechanical repetition, endlessly repeated, had the advantage of calming her and making the time pass. It was so simple, really! She just had to wait for nightfall.

And the night, as it should, finally arrived.

Tessa's room looked to the east, towards Grynow, and she thus didn't see the winter sun reddening as it sunk into a bed of clouds. All that she saw was the town, its roofs, its turrets which became intensely pink before melting into the night, and then the lights that, like stars, were lighted one by one. The men, she thought, the living . . . But that thought didn't sadden her. She no longer expected anything from them and already was not one of them.

She didn't even light her lamp. And when her great-aunt knocked on the door to see if she needed anything, Nikolaïa to turn down her bed, she didn't answer so that the two women would think she was asleep.

She had let the fire go out. She was cold now, but told herself that soon she would be even colder, so she should get used to it. And she waited for the last sounds, for her great-aunt who was getting ready for bed, the steps of the servants climbing upstairs to bed.

Outside the moon had come up.

She still waited a long time, until a little wind began to rustle the branches of the trees and the furniture in my rooms stretched, crackling. Usually those cracklings frightened her but why, now, be afraid of such things? She didn't even tremble when, going into the darkness of the hallway, she sensed she had been brushed by invisible presences. Or maybe she did tremble a bit. Because she was going to die, wasn't she? And she was only sixteen.

Below, outside, she breathed better. The moon cast its silver light on the paths, dissipated the shadows between the trees, illuminated the little stone bench where no one, at this hour, was sitting.

The moon also shone on the surface of the pond. The moon became double to stay with me, she finally told herself in order to gather strength. And without waiting, her heart heavy, she jumped into the water.

20

The water was icy, even colder than Tessa had imagined. The frigid water that instantly went through her clothes made her aware, probably for the last time, of every inch of her body, and that body protested, sought to lash out in a reflex of defence; her hands beat the air which was now only water, her mouth shouted and suffocated with it, her eyes opened wide onto a murky darkness—*it is in troubled water that one finds fish*, something inside her remembered . . . Her skirt rose up like the corolla of a large carnivorous flower and her legs, freed, beat frenziedly. They wanted to maybe make amends, those legs, repair their cowardice; but wasn't it a rear-guard battle? Wasn't the darkness more and more profound, more and more opaque? And what did it matter what her legs did if her mouth didn't breathe any more?

And then the child, very slightly, also stirred. Poor little one, thought Tessa, who had not yet felt it. He is choking, he's cold, he is calling me perhaps . . . A glimmer of pity awoke in her, then took hold and grew.

He is calling me to help him, and what am I doing? Poor little thing, he wanted to live . . .

In her thoughts everything became white like a field of snow—time stopped, the world no longer existed, there was only she and her child, only the two of them . . . the two of them?

But I don't want to die! She suddenly realized. I don't want to, I don't want to any more, there are two of us and I am his mother!

Her feet have just touched the bottom. With a vigorous push she propelsherself to the top, her hands sought, now, instead of struggling, and they found—a thick root, or a clump of rushes. She still has to fight to reach the banks. Her soaked clothing weighs her down and it is with all her strength that she pulls herself out of the water. But she stays only a few minutes—if she doesn't move the cold will kill them.

Quickly, return to her room, light the fire, crouch near the hearth and vigorously rub her shoulders and legs. Put on a dry dress, even if it no longer closed—a shawl wrapped around her waist will work. Then throw some clothes into a bag, a few little things, go into the library, to the drawers where they keep the money. It seems to Tessa that there is a lot, and she leaves two-thirds of it thinking of her great-aunt whom she is abandoning. What would become of her, that poor old madwoman, alone with her demons? But I chase that thought out of her. Forget your great-aunt, Tessa, you can do no more for her than she can for you! And don't delay, because in an hour or two the sun will begin to come up.

She wraps herself up in her hooded cloak, goes down the main stairs, turns the huge key and goes through the front entrance, pushes the little side door of the main gate, which creaks a bit, but it doesn't matter! By the time they wake up, she will be far away. She chooses the road to the station, and she is right—in twenty-four minutes, the first train will come by, the one that takes people into town at the beginning of the day. She sets off, places one foot, then the other, continues to advance . . . It is now, I sense it, it is now or never! She must turn around. Tessa, turn around!

She has heard me. That is, stopping for a moment to catch her breath, she is looking around her at the countryside still bathed in the moonlight, and thinks: My fields, my Galicia, will I ever see them again? Then her eyes rest on me, and a flood of emotion swells her chest—it is at that moment, with all the strength of my immaterial self, I break my chains to take refuge completely in her warm little body.

Oh, what a shock! Through her eyes, for the first time in my long, long life, I am able to see myself. A big building with three storeys, a mouldy roof, front windows on the ground floor alternating with somewhat chipped, round reliefs. On the front a once-white colonnade, now grey, and above, a little pediment vainly seeking to imitate that of a Greek temple. Paths invaded by weeds, trees planted one hundred sixty years ago, grown wild since, like at the castle of Sleeping Beauty that Elvire Denisot once told us about . . . And that's all? In the end, I am not very much.

And so, with a final sigh, Tessa sets out and I turn my back on myself.

Goodbye old world! And my sugar factory, goodbye . . . But what factory? It has been closed for six months, I must have forgotten to say. It doesn't matter to me, in any case—I have a new life to begin.

And this new life inside a human body resembles nothing I've ever known. This swaying of the gait, the shaking of the organs, the little fellow who wiggles as much as he can—yes, it's a boy, I'm the first to know—those corporeal fluids in which I bathe are unnerving and, mainly, somewhat disgusting. What am I doing there, I ask you!

But in a few minutes I get used to it, and, from then on, excitement takes over. What a marvel it is to move around like this in this landscape that before was static, to go around that cottage which I'd looked at for ever from the same side, to arrive under the chestnut trees on the main avenue which, I now admit, I will never see full-grown . . . (nor will I see Yosyp Pavlyk, or rather Joseph Pavlic, leave along this avenue in 1914 to join his regiment) but after all, why shouldn't the trees continue to grow in my absence?

And then there's the train station, still almost new, whose door Tessa pushes open and where she buys a third-class ticket because she has realized, the innocent, that otherwise her travel funds will not last long. The waiting room with its brazier, a few soldiers on leave, Ruthenian peasant women nodding off under their scarves, the ground strewn with feathers, straw and bits of tobacco . . . The world is dirty but it is beautiful, great gods, it is beautiful!

'Hey, is that you, sprite?' Tessa raises her eyes and recognizes Danylo—recently released from prison, he explains, and come to visit his sister's family before trying his luck in town. There he has contacts, friends, one of them works in a printing house where, it seems, they are hiring right now . . .

Danylo has lost weight. He looks his twenty-five years, even a bit more, he has laugh lines at the corner of his eyes, darker hair, but still the same turned-up nose. And while Tessa is looking at him, he looks at her and doesn't take long to understand—she is cold, afraid, pregnant and running away from home with a bag smaller than his. That's rough; yet Danylo seems happier and happier. As the train is approaching, he says, 'Give me your bag and get on in front of me, I'll find a corner where you can sleep. . . Sh! Don't cry, sprite. Don't cry. I'm here.'

I feel his warm hand under Tessa's; and shortly afterwards I feel the trembling, the jolts, the rolling of the convoy that is carrying us . . . I still can't believe it—so I have taken the train?! Then the immensity of the plain unfolds, the moving curve of the horizon, other farms, other churches, other towns, other people . . . And then the red, the orange, the red, because Tessa, huddling against the window opposite Danylo, has closed her eyes and fallen asleep.

IV
LIBERTY

There is another rolling—more gentle. But the sky is clear, the air is cooler, you need only to breathe it in to feel you are already on the way, the birds passing by, shrieking, are indeed sea birds, even if the real sea is still far away.

On this citadel of wood and metal with masts standing proudly, with billowing chimneys, so many little soldiers ready to attack! Some seem proud—in light clothes, they are waving handkerchiefs at their loved ones on the quay; and when they cry it is still a beautiful spectacle, as beautiful as the third act of a play or the finale of an opera.

Others, many more (I realize now that we have already crossed the gangway) evoke rather an army in retreat—poor soldiers clutching between their legs piles of rags and wearing, for lack of room in their parcels, two vests and three jackets one on top of the other. They too are waving their handkerchiefs, but it is for form's sake. They already said their goodbyes a long time ago, in a Russian town, a German forest or a little Greek village.

Their hearts are full of hope, hope and sadness. They are leaving everything behind them, all that they could they have sold except, perhaps, a violin, a pretty box or a lace headpiece, the headpiece that the girl to our left, probably a daughter of Frisian fishermen, promised she would wear when they arrive in America, because it is the best thing she owns . . .

I sense, next to Tessa, the shoulder of little Yosyp who is quiet and observant. Not that he is sad, strictly speaking. At five, you're not sad as long as you're standing between your mother and father (because Danylo is his father, it went without saying for him). He is just moved by the tears of the adults and by the noise of the siren that has just sounded, and worried at not knowing where he will sleep that night. His mother seems tense and unhappy, and there is reason to be. That morning, he forgot his lead soldier at the inn where they had been lodging for two weeks with other Galicians waiting for their boat, his nose had bled when she had already folded all their spare clothes, he had been hungry at the moment they were counting and recounting their bags . . .

The Pavlyks have quite a number of bags. A typographer and a teacher, they are not the worst off among the passengers in steerage. They even have plans, provisions for the trip, a bit of money for their first expenses over there. They have been saving for a long time to prepare for this departure, and, despite what Countess Wytocka's nephew might think, I fear that Tessa, in the interval, must have made her own hats.

And now the day has come, they watch, almost incredulous, as the port of Hamburg moves farther away . . . Is it a dream? No—the entire boat groans and vibrates to the rhythm of the machines, and the breeze picks up.

Danylo perches his adopted son onto his shoulders, then smiles at his wife who is now separated from him by a little empty space. She doesn't come closer. It has been like that since they have been together—she always stays at a bit of a distance, doesn't allow herself to be entirely possessed. '*Panienka*, little mistress!' he sometimes teases her. Then she gives him a punch for fun and he ruffles her hair. They get along well, she and he, they are two completely complementary friends and in perfect harmony but there still remains this resistance in her, that little hard core that (she is unaware) is nothing other than I.

What does Danylo really know, what has she told him? I won't tell you—a certain reserve has overtaken me since my incarnation. There are things, I've understood, upon which it is better not to dwell. I have learnt modesty, introspection, and it is not out of the question that one day I will be completely quiet, even though the life of the one who is carrying me will be long.

Between that man and the one whom he considers his son there is thus a complicity of males in the face of the woman; but not that alone. Because Danylo is easily playful with this nervous, not very robust little boy who is subject to nightmares and convulsions, to whom he thus hopes to give a bit of his strength. But would Tessa indulge in such playfulness? Never. She keeps too many bad memories of her childhood for that.

Now Danylo puts the boy back on the ground, enough laughing, becomes the head of the family again and the husband of a young woman almost ten years younger than he. At the sound of a bell, the first-class passengers go to lunch. For the others, it is time to go down to steerage and settle in.

This takes some time. People shuffle down the stairs, they shuffle in the passageways, they shuffle at the entrance to the dormitory, a huge, dark room with a low ceiling. There are no windows. Air? One assumes that it will regenerate by itself. After all, thousands of emigrants have already made this voyage and almost no one has died of it. On the one side, the men, on the other, the women and children—the boundary, which for the time being still appears important, even essential, is marked by old cloths hanging from ropes. At every turn the close ranks of beds with two or three levels, one bends one's head, there is very little room, the mattresses smell bad and already a few babies are crying. Fifteen days or more in here? That's what it will take. Moreover, for most of them it isn't any worse than what they have left back home.

Yosyp, who doesn't like to sleep alone, is happy—he will sleep head-to-toe with his mother in one of the lower bunks. He makes a little house between two parcels of clothes, takes over the mattress, its odour and its lumps; that's good, thinks Tessa, reassured.

But she misses Danylo already. She wanders along the hanging blankets, tries to distinguish him in the other forest of beds.

Over there, the settling in is stormier. A group of young fellows have laid claim to the beds closest to the boundary, because there are girls on the other side, girls they will perhaps see, at night, in their camisoles . . . Older men argue, the tone rises, insults and fisticuffs begin to be exchanged, because some are Protestants and others Orthodox, if I've followed well, or it is a story between Hungarians and Slovaks, or between Westphalians and Turkish Jews, or all of that at the same time, because the dispute now extends to the entire dormitory.

Members of the crew intervene, form zones of geographical origins, and families of religions. The captain must know something about schisms and territorial conflicts since the time he began transporting all the dregs of old Europe across the Atlantic. And calm returns, a calm heavy with resentments and furtive glances. Patience, think the pugilists. Soon they will be able to hate one another in less confined quarters in the vastness of the New World, where the trees and towers climb into the sky, where the streets paved with gold are lost in the horizon, where the land belongs to whoever wants it.

But well before that, in fact, they will forget their hatreds. Once we have reached the open sea and gone around the British Isles, there will pass among them a great pacifier before whom all men are brothers and equals—Slovaks, Westphalians and Czechens, ladies in First Class and old men in steerage.

They are told it isn't serious and they will survive, but for the time being they wish they were dead. It is a torture that confines them to their mattresses which have already been soiled many times, and a torture that lasts—those fifteen days will surely be the longest in all their existence. There is only one remedy for anyone who has the strength— to go onto the bridge to breathe in the pure air, cling to railings and then go back down when you can't stand the cold any more.

Only the young children are relatively spared, and from time to time I see one of them fishing in the barrel of herrings put graciously at their disposal in the middle of the dormitory. It is also they who go up to get water to make their elders, their ill mothers, drink—the maritime company had foreseen herrings, but not water. Some, since they aren't being watched, slip into the machine room where they become covered with dirty grease, or into the kitchen where they pinch a handful of raw noodles before a waiter shoos them out. For them, the crossing would be a wonderful memory, liberty, ah! They have tasted it even before reaching Ellis Island.

This is not the case for poor Yosyp, who doesn't have sea legs. And Tessa has been sick almost non-stop ever since our departure—she can hardly get up from her bed. I am sorry. I would have so liked to have spent the time looking at the sea, the sky, the walls of waves . . . But it is a bit my fault; because without me, she would feel better. I am a weight in her that she thought she had left in the port of Hamburg and which she realized on the first day at sea had not left her.

And what a weight! When one considers that this body of a young mother contains, in her still svelte thighs—a large Empire salon, a little green salon, a great number of bedrooms, hallways and cubby holes, not counting thirty ancestors, a struggle for independence, two religions and three or four failed insurrections, it is not surprising that she doesn't feel well.

Oh, she is vomiting again—we are crossing what seems to be a terrible storm in the North Atlantic, which the sailors are calling a 'squall'. She vomits up the few mouthfuls of bread and cheese she was able to swallow at lunch; but I and the thirty ancestors stay there, it takes a bit more to make us leave.

She thought she had left me in Hamburg. By the way, it is she who, in the beginning, wanted this great departure—Danylo had his misgivings.

'It's my country, sprite, I love it, can you understand this? . . . And we have struggles to fight here, my comrades depend on me in these times when the peasants are organizing, when strikes are being prepared . . .'

She understood him and resigned herself for many months. That desire to leave remained in her, and she knew well that in life one doesn't always have what one wants, Danylo is already so good to take care of Yosyp and to love him like his own son . . .

But Danylo, with his simple speech, his good face and his turned up nose, hides a true psychological finesse. He had not been duped. This wouldn't work, he saw, she would waste away. Why not leave? It was he who, a year later, spoke to her about it.

'But what about your country, your struggles?'

'There are also causes to fight in America, sprite . . .'

I was delighted with those words, worthy of a Zygmunt Borowski. After four or five years spent contemplating the back courtyards of a workers' neighbourhood, a classroom in a teachers' college, later school classrooms filled with close-cropped children who looked at us right in the eyes when they weren't writing, I was then going to discover the emigration offices, customs offices, a succession of Prussian trains, then the great blue sea!

Here we are on the great blue sea; and Tessa is doing worse than before. I feel guilty, but what can I do? Certainly I have powers but not that of disintegrating myself.

During those days at sea, however, I observe and I listen better to our neighbouring passengers, I get to know them. There is that skinny woman and her six children to whom she sings, at night, songs in a language that no one here speaks, where does she come from? No one really knows; those three young Jews, sisters, who huddle on the same bed redoing their braids, wearing the little badge of unaccompanied minors around their necks and jumping at the slightest noise (they say they were all three raped by Cossacks); the old peasant woman surrounded by her daughters and daughters-in-law who cries and cries, and says her rosary—she didn't want to leave but she couldn't stay alone in the country, and now she cries, the poor old woman, missing her four little chickens, her row of cabbage, the village cemetery where she was to join her husband . . .

And as I get to know them better, my guilt fades. Because Tessa is clearly not the only one in her condition, in fact, it is the rule. Who among these emigrants isn't dragging thirty ancestors, land, a hundred or a thousand years of history with them? Who doesn't carry in his body something very heavy and yet intangible—something like a *house*?

Two weeks have passed. We have slept and been awake, we have played dice and sewed, the sound of an accordion has caught our attention. We have all gone up on the deck to see a whale dive, large icebergs floating between the waves. Now the arrival is near, the news spreads, even the old lady near us has stopped crying.

The morning when someone shouts 'Land!' Yosyp is still asleep, tired from a bad night. Tessa stays with him in the almost empty dormitory. Finally he wakes up, rubs his eyes, and she takes him into her arms: 'Come quickly, let's go see! We're almost there.'

You can already see the land on both sides. It is land like any other, thinks Tessa, a bit disappointed. Low houses, docks, trees . . . But the spectacle is in front of her, at least if one is able to forge a path to see it.

'Ladies, gentlemen, I beg you, move back, you risk an accident!' bellows an adjunct of the captain. In vain—no one listens to him, they are too busy pressing against the railing. Tessa, when she arrives, remains stupefied in front of the view offered up to her; I am too. Is there truly such a concentration of people on the earth? Those roofs, those avenues, those huge buildings . . . When I think of Grynow and my little hamlet!

But now Yosyp, in his mother's arms, begins to struggle, his eyes rolling back in terror, his teeth clenched to the breaking point.

One of our neighbours offers him a handkerchief, another some water, Tessa, frightened, thanks them and whispers, 'Yosyp, what's the matter?'

Incapable of speaking, he points his finger behind her. Then she turns around and in turns sees the huge statue that we are passing by.

'It's the Statue of Liberty, my darling, don't be afraid. Look, everyone is laughing!'

Indeed, all around us, people are laughing and crying, crossing themselves, shouting. But Yosyp is still trembling and hiding his face, and when he is finally able to unclench his teeth, I hear him groan, 'It is too big! . . . too big!'

Luckily, Danylo has just joined them and his presence, as always, calms the little boy. He says 'tt, tt,' runs his fingers through his hair, picks him up in his arms to show him the sailboats that are unloading their cargo of merchandise, steamboats crossing the harbour, barges that are approaching to come take our first- and second-class passengers— they're lucky, after presenting their passports they can set foot on the land of Manhattan with no further ado.

For the others, real life starts again, and real life is often waiting for hours, enduring it patiently, hoping that all will go well. Some stand around above, fascinated by the spectacle, but most have already gone down to steerage to get their things together, nurse a newborn (he has time, he will even have time for the next feeding, even for the one afterwards), catch a last nap for the laziest.

Finally the ship docks, it moves in the water again, then stops. Everyone is standing and trying to move but, for the moment, no one, or very few, can move . . .

'What is happening?'

'We have to wait.'

In the standing crowd, there are already rumours circulating to explain the long wait: a criminal sought by the police was among them, everyone looks at everyone else suspiciously; no, it's cholera, there were three cholera cases on board and everyone is going to be put in quarantine. 'Impossible!' objects a man wearing glasses, 'they wouldn't have let the first-class passengers get off—Oh, them, with money you can do anything . . .' That last remark doesn't please people, and eyes turn with reproach towards the killjoy who spoke it: We are in America, for goodness sake, it isn't the time to speak of the rich and the poor, here everyone is rich, or will be one day.

Then the rumours dry up because it appears that we are indeed in the process of disembarking, but it takes a long time, quite simply, because each barge can only hold twenty or thirty people.

Then our turn comes. And our barge very calmly approaches Ellis Island.

Around us everyone is silent. Danylo rubs his hands over his cheeks, perhaps he should have shaved? How stupid, he had all the time in the world . . . Tessa is biting her chapped lips and, in her palm, I feel Yosyp's fingers become moist; he probably senses this atmosphere of condensed fear, a fear of adults, the worst, because if the adults themselves are afraid, things must be really bad.

The island is ugly, flat. You can make out a small building with a tall chimney that resembles a factory, scrawny trees, and in the middle something big and hostile, made out of wood, with a pyramidal tower on each corner—a sort of fortress drawn by a child.

Why, but why at that moment did Yosyp have to turn his head and see—even closer, even bigger than before—the metal Lady? He convulsively squeezes his mother's hand and continues to stare; since it is now a matter of going down the gangplank, Tessa doesn't sense anything is wrong. And why, but why, does an official have to stop and look at this young woman and her very pale son, and something, I don't know what, some vague feeling makes him insist that they pass to the front of the line, along with the husband?

And here are the Pavlyks the first to cross the threshold, they must be envied. But the main floor is only a warehouse of luggage, they have to climb the stairs.

'Advance, please, advance,' cry out men in uniform. Advance, but where? Up there the space is chequered with an infinity of gates leading to counters. How can you know? Don't worry, and advance, you'll be taken care of.

They pass, still in front, before a few gentlemen who say nothing to them and simply look at them from head to toe. I really should have shaved, Danylo must have thought, Tessa tries to smile, one of the men responds to her smile, then murmurs something in the ear of a colleague who marks an 'X' in chalk on Yosyp's jacket.

A bit further, other passengers from our boat file in front of a man with epaulettes and a kepi. I recognize one of the young Jewish girls whom her sisters must push in front of them—everything that vaguely resembles a soldier terrorizes her. She is, moreover, not the only one to be terrorized because the man, with an instrument, flips everyone's eyelids up and it seems that it hurts, at least that's what is said in the line where a few children have started to cry.

Yosyp doesn't cry when we file by the man—he is already beyond tears, petrified with fear.

We are sorted, we are counted, we are questioned and squeezed . . . Finally we are at the end of our misery, it seems, because we are seated in a huge dining hall. Signs everywhere remind us that this meal is free and that there is nothing to pay. To eat soup, and in a bowl, after so many days of dry bread and salted herring! Faces relax, tongues are untied, good spirits return.

Then we wait some more. And a female official comes looking for us—us, why us?—to take us into a room where, behind a table, a doctor and a man in a suit are seated. Another health exam, then; but I seem to understand that it only involves Yosyp.

At other tables there are other emigrants, also, with chalk letters on their backs or shoulders. And the 'X's, my goodness, are a sorry sight. Some are laughing all alone, two are afflicted with goitre, a woman is singing and trying to breastfeed a doll . . .

Tessa turns towards her husband but they don't dare say a word, in any case, their turn has come. Ruthenian? Fine, we'll find an interpreter who speaks Ukranian.

The interpreter, from his accent, comes from Little Russia. But he must have been here for several years—he does not have that sheepish look of the poor newcomers, he looks at us with the satisfied haughtiness of someone who has already made his way.

'Come on, little fellow, let go of your mother's hand and come sit here. You're a man, aren't you?'

This beginning doesn't soften Yosyp. They have to almost carry him to the chair, so tense are his muscles. He stays as he was placed, his back straight, his hands clinched on the edge of his seat; and Tessa, who has come to ask for mercy for him, is roundly ordered to return to her seat.

And the examination begins. The doctor speaks with a soft voice; one senses that the interpreter suppresses the kindly turns of phrase and the niceties, not seeing why one should treat this scum with kid gloves. When Yosyp doesn't answer, which happens most often, he adds: 'Come on, are you deaf?' so that the doctor has to stop him with a gesture before going on to the next question. And each time Yosyp's fingers, on the seat, turn white at the joints.

'. . . And tell me, son, do you happen to see little lights that dance around?'

The child raises his eyes to him, worried.

'Rays of light around people's heads, like on an icon, you know?'

Yosyp is breathing more quickly, stares at a point on the wall, responds as if in a trance, 'Rays of light, around her head . . . Points . . . Sharp points . . .'

'You see points. That's good, that's very good!'

He quickly translates with a knowing smile, the doctor makes a note, then pursues his questioning but more quickly, as if his opinion, henceforth, has been made up.

'Go on, little fellow, we won't bother you any more, go to your mother . . .'

We have only to wait for the verdict, and soon it falls, irrevocable, from the mouth of a functionary—mental troubles incompatible with entrance into the country. The Pavlyk child must go back on the same boat with at least one of his parents.

This was a completely unforeseen blow and Tessa, at first, remains stunned. Mental troubles? But that can't be right, a mistake, that interpreter was against them! With what she had left of German she tries to speak directly to the doctor, but he, still polite, indicates that he doesn't understand and turns to his next patient.

Not their protests, not their shouting, not their tears would have any other effect than to attract several members of the forces of order. Here and there, similar scenes unfold, without different results. Our former neighbour in steerage learns that two of her six children have croup and will be evacuated to the hospital on the island, while she will wait here with the rest of her brood, until the ill ones are cured or die of it. Those who have let themselves be taken in by the benevolent familiarity of the personnel are quickly disabused— there is no question of leaving, these walls and locks will see to that. It is a prison, in fact, for those who haven't yet understood.

And next to us I observe Danylo, who has seen worse prisons than this. He has put the distant descendant of Count Fryderyk on his lap and is caressing his hair with his scratchy chin. Poor little fellow, he is probably thinking. Too delicate, too young for this long voyage; but don't tell me he's epileptic! But now they are in some trouble. They have spent almost all their savings on train and boat fares, he has lost his job, she has quit . . .

I can see he is, for the first time, beaten down. And his face lights up when Tessa slides on the bench to fill the little space that had opened between them.

'We're not very lucky, are we sprite?'

She responds only with a sign of her head but she stays next to him.

They won't speak about it again until we have left the coasts of the New World. Is it habit, the milder weather, or another reason still? The fact is that Tessa, this time, endures the crossing much better. They spend a lot of time on the deck looking at the birds, the clouds, the little crests of foam. To tell the truth, down below the spectacle isn't very cheerful. Steerage holds all the other rejects, the mad, the infirm, children with trachoma still not knowing that they will end up blind, hidden passengers coming over who were rejected right away . . . It is a true portrait of human misery. The only ones who don't elicit pity are the temporary emigrants who are returning home. Their trunks are filled with gifts for the entire family, the women have hats, the men suits such as no one has seen in their village, they are already urbanized, worldly-wise—they are unbearable, actually, in their ostentatious happiness, and people keep their distance from them.

On the deck, for example.

In the midst of this plain without shrubs or fences, without men or past, which never ends and which belongs to no one . . . To the wind, perhaps? To the wind that sculpts the waves just as, at home, it used to sculpt the snowdrifts in the winter and to bend the tall wheat in the summer.

I hear Danylo's voice murmuring to Tessa, 'You know, we don't *have* to go back to our country . . .'

'That's true,' she answers. 'It's not good to retrace one's steps.'

And Danylo tells her his new plans—stay in Hamburg and, if they don't like it, earn enough to go to Rumania where many other Ruthenians have settled . . .

Or to France, I whisper to Tessa with all the strength of my will. I dream of seeing France, I've heard about it for so long!

'Or to France,' she says. Then she blinks her eyes, leans against the railing and watches the waves.

They are in the middle of the ocean, that is, nowhere. The sky is grey, they can't see the sun, and, if by chance the engines stopped, if the boat slowly began to turn on itself and go off course, they would be incapable of saying where is North, where is South, where is the East and West.

And I still hear Tessa who has turned towards her husband and observes, with a brave little smile, 'In the end, we can live anywhere, can't we?'

How good I feel in her—it seems I have recently lost my rough edges. It even seems that I am taking up less space, that I have melted a bit, like a polar iceberg lost in a tropical sea.

Live anywhere?

Live . . . anywhere.